THE HANGING OF MARGARET DICKSON

Alison J. Butler

THAMES RIVER PRESS

The Hanging of Margaret Dickson

THAMES RIVER PRESS
An imprint of Wimbledon Publishing Company Limited (WPC)
Another imprint of WPC is Anthem Press (www.anthempress.com)
First published in the United Kingdom in 2013 by
THAMES RIVER PRESS
75–76 Blackfriars Road
London SE1 8HA

www.thamesriverpress.com

All the characters and events described in this novel are imaginary
and any similarity with real people or events is purely coincidental.

A CIP record for this book is available from the British Library.

ISBN 978-0-85728-347-4

Cover design by Sylwia Palka

This title is also available as an eBook

In memory of May and Bob Caulfield

ACKNOWLEDGEMENTS

The research for *The Hanging of Margaret Dickson* took me many, many years. Basically, Maggie's story became an obsession of mine, and as the story is over 300 years old, I've had to fill in some gaps and use artistic licence. Extensive work went into researching and collecting birth and marriage certificates relating to Maggie's background, and of course I had to study eighteenth-century Scottish history, social history and maritime history. In short, I'm pretty confident that all historical details are indeed accurate – but then nobody is perfect, and if there are mistakes, I can only apologise.

I am most grateful to the staff at Haddington Library who provided me with vital information regarding Margaret Dickson, and also my gratitude to East Lothian Local History Centre. Many thanks go to the archivists at the National Archives of Scotland who located the original JC court records of Margaret Dickson's trial.

Adam Lyal of the Edinburgh Witchery Tours contacted me with vital information relating to Jock Dalgliesh, the hangman, and the botched hanging. David Stillie of the Old Musselburgh Club kindly took the time to answer some of my questions, my thanks to him also.

I am indebted to Caelin Charge, and all the staff at Thames River Press. In particular, a very special thank you to Kamaljit S. Sood, who discovered my manuscript and helped me to realise my dream of publishing Maggie's story.

As ever, I am grateful to my husband, Dave, my four children and all my friends and family for their support.

Finally, I've never been able to locate Margaret Dickson's grave. My research suggests she ended her days in Berwick. If anyone knows of Maggie's final resting place please contact me so that I can pay my respects.

You can find out more about me and Maggie at alisonjanebutler. wordpress.com and about.me/alison_butler, and on Twitter @halfhangitmaggy.

Alison J. Butler

CHAPTERS

1690 ACT ANENT CHILD MURDER

[T]hat if any woman shall conceale her being with child dureing the whole space and shall not call for and make use of help and assistance in the birth, the child being found dead or amissing the mother shall be holden and reputed the murderer of her own childe, and ordaines all criminall Judges to sustain such processes, and the lybell being remitted to the knowledge of an inqueist, it should be sufficient ground for them to return their verdict finding the lybell proven and the woman guiltee of murder tho there is no appearance of wound or bruise upon the body of the childe...

PROLOGUE

THE SCOTTISH BORDERS 1723

The maidservant drops to her knees in the attic room. There is little time and so she must begin. A tallow candle illuminates her pale face as she crawls beneath the box-bed; she inclines her head to the side and places her candle upon the floor. With a grunt of pain she inches forward. Her hands dart and flutter like trapped birds in a cage, not an inch is left unexplored. Soon a finger brushes against something soft and a small cry escapes her lips. The item sought is just within reach, and so she stretches and scoops it into a bundle to hide beneath her plaid.

A moment later, she descends the stairs. Fear burns her throat and threatens to choke her. She treads quietly, one hand against the wall to lighten her weight. Her breathing is laboured, as though a great weight is pressed hard upon her chest. For a moment she pauses to catch her breath. At the bottom of the stairs, the maidservant tiptoes through a cobwebbed corridor, into a sea of liquor-glazed eyes. All around her, the last of the tavern's stragglers scream and cavort, and so she takes care to avoid them and their one-handed assaults. In haste, she weaves and side-steps through them, holding her breath against their fetid odour until she reaches the scullery.

Beside the hearth is a wooden pail. A fire snaps and hisses, she moves towards its hot flames, basking in the warm glow. Smoky peat burns her eyes; she rubs them and looks left then right, all clear, not a soul in sight. In one swift motion, the maidservant throws the bundle into the pail and lifts it from the ground. For a while she stands there weakening at the knees, as if her bones have turned to mush. The moment passes, a door swings open and a shadow falls upon her cheek. Quick as a flash, the maidservant hides the pail behind her back and turns around. Her eyes follow Cook as she squeezes her fat rear through the scullery door, red-faced, arms full of filthy pots, a mangy dog close to her heels.

'What ails you?' Cook begins to scrape slop from the pots into a huge bowl.

The maidservant feels a hot flush shoot up her whole body. She tries to open her mouth to speak, but the words won't come out. After a while she tries again. 'Whatever do you mean? Nothing ails me. We're low on water; I'll fetch some shall I?'

'In this weather? Have you lost your senses?'

'No matter. Won't be long.'

Cook shakes her head and returns to her dirty pots.

With the pail safe in her hand, she exits the tavern and marches past kirk, downhill towards the river. Before long, the sparkling water is visible, its long snaking trail sheltered by twisted trees and naked branches stretched out like bony limbs. Beyond the foliage, the icy river seems to call to her, and so she obliges and follows its winding track to the promise of solitude.

The air is crisp and bitterly cold. The woman sucks in her breath through clenched teeth as her nostrils sting. Thousands of ice crystals descend from above, falling upon her lashes and nose, causing her to tilt her head backwards to the leaden sky. With arms open wide, she rotates in the flurry, mouth open so that snowflakes melt on her hot tongue, and every drop of colour evaporates from her face. The bleak landscape blurs, her ears begin to ring. She looks for something to lean against but there is nothing. She is weak, a sickly sweat covers her forehead, and as her hearing fails, her legs buckle as white turns to black.

The maidservant opens one eye, the one not frozen shut with ice and tears. She lies on her back upon the powdery snow, fingers and face blue. For just a moment she fancies she's in heaven, and that an angel has come to collect her.

The maidservant gasps: 'The pail.' She doesn't know if she has the energy to sit up, her throat is swollen and her heart pounds in her breast. As she pushes herself off the ground, she sways unsteadily on her feet towards a glimmer in a hedge. In the centre of a frosty bush, a handle protrudes from dead leaves. With her hand outstretched, she plunges it into the frozen hedge, curling her fingers around the pail, but it is stuck. She pulls harder, in the process disturbing a nesting bird, sending it spiralling aloft in an explosion of white feathers. Shadows lengthen on the riverbank. The maidservant shivers and exhales misty clouds into the air. One small hand wavers over the pail, deciding whether or not to pull out the bundle. Tentative fingers curl under the fabric to unravel the precious bundle; she can hardly bear to look. A fully formed child lies within her arms, its tiny head covered with fine golden hair. His eyes an odd shade of purple-blue, like a wild flower.

The maidservant is numb now. The water catches the fading twilight and she walks towards it as though in a trance. At the riverside, she lifts the tiny body and holds it over the ice-cold water. Arms outstretched and muscles taut, she maintains this position till her arms twitch and burn, no longer able to bear the weight. Hot tears roll down her frozen face as she sinks to her knees and places the baby boy farther beneath the reeds, her eyes taking on a faraway look, as though looking beyond the objects around her.

CHAPTER ONE

TEMPLE 1697

Folk travel from all around to sup at the Ten Bells Tavern, and not just for the frothy ale or riveting conversation. Most come to gawp at the innkeeper's wife and get a glorious view of the biggest jugs in Temple. Many a woman turns up at the tavern come sundown to drag her husband home, but not before casting a scathing glance at the main attraction.

Duncan Dickson sits at the rear of the inn, slumped behind a barrel, mouth wide open, snoring like a pig. The doors to the drinking house open and close like a barn door in a gale. At some point two link-boys scamper inside, dressed in ragged clothes, both of them covered in filth and dust. The younger boy limps, dragging his stick-thin leg behind him, a pitiful sight as the famine has left its mark on him. Their eyes search the room and widen at the sight of Duncan, the easy prey. The tallest boy conjures a plan while twitching his head in the sleeping man's direction.

'You empty his pockets while I keep watch.'

'Nae, I'm not doing it. You do it. He reeks. Probably peed himself,' the smallest boy wrinkles his nose.

The taller boy ignores his brother's protests and pushes him towards the drunkard.

'What if he wakes up?'

'Just do it and be quick,' the eldest boy raises a hand to slap his sibling with all his might.

The younger boy yelps, the blow snapping his head backwards. Tears of humiliation roll down the lame boy's face. He wipes them away with the reverse of his hand and grimaces back the tremor on his lips before searching the man.

'Nothing,' the boy shrugs at his older brother. 'He's got nothing.'

'We'll take his shoes then. If we're going to eat tonight we need a torch to light a gentleman's way and that costs money. We can pawn them.' He points at the shoes. 'And stop crying. Do you want to end up in a molly house?'

Like soldiers they drop to the floor to tug at the drunkard's feet, the stench that comes off him causes the youngest to turn a shade of pale green. They manage to take one shoe when a fierce highlander lunges at them from nowhere.

'Run, Angus. Run!' the eldest boy squeals like a piglet and grabs his little brother's hand. They flee carrying just one shoe before the highlander boxes their ears.

★★★

'Duncan!' the highlander screams into the inebriated man's ear. He repeats his friend's name twice before pouring the contents of his tankard over his head.

Duncan comes to, wiping the ale from his sopping head. 'What did you do that for?'

'You've been robbed, you idiot. Two beggar boys. If we go now we'll catch up with them. Give them a good hiding.'

'Nae,' Duncan slurs. 'It's not their fault. Leave them be, Johnny. They're a creation of society; the damned gentry making criminals of the poor. God knows, it's a wonder they're alive after the dearth.' Duncan wobbles on his stool, one eye closed as he rummages through his pockets. 'I've got no money.'

'You've spent it no doubt.'

'Aye,' Duncan looks over towards the bar. 'Seen the view?'

Johnny nods and twitches his head at the innkeeper. 'She's good for business mind, but I don't envy him. All those men drooling over my wife's charms would vex me something rotten. What's up with your eye?'

Duncan tries to focus. 'Nothing, there must be something in it.'

Johnny looks him up and down and sniffs the air. 'Lord above, Duncan, you stink like a day old chanty. Have you been sleeping in a privy? You're a disgrace man. Isn't it time you took heed of some wise words, "wine is a mocker and beer a brawler; whoever is lead astray by them is not wise"? You should pay attention in kirk and be a good Christian man.'

'Spare me the zealous nonsense and buy me a drink.'

Johnny shakes his head. 'I will not. When did you last see Ann?'

'Ann?'

'Yes. Ann. You know – your wife?'

'We had another quarrel a few days ago and I've not been back since. She's a shrew. You don't know the half of it. Anyway, I'm parched. Have you got a few coins for me? I need a drink.'

'Nae.'

'One for the road?'

'Get your hat.'

★★★

Two rowan trees flank Duncan's cottage, their warped branches stretch across the turf roof, as though to protect the inhabitants within. Johnny glances at Duncan ahead, walking his crisscross walk, made even more peculiar by the fact that he only wears one shoe. The sky is overcast and Johnny's keen to be inside, but not here – not near Ann.

Outside the cottage, Duncan cowers under the shadow of the rowan tree. Suddenly the orgy of drinking finally catches up with him, and he opens his mouth and unleashes a bellyful of vomit onto the floor. Johnny groans and points him in the direction of the door. But the prospect of entering his cottage and facing his wife is too much for Duncan, and so lacking in courage he clings to Johnny till they are safely inside.

The room is dark. Johnny half walks, half carries Duncan across the room, dropping the drunkard into a chair. Only then does Johnny dare to look at Ann's face. His eyes widen, her face has never looked like this in his mind; she has aged since he saw her last. He sighs and remembers how they met. The famine brought them together. The recent great dearth has caused many a highlander to venture miles from home; in droves across the Stirling Bridge to trade food. Most exchange excess dairy produce for Lowlanders' meal and Johnny's no exception. And so, this is how he became acquainted with Ann, long before she fell for the fine-looking Duncan.

The highlander glances at her from the corner of his wet eye, every so often her eyes flash with melancholy, tangible proof of her miserable existence. Johnny wipes his face, life is cruel he thinks. Why is it that Ann withers while Duncan matures like a fine wine? If only things could be different. Johnny inches forward, moving to the back of her as she toils, he leans over her, but not so far as to allow her to see his face, which is sickened with regret and something else – perhaps sorrow. She bends around to meet his gaze but he won't permit it, and therefore he twists his body around to face a dying fire, and thus the moment passes.

Ann claps her hands together and rubs them for warmth. 'So he's drunk again?'

Johnny nods. 'I found him at the Ten Bells. I can't stay long, lassie – I've work to do.'

Ann nods her head. 'The fire's low. I'll fetch more peat,' she ignores Duncan and directs her speech to Johnny.

'Duncan?' Johnny elbows his friend in the ribs.

'Ouch. What did you do that for?' says Duncan.

'Ann shouldn't be carrying a bucket of peat in her condition!'

Duncan turns in his wife's direction, his watery eyes settle on her swollen stomach. 'Just fetch half a bucket, Ann.'

Johnny chokes and his eyes widen. 'You're jesting?'

'Nae. Why?' Duncan asks.

★★★

The child came a week later. Ann gave birth alone. Her husband could not be found and so there was no one to send for the midwife.

Nevertheless, somewhere within the desert of Ann's black heart, a bright shining star gave her hope, for her child was as bonny as a mid-summer sunset, a baby girl with chestnut hair, thick lashes and the tiniest nose. Ann named her Margaret, but in time she would come to be known as Maggie.

One year later, true to form, Duncan missed the birth of his second child, a son named James. It was the last straw for Ann and a defining moment in their matrimony. Ann, a pious woman at the best of times, sought divine guidance. The kirk elders (in their desire to be rid of the drunken profligate, Duncan) were more than happy to assist them. And therefore, with the parish's support, they moved to Musselburgh, known as 'The Honest Toun.' They settled near Inveresk, a cold and rough land near the coast of the Firth of Forth. It was a land of gardeners, farmers and fishermen, and if none of these professions were to Duncan's satisfaction, there was always the nearby coalmine or saltpans. They departed at dawn, with the children wrapped up warm and testimonial of characters safe in hand. For a whole day they travelled by foot and hay-cart and together they left the horror of famine behind.

★★★

If truth be told, Duncan has to bite his tongue while the landowner talks down to him like lord to vassal. In consolation, Duncan devotes half of his attention to the gudeman's pretty wife, who snatches every possible opportunity to cast a swooning glance in his direction. While Duncan, his wife and children stand in rags, the shovel-faced landowner preaches to them in a new broadcloth coat, worsted stockings, silver buckled shoes and a silly little hat. He wastes no time in laying down conditions of verbal tack, thereby tying Duncan to the landowner on a short term lease.

'Is there a cottage...?' Duncan pretends not to notice the landowner scowling at having been interrupted.

'Yes, yes, yes. It has land on the in-field to sow oats or peas, and a kale yard. You'll be required to help with the ox team.'

'Is that all?'

The landowner grins and reveals yellow-brown teeth. 'I might need a man to help clear the middens once in a while, and there's a problem with foxes.'

Duncan nods, but deep down seethes inside. That's all he needs, chief shite clearer and ghillie. He hopes he won't be labouring morning till night, with no time for drinking and women. The landowner and peasant shake hands and the deal is done. Duncan smiles at the comely gudewife and tips his hat.

With the landowner now out of sight, he's alone with Ann, at a loss for words. What does a man say to a sullen wife with a face like thunder? He closes his eyes and imagines finer things, a woman's naked foot, long silken hair, pouting full lips. Without much enthusiasm he opens his eyes and searches for the figure of Ann. She stands beyond the run-rigs towards sloping ground, as if contemplating the labour yet to be done. Duncan sighs, the sad reality is, life for all but the privileged few is cruel, brutal and often short. These fields will claim their blood and strength. This is their lot. Duncan walks towards his wife, and as he does so his chest fills with air, and a deep sigh escapes his lips as a tentative hand reaches out towards her. She declines it.

'We can make progress here, Duncan, let's not waste this opportunity.' Her face turns towards the hills that swell to higher grounds. 'No more whoring, no more drinking or we'll lose everything. You've James and Maggie to think of now.'

Duncan's face tilts up to the sun, his eyes darting left and right to all four corners of the sky, as though searching for the right words. 'I cannot agree to that, wife. But I will work the land and keep us in home.'

Ann nods, her eyes flicker with emotion. 'Couldn't you try?'

CHAPTER TWO

THE HONEST TOUN

Of course, Duncan does not try. His roguish nature is fixed like limpets to rocks. And so, in the passing of ten years, Duncan Dickson does as he pleases and follows every decadent desire, and from this tree sprouts a branch, patterned with the same imperfect knots – Maggie. There is a pained expression on Ann's face, for Duncan and Maggie are one and the same.

Nevertheless, there is a vain hope for the child's soul. Strict moral guidance and hard work is to be the girl's salvation. And therefore, Maggie's doting but ailing mother begins to impart vital knowledge to her daughter, in the hope of making her a useful, God-fearing and conscientious girl. But Maggie is not in the least interested. The practical business of learning to cook and clean, to spin and sew, she likes not, but no matter, she *will* learn them all.

Therefore, Ann continues to guide her daughter, instructing her in all the domestic duties that are necessary to make her a good wife. Every day is dedicated to a new chore; washing clothes, making a fire, brewing ale and so forth. Thus, with the passing of time, and to Ann's delight, Maggie begins to make progress. Religious instruction can be concentrated on later, Ann decides, for the time being Maggie must learn how to make rush lights for instance, but today she cannot be found. A deep scowl line mars Ann's face as she searches the cottage, then the kale yard, but Maggie cannot be found. All day they search for Maggie across the moors and run-rigs, till Duncan finds her by the rugged coast, wild-haired and barefoot by the harbour, watching fishermen splice their ropes.

They keep her prisoner after that and the lessons recommence. On a warm sunny day, a day no doubt Maggie would prefer to be spending out-of-doors, Ann demonstrates how to foot a stocking. Maggie observes her parent with a critical eye, finding it hard to believe her mother was once bonny and not this crooked woman of many chores. After all, what has all this domestic diligence achieved except chapped hands and swollen legs full of black spots? Once a week, near the clear waters of the Esk, her mother and countless other poor women trample dirty laundry in tubs of cold water, after that they run home to warm their legs by the fire – the result is black spots and swollen legs. Maggie winces at the thought; she doesn't want to end up like her mother, old and wizened before her time. No wonder her father prefers the company of other lasses.

When winter comes, the Yule brings a deep snow. Upon naked moors, shivering trees yield to a storm of swirling snowflakes, and for many weeks people huddle by their fires. The wintry weather leaves its mark on Maggie's mother. Like the bent and twisted trees that cling to the landscape, she becomes more withered and worn. Her dull eyes only brighten at the sight of Maggie, such a spirited daughter, so different from her. Ann smiles and opens out her arms. Here she is, fresh from the harbour, and at fourteen years of age slender and comely. Men drool all over her like a dog for a flesher's bone. Ann sighs, what to do? What else but domestic service. The sooner the better as far as Ann's concerned, before she brings shame to their door. Ann gathers her shawl around her; of late there is a chill in her bones. Her breathing is laboured and as she holds a hand over her heart she thinks *life is pitiless, as my blood weakens, my daughter's strengthens*. A pious lecture is what is needed. Ann is decided; the path of righteousness is to be Maggie's salvation, because in her passing, Maggie has but one guardian, an incurable philanderer.

★★★

St Michaels sits at the top of a steep hill, the shining crown of Inveresk. It's an impressive structure surrounded by moss-stained gravestones and an abundance of weeds. At the crack of dawn, Maggie, her mother and James wait by two huge wooden doors patterned with metal rivets. To the right is a cutty stool and jougs, the collar all rusty and worn. Every Sabbath without fail the children dare each other to place it over their heads.

Once the doors open, folk flock into kirk, pushing and shoving for one of the limited amount of seats. Maggie fights through the crowd, determined not to stand. James walks slowly behind supporting his mother's arm. But all the seats have gone. All three of them huddle together in the dark. Rats and mice scurry over their feet, their tiny claws scratching their way around kirk fixtures in search of tasty morsels to eat. All around them, intricate wooden carvings adorn the alcoves, complimented by majestic buttresses, pillars and arches. Maggie bends her neck backwards and stares above, and she cannot be sure but she fancies that the grotesque gargoyles seem to sneer and mock the congregation below.

As the last person enters kirk the door closes. Ragged parishioners stand shoulder to shoulder as mangy dogs run up and down the aisles. In the thick of it the stench is unbearable, and many a person holds a clout to their mouth or wrinkles their nose. The quality gloat from the safe distance of their comfortable seats, holding their smelling salts or vinaigrettes to their faces, well away from the rabble. The minister enters. A quick head-count is done. Woe betides the Sabbath-breaker that dares to miss a sermon, if they're fortunate they'll spend a day in the stocks.

The minister begins his sermon with a typical bout of moral indignation. A feeling of dread bubbles within Maggie's stomach. Is it possible he directs this pious speech to her? Surely not, Maggie thinks, and then flinches as a bony finger points out towards her face. His voice cuts through the air and the sermon goes on and on...

'It is the congregation's moral obligation to root out evil and sinful behaviour. Failure to do so will lead to punitive divine intervention in human affairs,' he pauses for breath, 'I promise you this, my congregation will be rid of impiety, and drunkenness, idleness, and cursing will not be tolerated. I have no need to remind you that only the elect, who were the followers of the true church, will achieve salvation. The sinners or reprobate will achieve eternal damnation in hell.'

Maggie yawns.

★★★

Prior to the passing of Maggie's mother, a single event occurs that will determine her future. The incident in question transpires on a cold wash-day, under the Roman Bridge, near the sparkling waters of the Esk. Several lasses wash their dirty linen that day, in the Scottish way of course, with their dresses hitched up around their waists, treading away on their laundry with bare feet to trample away offending grime.

A group of men approach the river, fishermen looking for bait: the likes of lugworms, paps or mussels. As the men settle near the edge of the Esk, most of the women blush and pull down their petticoats and wait for the men to be on their way. But not Maggie, she hitches her skirts higher and treads on her laundry with much vigour, her pretty thighs on full display. The other women raise their eyebrows and tut-tut at her brazenness, but Maggie doesn't care, let the men have a good eyeful is what she's thinking. Before long, two of the fishermen stick to her like dung to a cross sweeper's shoe, and to the other women's amazement they even help her to empty a dirty pail and carry her washing.

★★★

Beneath the Old Roman Bridge an old fisherman spits out his pipe and stares at a young lassie passing by. Two fellow fishermen flank her; they are smitten, slavering all over her like rabid dogs. The old fisherman closes his gaping mouth. It's impossible to take his eyes off her. After a while he averts his gaze and presses a hand over his heart. There is a great weight pressing down on his breast, but to his utmost relief the pain soon passes. Damnation, she's stirred up feelings inside of him he's not experienced for years. He turns to the young lugger, Patrick next to him, busy sorting his bait.

'Look at those couple of Jack Tars with a lassie up yonder. Why don't you go with them, Patrick?'

'With that trollop? Not a chance.'

'But did you see her? What a beauty and did you see the size of her...? Well I expect you know what I mean, you'd have to have been blind not to notice that one.'

'I've seen her kind before; they bring nothing but trouble.'

The old mariner laughs revealing a toothless mouth. 'You've gone soft in the heid, lad. If I was but a few years younger, I'd rattle her bones, I would!'

'Not me,' declares Patrick Spence in a stern voice.

The old fisherman scratches his head. Nevertheless, he notices how the young man's eyes remain in the direction of the bridge long after the girl is gone.

★★★

Before Ann goes to meet her maker, she has but one dying wish – she asks her husband to take Maggie to see the new assistant minister, Robert Bonaloy at kirk.

'Why?' moans Duncan. 'You know Maggie. She's not one for kirk.'

Ann wrings her hands together. 'Aye and I wonder where she gets that from. Just do as I ask, please. I don't ask for much. This new minister will lead Maggie to the path of salvation. She must learn to obey God's will.'

Duncan shakes his head. 'Waste of time if you ask me.'

Ann persists. 'Our daughter must be brought up in strict attendance of the Worship of God. This is to be her salvation.'

The following day Duncan carries out his wife's dying wish. But such is life; things do not go according to plan because Maggie develops a wild passion for the new minister. And so begins Maggie's penchant for craving something that she simply cannot have.

'I could be at the Ten Bells now having a dram,' Duncan grumbles as he drags his daughter up the hill to St Michaels, 'you could pray till there's no skin on your knees, Maggie, but you'll not mend your ways.' He places a finger to the tip of his nose. 'Ask me how I know?'

'Please reveal all,' she replies.

'You and I are of the same mould, Maggie. You cannot change your true nature, lass. It's who you are.' He winks and pushes her in the direction of the minister.

★★★

Assistant Minister Bonaloy and the Dickson girl enter kirk after prayers. More than a few kirk elders cast curious glances at them as they walk briskly towards the cloisters. The new minister directs her to a small wooden bench and prompts her to sit. Against his better judgement he sits beside her and examines the girl. She has the kind of face that one simply must stare at, and so he does for the longest time, unable to process such beauty. Unconsciously he looks for flaws, and if he finds one it is that her mouth is too large, and her eyes too knowing for a lass of fifteen. He moves closer, but not so close that he touches her knees. Without thinking he stretches out a hand to her face. There's a slight tremble in his touch as tentative fingers settle beneath a bruised and swollen eye socket.

'You've a blackened eye. Why?'

'It's nothing. A farm laddie cornered me at the back of a cowshed.'

'And what were you doing there? On second thoughts, never mind, no matter. Does your father know?'

'Aye,' says she.

'And did he punish you?'

'Whatever for? I've committed no sin.' She crosses her arms and her bottom lip pouts like a sulky child.

15

The minister's face softens, his gaze drawn to her full lips. The girl's mother has a right to be concerned; he loosens his collar and crosses his arms. As he scrutinises her, he imagines the lassie's confounded, caught in the middle of woman and girl. He decides to change the subject and introduces himself.

'I expect you know who I am. I'm the new minister, Robert Bonaloy. And you are?'

'Maggie Dickson.'

'Well, Maggie. Your mother has asked me to have a wee talk with you. I'm under the impression she thinks you're in need of moral guidance, and I couldn't help noticing that she is ailing somewhat...'

'My mother need not be troubled. I am perfectly fine.'

The girl's face saddens. All of a sudden he becomes at odds with himself, craving to comfort her, veins bulging in his neck as he longs to lean forward. For a while this inner battle rages on and then he shrinks backwards to clasp his beloved bible to his heart, like a magic and godly shield.

'Have you learnt the catechisms, child?'

Maggie shakes her head.

'No? Why ever not? I'll read them to you.' His eyes look away as she removes her plaid. 'Come here and kneel with me.' He sinks to his knees and gestures for her to join him. Maggie kneels beside him, inching closer and closer, till one of her knees brushes against his, causing him to move away.

'May I ask you a question?' she asks with a bold stare.

'Of course,' he replies.

'Are you married, Minister Bonaloy?'

'Yes, yes I am. Betty and I have been married a year.'

'Is it a sin to look at another woman when you are married?'

'Whatever do you mean? Look at in what way, child?'

'As a man looks at a woman and acknowledges her as a woman.'

The minister shivers. 'It is sinful for a man who is married or betrothed to look at another woman, for to do so is to commit adultery in the heart.'

Maggie shakes her head. 'But 'tis a natural thing, is it not?'

'No. It is not,' he replies in a harsh voice.

'So, you've *never* looked at another woman since you became wed?'

The minister cradles his bible to his chest. 'No, well not in that way, to do so would be disrespectful to my wife. Can't you see that?'

Maggie raises her eyes and scowls; the action wrinkles her pretty face. 'Can't see the harm in it myself, isn't it the same as appreciating a beautiful sunset or the sound of a bird in song?'

'Lead us not into temptation, Maggie. We must remain chaste, wholesome and free of sin. Think of your eternal soul. Do you want to be cast into eternal damnation?'

'Of course not, but I have committed no sin,' Maggie huffs.

The minister suddenly feels a great weight upon his shoulders. 'You must learn to obey the will of God, Maggie. Now let us pray.'

★★★

At the river bank, Patrick sees her again, the bonny washer lassie from Musselburgh, sporting a black eye. Not that it detracts from her beauty in any way. He knows it is only a matter of time before she disgraces herself, so he keeps his distance and watches from afar. But despite his reservations he soon finds himself drawn to her – there is something earthy and iniquitous about her. Thus, it is with a heavy heart he departs from the river that day, for he would have liked to walk over to that girl, and push the other men away. But he has neither the courage nor conviction.

A week later he bumps into her at kirk. Her eyes gaze upwards to the new minister, attentive to every single word. Perhaps she's learnt the error of her ways, he wonders, or perhaps not. His heart swells as he stares; there is no doubt that she is a beautiful young woman, with waist length, chestnut hair and sloe-eyes rimmed with thick, sooty eyelashes. Her full lips are a vermillion red and her body already possesses the curves of a voluptuous woman. But when all is said and done it is her eyes that captivate him because beneath those long dark lashes is something evocative of pleasurable fulfilment.

After the sermon, as always, he prepares to walk home with his mother and father. But a compelling voice calls to him from within. *Go to the girl*, it chants over and over, until despite his reservations he contrives to meet with her near the kirk door. A great desire washes over him as she nears the entrance, and then to his dismay she turns and waves to the new minister instead. But Patrick persists and waits near the entrance. With much fortitude, he lingers close by and is soon rewarded with her presence.

'Aren't you one of the fishermen from Fisherrow?' she enquires in a loud voice.

Patrick's mouth opens, taken aback by her boldness and confidence. 'Yes, Patrick Spence. Pleased to meet you,' he stammers. 'And you are?'

'Maggie Dickson and this is my brother, James. He's apprenticed to be a weaver.'

'So you're a fisherman? What do you fish?' the brother asks.

'Herring.'

The brother grins. 'Maggie loves the sea. Ever since she was a bairn she's been running to the harbour to watch the boats…'

'Hush, James,' Maggie scolds and wraps her plaid around her.

'Well you have, Maggie. Clothes and hair soaked from the sea, always telling our mother you want to be a sea captain.'

Patrick is well aware of her harbour exploits. His mind reels, now is the perfect opportunity to get her alone with a pledge of sorts, but for the life of him he doesn't know what to say. He's lost his tongue.

The girl and brother bid farewell and walk away. Patrick opens his mouth but nothing comes out. At the very last moment, just before she disappears from sight, he manages to stammer: 'Maggie. Perhaps one day – if you are not – maybe I could take you…'

'Yes I would like that very much,' replies Maggie and walks swiftly away.

★★★

In January, a great gale of wind sweeps across from the moors, sending autumn leaves in a swirl of dead elm, oak and beech. It's a black month of the year, haunted by melancholy, and a plague upon the ill and weak. Maggie's mother, Ann, hovers between life and death, her paper-thin skin stretched over her bony face. Of course, in the wake of a great famine, Maggie is no stranger to death, but nothing can prepare her for the passing of her mother. When she dies, it is a bitter blow. There is no consolation from Maggie's father. Duncan remains indifferent, he labours, he gallivants, and little else. Maggie's only comfort is James.

As one season passes into another, buds of the rarest green begin to scatter across the distant hills and for Maggie life goes on. With the passing of her mother, she is now responsible for all domestic work, and Lord there is so much to do. Wash day in particular causes Maggie to moan and groan, but of course it has to be done. As Maggie walks to the river, her pail of laundry weighs her down and causes her back to throb and ache. Near a great expanse of mountain gorse, she bends at the waist to set it down near the river edge, and as she does so, from the corner of her eye she catches sight of the fisherman, Patrick Spence shading beneath an oak tree, its budding twigs spread out like a fan. A yellow yowlie chirps and flutters in the tree above him, competing with the song of a sky-lark. Maggie squints into the bright sunlight to observe him, curious as to why he's there. He leans against the tree bark, his leine open at the neck. For just a moment, Maggie's eyes linger over him, he's broadened since she saw him last. After a while her interest wanes, and for the most part Maggie ignores him.

The cold water is up to her knees. Maggie adds more lye and hitches up her skirts. As usual there's no shortage of scandalous gossip. All round her women chitchat, clucking like hens. Maggie has the good sense to take no part in it. After a while a fair fisher lassie scurries towards the oak tree to the broad-shouldered fisherman. To Maggie's surprise he welcomes her like a lost lover, throwing his arms around her and kissing her neck. And this, and only this, secures Maggie's attention.

For what seems like eternity the amorous couple remain pressed up against the tree. The young women giggle, the older women shiver and grimace. And all the while the women go about their chores till their hands and feet wrinkle to a bright pink. As the sun reaches its highest point it has a great power now, and Maggie's legs stamp up and down on her laundry, her mouth set in a tight scowl as the smell of soiled linen fills her nostrils. But no matter how often she turns her head away, her curiosity soon gets the better of her, compelling her to sneak a sly glance in the fisherman's direction. His sweetheart can't take her hands off of him, lingering all over him as she blushes like a rose. Maggie becomes rather animated then, dancing up and down on her washing and singing a rousing song which some of the other women join in on. The amorous couple remain oblivious to all around them, lip to lip, toe to toe, the sounds of their unmistaken passion competing against the droning tones of bored washerwomen.

Then something snaps inside of her, and for whatsoever reason she reacts. Fire burns in Maggie's eyes as she looks at the man and truly sees him for the first time – this unassuming man, suddenly attractive while wrapped around another woman. But that's still not it. There's coldness in the fisherman's face she would like to thaw. She's seen it in the angular facial lines of the Norwegian fisherman with their steely blue eyes that mimic the ice cold fjords of their homeland – and cruel lips that hint of danger. Suddenly he's all man.

In a trance she inches closer towards them, her slippery fingers curling tight around her soapy pail. In one graceful swoop she flings the water with all her might towards the oak tree.

'Jesus. Watch what you're doing. You've soaked us,' the fisher lassie gasps.

Maggie replies: 'I didn't see you there.'

Patrick breaks away from the woman and moves closer to Maggie. 'But you knew I was here…'

'No matter, I expect you will dry in no time.' Maggie turns her attention to the fisher lassie smoothing out the wrinkles in her clothes. She's a pretty girl with wispy, fair hair. Suddenly Maggie's interested in which of them Patrick will prefer.

'Is this your sweetheart, Patrick?'

Patrick's face reddens. 'No – Agnes and I work at the harbour together.'

'I'm pleased you mentioned the harbour. Remember that day at kirk when you offered to take me…'

'The offer still stands,' he says.

'In that case we will go at once.'

Patrick turns to face Agnes, a shadow of regret in his eyes. 'But I have to…'

Maggie stoops to pick up her pail. 'Well, if you have other plans…' she glares at Agnes.

'No, no plans,' he shakes his head, a look of embarrassment on his handsome face as he shrugs at Agnes.

Agnes pouts her pretty lips. 'But you said we would go to the fair.'

'I know I did, Agnes. But the press gang might be there. I can't chance it.'

'But you said that…'

'I will make it up to you, lass, I promise. You see, I did say to Maggie that I would take her to the harbour a while…' He reaches out and places one arm on Agnes's shoulder in consolation.

Agnes pushes him away. 'Don't bother.'

Maggie stretches a grin as Agnes marches away. 'I'll have to finish my laundry first.'

'I will wait for you.'

As they stroll towards the harbour Maggie allows his free hand to clasp hers and his fingers link with her own. As they reach the seafront a voice shouts out, that of a fisherman calling out to another or to some companion working upon the silted quay, and the sound flickers and ripples, blown away by the wind. Iron rings on iron, hammers striking nails as boatmen make repairs. The sea whispers on the ebb-tide sand and all above them, always clearly audible are the mewing cries of seagulls. This is Maggie's favourite place, it is here

21

that she loves to watch the mariners at work, smoking their pipes as they empty gear from their boats to unload their haul. Some of them sit cross-legged on the floor, surrounded by their baskets, creels, and skulls. Others redd their nets to discard unused bait, and many of them curse as they free their nets of seaweed. It's here that Maggie feels at peace, especially when she looks out to sea.

'What's the matter?' he asks.

'There is nothing the matter.'

'Come here,' he says and pulls her tight into his arms. For what seems like eternity her breath mingles with his own, until at last she manages to cry out, 'Get rid of Agnes.'

CHAPTER THREE

SKULLS, MURLINS AND CREELS

Up and down, Maggie paces the cottage, from one wall to the next, ears peeled for the sound of heavy footsteps. Maggie knows he will come. For a moment she steps outside, her hair soft-lifted by a gentle breeze. In the distance she hears lambs bleat and the rustle of leaves in the trees. She lingers for a moment, hoping to see his large frame appear along the brae, a pleasant smile upon his handsome face, but it is not so. She enters the cottage and closes the door.

'He is not here yet,' she complains.

'He will be,' James nods.

'How do I look, James?' Maggie twirls around so that her skirts billow out into the shape of a circle.

'You look bonny, Maggie. You always do, but you are the vainest girl in Scotland. And quit preening and fussing with your hair, and shouldn't it be hidden under a fillet or a cap?'

'I'll do as I please. No one tells me what to do, least of all you.'

James arches back his neck, and pinches the bridge of his nose. 'You're asking for trouble. You're not a bairn anymore, Maggie.'

'All right, all right, I'll put a cap on.'

A knock on the door interrupts them. And this sets Maggie off in a wild panic, running from one corner of the room to the next in search of her cap. After a while she finds it and with much reluctance places it upon her head.

'James, open the door will you?'

'Get it yourself. Why should I help you? No one helps me. All day long I've been working the run-rigs all on my own. I was supposed to be at the master weaver's ages ago. My back's gone and I've cut my hand. So open it yourself.'

'Please, James,' Maggie begs. But he shakes his head and pushes her away, nursing his injured hand.

'Fool,' she stamps her feet and crosses the room.

A series of knocks causes the door to rumble and shake. Maggie takes a deep breath and places her hand on the door handle. As the doors swings opens it creaks like a squeaky wheel, meanwhile a suckling pig takes the opportunity to escape into the kale yard, nearly tripping Patrick in the process.

'Get it,' shouts Maggie. 'The little swine will run away for sure.'

Together, Patrick and Maggie chase the piglet around the yard while James looks on with folded arms trying not to laugh. It takes them a good while before the pig is caught, and by the end of it Maggie's hair is a mess and her clothes are spoilt. It's not the best beginning to their first day of walking out, but nevertheless Maggie is determined to make up for the shaky start.

'Come in. Come in. Mind your head.'

Maggie conceals a smile as he bumps his forehead on the crumbling doorframe.

As Patrick steps inside, a couple of hens run over his feet and from the look on his face they're not a welcome sight.

'Don't mind them. They're roosting in the rafters and only come down for a while.'

'Come sit by the fire, Patrick,' calls James and pats his hand on a stool. 'Maggie, take his coat.'

The room's smoky. A pot of broth bubbles away on the hearth and the smell is delicious. Patrick takes a seat near the fire and nods to James. If he's nervous he does not show it and in truth he seems right at home. As Maggie takes his coat he removes a bunch of wild flowers concealed from within the fabric and smiles. A pleasing scent mingles with the smoky peat air.

'Thank you,' Maggie says and with a flick of the wrist she throws the flowers to the side, thinking the pig can eat them later.

An awkward silence descends upon the cottage. Maggie stares at her humble home, suddenly seeing it through Patrick's eyes. Not a pane of glass graces the crumbling wattle and daub walls, and the only light comes from fire or rush light. Any smoke escapes from a crude hole in the roof. But this is home, somewhere to eat and somewhere to sleep.

'Shall we?' Her eyes glitter with mischief as she holds out her hand to return his coat.

★★★

They walk hand in hand along winding tracks, their route pock-marked with the hooves of horses and dumb beasts. Maggie sniffs the pungent air, Beltane fires burn in the distant hills in celebration of the return of summer. For a while they walk in silence, past ancient dry stone walls and sodden ditches, and soon they reach an old castle ruin. A burn bubbles and gurgles nearby; its crystal waters trickling over smooth stones. A sparkling light reflects on the water's surface, casting a hazy glow on the two figures as they embrace near the water's edge. Maggie closes her eyes as fervent hands seek the cap that conceals her hair; her long tresses cascade around her shoulders. She shivers and tilts her neck backwards to look at the handsome fisherman. His eyes are rimmed with pale lashes and the bristles on his face do not match the colour of his hair.

As he leads her to the burn her heart thumps in her breast. All of a sudden her one and only desire is to run from this place and never return. He's immersed in the water now, waiting for her to join him; tradition demands that she mirrors his actions. And yet, all the while an image fills Maggie's head, an image of a fine-looking young priest, forbidden, out of reach, and thus more desirable. And so, it's with much trepidation that Maggie Dickson drops to her knees in the water to join hands with Patrick, to seal their fates forever.

'Will you marry me, Maggie?'

'Aye.'

Her heart sinks as she stands on her tiptoes to kiss him. *What have I done?* she thinks, but as his soft lips press hard on her mouth, Maggie becomes much altered and consumed with desire. As blood courses through her veins, he pulls away.

'We must wed in haste. I don't want to lose you to another man.' His eyes narrow.

Maggie reaches out to soothe him, already aware of the jealousy that lies dormant within him. 'Well I want a real shindig of a wedding, with pipers and fiddlers and dancing. And, Patrick, can the new minister wed us?'

'Why the new minister?'

'He helped me after my mother died. It would please me so, Patrick.'

'Very well.'

A nauseous longing stirs inside of her. How she longs to feel his lips on her own again and so she kisses him for the longest time till there is no breath left in her. After a while she drags him to the dry purple heather below, hitching her petticoats higher and higher to inflame his desire. The art of love comes as natural to her as the air she breathes. With her head thrown to the side she pulls him on top of her, the sounds of his groans and heavy breathing tickling her ear. A wave of pleasure washes over her as he fiddles with his undergarments.

'What's wrong?' she cries as he rolls off her and jumps to his feet.

'A noise, did you hear it? Pull down your skirts, Maggie.' He pushes her petticoats over her knees and forces himself into his undergarments.

'There's no one here,' she replies, continuing to caress his inner thigh. Her hands travel higher and higher until they settle near his groin.

Patrick slaps her hands away. 'Stop it, Maggie.' He pulls her to her feet. 'See,' he nods in the direction of two poachers.

A couple of poachers pass by covered head to foot in mud. Each of them holds a dead bird in one hand, a pistol in the other. A hunting dog yaps at their heels, sniffing the ground.

'We have to go,' Patrick mutters, his face red and breathing laboured.

'Can't we stay a moment longer? They'll be gone in a moment.'

'Nae,' Patrick snaps. 'We must go. If we stay here one moment longer you're in trouble.'

An awkward silence descends upon them as they wait for the poachers to be out of sight. As the sky darkens above Maggie sulks and will not meet his eyes. *How dare he reject me*, she thinks. Her tiny hands make a fist and her fingernails make crescent shapes upon her palms. Before they reach the cottage, they shelter beneath a rowan tree, its clustered branches dipping into a muddy stream.

'Maggie, I have to go away for a wee while, on the keels. I'm taking oysters on coble boats to Newcastle upon Tyne, and after that I'm bringing glass bottles to Leith. It's well paid work and we need the money mind to rent a cottage. But rest assured, when I return we shall be wed.'

'But, Patrick. I don't want you to go.'

'If we are to have a roof over our head I must.'

They walk back to the cottage in silence with Maggie moping the whole way home. At the cottage Patrick stoops to kiss her, but at the last moment Maggie turns away and runs off to her dwelling before slamming the door.

★★★

So begins a volatile relationship, and one that will bring Patrick Spence to his knees. Nevertheless, as is the custom, he arranges to meet with Maggie's father to ask him for his daughter's hand in marriage. But this proves difficult indeed, as Maggie's father is invariably gallivanting or inebriated from the effects of ale. And therefore, Maggie's brother, James takes the place of Duncan and gives the fishermen permission to marry his sister.

On a beautiful day in May, Maggie Dickson and Patrick Spence give their names to be proclaimed in order to be married in the old kirk of St Michaels in Inveresk. Their date of marriage set for 3 June, 1715.

★★★

Inside the Musselburgh Arms, near the tolbooth, patrons drink a toast to the betrothed couple. It's gaming night and so the wedding party huddles around an old beer-stained table, shouting to one another to be heard above the din. A serving wench brings a full tray of ale and points to a handsome man propped up against the bar. Duncan winks in their direction and raises a jar of frothy beer.

Patrick's father, George Spence shouts above the rumpus. 'Has the lassie got a dowry by any chance?'

'Aye, I have.'

James shushes her as though she's incapable of answering him. 'Allow me to speak for you, Maggie.'

'Damn men and their superiority,' Maggie curses to herself and sits back in her chair. A tight smile stretches across her face as she seethes inside. Patrick places a consoling arm around her; she brushes it aside and glares at her brother, unable to appreciate, as yet, the important role he is willing to play.

James clears his voice. 'Since Maggie was a wee lassie our mother, friends and neighbours have helped to collect and make bed linen, furniture, blankets and the like for Maggie's dowry. There's a suckling pig for her and other odds and ends. She's not coming to Patrick empty-handed mind; she's a fine catch.'

'Oh, I don't doubt that,' says George, his gaze remaining on Maggie's figure a fraction too long. His wife, Barbara, cuffs him around the ear with the back of her hand.

'What did you do that for, you daft bat?' George glares at his wife.

'You know why, and don't do it again or I'll slap your other lug-hole.'

In the midst of this quarrel, Maggie notices Patrick looking at her father with a curious, puzzled face. Duncan is on his feet, swaying back and forth, his hat on back to front, and he seems to have lost the use of one eye.

'Your father looks like he needs to go home.'

Maggie shrugs, indifferent to her father's behaviour. 'He's only just started. Once he takes one drink he has to have more. Oh no, here he comes.' She winces.

'Well, what's all this then?' Duncan slurs.

'Your daughter's getting married,' declares George in an offhand manner. 'And your son has taken your place giving her away. Haven't you heard?'

Duncan wobbles on his feet. 'Oh, the indignity of it. No matter, Maggie, he's a better man than I.'

'Well wouldn't you like to know when?' George runs his hand through what is left of his hair.

'When what?'

'When they are to be wed.' George shakes his head.

'When?'

George informs Duncan of the date.

'Perfect. You two choose to get married when the bastard Jacobites are planning an uprising. What timing!'

George sniggers and mumbles under his breath, 'What would a drunk know about politics?'

Duncan laughs. 'Every Scottish man should know about politics or those damned Sassenachs would run us out of our own country. Why do you think they don't want a Stuart to reclaim the throne? Answer me that, fisherman.'

'That's obvious, pal; they don't want a Catholic.'

Duncan shakes his head. 'Nae, the English couldn't care less. He's German, with a couple of mistresses to keep him happy. The Stuarts are of a *Scottish* line, and the Sassenach's would rather have a German running the country than a Scottish descendent. Anyway, where was I?' Duncan staggers back to the bar; carefully turning his hat until it faces the right way.

★★★

Long ago, on the east bank of the river at Fisherrow, there was once an old almshouse. It stood near the west end of Market Street and was a great comfort to the poor, ill and destitute. But those days are long gone and now Fisherrow has one main street, with soaring tenements built up on both sides. Beyond the tenements are a multitude of fisherman's cottages, in several rows leading to a busy harbour.

From Martimes to Candlemas, a school house operates here, recently built at the west end of Magdelen Chapel. Its traditional medieval roof thatched with turfs dug from the town's common lands. A saltwife cries out her wares and shuffles along with her creel on her back, unhappy in her toil. With much reluctance Maggie stops her and can't help but notice how her mouth slants to one side, as though she's suffered an injury of some kind. Before she loses courage, Maggie asks her if she could direct her to Watts Close where the fishermen dwell. The saltwife grumbles and directs her to halfway along the tenements to a group of white cottages.

'It's up there, by the sea mill.'

It takes Maggie longer than she thinks to reach it. Nevertheless, when she reaches Watts Close she realises how close she is to the harbour.

'Maggie,' a deep voice calls out.

About half way down the wynd, Patrick waves to her. Silhouetted by the sunlit harbour, he stands by a small cottage, his stance tall and proud. Maggie squints into the sun and walks towards him, with every step she resists the urge to run, and soon she has a better view of the dwelling. It has large stores at ground level for a good catch, and fishing gear with living accommodation above. At the entrance, near a little wooden door is a hook for drying fish. Below, an abundance of fishing nets, creels, baskets and skulls are on hand for line and sea fishing. Near the steps, Patrick waits, his eyes never leaving her face as she walks towards him.

'You took your time.' His forehead creases. 'Why is your hair uncovered? Shouldn't you have it under a cap or tied with a fillet?'

Maggie pulls a face at him. 'No, I like my hair like this,' she smiles, tossing her locks to one side.

'I really think you should keep your head covered in future, it's not fitting. Put it on now,' he squeezes her hand and guides her up the steps.

Maggie changes the subject. 'Why didn't you tell me it was near the harbour?'

'I did,' he says.

'Are you going to show me inside our new home or are we going to stay out here all day in the cold?'

'Aye, but no kisses, Maggie. My mother might arrive at any moment, says she wants to give this place a wee clean.'

Maggie huffs. The last thing she wants is an interfering woman. 'I can clean it myself.'

The wind in Musselburgh is like no other, blustering, bitter and incessant. Hand in hand they ascend the stone steps that lead to the fisherman's dwelling. The interior is surprisingly warm, fat walls keep out the cold wind and drown out all noise from outside. With bright eyes, Maggie skips around the dwelling to explore every nook and cranny, and to imagine hers and Patrick's possessions positioned inside.

'Patrick. Look here, there is a small window.'

'Aye, I've seen it. The glass isn't broken, it's just dirty and needs a bit of spit on a clout to clean it. Your chore,' he nods to her.

'More like your mother's.'

'Less of that, Maggie, you should be grateful for the help.'

'I just want us to be left alone.'

'There's no rush. Patience, my love.'

Maggie presses her finger onto the grimy windowpane; it feels cold and smooth to the touch. She draws a star in the dirt; it makes a squeaking sound with every line. Happy with her handiwork she wipes her finger on her skirts and crosses the room to his extended hand. A delicious shiver shoots up her spine as he takes her hand in his own and presses it to his lips. In a trance, Maggie follows him out of the dwelling.

'Next time we come here, I'll be carrying you over the threshold.'

Maggie smiles and then turns a frown. 'Aye, I can't believe it.'

★★★

Upon the ancient rocks at Joppa, Maggie observes white caps explode against rocks misshapen by a thundering sea. Is there a more beautiful place, she wonders? She fancies not. A solan goose circles above her head, and it seems to spread its wings like a majestic angel to a dying sun. For a while, she follows its progress and becomes lost in thought. A bitter taste fills her mouth – in a short while her husband will be her master and she must do his bidding. With a sickened heart Maggie stands to leave. Beyond the rocks she catches sight of a splendid ship on the horizon, its intricate rigging and a fine figurehead cutting through the wind. There's a wild desire in her heart to be on-board the ship, as one with the wind and sea.

'If only I were a man,' she whispers into the salt breeze.

A hungry guillemot mews above her head, soaring towards the fishwives who gut fish near the shore. The fishwives are a fearsome lot, feisty, outspoken and coarse. Maggie observes them from the corner of her eye and notes the muscles in their arms as they lift huge creels of fish onto their backs. Curious about a fisher lassies lot, she'd asked Patrick about the fishwives, and he'd told her that they're strong independent women, used to being alone while their men are at sea. Maggie approaches the boat shore, her legs trembling and shaking, feeling as though she's approaching an unknown barbaric land. As she stoops by some rocks, one fisherwoman in particular catches her eye. She has dirty clouts tied around her neck and a masculine weather-beaten face. There're all kinds of fish set out around her, and the fisherwoman has spread them out on the rocks in neat little rows. Maggie takes a deep breath and steps towards her.

'Hello, missus. What you doing?'

'What the devil does it look like? I'm sortin' the catch. You're Patrick Spence's lassie, aren't you? Going to be a fisher lassie soon?'

'Aye, I am,' replies Maggie. She lifts some seaweed to her nose and inhales its bitter scent.

The fishwife stops what she's doing and stands still. A dangerous looking knife dangles from a belt tied to her apron and skirts. Her gaze is intense as though she's deciding if Maggie's up to the job. 'So you've decided to come to the harbour and take a wee look at what we do then? That takes some guts, girl,' she nods.

The fisher lassie's nimble fingers slice through a slimy fish. Greedy gulls swoop from above in pursuit of tasty morsels. She stops again and peers at her abruptly, as though vexed at being interrupted in her work. 'Are you still here?'

'Aye,' says Maggie.

'Do you want me to show you the ropes, is that it?'

Maggie stares at the woman's torn fingers covered in strips of cloth. 'Aye, missus. If you're busy, I'll return later.'

The fishwife cackles. 'Lassie, you'll get nowhere with that attitude. Be bold. I've seen you with the fishermen. You're not shy with them now, are you?'

'What's your name, missus?' Maggie asks.

'That's better. My name is Isobel, Isobel Tait. That's my husband over there, Jack bastard Tar,' she laughs and waves at a short, stocky man baiting a six-stringed line into a wicker skull. 'Aye, we know your Patrick, he's a good man. You've much to learn, lass. I'm busy now but if you come here tomorrow, I'll try and help.'

Maggie smiles and thanks her, pleased that someone is willing to teach her. She walks away and then realises that she's not asked what time. She turns and calls out, 'Isobel. What time should I come to the harbour?'

'Sunrise, and don't be late.'

★★★

On the horizon, where the light blue heavens meet a turquoise sea, a beautiful sunrise streaks the sky soft yellow, pink, and blazing orange. Shadowy silhouettes of sailing boats bob on a glittering water, and the warm sun reflects off its surface, casting a soft glow on the ebbing tide. A hissing noise fills Maggie's ears as a current of air whips up the sand, with both hands she covers her eyes and rubs away the grit till her vision returns. When she opens her eyes an astonishing scene greets her. Into the wading waters go the fishwives. Their skirts hiked up and tied around trim waists so that their bare legs are exposed. But it's the sight of the fishermen sat on their backs that surprises her, clear of the water until safely aboard their boats.

'We carry the men to the boats so their clothes and sea boots don't get wet. You see, if they board ship with wet clothes, they'd never get the damned things dry.'

'You startled me,' says Maggie. 'When did you get here?'

'Just got here. Saw you gawping at the women carrying the men to the boats. It's not as difficult as you think you know.'

'You're jesting. You've seen Patrick and the size of him.'

'You'll be amazed what you can do.'

A swallow circles above. Maggie peers at it as it swoops into the waters before soaring off again into the sky.

'The swallow's a sign of good weather, lassie. See the gulls too?'

Maggie cups one hand over her eyes, squinting into the bright sky. 'Aye. What of them?'

Isobel's face turns grave. 'Seagulls are thought to be the souls of those drowned at sea.'

Maggie continues to stare at them. As far as she's concerned they're noisy flying rats, forever in pursuit of food. And yet the harbour or any shore for that matter would seem desolate without them.

Isobel prattles on. 'Fisher folk are a superstitious lot, Maggie. Have I mentioned nets? Don't ever step over fishing nets barefoot; otherwise the nets cannot be used again. And don't say any of these words in front of the fishermen: pig, that's a bad one. Oh and rabbit or hare, fox or salt. Do you want to know more?'

Maggie shakes her head.

The women return from launching the boats, their clothes soaking wet and skirts tied around their waists. A group of them walk over to the rocks. From the look of them they seem to have lost something and then Maggie realises that they're searching through the rocks. But why, she wonders? They are quite odd; perhaps they are looking for crabs or starfish, she thinks.

'What are they doing now?' Maggie asks.

'They're collecting heavy rocks to act as ballasts; those rocks weigh a boat down and control buoyancy. It can mean the difference between life and death choosing the right ones.'

'Should we help?'

Isobel shrugs. 'You're not one of us yet.'

Maggie looks out across the shingle, a determined look in her eyes. 'Can I carry your creel?'

Isobel shakes her head and explains, 'It's full to the brim. You'll never take the weight. These things take time, Maggie.'

Maggie ignores her and strolls over to the willow creel, its hessian strap all withered and worn. A glazed look crosses Maggie's face as she bends to lift the creel. To Maggie's utter displeasure, Isobel follows her and barks out an order.

'Don't you be lifting it yourself, you daft beggar. You'll be falling on your backside. Wait. I'll help to attach the strap to your shoulders, so keep still.'

Maggie whines, 'I can do it. I can do it.' She holds out her hands in front of her to carry the creel.

Isobel cackles. 'Nae, you don't carry it like that. Like this.'

A glitter sparkles in Maggie's eye as the heavy creel is lowered onto her back. For a short moment Isobel faces her, as though waiting for her to drop the creel. But to Maggie's amazement she takes the weight and takes a few steps. 'See, it's easy.' But Maggie's progress is short-lived; it starts with a buzzing in the ears. After that an explosion of bright colours burst from beneath her eyelids. However much she ignores the pounding in her ears, it's to no avail and all colour drains from her face.

An amused expression crosses Isobel's face as she removes the heavy load. 'You're trying to run before you can walk, Maggie. Don't be too disheartened.'

Maggie slumps to the floor, perched atop a mound of rotting seaweed. A cold sweat covers her whole body. And as she looks out to sea, for no reason at all she thinks of her mother.

★★★

Maggie returns to the boat shore every day after that, eager to learn. She meets up with plenty more fisher lassies and they're a lively lot. Most of all, Maggie's astonished by the women's strength and the manner that they talk to one another. They employ a rude kind of eloquence and witticism that's crucial when selling fish in Edinburgh or at local fish markets. But when all is said and done they're a rowdy lot; loud, crude, bawdy and absolutely hilarious.

With the fisher lassies' help and guidance, it takes just one week for Maggie to learn how to sort a catch. In no time at all Maggie learns to gut, clean, split open and salt the fish and before long her fingers and hands are red raw. With a knowing look the fisher lassies show her how to bandage her fingers to protect them but to Maggie's mind they never seem to heal, because every time she dips her hands into salty water it feels like her flesh is being torn apart. Then there are the dreaded creels – she carries a small one at first and then progresses to heavier loads and bigger creels. In time, Maggie builds up her strength and learns to take the jeering banter when she falls on her behind. The more thick-skinned she becomes the more they accept her. One thing is for sure, there's no room for sentimentality or mollycoddling with this bunch.

CHAPTER FOUR

ST MICHAELS, INVERESK – 3 JUNE 1715

The first wild roses bloom in June. Soon follows a scorching sun, drying out the grass and making the earth hard and dusty. When the land is like this, Maggie shivers in her bones because there's no question her father will require her in the fields to perform backbreaking labour from sun-up till sun-down. God knows the only saving grace is when James lends a hand, when he can, subject to his weaving. Nevertheless, before long, Maggie will leave this kind of work behind her. She will not miss it because to her mind the land and toil killed off her mother, that and her thankless role of wife, mother and serf. Aye, Maggie's certain all that heavy lifting and bending over a cooking pot sent her mother to an early grave, either that or a broken heart.

The evening of the hen night arrives. And isn't it typical of her to get in a muddle, spinning over long outside and panicking about the time. On one bended knee she stoops to the ground to pick up her yarn. Maggie's so engrossed in her task she does not sense Patrick behind her.

'Maggie,' Patrick calls out. 'Didn't you hear me?'

'No. Help me with the spinning wheel will you and where have you been?'

Patrick silences her with a kiss and drops to his knees in front of her. Next he opens out one of her palms and places a gold ring within it.

'Where did you get that from?' she gasps, placing it onto her right finger.

'A Bilbao fisherman trading in whitefish. Have you missed me?'

Maggie shudders and presses her body against his. 'Aye, but I must confess I was beginning to think that you'd changed your mind.'

Patrick laughs and shakes his head. 'Not a chance. You look exhausted, lassie. Are you all right?'

'Aye, it's just I'm worn-out from all the upheaval, Patrick. The disagreements, the altered plans. Oh, and your mother, Patrick. Now she's really beginning to vex me...'

'Hush, Maggie. You know how folk are. Any excuse for a party. Weddings are community property, lass. A time for neighbours and friends to make gifts, bake bread and brew ale for the feast. And don't mind my mother, she means well. She's baked enough bannocks to feed an army. There's not a surface clear in our cottage.'

'Why didn't you come to me yesterday, once you were off the boat?'

'The men folk abducted me and took me to a tavern. You wouldn't believe what they did.'

'I can imagine.' She kisses him and he tastes of alcohol and his face is all smudged with soot. 'You'll have to go. It's my turn tonight.'

Patrick places a hand to his brow and then scratches his head. 'Your turn for what?'

'My hen night. It'll be like a bare-knuckle fight before the night is over. In one corner the farmwomen and the other, the fishwives.'

Patrick shudders as though a sack-'em-up man has dug up his grave. 'I'll be off then.'

★★★

Hen nights are normally sedate occasions, a time for woman folk to come together and pluck hens in preparation for a wedding feast. Maggie yawns. She's not really in the mood for a get together. To her mind, the night does not bode well, and just the thought of what's to come causes her to shiver inside.

They arrive at dusk in droves, with hens and other victuals tucked underneath their arms and skirts. James and Maggie's father are promptly banished to a tavern and told not to hurry home. The hens are piled on a crude wooden table, begging to be plucked. Around the poultry, a cloud of flies buzz, causing several of the women to swat them away. Above them, Maggie's roosting hens cower in the rafters, not wanting to join them.

'Where's the ale, Maggie?' a fisherwoman calls out in a coarse raspy voice.

'At the far wall. There are a couple of kegs brewed by old Widow Arrock. Strong stuff too,' Maggie shouts through the din.

Isobel Tait smirks. 'Aye, that ugly old cow's ale will put some hairs on your chest!' She pours out some ale and hands it out to the fishwives, interrupting them as they pull out their snuff, pipes and tobacco.

At the other end of the room, a wizened old farmwoman raises her shaggy eyebrows and glowers at Isobel and the other fishwives. Several of her chins wobble as she sniffs up her nose in a stern manner. A group of young farm lassies surround her, licking their lips at the prospect of frothy spiced ale, their eyes fixed on the old woman in the hope that she might allow them to join in with the drinking. But alas, the young lassies' hopes are to no avail, because soon the old woman claps her hands together and yells, 'Come on ladies, it's time to pluck the hens.'

One young farmwoman in a striped apron and petticoat complains out loud, 'Why can't we have a drink first, Ethel?'

'Once we've done our chores and not before.' The older woman extends a flabby arm and shuffles her way over to the table of hens.

The fishwives pay no heed to the farmwomen making their way to the hens. They're far too busy tittering and telling crude jokes. The smell of pipe smoke wafts across the room, along with lewd laughter and scandalous talk. Maggie takes a deep breath and hurries over to them with a nervous smile. She pauses to brace herself, opening out her hands in front of her, palms up.

'Come on lassies. Now is not a time to be idle, we must pluck the hens!'

Isobel points at old Ethel and says, 'Aye, we will if she stops turning her nose up at us. Has she got a cane stuck up her backside?'

Maggie sighs deeply. 'Don't be daft; it's just the old woman's way. She's all right once you get to know her.'

The fishwives look to one another, as though unsure of what to do. Nearly all of them are up to their elbows in ale, snuff and tobacco. But now, to Maggie's relief, they put their drinks down along with their pipes and roll up their sleeves.

'Come on girls,' Isobel says. 'The quicker we have them plucked, the quicker we'll be back on the ale.'

One of the women jests. 'Aye and we all know you're the best plucker around, Isobel!'

And just like that the women come together as one. In no time at all they create a snowstorm of feathers and pluck enough hens to stuff a dozen or so mattresses.

'That was damn thirsty work,' declares Isobel while hurrying back to the ale. The other fisher lassies follow close behind.

The young farmwomen remain busy. They sweep up the last of the feathers and cover the hens to keep off the flies. Every once in a while they glance at old Ethel with expectant eyes. Despite the heat, Ethel huddles in a corner, wrapped up in her shawl. At long last, a loud groan escapes her fleshy lips as she mutters, 'Go on then. But mark my word you'll be sorry come morning and don't say I didn't warn you.'

It isn't long before the hen party is merry and Maggie's dizzy from it all. Blood rushes to her head and her eyes are throbbing with fatigue. A blend of odours fills the small cottage; sweat, brackish fish, and the ever-present smell of a peat fire. One of the fisher lassies, Mary Brock, is up for some antics, doing her best to impersonate daft Davie from the village. She shuffles her feet and closes one eye, then does her best to mimic his childish way of talking. It comes out like gibberish and the other women laugh and slap their knees. Then, all of a sudden all hell lets loose when Mary Brown, a relative of daft Davie, overhears the banter and punches the offending imitator square in the eye.

'Never mind them, Maggie. Have a drink of this. It's my own special brew,' one of the women shouts.

The ale's delicious. Maggie closes her eyes and throws her head backwards to catch the dregs in her mouth, a quantity spills down her chin. She proceeds to wipe it away when the women grab her and secure her to a stool, clamping her head with strong hands and arms. It's useless to struggle, the reason being that when she does it makes their sharp fingernails scratch even more, and so the women hold her still to pour ale down her throat. All the while they chant, 'Drink, drink, drink…'

The room begins to spin. Someone plays an instrument, a merry tune on a Jew's harp, a foot tapping melody, pleasing to the ear. Maggie's breathing becomes shallow and suddenly it's as though everything's in slow motion. All around her the room is a blur of vibrant colours, as dancing figures and swishing skirts fly through the air. The pain behind her eyes causes her vision to blur and she squints into the haze. The two Marys: Mary Brock and Mary Brown are fighting again, this time over a bottle of whisky. A circle forms around them as they roll on the floor, fists flying and nails scratching. Several articles of their clothing scatter across the floor alongside a broken bottle. They look a sorry sight, hair wild like they'd been dragged through a hedge backwards. Soon they both sport thick bloody lips, and the language that comes out of them, well they would put a drunken sailor to shame.

It's this rowdy scene that greets Maggie's father and brother as they enter the cottage. Near the open door, they stand shoulder to shoulder with open mouths, rooted to the spot. So intent are the two scolding women in their fight, they haven't even noticed them.

'I'm so sorry Father, James. There's no point trying to separate them. They've been quarrelling like cats since they got here.'

'Don't stop them on my account,' Duncan winks at James. 'This is quite a show.'

Maggie's attention returns to the fight. It's really getting out of hand now. The two women are like wild animals and no one dare go between them, least of all Duncan who's enjoying a spectacular view. For a while longer they roll about the floor, teeth bared and breasts popping out from stays. Maggie makes eye contact with her father, one eyebrow arching as an understanding passes between them.

Eventually, to everybody's relief they break apart. Duncan holds out a hand to the prettiest girl, Mary Brock. 'Lassie, you look a little worse for wear. Let me walk you hame.'

'I'd rather walk with the devil himself, Duncan,' she scoffs, hands on hips. With the back of her hand she wipes blood from her mouth.

James bites his lip to stifle his amusement. 'You must be losing your touch, Father,' he smirks.

'I think not, son. Watch and learn,' he places a finger to his nose.

The room looks an almighty mess; the only thing Maggie wants is for them all to go home. She bangs on a table and shouts at the top of her voice, 'The hen party is over everyone. Come and fetch a hen.'

The women form an orderly line to collect a bird; it helps that the cooking is shared for the wedding feast, and Maggie is eager to get each and every one of them to take one home. First in the queue is Patrick's old sweetheart, the one he had up against the rowan tree, Agnes Lecke.

'I haven't got a dangle spit in my cottage, so there is no point me taking one,' Agnes whines.

Isobel pushes Agnes aside. 'Hah! Trust you, Agnes. No matter, I will take two, Maggie. It's no bother.'

And so, as a cloud uncovers a half-moon in the starless sky, a line of women march up the brae from Maggie's cottage. All but one of the women carries a hen in their hands. At the very end of the row, there is one man, Duncan, with a spring in his step and one arm around Mary Brock.

★★★

At twilight on the next Sabbath, a childhood friend pays Maggie a visit, carrying a mysterious brown parcel under her arm. For the past year, Maggie's friend, Alison Beutson has been employed at the local manse, probably to avoid working the fields (just like her). Maggie lets her in, ignoring her father and James gawping at the girl and her hessian bag.

'Aren't you supposed to be at the manse, Alison?'

'Not on the Sabbath.'

'Oh, so what brings you here on your one day off pray? There's not much going on here except mending stockings and spinning. Sit yourself down near the fire.'

'I wondered if you'd be interested in this.' Alison sits down and unfolds the parcel. A beautiful amber silk dress spills out onto her knee.

'Would you look at that? Where did you get it? I could never afford it.'

'It's beautiful, isn't it?' Alison pats the dress. 'It looks bonny on me, mind, and I'm tempted to wear it – you know, for your wedding. But I'm not the bride, am I?'

'Couldn't you sell it?'

'Aye, I thought about pawning it. It would fetch a fortune. But then I thought about all the questions the pawn man might ask me and so I daren't, Maggie. He'd probably declare me a thief and have me locked up in the tolbooth.'

'Come on then, where did you get it?'

'Well, I was cleaning one of the spare rooms in the manse. On my hands and knees I was, minding my own business when I heard a rustling sound.'

'What was it?'

'A holy man. He was standing in front of a one of those looking glasses and he was admiring himself.'

Maggie frowns. 'Aye. Go on then, what's so strange about that?'

'Hah. He was wearing this dress! Of course, once he caught sight of me he tore the garment from his body and ran stark bollock from the room. Can you imagine that?'

'You're jesting.'

'Hah. I swear to God it's true. A bearded man in a dress,' she giggles.

Maggie raises her eyebrows. 'I can't believe it. I wonder who it belongs to.'

'I don't know. No one's asked for it and the man with the beard's surely not going to ask for it now, is he?'

43

'Nae, give us it here.' Maggie stretches out her arms for the dress.

'I attach one condition to you wearing it.'

'Anything,' Maggie smiles.

'I'm your chief bridesmaid.'

'Done.'

***

Widow Arrock lives in a henwife's cottage. It has the only indoor privy in town and is the envy of the whole of Musselburgh. The widow's hen-pecked husband built it just before he succumbed to smallpox, and it was to be his greatest achievement and testament to his place of refuge, away from his nagging wife. To be sure the widow's a feisty character, well-known for her wicked temper, quick tongue and strange appearance. Folk either love her or loathe her and Maggie falls in with the former.

When the Lord was handing out good looks, sadly Widow Arrock was not in the queue. Her face and body have no symmetry, everything's twisted and out of kilter. The widow has beady eyes, one placed higher than the other, ears that resemble cauliflowers and thin lips that stretch inwards to form an ugly grimace. And if that isn't bad enough, her skin is so bad it resembles the peel of an over-ripened fruit, spoiled by a hot sun. For sure, Widow Arrock is the ugliest woman in Musselburgh, and probably the whole of Scotland. But nevertheless, Maggie is proud to call her a friend.

Upon an old wooden stool, Maggie stands, fidgeting as the widow pins her wedding dress. With nimble fingers, the widow makes the necessary alterations all in her own good time. Maggie draws in her breath and clamps her teeth together. A searing pain shoots down her back as she struggles to hold her position.

'Be still, Maggie. If your poor mother could see you now, she'd be having kittens. You look a mess; a blue-gowned beggar would put you to shame. Look at me up to my oxsters in pins and material, but I'm well turned out.'

Maggie glances at the widow and can't help having visions of ugly toads crawling on their backs in muddy swamps. 'I was too busy to comb my hair.'

The widow slaps Maggie on the leg and puffs out her cheeks. 'That's no excuse girl; you should always look your best. You're bone idle.'

'Ouch, that hurt! Anyway, today is not my wedding day. Does it really matter what I look like?'

The widow stops to stare at Maggie, her one good eye slightly slewed, so that it bores into Maggie. 'Now listen to me, girl. You youngsters are an absolute disgrace. In my day we would not be walking about with our hair unbound, even in private. You're slovenly, Maggie. You should always look your finest, not just for your husband, but for yourself. You're a very fortunate woman, because you were born with the gift of beauty. God never shined on me, but that didn't stop me trying to make the best of myself! Nae, it did not. I'm a handsome woman and not the hag people claim me to be.' She pats the rear of her head with a haughty look.

Handsome, Maggie thinks. *The widow's finally gone insane.*

'How much longer will it take? My feet are killing me and I'm starving.'

The widow scoffs. Her eyes near pop from her head and a vein bulges from her neck as she rants. 'Starving? What nonsense, you wouldn't know starving if it slapped you in the face. My generation was born hungry. You probably don't remember the great dearth, but your father would, that's if he wasn't too drunk to recall it. Anyway, it's patience you need a lesson in, young lady. I'm nearly done,' she says with a pin between her teeth.

'I'm going to pee myself if it takes much longer.'

'Be quiet, lass. The dress will be ready for you tonight. I've never seen so many petticoats in my life, what a fortunate lass you are to wear a dress as fine as this on your special day. Where on earth did you get it? On second thought I don't want to know. I wish your poor mother could see you now.'

It takes Maggie just a moment to take off the dress and run to the much envied indoor privy. When she returns she feels much better. 'All cottages should have indoor privies. I wish Father would build us one.'

The widow presses her hands together. 'Never mind the privy. I wish to God someone would knock it down now, it stinks rotten. The dress is perfect for you, lassie. The colour compliments your eyes. Oh, I almost forgot, I have to leave one stitch undone.'

'Why?'

The widow shrugs. 'How should I know? It's the done thing, lass.'

Maggie folds her arms over her chest, opens her mouth to ask something and then thinks better of it. At the front door she reaches out tentatively and touches the widow's hand. 'Thank you.'

Widow Arrock smiles and leans forward, her lips are dry and hairs stick out of her prickly chin. 'It's a pleasure, lassie. Now make sure you look after yourself. Dress respectable and keep your hair bound. You're going to be a married woman soon, so start behaving like one.'

★★★

At long last, on the night before her wedding, Maggie gathers her last remaining things together and places them in a bundle. Dusk falls, and soon the cottage becomes a place of flickering shadows as silence descends within. Suddenly it hits her. On the morrow she will be married and the thought terrifies her. A bottle of Johnny Notions's home-made fire water stands on the table near the furthest wall, the very sight of it makes her mouth water. Without a doubt her father will be cross if she takes but a single drop. But the blasted bottle is glinting in the firelight; she paces the floor up and down and eventually her footsteps stop at the far wall. The bottle makes a strange popping noise as she pulls the cork. The clear liquid burns her throat as she takes her first sip, like fire it spreads through her belly to the tips of her toes. And then, before she has the chance to take a second taste, a great crash causes her to jump from her skin.

'Damn. Don't you two know how to knock on a door? Is it the bridesmaid's job to scare the bride to death before her wedding?'

'Sorry,' say Isobel and Alison in unison.

'Where's your chanty and tocher?' Isobel looks around, her eyes settle on the bottle clutched between Maggie's hands.

Maggie places the bottle down.

'Whisky? Can we have some?'

'Nae, my father would skin me alive. Here's the chanty to fill with salt and all my belongings.'

'Go on. Just a wee dram,' whines Isobel.

'Aye, go on Maggie. Just a wee dram for us both,' Alison repeats. 'I'm chief bridesmaid and that means I should get first sip.'

'Nae, be off with you.'

The two women shrug and proceed to collect the bride's goods.

'Be careful with those, it's not just folds of old dusty linen. My mother's arasaid off Johnny Notions is in there and...'

'Oh, don't concern yourself,' Alison replies. 'We'll take care of everything. After we're finished here we're going to make up the bridal bed and collect petals to scatter over your blankets, and Isobel collected willow earlier. Didn't you, Isobel?'

Isobel nods. 'It's for fertility you know.'

'I know, I know.' Maggie puffs out her cheeks.

★★★

Before the men return, Maggie heats up some water to pour into a large bowl. Once out of her tight-fitting stays and pinching shoes, she feels wicked and free to explore the contours of her own body. The water discolours as she washes the filth from beneath her fingernails. A saponaria plant sits beside a water jug on the old mantle; the widow dug it up from her kale yard, claiming it does wonders for the hair. As Maggie crushes the roots and leaves, the fresh scent of luscious grass tickles her nostrils. To her amazement the roots produce a small amount of foam; she takes the water jug and wets her long hair. Next she applies the saponaria to it, massaging it into her scalp.

With a steady hand she holds the jug high above her head and pours the last of the clean water over her hair, rinsing the plant extract from it and sending a thousand glistening water droplets down the length of her naked body. An old plaid hangs from a nail on the wall; she takes it to dry herself and stifles a yawn. Finally, she cleans her teeth with a clout full of wood ashes and falls asleep by the glow of the peat fire.

★★★

Morning comes at last, and the sun rises bright in a clear blue sky. James, as usual is up first, to throw open the door and let the hens and pigs out. Maggie turns in her bed; her eyes glued shut with sleep as brilliant sunlight streams through the open door. Cursing in her slumber, she pulls a blanket over her scraggy head to shut out the light.

'Maggie. The sun is shining. Get up. You're to be married.'

But Maggie's all warm and cosy; she pulls the cover further over her head and ignores his voice. But James persists, and soon she feels his foot upon her backside.

'Don't kick me or I'll tell Father,' Maggie screams.

'He isn't here.'

A sinking feeling begins in the pit of her stomach. Just for once couldn't he have behaved and acted as a father should. 'Who's going to give me away? Oh no, where is he, James?'

With a thump, James sits beside his sister. 'I don't know. He could be anywhere, a ditch or a brothel. Who knows?'

Maggie shakes her wary head. 'Perfect.'

★★★

By the time Isobel and Alison arrive, all dressed up in their Sunday best to arrange Maggie's hair, the bride-to-be is in a right state. The cottage bustles with activity. Hens and pigs scuttle around in the dirt, and then to top things off, Duncan returns in search of his bottle.

'Who's been drinking this? I was saving this for me and Johnny.' With one hand he holds up the bottle to examine the contents, sloshing the liquid inside.

'He'll be fortunate if he gets a drop,' Maggie remarks.

'I heard that. Did you two drink some?' He points an accusing finger in the direction of two red-faced bridesmaids.

'No. We've come to dress the bride and arrange her hair. We haven't touched it, have we, Alison?'

'Well get on with it,' mutters Duncan, before picking up the bottle.

It requires much patience to place wild flowers into the fine net that covers Maggie's hair, but the bridesmaids persist, and it was well worth the effort. After that they help her to dress, fluffing out her petticoats so that the skirts billow out to resemble the shape of a bell. Beneath the silk fabric they place a ribbon garter, and when the bride isn't looking they hide a coin in her left shoe for good fortune.

At long last, the bride is ready, it doesn't matter that her shoes pinch and the hem of her dress is slightly over long. It's time. Maggie takes a deep breath and tries to show some enthusiasm. Her father's singing an old Scottish folk tale, his bottle clutched tight to his heart. How she loves him, despite his faults.

Maggie gets to her feet to be promptly pushed down. 'Just one more thing to do now, stop moving, Maggie – and stop pulling a face, close your eyes while I put some soot on your eyelashes.'

'Give us that bottle, Father?'

'No chance,' replies Duncan.

★★★

Many months ago, in a vain attempt to keep his wedding attire safe and clean, away from the incessant smoke from the peat fire, Patrick hid his clothes. The trouble is, for the life of him, he can't remember where. They're by far the finest clothes he possesses and so he turns the whole cottage upside down looking for them, until his mother holds them up over her head and says: 'You daft oaf! You told me to move them the other day to a better hiding place.'

It's a beautiful morning; a gentle breeze blows into the cottage as he pulls on his new worsted stockings. Next he picks up a hessian bag and pulls out a pair of new black shoes, a present from his mother and father. They seem out of place on his big ugly feet. Patrick's only ever worn scuffed homemade brogues, usually with holes in them, or his trusty sea boots.

William Cass, Patrick's best man, arrives at dawn. They spend most of the morning reminiscing about their days at sea, until Patrick's father pokes his head around the door and roars at them to hurry.

William whistles. 'Look at you, all dressed up in your finery. Are you sure you want to go through with this, lad? Marriage is forever you know, no more gallivanting. Remember our days at sea?'

'We were just boys at sea, years and years of sailing – but gallivanting? No. I'm as quiet as I was then.' Patrick fidgets, his face contorting and wrinkling as he pulls and tugs at the new clothes.

'Stop fiddling and scratching, man. You're like a dog with fleas. Oh, I almost forgot. I need to check you've no knots about your person.'

Patrick groans out loud.

'Come on, once the ceremony is over, we can tie the knots again.'

'All right,' Patrick says, holding up his hands.

★★★

The bride's party set out led by the bride's father; unfortunately he's blind stinking drunk. Therefore, James makes sure Maggie approaches the kirk from right to left, to circle the kirk three times, before entering. Duncan staggers behind, looking like something the cat's dragged in. At the kirk gates, they're informed by a kirk elder that Patrick's arrived with the bridesmaids, preceded by a piper.

At the door, Maggie's met by a kirk officer, who takes one look at Duncan and decides James, not Duncan, should walk her up the aisle. Maggie cringes inside; her cheeks flush as she walks at a slow pace, head dipped to the floor until she stands to the right of her groom. When the service begins, there's not a sound as the betrothed couple exchange vows.

★★★

Patrick stands with his legs wide apart, breast puffed out with pride. It's finally happening. Soon she will be his and the faint flutter of anxiety that constantly irks him will be no more. He can't take his eyes off her as she stands beside him, looking like a fine lady in her fancy dress. It doesn't matter that he has no ribbons or pearls to give her; a woman like Maggie doesn't need any ornament or decoration. She'd look beautiful in a sack of cloth. As he places the gold ring on her left finger, there's a great swelling in his heart and at long last they are man and wife.

As the church bells ring out, the customary rush to kiss the bride is won by Minister Bonaloy since he's the nearest. Patrick watches her with proud eyes, his heart thumping as he takes her image in. She's breathtakingly beautiful, but it's her eyes that do it for him. Dark, smouldering eyes, feline and predatory, Maggie's eyes hold the promise of carnal delight.

Outside kirk, Widow Arrock has a major disagreement with the miller's wife. Together, they make a hideous sight and it's difficult to decide which of them has the prickliest chin as they point and curse at one another. Folk gather around them to get a good view in case it develops into a fist fight, but then the minister breaks them apart and threatens to fetch the scold's bridle. It's at this moment that Duncan suddenly comes to life and removes one of his shoes to throw in Patrick's direction.

'Hah! I've thrown the shoe and you know what that means don't you, laddie? She's your responsibility now, and good luck to you because God knows you'll need it.' Duncan skips away to retrieve his missing shoe, stumbling as he replaces it on his foot. 'And bloody good riddance,' he mutters before bumping into Johnny Notions.

Johnny embraces his old friend and bellows, 'Doesn't she scrub-up well, Duncan? A bit of tallow soap and she looks good enough to eat. No mangy Maggie.'

'Mangy Maggie?' Patricks asks the highlander.

Johnny turns to Patrick with a twinkle in his eye. 'Aye, that's what I used to call her when she was a wee bairn. Maggie was forever climbing trees all day, or running along the harbour to the rocks. Always covered in bruises, she was.'

Patrick smiles at Johnny, noticing his mass of wild ginger hair. He likes the strange Highlander; and from what he can gather he appears to be a father figure to Maggie. The same cannot be said for Duncan. The man's a bloody disgrace, he thinks, can't even stay sober long enough for his only daughter's marriage ceremony. He places a protective arm around his new bride as they walk to the wedding feast.

The wedding party walk downhill towards the sea-mill, to the bottom of Kerr's Wynd, and soon they come to a tall barn. The miller has kindly let them use one of his out-buildings, much to the displeasure of his bad-tempered wife. As the guests flock in, Widow Arrock, along with a number of the women, uncover the food. It's taken all morning to prepare the feast under the watchful eye of the miller's wife, the cause for the widow's bad temper. Before the food is served, Minister Bonaloy gives a good speech, spinning yarns and telling jokes before introducing other speakers and proposing the first toast.

★★★

The pipers and fiddlers assemble themselves at the back of the barn, some of them tuning up their instruments, others supping their ale. Meanwhile food and drink is served on long tables, and the delicious smell of the cooked chicken wafts around the room. After folk are fed and watered, a space is cleared on the floor, and before long people dance and children play fight on the dirt floor.

Maggie grins at Patrick as he takes her hand in his own and leads her to the centre of the room. All around them people dance with the bleary look of people heading towards drunk but are not quite there yet. But alas, the same cannot be said for her father. He reached the point of inebriation long ago and to Maggie's dismay he's walking towards them.

'Allow me a last dance with my daughter, Patrick?' he slurs.

Patrick stands aside to let father and daughter say their goodbyes.

As they begin to sway in time to the music, Duncan steps on her feet. Maggie grits her teeth and hopes for the tune to come to an end.

'We may not have seen eye to eye, Maggie, but I've done my best and I wish you well.'

Maggie nods and turns her face away from him. 'I know.'

'I'm proud of you lass, and I always will be. You're a free spirit, just like me. So don't let anyone change you. Do you hear me?'

Duncan leans in close, so close Maggie can smell his alcoholic breath. 'And before I depart let me give you a wee bit of advice. Learn to accept change, lassie, because nothing in this world remains the same. Remember that.' He ruffles her hair as though she's a dog and turns on his heel.

★★★

A moment later the fiddlers pick up the tempo. Maggie searches the barn, eyes darting right and left for one man in particular. *That kiss at the altar.* She places a finger to her lips, her head's still in a spin and there's fire in her belly. After a while, she catches sight of the handsome minister and as usual he has a small crowd of adoring fans around him. She approaches him with conviction and holds out one hand.

'A dance with the bride, Minister Bonaloy?' Maggie asks before taking his hand. A new jig begins – a lively one that requires them to link each other's arms. After a while she clings to him, feigning exhaustion. From beneath her dark lashes she looks boldly into his green eyes.

'I'm not much of a dancer, Maggie. Sorry,' he apologises, releasing his grip.

'Don't go.'

'No, no,' he musters. He can no longer meet her eyes.

'Are you committing adultery in your heart, Minister Bonaloy?' she enquires, moving closer to him so that they stand inches apart. Maggie watches his face crumple into a mixture of emotions; confusion, disappointment, perhaps disbelief – she's not sure.

'You flatter yourself, Maggie,' he replies, suddenly taking control. With a firm hand he grabs her elbow and guides her across the room to her husband.

★★★

From across the room, Patrick watches his wife dance with the minister. He can't take his eyes off her, and his loins ache with desire at the thought of the night ahead. It's more than he can bear to watch them. His jaw twitches as he pushes his way through a group of dancers to get to her. He's nearly there, only a whisker away, when strong arms grab him from both sides and place a large creel upon his broad back.

'Oh no, I'm too weary to carry the creel. Can't we just miss this part out…' he complains, looking at Maggie with yearning eyes.

Patrick's father laughs. 'Tired? You'll be weary come morning, son. All fishermen carry the creel on their wedding day, to symbolise sharing life's burdens together. There's plenty of time for you and the lass later on,' he winks.

★★★

At Watts Close, on a sultry evening, Patrick Spence carries his bride over the threshold of their front door. And he's careful not to trip, mind, as this is deemed unlucky, and so as they enter the cottage, folk scream and cheer and throw petals over the married couple.

Patrick's mother, Barbara is a little worse for wear. With a clout held up to her eyes she whines in a shrill voice: 'You know in some parts of the highlands, a newly married couple lives with the groom's parents for the first week of their marriage. Oh and look at the state of this place, it's got no homely touches; it's not fit for my Patrick to live in. Perhaps you two should…'

Johnny Notions scowls. 'Nonsense, woman. And it's the bride's parents they live with the first week, not the grooms. And where I come from, they spend their first night in a barn.'

'How awful,' replies Barbara still dabbing her eyes. With much reluctance she passes Maggie the keys to the house and some fire tongs to place a peat on the fire. A look of resignation crosses her face as she embraces the bride, like she's finally realised that she's not the only woman in her son's life.

'Right,' says Barbara clapping her hands. 'Get out of here, Patrick. Go on. We've got to get on with the beddin' o' the bride.'

An air of expectancy fills the room as the women strip Maggie of her dress and petticoats, until all she wears is a thin sark. With nimble fingers they remove the wild flowers and pins from Maggie's long hair, so that it tumbles around her shoulders. Before they fetch Patrick, one of the women makes up a fire.

'Right, Patrick, she's ready. Time for you to undress and lie next to your bride,' the women giggle and sneak sly glances as he undresses.

Side by side, Maggie and Patrick sit on their bed of straw as the men re-enter to claim a kiss from the bride. Patrick grits his teeth, uncomfortable with the custom. How he longs to be alone with his new wife. But when the left stocking is thrown and hits old Widow Arrock on the nose, everyone laughs, and this lightens his mood, as one thing is for sure – no one in their right mind would marry old Widow Arrock.

At last the wedding party leave and all is quiet. Patrick turns to his bride, and right away all his blood seems to rush to his loins. They're finally alone, but he can still hear folk chatting and jesting outside. But Patrick's passed caring now and he pulls Maggie into his arms and kisses her passionately, his coarse hands exploring her body, feeling every inch of her soft skin.

'I thought they would never go,' he groans, covering her body with ardent kisses while wrapping one hand around her throat. He teases her with his tongue as his knees force her thighs further and further apart. She groans beneath him as he places his weight on both hands, pinning her arms outstretched aside of her to kiss and tease her breasts. 'Say my name,' he demands, shivering as her breathing becomes heavier. 'Say my name.'

'Love me, Patrick,' she cries.

It's more than he can take; he can't wait any longer. He has to claim his bride and make her his own forever. Patrick's a large man and knows it has to hurt, but as his knees force her thighs wider apart to enter her, he's at the point of no return.

'Hush, they will hear us.' His lips crush her mouth and stifle her cries. His hand returns to her throat as he pushes deeper inside of her, almost exploding as she opens her legs wider, fingernails clawing into his skin.

A moan escapes from her swollen mouth. The very sound sends him over the edge, and his hot seed spills inside her. He rolls off and stretches out a hand to cover her stomach, and a pulse beats within her groin. 'Are you satisfied, wife?'

'Aye.'

As they lay entwined, limb twisted around limb, recovering their breath, a loud cheer roars from outside. Patrick jumps off the bed and throws a blanket around him to peer outside.

'Haven't you lot got anywhere to go?' he shouts, before slamming the door.

★★★

'I love you,' he says. It's barely a whisper.

She kisses his mouth and shivers at his touch. A gasp escapes her lips as she examines his back criss-crossed with marks. 'How did you get those scars?'

'I went to sea as a boy. By the age of sixteen I was rated a seaman. But along the way I got the scars…'

'Who gave you them?'

A knock at the door interrupts them. Maggie sighs and cringes inside. She knows it's the womenfolk; they've come to roll Maggie's hair with wooden bodkins and cover it with a kertch. As Patrick sleeps quietly in bed, they place a fine piece of linen on her head and fasten it behind her ears, and all the while Maggie fidgets and curses.

'Do I have to wear this ridiculous thing on my head?'

One of the old women gasps.

Another old biddy can't hold her tongue and grumbles. 'You're married now, Maggie, and you should behave accordingly. There can be no more prancing around with your hair flying about your face like a wee bairn.'

Maggie pouts her lips, her forehead wrinkling into a frown. She loathes being told what to do. 'If I want to run round naked with my hair unbound, I will.'

The women cluck, shocked at her scandalous words. A smack around the side of her head sends her kertch flying through the air, causing the women to titter.

'Put it on, woman. And never let me hear you talk like that again.' Patrick returns the kertch to her head.

The air crackles with tension. Maggie lowers her lashes and stares down at the floor; she ignores the women, too humiliated to look any of them in the eye. She nods and wipes a tear from her face. *You will never be my master*, she thinks, *nor my keeper or insult me in front of the other women again*. She continues to stare until he walks away and then rips the cloth from her head.

CHAPTER FIVE

THE FISH MARKET

The harbour smells of seaweed, tar and brine. It's a noisy place once the seamen begin to work on their boats, banging their hammers with swift rhythmic movements. Seabirds swoop and dive from above, their shrill mewing cries piercing the air as they plunge into icy waters rich with fish. Concealed within the bruised sky is a winter sun, trapped in dense clouds, unable to break through.

Maggie stands at the edge of a rock pool, wild hair streaming behind her like a mass of tangled brown ribbons. Clothes soaked by wind and sea, laughter on her lips; she's never felt so alive. It's here that Maggie's one with nature, trancelike and content. An old seaman sits nearby on the rocks, a meerschaum pipe carved into the figure of a naked woman protruding from his cracked lips. Maggie observes his weathered face as he redds his fishing line and winds it into an old murlin basket that's seen better days.

Maggie turns away from the rock pool, moving barefoot effortlessly across the rocks towards the shore. She recognises him by the set of his broad shoulders and fisherman's garb. A woman stands close to him, linking his arm, head thrown backwards in laughter. Maggie marches in their direction towards the boat shore. *Damn and damnation*, Maggie thinks as they break apart.

'Hello, Agnes.' Maggie turns to Patrick, hands on hips. 'Well?'

Awkward silence follows until Agnes coughs and raises her hand to her red face. 'I was just asking Patrick how married life…'

'Get gone, will you, Agnes? And while you're at it, get your own man, hussy.' Maggie's gaze remains on her husband's face as Agnes saunters away.

'What's going on, Patrick?'

'Hush.' He places a finger on her tight mouth.

'Don't hush me!' She takes a swing at him but misses. 'I don't know what you're grinning at. I'll wipe the smile off your face before sundown.'

'I was just being friendly.'

'Do you think me a fool? The lassie was crawling all over you. You should've told her to be off the moment she turned up fluttering her lashes.'

'Come here, Maggie. You know you're the only woman for me.'

'Do I?'

'You know you are. You mean everything to me. Come here.'

Maggie hesitates before walking into his arms, but once his arms are around her all is forgiven. As she presses her cheek against his, her hair whips up into her face.

'Why aren't you wearing a cap? How many times have I told you to wear one?'

She pulls away, her face contorting at his displeasure. 'I forgot it. Anyway, how long have you been talking to Agnes Lecke?'

'Oh, I see. You're jealous.'

She shakes her head, teeth chattering from the cold wind. 'No, not of that one.'

He frowns. 'What's wrong then, lass? You've never been short with me before.'

'I'm to have a bairn.' Maggie kicks her feet in the sand and pulls a sulky face.

'Well, that's great news. Aren't you happy, lass?'

'No, I am not. I'm too young to have a bairn.'

'Nonsense, you're seventeen, nearly eighteen, that's old enough. It is natural, lass. Haven't we just tied the knot?'

'Aye.'

'Good. Now stop complaining and let's go home.'

★★★

Maggie's in a foul mood as she clears up the room. And what a sight she must look with her face streaked with tears and flour. The cooking pot's on its side, and all around her is an almighty mess, half-peeled vegetables, utensils and a cooling tray as if she hasn't been able to decide what to cook.

The door crashes open, and she hopes it's not Patrick.

Widow Arrock doesn't wait to be invited in and sits herself down. 'What's happened in here? It looks like you've been raided, have you had a couple of gaugers in 'ere looking for brandy and baccy?'

Maggie interrupts her. 'Chance would be a fine thing, but no. Patrick was hungry, and, well, the smell of the food was making me gag.'

'And...'

'Well I might have become a wee bit careless and tipped a pot over.'

'Aye, he told me.' The widow nods and crosses her flabby arms.

'And now he's gone off fishing without a meal in him, and he's in a fierce mood with me, ranting and raving at me and calling me a terrible wife. Oh, and I've spoiled most of the food now. What shall I do? I've no fish to sell at market until he's home, and now I've hardly any money to buy food.' Maggie's bottom lip quivers.

The widow's face is indifferent, Maggie expects no less. The old woman probably thinks she has a lesson to learn no doubt, she'll show her. With a stiff face, Maggie picks up her boots and creel and grabs her shawl.

'Where are you going?'

'To buy fish off the boats.'

The widow's eyes shine with mirth. 'You're learning fast my girl.'

But alas, Maggie has much to learn. Her first mistake is to buy an old batch of herring off Billy Swindles who unknown to her, is a worse drunkard than her father. The money Maggie gives him no doubt goes towards his next round of ale. Her second mistake is to carry her fish in the midday sun all the way to Edinburgh, a good three or four hour walk. By the time she gets there Maggie's hungry and thirsty and her back feels as though it's about to cave in.

She follows her nose to the fish market. Until now, Maggie's only hawked at Fisherrow, and the crowded market is packed with people pushing and shoving one another. Her eyes frantically dart left and right for a familiar face – Isobel, even Agnes, anyone will do – but alas everyone's a stranger and everyone's in a hurry. The market hawkers gawp at her with evil eyes. A fat fisherwoman gives her an almighty whack on the arm. 'Your herring is rotten, get rid of it before you give us all a bad name.'

'But...' Maggie stutters.

The woman doesn't wait around. In an instant she cuts the strap of Maggie's creel, spilling her rotten fish to the ground and after that she holds a knife to Maggie's neck. 'Pick up your creel and your fish, and be off with you before I slit your throat.'

Maggie's heart thumps in her chest as she falls to her knees, scooping up the slimy fish with slippery hands, and all the while her eyes swim with tears. The stout woman hovers above her stinking of sweat and onions and rotting teeth, and the smell mingles with the scent of putrid fish guts and brine.

'Hurry, shift yourself or you'll be sorry,' she says, prodding Maggie's shoulder with the handle of her knife. Without hesitation, Maggie flees, taking her rotten fish with her. At the end of a fleshers market she dumps her fish on a stinking midden and hurries away. A moment later at a street corner, Maggie presses her fingers to her neck and heaves a great sigh – there's no blood.

'Could this day get any worse?' she says to herself. She has no fish to sell, no money and nothing to eat. Maggie's shoulders sag, everything's gone wrong. She picks up her empty creel and starts to walk home; at the first bend she dodges an old woman shouting out 'gardy loo' as she throws out her slops from a chamber pot. At Canongate, a pie seller cries his wares from beneath an old stone bridge; the sight of the food makes her eyes bulge and her mouth water. Maggie edges closer and closer, by God she will have something to eat by the end of the day. She stretches out her hand and curls her fingers around a juicy mutton pie, but the pie seller's a canny man with eyes in the back of his head.

'Stop thief!' he cries, as Maggie runs away clutching the pie. At Joppa, she wolfs down the food and vows to never venture to market without the Fisherrow fishwives again. What was she thinking going alone?

★★★

Just before New Year, Maggie cleans the cottage. She sweeps, washes utensils and empties the rok of yarn. Patrick's fishing gear she daren't touch, so she cleans out the pigsty instead and collects weeds for the new goat. When she's finished she crosses her arms and looks around the room, then notices the pipe. It sits on an old bedding box and is in a shocking state. So much so, that when she lifts it to examine the carved detail, it's smothered in dirt. Maggie goes to work on it, scrubbing and cleaning until it gleams. By the time she's finished her arms feel like lead. Pleased with her handiwork, she replaces the pipe and returns to her chores.

'Shut the door, it's freezing out there,' she shouts as Patrick strolls through the door. Her gaze follows him as he walks to the fire.

'You'll get chapped skin. How many fish did you catch?'

He grunts. 'Not many, it's still too cold for a good catch. I tell you what, Maggie, those bairns from the bottom of the brae have been playing tricks again. They've been throwing seaweed through keyholes and door rapping.'

'Widow Arrock will sort them out.'

He walks towards her and then stops dead. 'What have you done to my pipe?'

Maggie puffs out her bosom with pride. 'I cleaned it,' she declares in a proud voice.

'You cleaned it?' he roars.

She begins to panic inside. 'Aye, with the tallow soap Johnny gave me.'

His eyes bore through hers as spidery veins bulge in his neck. Without thinking she begins to walk backwards. 'Well, it was filthy.'

'Ah lass, you shouldn't have done that to my pipe.'

Maggie swallows hard, teeth gritted together as one small hand forms a fist. A barrage of angry words spew from her mouth, 'I thought I was doing you a favour, a good deed. It was all dirty. You are one ungrateful swine,' she sobs.

He points a finger at her. 'Be careful what you say, woman. I've a mind to send for the lockman to fit you with the branks. You have the tongue of a shrew.'

'I despise you!' she screams and smashes the pipe against the wall.

★★★

After that, Patrick can't do anything right. His wife's gone and in her place lives an irrational, weeping woman, quiet and moody. The widow shakes her head when he confides in her. To his consternation, she says it's common for women to be this way when carrying a child. *Oh, the horror of it*, he thinks. The slightest little thing can set her off, crying for no damned reason. Patrick's had quite enough of it and so he keeps well away.

To his utmost relief, Maggie's temperament improves when she begins to conceal her widening girth. From the corner of his eye he watches her tightening her stays over her bulging stomach. And if this makes her feel better and puts her in a better mood, that's grand with him.

The following Sabbath, Patrick and Maggie attend kirk at St Michaels. The congregation is packed full because the miller's wife, Bessie Ruchat has summoned Janet Hogg before the kirk session for slander, and so poor Janet has to stand for several Sundays to be rebuked at the stool of repentance. And if that's not enough humiliation she has to go down on her knees and beg Bessie's forgiveness in front of the entire congregation. And thus, there is the inevitable finger pointing and sniggering. Patrick tears his eyes from the miller's smug wife and nudges Maggie. 'Poor Janet, the miller's wife is a right scold…'

But Maggie's attention is elsewhere, her neck is turned and she appears to be looking at something at the back of kirk. As he twists his head to see what she's looking at, his heart sinks. Maggie's looking at the young McDougal brothers. Patrick seethes with rage; he scowls and presses his lips together, but for now he lets it go.

The sermon drags on and unbelievably she does it again. 'Stop looking at the men over your shoulder,' he hisses through his teeth.

'What men?' She frowns and crinkles her pretty face.

'You know what men.' His face reddens as he begins to wonder if he really knows this woman standing next to him. He thought he did – until now.

★★★

Maggie unlocks the door and descends the cottage steps. She's eager to venture outdoors. It's a fine day and there's a number of flowers just opening, golden gorse and violets too, uncurling their buds under fresh green leaves. No amount of tightening her stays can disguise her pregnancy now, and so she's waddling about like a fat duck. It is market day, and she's already late, lagging behind the Fisherrow fishwives. Soon her body glistens with sweat, and her hair's stuck to her face, sopping wet.

Just before the high street, Maggie struggles with her full creel of fish. She can't take a footstep more. And so, with weary legs she fights her way through a barrage of pedlars, hucksters, and buyers to the quiet corner of a fine house. At a stone doorstep, she eases her swollen frame to the floor, a joyous expression lighting her face. *I'll just stretch my legs for a moment*, she thinks.

A sedan chair comes to a halt in front of her. Two red-faced bearers lower the long poles that support the passenger's box. The men sag with fatigue, beasts of burden, removing leather straps from sweat drenched bodies and fighting for breath. The front bearer knocks a firm hand on the passenger door.

Heavy brocade curtains open. A fine gentleman leaps out; his hat tipped forward, no doubt to conceal his identity before his secret liaison. He lands on Maggie's feet, but seems oblivious to her cries.

The front bearer throws up his hands and exclaims: 'You stepped on the fisherwoman's feet.' His thick Irish brogue is musical to the ear.

'What woman?' the gentleman mutters, and scarpers into the fine house.

The bearer holds out a calloused hand to Maggie. She wonders whether to take it.

'Are you all right?'

'Aye,' replies Maggie. She allows him to help her to her feet.

'Take this coin. You look like you need a bite to eat.'

'Thank you,' she says, and can't help smiling when she overhears him saying, 'I'm glad the last one wasn't one of those fat pigs, aren't you?'

★★★

By the time Maggie returns home, the heather on the hills are drenched with fine rain and cling to Maggie's clothes like wet rags. Near a roaring fire, she removes her damp clothes to get warm, and soon falls asleep. In her dream she's swimming in a cool turquoise sea, like a mythical mermaid with long hair swirling around her face. And then, something interrupts her reverie, a twinge in the base of her back that wakes her with a start. The bed's wet and she can't understand why. She shifts her bottom and reaches beneath her legs before drawing up her hand.

CHAPTER SIX

THE TAIBSEAR

There's no blood.

But her clothes and bedding are soaked. A searing ache tears through her stomach as she gathers the blankets to dry near the fire. Just as the pain is almost over, Maggie clenches her fists and then drops them to her side.

'Why is this happening to me now?' Maggie groans. 'God no, not now while I'm all alone,' she curses out loud. Sweat covers her entire forehead and she's near bitten through her lip. Damp earth embeds between her toes as she staggers through the cottage. As she pushes open the door she catches her neighbour's eye.

'Mrs Johnston, can you fetch the midwife? I think I'm having the bairn.'

The neighbour's wizened face wrinkles with concern. 'Where's your man? He should be with you.'

'He's at sea. Can you send word?'

'Of course, lassie, I'll be with you in a moment. Now get yourself inside and cross your legs.' She cackles.

Maggie staggers inside. She's cold now, so cold her teeth have started to chatter. She wraps a blanket around her and suddenly feels nauseous, and so she bends over her knees and vomits onto the floor. When the retching stops, Maggie rolls on her side, and in this odd position her thoughts turn to her mother, and the tears begin to fall. 'Please somebody come now,' she whimpers like an injured animal. 'Oh why won't someone come?'

After a while the sound of footsteps and whistling comes from outside. Maggie rolls onto her swollen stomach and pushes on her knees, her eyes constantly watching the door. In a flash, Isobel bursts through the entrance carrying her creel.

'Maggie, I came at once. How are you, lassie? I got here as fast as I could, honest I did. Where's Patrick, is he at sea?'

'Aye.'

'As soon as the saltwife told me, I ran here as fast as I could.'

'But I asked her to fetch a midwife.' Maggie whines, grimacing as a pain passes.

'Don't fret, the midwife's on her way. Are the pains coming fast?'

'Aye, they started this morning, and to be honest I thought I'd wet the bed and that's when they started.'

Isobel nods. 'Your waters have broken. I've seen it before; my mother's had plenty of bairns. Ah, here's the midwife.'

Maggie almost cries out with relief. The pain is more than she can bear now and the sight of this no-nonsense woman with a kind face is a sight for sore eyes.

'Now then, let's see what have we here,' says the midwife, rolling up her sleeves. A timid lassie peers over her shoulder, carrying a linen bag.

'My name's Jean Ramsay and the lassie behind me is my niece, Betty. She's here to see how things are done if that's all right with you. Your name's Maggie, isn't it?'

Maggie nods and gestures to Isobel. 'That's...'

'I know who she is, used to be a fishwife myself many a year ago. I knew Isobel when she was this big.' The midwife places one hand waist height before adding, 'And what a little beggar she was! Now then, I need you to loosen your garments for me. Lift up your skirts and let me take a wee look. You're doing a grand job, lassie, now don't be getting upset, Auntie Jean's here now to sort all this out. Is this your first? You're awful young.' She coats her hand with duck fat for lubricant and fletches her fingers, preparing to stretch the neck of the womb.

'Aye, it's my first. Oh, ouch. It hurts. Don't do that. Please stop.' Maggie tries to slap the midwife's hand away.

'Hold her still, Betty.'

Betty places two firm hands on Maggie's arms and holds her down.

The midwife continues with her examination. 'Be strong, lassie. I can see the head already so the baby will be born within the hour. You've done most of the work alone.'

The midwife gestures to Betty. 'Pass us that bag, will you, Betty? And after that fetch us some hot water.'

The midwife grumbles as she rummages within her bag. Each time she pulls out an object she curses and drops something back in. This goes on for a long while, tugging out one thing and then another, until suddenly she finds what she wants. She moves quickly and with a sense of urgency. 'Where's your linen?' She asks.

'In the chest over there. My mother put all of it together for me before she died.' Maggie's face contorts and her teeth grind together as she fights one last pain. And then suddenly she flops backward and everything goes black.

A dull buzzing noise rings within her ears. When she opens her eyes, a dark velvety blackness fills the room. Occasionally, the firelight glows to reveal blurred, distorted shapes of women busy at work. Above the incessant chatter, she can make out the midwife barking out orders.

'Now Betty, we must wait for the afterbirth. Keep kneading her stomach like a baker kneads bread. And after that give her an herbal wash and make a poultice, the way I showed you. It will slow the blood flow.'

'Where's my baby?' Maggie croaks. Her mouth feels like sand.

'She's here, lass. Look at that face and those eyes. What a bonny wee girl.'

'I feel ill. I need water,' Maggie murmurs, covering her mouth in a vain bid to stop retching.

'Drink this ale,' Jean places a wooden cup to Maggie's lips, then promptly takes it away.

'Gather your strength together, lass. The baby needs you to be strong.' She gives Maggie one more drink from the cup before placing the baby in her arms. 'That's it, lass. Support the child's head; let it nuzzle into your breasts.'

Maggie gazes down on the wrinkled pink flesh covered in slime; she holds it clumsily in one arm. It feels completely unnatural, and so she fidgets and adjusts it with shaky arms, almost dropping it in the process.

'Isobel? Could you take the child? I don't feel well.'

★★★

For the most part, Isobel's delighted to take the child off Maggie's hands. The baby's covered in blood and could do with a wipe anyway. But the way Maggie turned away from it; Isobel can't help but wonder if that's normal, so once Maggie's asleep, Isobel seeks out the midwife.

'What's the matter with her, Jean? She looks right through it like she doesn't want it. And she's such a bonny baby with the darkest eyes. The poor wee thing's hungry, see how she's sucking on my little finger. She should have her on the breast now.'

The midwife crinkles her eyes together. 'Don't be troubled so, Isobel. Maggie's just worn-out. You'd be surprised how many women don't want to hold their babies after a birth, and not because their exhausted mind. It's like all those days and months of carrying the child have gone by and, well what can I say? It's just too much for them.'

Isobel sighs. 'So she'll be all right when she wakes then?'

'Aye, and she can feed the child then,' nods the midwife, crossing her arms.

A smile lights up Isobel's face as she stuffs a coin in the midwife's hand. 'Thank you, Jean. You've been grand... and Betty.'

'It's nothing, Isobel, all in a day's labour and a damn sight easier than carrying creels full of herring, I can tell you. Now then, remember to get her to put the baby on her breast when she wakes. And tell her not to feed it spirits to prevent it crying. I don't agree with that. A child needs the breast and nothing else.'

'Aye, I'll tell her.' But Isobel's mouth gapes open. 'Surely a bit of strong stuff on a babe's tongue won't do any harm. Sometimes it's the only way to get them off to sleep. My mother fed all of us on a sugary pap laced with alcohol.'

The midwife clucks her tongue and points out a bony finger. 'Aye and how many of your brothers and sisters lived past the age of two, Isobel? How many?'

'Two.'

'So your mother lost how many weans? Speak up, child.'

'Me mam lost four babies. But there's nothing unusual about that. It was God's will.'

'God's will? More like the stuff she poured down their poor wee throats. Don't tell her I said that, mind. Ignore me and my big mouth. No spirits for the baby, have I made myself clear?' The midwife waits for an answer with crossed arms.

'Aye, no spirits for the baby.' Isobel nods her head.

'Grand. Now come on, Betty. It's time to go, our job's done here. The dry nurse can take care of the lying-in, until the up-sitting and churching that is.'

'Up what?' Betty frowns.

'Oh never mind.'

★★★

'Isobel, where are you?'

'Wait there. I won't be a moment, Maggie.' Isobel picks up the baby. 'Here, put it to the breast.'

'Must I?'

'Well if you don't, it will starve,' Isobel tuts.

Maggie holds out her arms for the child. It feels odd and awkward as Isobel places her in her hands. She's unsure of whether to hold it to the left or right and so she tries both ways, finally resting its head in the crook of her left arm. Her skin crawls as Isobel guides it to her breast.

The child hiccups and jerks in her embrace, as though something disturbs her sleep. Maggie gazes at her with drowsy eyes. Already she prefers it asleep, silent and undemanding. Suddenly, a hoarse cough startles Maggie, causing her to clinch the babe tight in her arms.

'Oh, it is you, Patrick. Where have you been? I was frightened to death.'

'At sea. Where else? I got here as soon as I could. The midwife got here in time then?'

'Aye, but the birth – oh Patrick, I never want to go through that again.'

Patrick shakes his head. 'Was it painful, lass?

Maggie nods and slumps her head back. 'Do you want to hold her?'

'Aye. It's a girl child then? What have you called her?'

'I haven't called her anything.'

'Why not?' He walks the length of the room and sinks to his knees beside her.

'I was waiting for you, silly beggar.'

He kisses her forehead. 'We'll call her Anna, in remembrance of your mother.'

She lifts her head to find his lips. He tastes of the sea.

'Anna Spence it is then,' she agrees.

They christen her on 29 July 1716 at St Michaels Kirk.

★★★

Motherhood does not come naturally to Maggie. Why didn't anyone warn her about the trouble bairns bring? And how many more sleepless nights must she endure? The incessant crying grates on her nerves now and, to make matters worse, the child seems to be permanently on the breast like a huge sucking parasite.

A rapping noise from the door startles her. Maggie's not really in the mood for visitors but nevertheless she crosses the room with weary legs to answer the door. It's the midwife, Jean Ramsay, waiting to be invited in. She opens the door and ushers her inside, offering her a chair near the fire.

'How's the child?' asks Jean, glancing at the baby and giving the cottage a once over.

'She's feeding well that's for sure and she's a healthy pair of lungs on her.'

'And you?'

'Grand,' Maggie tells a falsehood.

Jean scrutinises her with penetrating eyes. 'Hmm, you look a bit sickly to me. Have you taken the child outside yet?'

Maggie shakes her head and shudders; the thought of going out with the babe irks her, and to be honest she has neither the energy nor the desire to venture out-of-doors. 'No, I thought I'd leave going out for now.'

'Nonsense. The child needs fresh air, and by the look of it so do you. You can't stay within these four walls forever you know, you'll be off to Edinburgh soon with the other fishwives to sell your fish. And look at the state of this place. I've seen cleaner pigsties. Do you want me to help you give the place a wee clean?'

Maggie lowers her head. 'Aw, no need, Jean. I'll have this place spick and span soon; it's just I've been so weary and Widow Arrock said she'd come by to lend me a hand after kirk on Sunday.'

'All right then. I'll be off now, but get yourself out in the fresh air, do you hear me? You need to get some colour back into those cheeks.'

★★★

The rush is on. Market day at Fisherrow and the fishwives labour hard to sort and gut their fish. Agnes Lecke toils slowly, in her typical precise manner. She sits apart from the other fishwives, happy in her own company, sometimes chattering to herself. Wispy fair hair spills from her cap as she leans over her fish, a razor-sharp knife twisting in hand as she guts her fish. She senses the woman and baby before the others. Her nostrils flare and her upper lip rises as she turns away, Agnes can't bear to look at them and her heart aches as though a cold dirk twists beneath her breast.

Agnes sucks in her breath; her eyes narrow as Patrick's baby begins to cry, instinctively she turns to look. She's the image of her father, the man *she* should've married. The taste of sour bile fills her mouth. She swallows it away and proceeds towards the infant, but before she gets there the voices begin.

'Not now,' she groans. Agnes doesn't want to hear the voices. But they keep talking to her in a jabbering incessant fashion, conjuring up images of death and vengeance, violating her mind. She screws up her eyes into narrow slits hoping they'll go away, but they won't leave her alone. And so, she sways to and fro, humming aloud.

★★★

The baby cries all the way home. The child was as good as gold at the harbour with the fisher lassies, but as soon as she's alone with her mother she wails and screeches, grating on Maggie's nerves. So Maggie tries singing, rocking, and even pulls funny faces at it, but nothing seems to work. Near the harbour wall, she grinds her teeth together and tries to control a building rage that bubbles inside. How she longs to be free again, to walk barefoot upon the rocks, the sea breeze in her hair.

The midwife calls again at the crack of dawn, carrying a linen bag full of bannocks and a bone teething ring. Anna sits upon the old woman's knee by the hearth, fidgeting and cooing in her strong arms. Maggie observes the woman with curious eyes and notices how the child seems content, not at all like when she holds her. It's as though when the child is with her, it senses her anxiety and discomfort.

Jean clears her throat. 'When's Patrick home?'

'Don't know, a few days, next week. Who knows,' replies Maggie. The cooking pot is bubbling over; she stirs it and throws a dirty spoon on the table. 'Have you anything for a broth? I've nothing here except turnips.'

'I've kale and some herbs, and you are more than welcome. I'm sure your man will be back soon with a bag full of coins.'

'I hope so. I'm beginning to wonder if he's a part of my imagination.'

The midwife laughs. 'Do you know Sarah Clerk from the village? She had a baby around the same time you had Anna?'

Maggie nods. 'Aye, I know of her. How is she? Isn't she the lass with the fancy house?'

Jean continues. 'Aye, that's the one. She's not good; I was there at the birth and she had an awful time. In labour three days, she was, and when the bairn came it had a swollen head. And now folk say it's a changeling.' Jean crosses her arms.

Maggie shudders. She's taken every precaution to avoid fairies entering her home and spiriting her baby away. She's even got Patrick to place a large iron pin in the baby's cradle and warned him not to cut the baby's nails or hair.

'A changeling? That's terrible. Why do they think it's a changeling baby?'

Jean shrugs. 'The child's an imbecile and has distemper in the brain. The father wants to be rid of it and his family are urging him to bury it in a shallow grave come Martinmas so that the fairies will take it away. But his wife, Sarah will not hear of it. She doesn't believe that when they dig it up a few days later, the real baby will be returned.'

'I don't blame her, Mrs Lewis from the dame school in Haddington buried her baby because she thought it was a changeling, and when they dug it from the ground, it was dead.'

Jean's brows lower as though she's deep in thought. 'Aye lass, I understand. But it was the changeling that was dead not her real baby.'

'What is she going to do then?'

'She thought about throwing it in the linn, but she can't bring herself to do it. Do you know the foxglove plant with the pretty purple flowers?'

'Aye, I've seen them.'

'Well, some folk around here call them witch's thimbles. A wise woman told Sarah to scatter the foxglove flower heads over the changeling's body. Boil the flowers and feed it the boiled potion before leaving it in a barn overnight. The wise woman said come morning the real baby will be found in its cradle.'

Maggie's eyes bulge in her head. 'Leave it in a barn overnight for foxes and God knows what else to get at it?'

Jean adjusts baby Anna in her arms, the child's head is tilted backwards, and her tiny lips press together like a rosebud. 'Well, we've no reason to trouble you about this little one; she's perfect and fast asleep for now.' The midwife holds out her arms.

'Aye, for now, just the way I like her.' Maggie places the child within her cradle. 'Have you seen this contraption? My Patrick made it out of some wood from an old table. It looks more like a pig trough!'

Jean chuckles and slaps one bony knee. 'A pig trough maybe, but it's a perfectly formed wee baby girl you're placing inside. Count your blessings, lassie. How many babies die before they reach their first year? Near every month a poor mother buries a little one.' She places her hands together in a silent prayer. 'Anyway, I must be off, Maggie. It's time I filled my belly with some oats. I'll bring you some kale later to make some broth once I'm fed and watered.'

Maggie thanks Jean and places a hand over her rumbling stomach and with a sinking heart she realises that she's low on peat and must scavenge for wood. After all, when all is said and done, she cannot boil broth without a fire.

★★★

After countless sleepless nights, in the sixth month of little Anna's life, a marvellous thing happens: she sleeps through an entire night. And therefore a new wife awaits Patrick when he returns home. Once Maggie learns that Patrick's on dry land, she dresses for the occasion with the utmost care. Her white shift is tight after the birth and clings to her curves. With her hair unbound, she loosens the laces at the front of the shift and smooths the material over her generous hips.

They make love till the break of dawn and it feels like their wedding night all over again. That morning, as she dresses near the fire, Maggie stares down at her thighs and notices several black bruises from the top of her thighs to the inside of her knees.

'Look at this, Patrick,' she points at the bruises.

'What?'

'Look at the bruises. You need to be gentler, Patrick,' she declares in a high pitched voice.

'I thought you liked it rough,' he replies, grabbing her around the neck and pulling her into a fierce embrace.

'Stop it,' she demands.

He laughs. 'For better or worse, Maggie – you are mine.'

★★★

Maggie's starving, her breasts are empty of milk, and the child's not been fed for a good few hours. Outside she digs up a few kales, ignoring the child's wails as she bends on dirty knees. Maggie takes a few leaves and jams them into her mouth, chewing the lot so that her cheeks bulge out and a quantity of green mush spills out onto her chin; she wipes it away with the back of her hand.

At the mouth of the Esk, Maggie gathers mussels. She loathes shellfish but when her belly rumbles she's not so fussy. Above and beyond, Anna needs feeding, and if Maggie's not careful her milk will dry up. Without a doubt the child will need weaning soon, but Maggie daren't feed it floury pap yet, just in case it gets sickly. And so she collects a basket full of mussels and hurries home.

The following day Patrick returns and his face sun-tanned and covered in bristles. For once Maggie makes a real fuss of him; kissing his face and helping him carry in his nets and fishing gear. From the corner of her eyes she notices him looking her up and down, a frown upon his weathered face.

'You're getting thin, woman. And no wonder if all we have to eat is kale broth. This tastes awful; didn't your mother teach you how to cook?'

Maggie puffs out her cheeks. 'Aye, but I wasn't listening. Anyway I can't buy good food if I've no fish to sell, Patrick. Have you caught anything?'

'Aye, there's a creel-full for you to sort out. But no matter, come here, let me give you a kiss.'

'Nae, I must sort the fish,' she says and heads for the door.

'What's wrong with you, woman? Your husband should always come first.'

Maggie stands with her hands on her hips and shrieks like a scold. 'I'll tell you what's wrong, Patrick Spence. I've had nothing to eat for days and I've a weary heart. For days now, I've had no money, no food, and the child needs feeding…'

'For God's sake, woman, my head's beginning to ache. And what do you think I've been doing? Sitting on my hands?'

Maggie shakes her head, eyes flashing. 'Well a couple of lasses at the harbour said they saw you near the links with Johnny Notions. How do I know that you've not been throwing all our money on a cock-fight or the horses?'

'That's nonsense. Here, go and buy something tastier than this awful broth,' he utters, tossing her a few coins before reaching out to embrace her.

Maggie pushes him away.

Patrick lets out a loud groan and puts his head in his hands. 'For the love of God, woman, what's the matter with you now? Come here. Now listen to me. I'm going to give you some practical advice. So listen to me for once. You're going to have to learn from the other fishwives, Maggie. And I'll tell you why, a fishwife's life is a tough one and you must learn how to survive while I'm gone. Are you listening, Maggie, because if you don't, you and Anna will starve? Is that clear? Make do, scavenge, and don't be too proud to ask for help,' he pauses for breath. 'I must say, I'm surprised, Maggie. I thought you were made of sterner stuff. Is something else the matter?

'Aye,' Maggie says and sits down, her eyes looking down at the floor and her feet. 'I'm to have a baby again,' she heaves a great sigh.

'Oh, lass,' he says taking her hand. 'Is that so bad?'

Maggie slaps away his hand. 'I told you the last time I never wanted to go through that again. And Anna's just a few months and I'm to have another.'

Patrick runs his hand through his hair. 'Well, there's no use whinging about it, woman, what's done is done and you'll just have to make the most of it. Now then, when you've seen to the baby, fetch me something to eat.' He smacks her backside and proceeds to fill his new pipe to the brim. His long legs stretch out in front of him to be warmed by the fire. And with that he dismisses her.

Many thoughts sift through her head as she feeds the child. The very act irks her. If she'd have been born a fine lady, she'd have hired a wet nurse from the day of its birth. But alas, she's poor. And so, she plods on, till the child's sated and then puts her down to sleep. While Patrick lazes by the fire, she decides to take his advice and make do, so she calls on the widow to ask for some food. In no time at all, she had a quantity of vegetables and a chicken carcass to flavour the broth. Soon the delicious aroma of chicken broth fills the room; Patrick practically salivates over the pot. And yet, none of this domesticity gives her a sense of purpose or fills the void inside her. In her heart Maggie knows something else out there awaits her, and it seems to call to her like a tantalising whisper of a thrill.

Before long, Patrick falls asleep again by the fire. Maggie would have liked to rest too but she has things to do. She clears up, washes the pots and generally bangs about the room, making as much noise as she can, no doubt to announce her displeasure. For the longest time she continues to make an almighty din until Patrick sits up, rubs his eyes and shouts: 'For the love of God, woman, stop making so much noise.'

Maggie scoffs. 'While you sit here and do nothing.'

The look that crosses Patrick's face is frightening; Maggie steps backwards till her back faces the door.

'You've got some nerve. All you have to do is look after one bairn, sell fish and keep home…'

'Aye, and what do you do except constantly disappear?' she screams.

'What do you think I do, Maggie? So you gut and sell a few fish. Pah! Near every day I climb in a lug-sail boat with an open hull. At any moment I can be thrown overboard and drown. Are you even listening to me, woman?'

Maggie twitches her head to signal a yes but it somehow comes out as a no, she's never seen him lose his temper before and for some reason it gives her a thrill. A shiver of pleasure runs up her spine as he approaches her, one calloused hand taking her by the shoulder to take her in hand. She leans into him and presses her body against his, arching her neck backwards in anticipation of his kiss. His head moves closer, till their lips are barely a whisker apart, and then with a violent shove, he pushes her aside.

'I'm going out!' he shouts, before slamming the door.

***

Patrick does not return that night, or the night after. So Maggie decides to put him out of her mind, and go about her business and *to hell with him*, she thinks. The following day she takes the money he gave her and stocks up on food, the rest she puts away for a rainy day.

At dusk, the widow calls round and Maggie can't resist telling her of her quarrel with Patrick. It's the first time Maggie's confided in anybody and she's curious to know if all women feel such disappointment in married life, and for some reason this causes the widow to laugh till she's red in the face.

Maggie frowns. 'What's so funny?'

'It's a woman's lot. Drudgery, looking after your man and your children, what did you expect? So you're feeling trapped, is that it? Feel like you've got the raw deal because you're a woman and a peasant one at that?'

'Aye,' Maggie nods.

'Hah!' the widow mocks her. 'What's your occupation?'

'I'm a fishwife.'

'Well let me tell you something, Maggie. Fishwives are probably the most independent women in the whole of Scotland because their men are always at sea, and therefore they can do as they please. There's no one around to tell them what to do, most of the time that is. They drink, they smoke, and their language would put a navvy to shame. So why on earth are you whining about nothing? You are as free as a bird and not many women have that.'

***

A shrill cry pierces the air as Anna wails at the top of her lungs. Her linen needs changing, so Maggie bends over the crib to remove her soiled napkin, screwing up her nose as the offensive smell wafts up her nostrils. Maggie lifts the child's ankles up in the air, her bottom's red raw and covered in sores, so she rubs in some fat onto her chubby buttocks and it seems to ease Anna's pain.

As always, she senses him behind her; it's his smell, like fresh air, seaweed and tar. A shiver of delight runs through her as he wraps his arms around her and kisses the back of her neck.

'Oh, you've decided to come home have you? Well, I'm busy, Patrick, so stop that now and let me see to the baby,' she makes him wait.

Patrick ignores her and continues to kiss the nape of her neck. 'Oh, come on, Maggie. I'm exhausted; perhaps you and I could have us an early night. I'm off in the morning to the keels to Newcastle.'

A red light flashes behind her eyes as she turns to face him, pointing a finger in his face. 'Oh, no you're not. They'll be no more gallivanting for you. You've only just walked in the door. I want you to stay here with Anna tomorrow while I hawk fish in Edinburgh.'

Patrick shakes his head. 'No, it's arranged. Things are quiet here at the moment so it makes sense for me to go where the work is and put food on the table.'

'But you're never here to eat at our table!' Maggie sobs.

Dark clouds gather over her shoulder as she clambers over rocks to reach the sea. She can almost smell rain as she settles near a rock pool to pull off her shoes. *To hell with him*, she thinks, and sniffs back tears. *I'll not moan at him anymore or beg him to stay. Nae, what's the use?* She finds that her hands are shaking, the way her father's do when he needs a drink, so she tucks them under her plaid and gazes up at the clouds.

When she returns to the cottage, he's gone.

★★★

On New Year's Day, Maggie spends another day alone. And on that day it happens the fire is low and so she ventures outside to fetch the last of the peat. As she descends the steps of the cottage she takes care not to slip on the icy floor, when suddenly a familiar voice calls out to her.

'What are you doing out here in the freezing cold, Mangy Maggie?'

'Johnny. Is that you?' She peers down from the steps to the ground below.

'Who do you think it is? Get that door open, I'm frozen to the bone.' In two strides he's half-way up the steps holding out his arms.

He looks at her with a puzzled expression and places a hand on her protruding stomach. 'I thought you'd have dropped that by now?'

'You feckless fool, this is a new baby. My baby girl's fast asleep inside; you must come inside and see her.' She stretches out one arm to the door.

Johnny ruffles her hair, exactly the way he did when she was a child. 'You have a wee baby girl? What did you call her?' He asks and follows Maggie through the front door.

'We named her Anna after my…' she beams.

Johnny's bottom lip trembles. 'Of course…' he replies in a broken voice, a tear rolls from the corner of his eye, and he wipes it away with his dirty sleeve.

For a while Johnny shuffles near the door and then he raises a hand to his face and laughs. 'I knew I'd forgotten something. Can I ask you a favour, lass? My friend's waiting outside by the harbour. Can he come in by the fire? It's a cold night.'

'Aye, bring him inside. I won't be a moment, I need to fetch some peat.'

When Maggie returns with the peat, a strange looking man enters the cottage. A cloak of sea mist swirls around his body as though he's wearing a magical cape. Maggie stares at him in awe, mouth wide open.

Johnny claps his hands together and walks over to the odd man. 'This is a good friend of mine, Maggie. This is Kenneth Laing.'

Kenneth wastes no time in getting close to the blistering hearth. A quantity of steam rises from his trews as he warms his rump by the fire. And as he does so an expression of extreme relief crosses his face.

'Kenneth's a taibsear.'

Maggie's eyebrows lower. 'A what?'

'A taibsear. Oh, you lowlanders are an ignorant lot. A taibsear – a seventh child of a seventh child. Kenneth has a gift; he can see into the future and has premonitions.'

Maggie's not one for such nonsense and narrows her eyes. 'And how did he get these powers?'

'How do you think? Through the power of the fairies, Maggie, how else? Don't you ever leave gifts out for the little people – milk or…'

Maggie interrupts him and says under her breath. 'Isn't that a load of old nonsense, Johnny?' she replies, ignoring the dagger-like look she receives from the strange little man.

For a while, there is silence, except for the crackling fire. When the taibsear opens his mouth, he directs his speech to Maggie, his tone smooth and rich like warm honey. 'The gift of prophecy is not nonsense; you should learn to curb your tongue, woman. The gift is not something to be taken lightly and comes with a price.'

'I meant no offence. So if there was a price, sir – what was yours?'

'I paid with my eyes.'

'He's blind in one eye,' explains Johnny.

The taibsear clears his throat. 'The sight comes to me in visions and dreams. Do you dream, Maggie?'

A feeling of unease comes over Maggie. Her hands reach for her neck, nervous fingers scratching at her throat. 'Aye, I do. It's very strange. I have the same dream, over and over again.'

Kenneth nods. 'To dream the same dream again and again is commoner than you think. What's in this dream, Maggie?'

Maggie swallows, unsure of whether to reveal the nightmare that plagues her sleeps. She looks to Johnny for reassurance and when he nods his head she utters. 'I am stretched out on a dirty floor and rats crawl all over me. And there's this banging noise in the dream, as though a hammer is banging in the distance and the noise drives me insane, so that I scream at the top of my lungs, and that's how the dream is – every single time until I wake up.'

The taibsear's face appears troubled. He turns to Johnny and then to Maggie as though unsure of who to address. 'My premonitions are spontaneous and come of their own accord. I see nothing of your future, but I do feel uneasy in your company. I sense a dark…'

Johnny Notions interrupts here. 'You'll be giving the lassie nightmares, Kenneth.'

Johnny pokes Maggie in the arm and twitches his head in Kenneth's direction, swirling a finger in a circular motion around his head. 'Pay him no heed, he's been at the fire water again and is not making much sense. I think we should be on our way now, Maggie, we've a long journey ahead of us.'

Maggie's shoulders sag. 'But you've had nothing to eat. Sit down and warm yourself by the fire.'

Maggie pulls a stool out for Johnny and another for Kenneth, gesturing for them to sit down. 'I've some broth and a couple of bannocks.'

Johnny shakes his head. 'Nae, lassie. You need the food for yourself and the coming bairn; you've not enough for everyone.'

'No, I insist Johnny. Let me give you a bite to eat and then you can be on your way.'

Reluctantly, Johnny nods his head. The two men sit by the fire and make conversation. Maggie sets about bringing the broth to the boil, all the while watching Johnny's kind face glowing in the firelight. Taking her time, she places the food on the table and then pours out two cups of small ale.

'Eat up,' she says.

'Where's yours?'

'I ate earlier,' she lies.

But Johnny's no fool. His brow furrows into a frown as he picks up a wooden spoon. 'Are you sure?'

'Aye,' Maggie replies as a look passes between them. 'Honest to God.'

She watches them eat and fusses all over them, fetching more ale and even some of Patrick's baccy. When they finish she places the last of the peat on the fire and signals for them to come near the hearth.

'Oh no, Maggie, we must go now.'

Maggie's eyebrows droop and the corners of her lips pull down. 'But I've just put more peat on the fire…'

Johnny crosses the room to embrace her, pulling her face to his chest. He smells of heather and tobacco and his coarse hair tickles her chin. Maggie sniffs up in her nose and swallows back the pain in her throat. He'll forever be the father she wishes she had.

'Your man will return soon lassie and when he does pass on my good wishes.' He kisses the top of her head and pulls away. 'Now kiss the bairn for me and keep a place for me near the fire.'

Maggie nods and places a shaky hand across the front of her mouth. 'Don't leave it long now coming back, Johnny,' she tries to smile but it somehow turns into a sob.

'I won't.'

'Goodbye, Kenneth. It was a pleasure to meet you. Look after Johnny, he's like a father to me you know,' she says and closes the door.

★★★

With her belly full of baby, Maggie follows the other fishwives downhill to the Westbow. Her throat's dry and raw. She catches sight of a water fountain and is so distracted she pays little attention to the familiar cry of 'gardy loo.' Suddenly a dirty rascal throws raw sewage from a tenement above. At the last moment, Maggie manages to avoid the offensive shower and hurries away, but in the process loses the other fishwives.

'No matter, I will catch up with them later,' she says under her breath.

At the water fountain she drinks her fill, wincing at an incessant snapping sound. All the while she wonders what is causing the noise, a carter's whip or something more sinister.

Near the market square, the snapping noise grows louder. A small crowd congregates near the Grassmarket. Maggie pushes her way through them until she comes to a break in the crowd, suddenly she freezes. The whip has nine lengths of plaited cord, attached to a leather baton and lashes the back of a half-naked woman. A length of hempen rope dangles from her neck as the bailie reads out her crime. And all the while, as her crime is being proclaimed to the crowd, they drag her around the market square before hacking off her hair.

'Name the father, and we will be merciful!' The bailie shouts.

The woman shakes her head and retches, her vomit spewing onto the floor. The bailie nods to the hangman to continue the flogging, Maggie turns her head away in disgust, wishing she was far away. A couple of linkboys scurry past her to the market square. Homeless and desperate for food, they beg all day till they have enough money to buy a torch to light a fine gentleman's way, come nightfall, for the price of a few coins. Maggie's face softens at the sight of one of them. He's fair haired and barely four summers old.

The whipping noise halts. They untie the girl from the market cross. She lies face down on the cold dirt floor. The blood speckled face of the hangman gleams with sweat as he delivers his final lash. Be it fascination or horror, Maggie's compelled to stare, her eyes drawn to his coarse hands running along the length of the whip, squeezing and wringing out the blood to form a large scarlet puddle on the dusty floor. The flogged woman is motionless in the dirt. All around her are long ribbons of skin, and her torso resembles a hunk of meat on a fleshers chopping board. The bailie kneels beside her to turn her over; places one ear to her breast and shakes his head. With a pale face, Maggie turns to leave and then stops in her stride, her chest feeling as though it's about to cave inwards. It's the lockman, calling out to her in his loud voice.

'You, fishwife. Come here.'

'Me?' Maggie points a finger to her chest.

He nods. 'Aye, you, fisherwoman. Don't be shy.'

Maggie walks towards him, with each step the smell of sweat and blood gets stronger. Almost immediately she has to resist the urge to retch. As she pauses to adjust the creel on her back, Maggie's swollen stomach protrudes in front of her.

'Come on, fishwife, I haven't all day. You know the rules, wench. I'm entitled to one fish from every creel on market day.' He stretches out one bloody hand and takes a fish from her creel.

Maggie recoils as he scrutinises her. For a short while his eyes move along the length of her body before finally settling on her face.

'Till we meet again, fisher lassie,' he utters in a menacing tone.

'Over my dead body,' she cries and races down the West Bow, running until there's no breath left in her. But the swelling in her stomach makes it hard for her to run and so she has to stop and lean against a door, bending over her knees and gulping like a fish.

After a while she feels well enough to go on, and in no time at all Maggie's at the fish market selling her fish, but alas the other fisher lassies have already gone. With her creel near empty she hurries home, stopping at Joppa to sell the last of her fish. But she can't get the image of the hangman and the woman out of her mind. At the coastal path, the sea soothes her nerves, but as Watts Close comes to sight she breaks into a trot.

'What's the matter with you, lassie? You are awful pale,' Jean says with a look of concern.

'A poor woman flogged to death at the Market Cross.'

'How awful. No wonder you look queasy, sit yourself by the fire. I'll get you a drop of the strong stuff. Where do you keep it?'

'It's all right, Jean. I'll be fine. How's Anna?'

'She's no trouble. And her teeth are much better I see. Now I best be off, you never know when a new baby's coming, Mrs McCoist is due any day.

Maggie thanks her and follows her to the door. 'Oh, before you go. The last time you came to visit me you mentioned Sarah Clerk and the changeling.'

Jean grimaces. 'It's not good news. The baby died, lass. So it was definitely a changeling. The fairies have her real bairn now.'

Maggie bites her lip. 'Oh, that's a shame; but I expect she can have another.'

'Aye, but you know how it is. Folk have started pointing the finger. They're saying it's her fault the baby's a changeling and that she's being punished for her sins.'

'What sins? She's a good woman. And does her husband blame her too?'

'Aye, he does. He's beaten her, gave her a black eye and a thick ear,' Jean shakes her head, unable to contain her anger.

Maggie looks at Jean and puffs out her cheeks. 'For goodness sake, as if the poor woman hasn't been through enough!'

★★★

When Patrick returns, he thinks he's entered the wrong cottage. Everything is neat and tidy, and not a thing out of place. Maggie's even took care not to tamper with his fishing gear and covered it with an old sack. And for once, his young wife appears to be in a merry mood.

'Come sit with me, wife.' He pats a stool beside him.

Maggie removes her kertch and joins him near the fire.

'What the devil have you done? Where is your hair?'

'I had no money, so I made do.'

'You sold your hair?'

'Aye, to the wigmaker on the mile.'

'But, Maggie, your beautiful hair. I can't believe it. It was down to your waist, and now it barely reaches your shoulders.'

'It'll grow back,' she stares into the fire.

A feeling of dread fills Patrick's bones and he shivers as he stares at his wife's pale face. There's a sorrow in those eyes he's not noticed before.

'Will you be here for this one?' she asks, patting her swollen belly.
'Oh, lass.' He pulls her into his arms and kisses the top of her head.
'I will. I swear I will.'

★★★

At the harbour, Maggie has a burst of energy, and the fisherwomen
tell her that it's a sure sign that the child is about to be born. She
labours all day until her back aches and her hands are red raw from
sorting fish on the rocks.

Maggie's pains begin the following morning and last till the wee
hours of the night. Jean Ramsay arrives in the afternoon, along with a
barrage of women folk. And soon the house is clacking with gossips,
for as the old saying goes, 'for gossips to meet at a lying-in, and not
talk, you may as well dam up the arches of the roman bridge, as stop
their mouths at such a time.'

Nevertheless, Patrick keeps his word and does not miss the birth.
And so, on a cold February morning he holds his second born, a
son, and listens to the child's lusty cries. Young Anna has a brother,
a strong wee baby boy, and they name him Patrick after his father.
For a month after the birth, every day the gossips return, much
to Patrick's distain. Intimate relations between man and wife are
forbidden, since it's believed a woman is defiled by childbirth. Thus,
the women's job is to ward him off until churching and purification
is obtained.

★★★

'What's the matter with you? It's time you sat up, Maggie. The sooner
the dry nurse goes the sooner the churching, and then you'll be back
to your old self.' Widow Arrock crosses her arms over pendulous
breasts. She knows what's wrong with Maggie. She's seen it before.
It happens sometimes after a woman has a bairn. And in short, it's
worse for some than others. Maggie, thank goodness has a mild form,
the type that makes women irrational, weepy and unable to sleep.

After the churching, Maggie wakes up each day in a daze to carry out her day to day chores. And as she does so, there's a brooding look upon her pale face as her mouth droops down, looking like for all eternity that it will never lift up again.

***

During the summer of 1717, just as Maggie's melancholia disappears, a strange thing happens. Patrick's old fancy, Agnes Lecke, begins to call at Watts Close to help Maggie with the children. It's an unlikely alliance, but nevertheless Maggie welcomes the company and the extra pair of hands. Today, with Agnes's help, Maggie will venture outside with both children for the first time. Up till now Maggie's relied on the widow or Jean to look after the children, so she could collect water from the river, peat from the bogs, or to hawk her fish.

Patrick's old fancy is a pretty girl, but she can only be described in one word – peculiar. Agnes's eyes are empty and cold, so unlike Maggie's large eyes, like wild unearthly fires. They are an odd pair as they walk side by side towards the harbour. The air is fresh and breezy outdoors, and in no time at all they are at the boat shore. Near the rocks, sunlight reflects on the sea, like a thousand sparkling wavelets. A catch of fish is brought ashore, and so Agnes looks after the bairns while Maggie helps sort the fish. After a while, when there's no sign of her husband, Maggie buys some of the fish and decides to go home. Later she will dry the fish on hooks outside her door. A quantity of fishing nets, creels and baskets litter the entrance to Watts Close. Maggie shakes her head and groans out loud: 'Mind your feet, Agnes. Patrick's left his fishing gear all over the place again. Don't want you to trip and fall.'

They settle the children down and sit near the open door, enjoying the cool summer breeze and waving to passers-by.

'Was Patrick not at shore?' Agnes enquires in a soft voice.

'No, why?'

'I just haven't seen him in a while, that's all.'

As Agnes crosses her legs, Maggie notices that her stockings are odd and her stays aren't laced as they should be. And even more alarming, there are scars and strange scratches up the length of her arms.

'I've a feeling that he visits the links. It's either that or he's playing with the lads kicking a ball. Comes in he does with mucky legs and gets into bed dirtying the blankets. And that's not all…'

Agnes yawns.

'I'm sorry. How rude of me. Would you like a bite to eat? I've some bannocks on the cooling tray near the hearth.'

Baby Patrick begins to wail, Maggie huffs and wonders if the lad's stomach is a bottomless pit. 'Agnes, did you hear me?'

'What?'

'I asked you if you want a bite to eat.'

Agnes nods and picks up little Patrick.

★★★

With thoughts of her old love, Agnes Lecke feels a shiver of anticipation as she crosses the room. A table and two stools stand by the far wall, everything's neat and ordered and not at all as she imagined it be. A clay pipe protrudes from a horn beaker on a wooden chest; a pair of sea boots that need mending lay upturned on the floor. And then her eyes become drawn to an old wooden chair, the seat of which was made up from thick rushes. She scrutinises the chair for the longest time, a quantity of its binding is frayed, but that's not what holds her attention. It's the coarse linen shirt that hangs on the chair's back.

With nervous eyes Agnes glances across the room. Maggie's busy warming bannocks so, in haste, Agnes places the child in its crib and sneaks off to the chair. Her hands shake as she lifts the material to her nose, inhaling Patrick's musky scent; a shiver of pleasure shoots up her spine. Agnes is greedy for his scent, how she longs to possess it, devour it, and suck it up into her own being, so that they mingle as one. And so, for what feels like eternity, she holds the shirt to her body and weeps like a child.

A voice calls out to her. Agnes drops the shirt and focuses hard, after a while a blurred image sharpens into the shape of Maggie holding out a plate of food.

'What's the matter? You look like you've seen a phantom.'

'I've a pain in my heid.'

'Oh dear. There's a plant that cures headaches, looks like a daisy, it does. Do you know of it? It's called feverfew. My mother taught me how to recognise it when I was a wee girl.'

Agnes stares at Maggie, her bottom lip quivering all the while; she can see two Maggie's now and demons, familiars, and strange beasts with forked tongues. 'Feverfew you say. Where will I find it? And if I take enough will it send me to sleep? My head hurts. I need to sleep, Maggie.'

'Feverfew works miracles. You can find it on barren land or growing at the bottom of stone walls. I have some. Do you want me to make a tisane?'

'Please, will you? Will it make me sleep?' Agnes repeats. The voices are returning now and her visions are becoming distorted. Everything's a blur, colours and shapes all merging into one. She can just make out Maggie's voice.

'No, camomile and hops will help you sleep, but be careful though. You need to know how strong to make it.'

When Maggie isn't looking, Agnes staggers out the door.

CHAPTER SEVEN

LEAD US NOT INTO TEMPTATION

Excited cries fill the harbour as a huge catch of fish is brought ashore. The fishwives work fast on the rocky foreshore, each taking their share and spreading them across craggy rocks. They move fast, fingers busy, sorting the fish as hungry gulls circle above. Once the catch is gutted, the women wash and scrub their fish with a brush of heather stems bound together. Maggie and Isobel work shoulder to shoulder. All morning they wash, scrub and remove all traces of blood from flesh and bones. Next comes the splitting and salting, this can take up to six hours. Finally, they can be placed in a circle, head out, tail in centre, and laid on racks or hooks to dry in the sun.

★★★

At the crack of dawn, Patrick creeps from his bed, taking care not to wake Maggie or the children. He tiptoes softly across the room, eyes darting left and right in search of his sea boots and fishing gear. But he can't find them anywhere. He steps on a sharp stone and curses, one of the bairns stirs in their sleep. Patrick screws his eyes together and holds his breath, and to his utmost relief the child settles down. He tiptoes back to his bed.

'Maggie. Where is my fishing gear?' he whispers.

'Outside.'

'Outside?' he raises his voice. 'And my boots?'

'Aye, I've had quite enough of you leaving them near the door for me to trip up on – so I threw them out the door.'

Patrick's mouth gapes open. 'You're jesting. What if it's rained? Or what if someone's taken my stuff? How could you be so foolish?'

Maggie ignores him.

'I'm going then,' he says through gritted teeth and strides across the room to open the door. He's just about to leave when he remembers that he needs some bait.

'Maggie.' He taps her shoulder.

'What now?'

'I need a line baiting for when I get back.'

Maggie groans and turns over in her bed.

'Maggie.'

She pulls the covers over her face. With an almighty push Patrick slams the door behind him, no longer caring if he wakes up the children. It's a clear morning and fortunately it's not rained. He gathers his fishing gear and picks up his sea boots. They're covered in fine dew; he wipes them with a clout, places them on his feet and is on his way. At the harbour he fills his lungs with sea air, thinking there's nothing better than a spot of line fishing to clear the head.

His lugger boat is close by. Into the deep blue sea he drops his baited lines. The sky is clear ahead, he stretches out his long body in the hull and waits for the fish to bite, not a care in the world. It might be a good six hours before he needs to haul it up.

★★★

Maggie's exhausted. Before Patrick left this morning he asked her to bait one of his unused lines. But for the life of her, she can't remember what he uses – lugworms, paps, anemones or mussels? She seems to recall it depends on what time of year it is. A cockerel crows in the distance as she rubs her drowsy eyes. The baby kept her stirring all night and she feels dreadful. Underneath a mountain of ropes and nets she finds a sturdy creel. She has a good mind to make him collect his own bait, the lazy swine! As if she hasn't got enough to do.

By the light of the fire, she dresses quickly, fastening her stays with nimble fingers. Her clothes reek of fish and brine, but Maggie's oblivious to the stench. A stale oatcake lies on the table; she eats it quickly before banking up the fire. After that, she covers her long hair with a clean striped kertch, pulls on her scruffy boots and feeds the bairns.

Young Patrick fits snug inside the creel. It's a warm day so she swaddles him in fine linen spun for her bottom drawer. Before she leaves Maggie looks around the cottage and wonders if she's forgotten something.

'The baby,' she says out loud. And then realises the creel and baby are perched upon her back. She takes Anna and a basket in her arms and walks out the door.

'Hold the willow basket for your mother, Anna?'

'Anna hold basquit,' shouts Anna.

Maggie smiles as the child struggles to hold the object in her chubby arms. It isn't long before she has to take it herself. Anna drops everything eventually; she's all fingers and thumbs.

At the Esk, Maggie lowers her creel and basket to the soft ground. And so, with Anna on her hip and the baby safe in the creel she begins to look for mussels. Several women are scattered around the river bed. It is wash day and the gossips are out, ears wagging, listening for mindless tittle-tattle. To Maggie's consternation, baby Patrick begins to cry before she's found one mussel. With a thump she drops to the floor and traps Anna between her legs as she feeds the child. Before long a shadow looms over her.

'You've got your arms full, Maggie. Do you need any help?'

'Just here to collect some bait, Agnes.'

'I'll collect some bait for you or hold Anna.'

Maggie stares upwards into Agnes's face, suddenly her stomach lurches. Just the sight of her makes her wary for some reason. There is something odd about her face and the way her eyes gaze into empty space. 'That's very kind of you, Agnes, but no. I'm fine. I'm in no rush. I'm just here to collect some bait and go home.'

'No washing then? It is wash day, you know.'

'No. Like I said, I'm fine; the laundry can be done tomorrow.'

Maggie glances at Agnes from the corner of her eye, her stockings are odd again and there's a quantity of heather and gorse in her hair.

Agnes persists. 'I am free to look after the children tomorrow if you want. You could collect more bait or go to market.'

'There's no need. The widow is always on hand to take care of my bairns.' Maggie breathes a sigh of relief as Agnes walks away.

It isn't long before an old farmwoman takes pity on her and watches the two little ones while she collects bait. With a double-bladed knife, Maggie shells a quantity of mussels until she's satisfied she has enough.

At the cottage, Maggie places little Patrick inside the cradle and collects some gear together. Into a fishing basket she adds a knife, a heather brush and some strips of cloth to bind her fingers. With Anna safe in her arms, she picks up the basket and makes her way to the harbour. Patrick's boat is in, beached on the shingle shore. She runs towards him.

'What's wrong?' he asks.

'I left the baby sleeping. I thought you might need a hand with the boat and your catch.'

'I managed without you,' he says gruffly. 'I've already sold most of the fish but I saved some for you. Did you bait the other line?'

'No, I forgot. I'm sorry, Patrick. I did get the bait though.'

'It's all right. I know it's sore on the fingers, lassie. I'll bait the lines later. I shot six lines from the skulls today and there's still plenty of fish for you to hawk.' He takes Anna from her arms so she can sort the fish.

Maggie's apron is soaked by the time she's done. 'I'll see you later,' she hesitates, deciding whether or not to kiss him, but packs up her creel instead.

'Don't forget Anna,' he frowns, holding out their child to her. 'And Maggie. I'll be off in the morning again and I don't know for how long.'

Maggie swallows a lump back in her throat and turns away.

The mariner, Billy Swindles, blocks her path as she makes her way home. He's stinking drunk as usual, and carries a bottle of grog under his arm. 'Where's your father?'

'In the tavern I expect, in a similar state to you.'

He laughs and displays teeth, green with algae. Bloodshot eyes ogle her as if she's a dockside whore.

'Your father's a good man. Heart of gold has Duncan. Well I'll expect he'll be home soon.'

'The tavern *is* his home,' she says through clenched teeth.

The baby's still sleeping when she returns. She places Anna next to him and crouches near the hearth, clutching her empty stomach. A soothing glow radiates from the fire; Maggie stares into the crackling flames and allows her weary head to slump to the soft ground.

★★★

Lammas is the last of the three fishing seasons after Beltane and Johnmas, a quarter day in Scotland. It's time for fairs and a welcome rest for farming folk. In bygone days, couples used to meet up at Lammas for the handfasting ceremonies. Many couples married this way, by a wandering priest or over the blacksmith's anvil.

Folk bring their horses to swim in the sea at Lammas, and the kirk ministers always kick up a right fuss as it's thought to be a pagan tradition. But when all is said and done, it's a time for good cheer and festivity, and for folk to dance by bonfires as pipers play a merry tune. Maggie waits for Patrick near the foreshore, amidst the revelry. He agreed to meet her and the children, but as the sky darkens, she realises he's not coming. While her attention is momentarily elsewhere, a hand taps her shoulder.

'Hello, Maggie,' calls a familiar voice.

'Hello, Minister Bonaloy,' Maggie beams, more than pleased to see him.

'Are you all alone? You could do with some help I see. Allow me to walk you home. But first of all, allow me to get you and the children something to eat,' he holds out his hands to Anna.

★★★

The baby is crying as Maggie drags on her old boots. She ignores the shrill wails and pulls up her stockings at top speed, before grabbing her plaid. When Jean Ramsay arrives to look after the children, she flies out the door.

In record time Maggie reaches Edinburgh. It's a busy day and the air is hot and sticky, and so she proceeds to a well for a drop of water, before she hawks her fish and returns home. A mixture of folk wait in the line, women, young boys, exhausted water-carriers. Before long, Maggie grows impatient, keen to be on her way. As she waits in the queue, one of her stockings fall down.

'Damnation,' she cries and tilts forward, lifting up her petticoats to reveal a shapely thigh. With one leg stretched out in front of her she pulls up her stocking and ties it with a knot.

Intent in her task, a wisp of hair tickles the back of Maggie's neck as she secures her stocking. And then, all of a sudden the tickling becomes stronger, like a prickling sensation, and to be sure she has the distinct sensation that someone or something is watching her.

'May I help you?' asks a strange voice.

A mature man of quality stands before her offering his hand. He wears a powdered white wig that makes it impossible to determine his age. Maggie stares into his eyes. He's handsome, aristocratic and superbly arrogant, and when he smiles he sends blood rushing up her veins. With an open jaw she examines his clothes; they're simply stunning – silken blue knee-breeches decorated with tiny gems, and an exquisite velvet coat, embroidered with silver thread.

'What fine breeding stock you are. What is your name, pretty wench?'

'Maggie,' she answers, tugging down her petticoats and skirts.

The man takes a step forward and pulls out from his pocket a silver egg-shaped vinaigrette containing smelling salts. 'A pretty name, indeed,' he leans forward and unscrews the top of his silver egg, picks out a sponge and holds it to his nose. 'I'm not in the habit of conversing with young ladies of your station, but I happened to notice that there was a problem with your…' Suddenly he seems lost for words. '…attire.'

Maggie drops the prettiest curtsey and steals a half-shy glance at him. 'My attire is in perfect order now, sir.'

The man leans in closer and whispers in her ear. 'I do believe that you are the prettiest wench I have ever seen. How old are you? Fifteen or sixteen?'

'Nineteen.'

'You look much younger,' says the gentleman, holding the sponge to his face. 'I was just on my way to the pleasure gardens near Queen Mary's bath house. Would you care to join me?'

Maggie points to the creel of fish. 'I'm busy, sir. I have fish to sell.'

The gentleman turns a frown. 'Are you sure? It's not far. If one wanders towards Holyrood Palace, one is bound to come across it. You won't be disappointed.' His voice is persuasive and pleasing to the ear.

'Aye, I might do that one day,' Maggie nods, watching him walk away.

She watches him walk into the distance for the longest time, wondering if she's being foolish in refusing his invitation. When all of a sudden, a fat woman in the queue for water nudges her in her ribs and says: 'You're an ignorant sow! Why didn't you go with him? You must be insane. I'd have gone with him for sure. And it's a wonder he came within an inch of you with the smell of that fish.'

Maggie shrugs. 'What's does someone like him want with a lassie like me? And besides, I've fish to sell,' replies Maggie, pointing to her creel. 'And a husband at home.'

'Haven't we all, lass, haven't we all. Where is he now? Have you any little ones to feed?'

Maggie nods, 'Aye, I have two.'

The fat woman shrugs. 'Have they any food in their bellies? You're all skin and bone! Look at me, fat and content, because I take what I can in life.'

Maggie stands rooted to the spot, suddenly regretting her decision. She drinks water from the well and strolls towards the fish market. The usual banter, eloquent speech, a pert tilt of the head, and her fish is sold. With her creel empty, she takes her time walking home, and without thinking her gait gravitates towards the pleasure gardens and the whisper of a thrill.

★★★

It's as though she's stepped into another world. A magical courtyard flanked by luscious greenery and vibrant flowers, such a contrast to the drab grey vista of Edinburgh. The air's heavy with the sweet scent of freshly cut lawns, she raises one eyebrow and observes one, two, no, three couples in the act of copulation. Maggie shudders inside, her breathing's shallow and her legs tremble with guilty pleasure. As she drinks in the rhythmic movements, the stolen kisses and fervent desire, her gaze becomes drawn to one couple in particular. She can't take her eyes off them, and her hand instinctively begins to caress her own neck and trail downwards to her décolleté.

'Enjoying the scenery?'

Maggie turns around, her face flushing a shade of deep ruby claret. 'You startled me,' she says, removing her hand from her hot skin.

'I'm sorry. I didn't mean to frighten you.'

Bells ring in the distance as her eyes return to a courting couple, lost in the throes of passion. 'I've never seen anything like that before.'

'It's perfectly natural,' he licks his lips.

'For dog or swine perhaps, but not folk – and in plain view for all to see.'

The gentleman's eyes widen and sparkle with mirth. 'You are quite the innocent, how delightful.' He pauses and pulls a gold fob watch from his jacket. 'Anyway, I must bid you farewell. I have business at the coffee house.'

'What is your business, sir?' Maggie doesn't want him to go.

'My business?' His expression is one of amusement. 'Oh, this and that, my dear. I suppose I do what most gentlemen do to pass time away: I gamble away my inheritance. Good heavens, you are the most desirable thing but that dreadful smell,' he coughs into a handkerchief.

'Tis the fish,' she shrugs and points to the pail. Maggie can't take her eyes off him. He's utterly fascinating to observe, his manner and speech so different from common folk.

'Of course, of course,' he repeats and moves towards her, one smooth finger tilting her chin backwards so that he can peer at her face. 'Beautiful.'

'Despite the muck and stench?'

'I could tell you were a beauty through six layers of dirt,' he adds with a fixed look.

Maggie's canny. She bends at the knee and bows forward to allow him a splendid view; her eyes face the floor then flicker upwards at the very last moment to meet his eyes.

'That's very kind of you to say so, sir. But I'm taking up too much of your time and so I'll be on my way.' She turns to walk away.

'Maggie,' he walks after her, blocking her way. 'I've been frightfully rude. Allow me to introduce myself. I am Alexander McGregor. I am very pleased to meet you, Maggie.' He holds out his hand.

She pauses for a while before taking his hand. 'It's a pleasure to meet you, Alexander. But now I really should be on my way.'

'But I simply must see you again,' he demands.

'I'm very busy, sir. I have a family and my fish to sell.'

To Maggie's utter amazement, he dips at the knee in an elaborate bow and brings his soft mouth to her hand, kissing it as if she's a lady. If the fishwives could see her now, they would pee themselves with laughter. She shakes her hand away, suddenly ashamed by their coarseness and filth.

'Please allow me the pleasure of your company again?'

'I don't know. Perhaps...'

'Until we meet again. I will not take no for an answer, Maggie.'

CHAPTER EIGHT

THE SINS OF EVE

The sound of the widow's cane tapping on the wattle and daub wall is by far the most vexing noise. *Tap, tap* goes the cane as Maggie crosses the room, wiping sleep from her eyes and stubbing her toe on a wooden toy.

'All right, I'm coming,' Maggie screams, thinking how much she'd like to stick that cane up the widow's backside. 'Stop banging the damned cane,' she whines as she opens the door to usher the old woman inside. 'The bairns have just gone back to sleep so be quiet.'

'It's the middle of the day and don't curse. Your poor wee mother will turn in her grave.'

'Midday? Surely not. The sun's not even over the brae.'

The widow clucks. 'Been up since the crack of dawn, I have, unlike some. My poor feet are killing me. I bring gifts, a chicken for the pot and a parsnip.' The widow's brows knot together, her face scrutinising the vegetable in her hand. 'Look at that, Maggie; it's like the shape of a man's...'

Maggie pushes her towards the fire and smiles. 'Aye, a fine maypole that is, Widow. Put it to the side, I'll save that for later.'

'Maggie, you're a wicked girl. Anyway, have you heard the news?'

Here we go, thinks Maggie. It's no wonder the widow's always getting into trouble, spreading gossip and causing trouble. And so Maggie says: 'No, I've better things to do than listen to idle gossip. Sleeping for instance, that's a more enjoyable pastime.' Maggie pulls a face.

'Nonsense, lassie. What woman can't resist a bit of gossip?' says the widow, slapping her warty forehead. 'You know the brewster woman from near the Old Roman Bridge?'

'There are lots of brewster women. Which one?'

'You know – the one with the bad leg and red hair. Well she was beaten by her husband for drinking too much of her own strong brew. And do you know that farmer at Inveresk? Peculiar fellow, you know, the one with the wife who looks like she has a beard. Well he's been caught interfering with his cows again.'

'Hah! You've seen his wife? I don't blame him,' Maggie laughs.

'Oh, Maggie, that's shocking talk.'

'Well, she's a right sour-faced cow.'

'Cow? You said cow and he's been...' Widow Arrock cackles and then covers her mouth, suddenly ashamed of her jesting.

Maggie pats her on the arm. 'I did hear something.'

The widow's ears prick up like a ravenous hound. 'What did you hear?'

'About a Quaker. Have you heard? Near Haddington, I think. He wouldn't let folk graze their animals on his land. So they flogged him and cut through his tongue with a red hot poker.'

'Did he have a family?' the widow enquires.

'Aye, banished.'

'That's a sad business.'

'Have you seen my father?'

Maggie fixes her eyes on the widow, watching the widow's face turn crimson and her lips purse together. A moment passes before she replies.

'Aye, I have seen him, Maggie and he's a devil as always.'

'Where did you see him?'

'I caught him coming out of the manse one morning tucking his shirt in. He's been dallying with one of the minister's daughters again.'

'Again?' Maggie sucks in her breath. 'And they're both so young, surely not?'

The widow clucks her tongue. 'Aye, well when your father's concerned nothing surprises me. I gave him a right tongue lashing, I did. But he told me to mind my own business and assured me that he was merely trying to educate the lasses, making them think for themselves instead of following the flock, whatsoever that means.'

'Was he drunk?'

Widow Arrock laughs. 'Hah! Of course he was drunk. Your father's always drunk. God knows how he does it. Even when folk think he's sober, he's half-cut. Never been any different since the day he moved here from Temple. Your mother told me he stayed sober long enough to secure a cottage and then slowly drifted to his old ways.'

'No one can accuse him of not knowing how to have a good time,' Maggie shrugs.

'He drove your poor mother to her grave.'

'Now that's not true. She was ill and nature took its course. It was God's will.'

'All right, all right, I'll mind my own business. Some things are best left unsaid,' whines the widow as she reaches for her wooden cane.

'Aye, they are. Thank you for the chicken.'

'You're welcome, my lovely.'

The widow places one hand on the table, putting her weight on it before bending her knees. 'My, I'm getting old.'

★★★

More often than not, before Maggie reaches the High Street, a barrage of hucksters and forestallers hinder her way. But with brute force she pushes and nudges her way through them, eager to reach her destination. *Nearly there*, she thinks, a pain in the pit of her stomach as she sprints along the wynds. A cross-road looms ahead, the palace grounds clearly visible beyond. But before she reaches it something prompts her to stop in her tracks and stare up into the sky.

Against the backdrop of a leaden grey sky, a gibbet creaks back and forth in the wind. A pale woman stands beneath it, waiting to catch his bones. Maggie closes her eyes to block out the eerie spectre – the image of a decomposing man, birds feasting on his rotting and putrid flesh.

★★★

103

The air smells of rain. Soon a fine drizzle covers her face, washing away the grime and filth. Without thinking she walks to the pleasure gardens and then the coffee house, but the fine gentleman is not there. With drooped shoulders Maggie walks towards the fish market and sets down her creel. Along the way, the lassies at the fruit market cheer her. They're as bawdy and vulgar as the fishwives and always have a funny tale to tell. Creel empty, she heads away from the fish market and crosses the street, proceeding downhill towards Anchor Close. There's a little tavern there by the name of Dawney Douglas where the rich folk are said to frequent. Outside, a small group of gentlemen sit playing dice.

★★★

Sir Alexander McGregor recognises her immediately. It's the beautiful peasant girl, with huge breasts and dark eyes.

'Look at the jugs on that wench,' remarks one of the gaming men, sucking in his stomach to reduce his portly frame.

'Cecil, do you really think the act of pulling in your stomach would make her interested in the likes of you? You're fat, bald and have rotting teeth… and then there is the wart on your nose,' Alexander scoffs.

'Mercy. A girl of her class would find a leper attractive. Remember that whore in Paris while we were on the grand tour? She looks just like her, don't you think?'

'She's not a whore,' declares Alexander. 'She's a fishwife.'

'Same thing. Although whores smell better,' sneers Cecil.

'Really, Cecil? You're an incurable buffoon. Run along to the cockfight or the bear-baiting will you, good chap.' Alexander springs to his feet and beckons to the girl, ignoring the men's guffaws as he takes her small hand.

★★★

They travel by horse and carriage, and for the most part Alexander holds his vinaigrette sponge to his nose. Maggie realises it's because of her fishy smell, but he insists it's because he has a cold. The carriage comes to a halt. Alexander opens the door and points to a grand building outside.

'Here we are. This is Queen Mary's bath house. And do you know, Maggie, Queen Mary is rumoured to have bathed here in a bath of sweet white wine?'

Maggie couldn't care less, but nevertheless nods her head. She takes his hand and steps out of the carriage. To her mind the building resembles a tolbooth but as he guides her up stone steps that lead to a second floor, she's pleasantly surprised. At the top of the stairs, amidst tapestries and a wood-panelled corridor, they're greeted by a maidservant. Alexander immediately takes charge, barking out orders in a commanding tone.

'Bring us some food at once and have someone make up a fire.' He turns to Maggie. 'Do you need a maid to assist you in removing your clothes?'

'Whatever for?'

'But you must need assistance with your stays?'

'They fasten at the front.' She smiles and wonders if he wants her to disrobe now in front of the maid.

As Maggie decides whether to disrobe or not, Alexander pushes open a door to reveal a wondrous sight. Beyond the entrance is a magnificent tiled room; in its centre a magnificent octagonal plunge bath, hot steam rising off its surface.

Maggie gasps. 'It's beautiful! So this is a bathhouse. Can I get in it?' she asks, removing her plaid.

'Of course.' He gestures towards a small changing screen.

Behind the changing screen there is a mysterious door. She bends to peek though the keyhole, but someone has stopped up the hole so that the view is obscured. Maggie's heart thumps in her chest as she removes her soiled clothes; soon she is completely naked behind the screen. She peeks out at the bath again; a tall man-servant has entered the tiled room. He has shiny brown skin the colour of rich coffee, and upon his head is a bright coloured scarf. Maggie watches in awe as he places a small white block and a drying cloth on the edge of the water.

★★★

A sweat breaks out on Alexander's face as all his blood seems to rush to his groin as he waits for the peasant girl to emerge from the screen. Never in his life has he felt so aroused, like a randy groom on his wedding night. His breath catches in his mouth as she materialises before his eyes, a naked voluptuous goddess, like one of the tantalising Lely paintings in his father's study.

'Aren't you coming in?' She plunges into the water, takes the soap and inhales its floral scent.

He shakes his head, unable to take his eyes from her. 'Later.' He smiles and notes that she's completely at ease with her nakedness.

'After you've bathed, enter the room next to the changing room. It's behind the screen.'

Maggie laughs and splashes, rubbing the soap into her body in a deliberately sensual manner. Steam rises around her, obscuring her figure into a misty haze. His eyes narrow and work harder to see the shape of her body, and then suddenly she emerges in front of him, floating on her back so that her hair fans around her in a dark halo.

The tingling returns, at the top of his thighs and spreading to the tip of his desire. The girl is like a precious flower unfolding her petals to a scorching sun, waiting to be plucked. Before long, he can bear it no more. With a sense of urgency he bends on one shaky knee and signals for her to come to him, holding out the soft cloth in open arms.

'Hurry,' he says stretching out his hand.

For just a moment she stands naked before him, every inch of her body covered in water droplets, giving her skin a glossy sheen. It pleases him the way she stares at him with those flashing eyes, and for an instant he wonders whether to take her there, right now on the cold wet floor. But he picks her up instead and throws her over his shoulder, carrying her off to his secret nest.

The room's sultry; a fire rages and crackles as Alexander edges her backwards onto a four-post bed. How tempting it is to enter her now to satisfy his wants and desires, but he's a patient man, and with a beauty such as this, he will be sure to take his time. However, it's more than he can endure as he binds her soft wrists with scarlet silk, such torturous exquisite agony. The very act only serves to heighten his impatience.

'Drink this.' He lifts her pretty head to place a crystal glass to her lips. 'Spanish fly.'

'Spanish fly?'

'It enhances the senses.'

'What for?'

'No matter. Just drink it,' he commands and watches her eyes widen. 'There will be nothing but pleasure and just a little pain.' He picks up a candle and drips some wax onto the tips of her nipples.

'Stop. I don't understand.'

'I think you understand very well, Maggie.' He kisses her then, his tongue forcing its way into her mouth as he opens her legs wide.

And then Maggie begins to understand.

★★★

The bed's like something from another world, as though it was made for a giant or to sleep a dozen or more people. It has four wooden posts carved with chubby-faced cherubs and heavy brocade drapes that sparkle with shiny threads. She removes the scarlet binds and sits up in the bed; Alexander lies beside her, gasping for breath.

A beautiful ornament sits on a nearby sideboard. Maggie can't be sure, but she imagines it to be the naked figure of a king or a god with a tall crown perched upon his head. Beneath the figure are four white unicorns rearing into the air, their nostrils flaring like savage beasts.

'What is that?' Maggie enquires.

Alexander catches his breath. 'It's a present for my parents. It's a sugar sculpture. The entire object is made from sugar.'

'They're going to eat that?'

'No, no, it would make them quite ill. There are metal wires holding the whole object together. It's not edible.' His eyes crease at the corners in amusement.

Maggie shifts and reaches for her clothes. How's she to know that the damned thing is made from sugar? Her cheeks flush a deep red.

'My dear, you cannot leave now.' He pats the bed.

Maggie ignores him and picks up her clothes. 'But I must, sir. It's late and I must be getting home.'

'What a pity. I wanted to see you pin up your hair – I must see that pretty neck free of grime and filth. You've such beautiful hair. How I loathe those ridiculous lice-ridden wigs. No matter how many times I send them to the nit-picker they come back crawling with damn mites.'

'Why do you wear them then?'

'Fashion my dear – why else?'

'I prefer you without it,' she runs her fingers through his closely cropped hair. 'Makes you look much younger.'

'You are a darling. But you see a wig is like a status object. Big wigs are worn by important and privileged men.'

'Oh!' says Maggie. Her mouth makes the shape of a circle.

Alexander groans. 'Give me strength.'

Maggie pulls on her clothes. 'My hair used to be much longer. Passed my waist. I sold it.'

'You sold your hair?'

'Aye. But it will grow back; it's already past my shoulders.'

'Oh, do you have to put on those dreadful garments?'

Maggie shrugs. 'Aye, can't be walking around naked can I?'

'More is the pity,' he utters.

★★★

Before returning home, Maggie rids herself of all feelings of guilt and remorse. And anyway, why should she feel guilty when he's never around? Aye, it's all Patrick's fault, she decides. If he'd been a better husband and provided for them all, she would never have acted in such a way. Or would she? In her heart she knows the answer.

Black clouds linger over the Esk as she nears Musselburgh. And Maggie can swear that St Michaels spire is mocking her in the distance, begging her to confess her sins. She turns her cheek and trudges on. Behind a hedge, she crouches, legs trembling as she takes a handful of soil and grass to wipe between her legs to mask his smell. But she's not ready to go home just yet. She takes another handful of dirt and smothers it over her arms and face. Now she can go home.

★★★

The children sense all is not well. Anna and Patrick huddle together once the quarrelling begins. As always, one of their parents leaves the cottage, slamming the door behind them. This time it's mother.

'Why did mother shout and say you are not a man?' Anna screws up her little face and bites her lip, determined not to cry.

'She's troubled. But it will pass. All will be well come morning.' Patrick strokes his daughter's head.

'But she hit you and now she's gone.'

'I know. I know. But she'll be back soon and then I must be off again to catch more fish.' Patrick tickles his daughter's cheek with his beard, and the sound of her giggles warms his heart. But then his eyes cloud over as his thoughts return to Maggie. He's wondering where she might be, because if he knew, he'd be tempted to wring her damned neck.

★★★

It's a potent thing deceit and treachery. Especially when it involves such savage passion and forbidden pleasures. Addiction can be resisted or gradual, but for the likes of Maggie, the craving is instantaneous. Time after time she entertains him, until the fruits of her labour land at her feet or stomach, so to speak. 'You reap what you sow.' Wasn't that the saying? And so, if Maggie's to continue this dalliance and pursuit of pleasure, she must play her lover like an angler would a trout, until she became uninterested in him, or him of her?

A savage wind blows from the north and tears at the landscape. Next comes rain and hail, and still she contrives to venture outside. There's no choice. She has to. Maggie leaves the children with the widow. The force of the wind and rain stings her face, and by the time she reaches the wise-woman's cottage at the top of fairy brae, her lips are blue. It's a most pitiful structure; the dwelling's virtually crumbling to the ground. Some cured well-wisher has tried to patch up her roof with a piece of turf, but unfortunately it's become dinner to a multitude of vermin.

Maggie knocks twice. Footsteps shuffle slowly towards her, until at long last the door creaks open and Maggie's confronted with an old woman. Maggie rubs at her eyes, can she be seeing right? Around the old hag's throat is a necklace of dead worms. Without a word she beckons for Maggie to come inside and reaches for a large jug on a nearby shelf. Next, she pours a quantity of liquid into a small cup.

'But I haven't said what…'

'I can guess,' replies the wise-woman with a knowing smile. 'The pains will begin in an hour or maybe less. Be sure to have lots of linen to catch the mess.'

Maggie hands her a coin, sips the mixture and is on her way.

★★★

The pains come much quicker than she anticipates, so with the wind howling in her ears, Maggie ties her body with a napkin to catch the blood before returning home. A dull light radiates from the cottage. Patrick waits at the door with his arms crossed, a pipe in his mouth.

'Where have you been, woman? Are you insane?'

'Nae, we've no food. I went out for eggs.'

'What do you mean, no food? Never mind, you're soaked through. Get yourself inside.'

Maggie warms herself by the fire hoping he won't ask to see the eggs. A dull pain throbs in her back and groin. With her back turned to him, tears roll down her cheeks, and no matter how much she rubs her stomach, the ache will not go away.

'What ails you, wife?'

'Ague I think.'

'I'm not surprised if you're going out in weather like that.'

With the back of her hand she wipes away tears and turns to her husband. He's holding out a warm blanket to her, a doubtful expression on his face. Maggie averts her eyes, damnation she cannot meet his gaze and so she turns away again, shuddering as he places a blanket over her.

Near the hearth Maggie slumbers, hugging her knees to her chest. Face streaked with tears, eyes red and swollen, she thinks to die will be a blessing. For only a wicked and selfish woman could act as she does, indifferent to her husband and children.

★★★

A week later, all is forgotten. With her husband at sea, Maggie's up to no good again, and one thing's for sure, she no longer cares when her husband returns home. Maggie cares even less about keeping a tidy cottage; nothing is in its place. Dirty pots and clothes are scattered everywhere, the pigsty is a mess, and she's let the fire burn out. But no matter – Maggie has only one thing on her mind.

With haste, she washes the children's faces, sticks a bannock in Anna's hand and trudges off to old Widow Arrock's. Anna runs ahead, Patrick's still unsteady on his feet, so she carries him in the crook of her arm. A tight smile masks her impatience as she chats to the widow; Maggie's not listening to a single word that she says. Nevertheless, all the while she nods and pretends that she's all ears, but in truth in her mind she's already in Alexander's bed.

'Won't be long, children.' Maggie avoids her son's eyes.

'Don't go. Please mother stay,' little Patrick cries and tugs at his mother's skirts.

Maggie turns to leave, a sudden attack of guilt surfaces and disappears as quickly as it appears, but niggles and festers inside of her. The ground crunches beneath her feet as she drops to her knees to clasp her son to her. 'I'll bring you and Anna a mutton pie, how's that?'

Anna smiles and rubs her belly.

★★★

A sense of exhilaration courses through her veins as she approaches Queen Mary bath house. Every time she visits him he introduces her to more decadent desires. She wonders what he has in store for her today, more acts of domination or perhaps some play-acting. His favourite is for her to touch herself while he watches from a secret place, whipping him up into frenzy, until he can bear it no more. The list's endless, and Maggie's an avid pupil, and more than eager to please.

★★★

To George's mind, it's like any other Sabbath, until his son walks in. The sermon drags on and on, prompting many a woman and child to pee where they stand. Like all kirks of Scotland, St Michaels congregation demands diligence and punctuality, and so when Maggie, Patrick and the children walk in long after the doors have closed, fingers point. Once or twice they receive a dagger-like stare. George winces as Barbara nudges him in the ribs and whispers to him. 'Look at the state of them, George. I knew he shouldn't have married that one.'

'Shush,' he silences her with flashing eyes. 'I'll speak to him, mark my word.'

After the sermon, he takes his son to a quiet corner.

'You've lost weight, son.' He tugs at his son's shirt. 'Doesn't your wife feed you?'

Patrick laughs. 'Have you tasted her cooking?'

George Spence glances at his son's gaunt face. 'It's that bad? Your mother's worried about you. It wouldn't do any harm to call around to see her once in a while. Eat a decent meal ...'

'I'm fine. Tell mother all is well. I'll see you next Sabbath.'

George nods and returns to Barbara, he places a hand around her shoulder and whispers in her ear. 'Your son is fine; nothing ails him, except his wife's cooking.'

But Barbara's not listening to him. Something else holds her attention. The minister and Maggie stand barely a whisker apart. Her manner towards him is familiar, enticing even.

'What did I tell you, George? She's a jezebel.'

★★★

Patrick looks around the cottage with weary eyes and to his consternation he can't find anything. The place no longer resembles a home. All around him is chaos, dirty pots, clothes, a half-eaten bannock, and for the life of him he cannot find his sea boots.

'Get your boots on, lass.'

His wife shakes her head.

'Aren't you coming to the burning of the boat? The children have been looking forward to it.'

'Nae, Patrick. I'll give it a miss. I said I would visit Jean Ramsay; she needs my help spinning. She's hurt her arm.'

'Can't it wait until tomorrow? The women are playing football and golf. I thought you liked the games?'

Maggie ignores him.

'Well don't expect me to take the children.'

'Do as you please, Patrick. I really don't care.'

★★★

At the bath house, she bathes and gives herself to Alexander. There's nothing she won't do for him. Maggie's more than happy to satisfy his every need. Naked, half dressed, on her knees, sat up, stood up, bent over with red painted lips.

Today he requires that she wear a fine dress. A low-cut velvet one with a ribbon trimmed smock. The short tight boned corset forces her breasts high and squeezes her waist so tiny that it accentuated her generous hips. He demands that she wear a black beaded choker, high heeled satin shoes, no shift and no stockings.

Maggie feels his gaze as she admires herself in the looking glass. She could gaze at herself all day. Alexander's hands encircle her waist; she slaps them away and smooths out a wrinkle on the bodice. But he will not be deterred and presses himself against her, grabbing her corset laces with both hands.

'You are quite lovely.'

'You haven't fastened it properly,' she scolds.

'It doesn't matter. It'll be on the floor in a moment,' he replies, kissing her neck. 'You look absolutely ravishing.'

At that moment, for whatsoever reason, he changes his mind and proceeds to fasten her up extra tight till her ribs feel like they might break and her lungs explode.

Maggie's face turns crimson. 'Damn. I can hardly breathe. What are you doing now?'

'Putting patches on your face.' He places one black crescent high on her right cheek and another on her chin.

'What do I want these on for?'

'Put this cape on. We're going out.'

***

Dawney Douglas's has all manner of clientele. A motley crew of gentry, peasants, artisans, poets and libertines frequent the inn. Aldermen talk treason, smugglers talk wine and brandy, and gamesters of faro and hazard. It doesn't matter whether it is night or day, the inn-keeper and his wife are open all hours, and for the most part the atmosphere's always merry.

With his arm wrapped around her, Alexander guides Maggie through a long narrow hall. Several rooms jut off it and in one a fiddler plays an Irish jig while a semi-naked girl dances on top of a looking-glass. In another, a pinching fight entertains the crowd and all the while Maggie keeps her head high and contrives to look neither left nor right. Maggie's hand clutches Alexander's arm, her heart pounds so hard she's breathless. The majority of men, young, old, rich and poor look about in surprise and sudden interest at the beautiful woman on the gentleman's arm.

'Here we are, darling,' Alexander prompts Maggie to sit near a group of rowdy men playing cards on a green table. 'Allow me to introduce my dear friend, Cecil.'

Maggie nods at the bald and warty man. Alexander cannot help but notice her displeasure as he takes her hand to kiss it.

'And this is my younger brother, John.'

A broad-backed man sits with his back half turned from them; he does not glance around but continues with his game. Maggie thinks him quite ill-mannered and rude.

'John,' Alexander taps him on the shoulder and then again.

'Not now,' says John.

'But I want to introduce you to a friend of mine.'

John curses and turns around. The colour drains from his face and his eyes widen.

'This is Maggie.'

Maggie bows her head. Meanwhile, with a flick of the wrist, John tosses his hand of cards aside. Next he embraces his brother, his eyes meeting Maggie's as they draw apart. There's a likeness between the brothers, accept that once they stand side to side, every flaw of Alexander's is magnified. John's younger, taller, his jaw more square.

'Sit with me, Maggie,' John beckons.

★★★

The brother is persistent. Maggie obliges without a thought for Alexander. John sits close beside her, so much so that she feels herself edging backwards as blood rises to her neck and face. His eyes dip to the swelling peaks at the top of her dress. Damn, he is a bold one.

'Where's Alexander?' Maggie's eyes scan the room.

John looks into her eyes, a half-smile on his lips, one eyebrow lifting as his hand caresses her knee, and then her thigh. 'Oh, forget him,' John says. 'He doesn't mind sharing his whores.'

'How dare you!' Maggie springs up to face him, almost bursting into wild helpless angry tears. Without thinking she raises her hand to slap him and then remembers herself, a lowly fisherwoman facing an aristocrat. A blur of tears obscure her vision as she searches for Alexander, but he's nowhere to be seen. In the end she finds him near the tavern entrance taking some air.

'I want to go to the bath house. I need to go home,' she sobs. 'I don't belong here. This is not the kind of place for me.'

'I beg to differ,' he remarks before taking her arm.

★★★

As they walk hand in hand along the mile, Alexander takes her aside. With gentle hands he wipes away her tears before walking to a carriage.

'Remember when you were facing the looking glass earlier?'

'Aye.'

'Well I'm holding one up to your face now. Take a look.' He mimics the act of holding a mirror to her face. 'You're a minx, a natural tease,' he whispers in her ear.

'No I'm not.'

'You can't help yourself, Maggie. It's just your nature to be, well, how can I put it? I knew the moment you set eyes on John that I would be a distant memory. You gravitate towards handsome men like a moth to a flame.'

'What I do is my business, sir. And your brother is incredibly rude. He called me a whore.'

Alexander raises one eyebrow. 'You met your match in him.' He stifles a yawn and climbs into the carriage. Before long they arrive at the bath house.

All is silent as they climb the stairs. He can't resist one more glance at that rounded bottom as she ascends the steps, and so he deliberately falls behind to enjoy the view. With one hand clutched to his heart, he struggles to keep up with her and she's already at the top of the staircase. Beyond the changing screen, she disrobes and changes back into her fisherwoman garb; her face turned away from him.

'You may take the clothes and shoes.'

Maggie shrugs and stuffs the items into her creel, a tense look on her face. 'Are you vexed with me?'

'Heavens, no. I'm afraid my time in Edinburgh is over. I must return home.'

'Why?' Maggie whirls around to face him.

'My parents demand it. There is to be no more gambling, drinking or whoring. I am to go to London to find a suitable vocation and a wife.'

His cool green eyes watch her feign sadness and distress, but he has the measure of her. She's an utterly selfish being, a woman who cares little for those she hurts, as long as she gets what she desires. 'Don't fret,' he opens his arms and kisses the top of her beautiful head before handing her a bag of coins.

'I'll miss you, Alexander. Truly – I will.'

He cringes at the falsehood. 'I know. You must learn to be happy and accept who you are. You've a long hard road to travel; it would have been an easier life for you, Maggie if you'd have been born a man.' He nods and turns away.

For just an instant he feels a pang of sorrow as she walks away. And then he laughs to himself and wonders why such a common strumpet could make him feel this way. Nevertheless, he decides to take one last look at her, and as she turns her head to reveal just a hint of her profile, he catches a glimpse of the black patches still glued to her face.

★★★

The world had grown two years older since the night Maggie Dickson returned home stinking of whore's scent, wearing patches and clutching a bag full of coin. Patrick never did ask where the money came from, but like any wronged husband he'd taken a stick no thicker than his thumb and given her such a thrashing that she couldn't sit down for a week.

He's no fool, but she obviously thinks him one, and so he's taught her a lesson she most richly deserves. After that, she's dutiful and kind, and eager to please him with hearty food. There are plenty of kisses and praise, and so once again he becomes complacent, at least for a while. Because suspicion is a terrible thing, like wormwood it can eat away at a man, and so in the depth of his heart, doubt and mistrust weaves an intricate web.

★★★

Maggie exits the bath house with a new man's arm around her waist. Just like his brother, Alexander – John will return to London soon, back to his ancestral home. But no matter, she thinks, there are plenty of other men to take his place.

At Dawney Douglas's John lifts his glass and drinks to their health. After that he gives her a quantity of money. John's very generous and she's more than happy to accept his gratitude. Later, when she returns home and there is no one around, she will be sure to hide the money away in the pigsty.

A string of men come after that, athough none as exciting or handsome as the McGregor brothers. Their company proves lucrative and is preferable to selling fish. She chooses her men carefully; steering clear of the unhealthy ones – Maggie doesn't want the pox. For the most part the majority are too old and fat for her liking. Worse still, many of them tend to talk politics, their favourite subject the south sea bubble, of which she knows nothing and is the most frightful bore as Alexander would say. By the end of the year Maggie's with child again.

This time the potion is unsuccessful. The wise woman complains that she has no ergot and gives her hemlock instead, which has little effect. Maggie's figure becomes rounded. In a vain attempt to disguise her condition, she ties her stays tighter and always wears her plaid. And all the while she cringes as the older women point and whisper.

'If all else fails use a sharp stick, lassie. It'll pull the baby out from inside you.'

'Is that safe?'

'Aye, works every time.'

Maggie shakes her head and winces. 'Isn't there any other way?'

The old woman cackles. 'You can always drink strong liquor and bleed your feet or better still…' she pauses for effect. 'Learn to keep your legs shut.'

In the end, she obtains some pennyroyal and to her utmost relief it is successful and the gossip is no more.

★★★

One day, after a long country walk, Maggie, a troubled spirit of late, begins to look into her own heart. *What makes me act so wanton?* she thinks. And then, Alexander's words come back to haunt her: 'If only you had been born a man.'

This is my curse, she ponders. *I am a weak vessel, a mere woman, and a poor one at that. Now if I'd have been born a man, I could do as I please, bed as many women as I like, and to hell with the consequences.* Her lips curve at the memory of Alexander and his brother, and their overt masculine prowess; men encourage such conduct and praise virility. But if women act the same way, their sex brings them down through gossip, denouncement, or condemnation.

A coughing noise interrupts her thoughts; a chubby-faced Anna holding up her shoes.

'We go to the long water, Mama?' she asks as her little brother pulls her hair behind her.

'Aye,' Maggie nods, 'why not?'

★★★

They paddle in the sparkling waters of the Esk, and in no time at all their feet become numb from the icy cold water. For a while all three of them sit together at the river's edge and watch a pearl fisher go about his work. He whistles a merry tune and digs mussels from the river bed, tossing some aside and examining others in his weathered hands.

'He's looking for a black river pearl.' Maggie points at the pearl fisher.

'What's a pearl?'

Maggie looks to the cloudless sky, thinking best how to describe it. 'Like a black or white pea, but shinier.'

Anna throws a small pebble into the water. She's a bonny child and the image of her mother, according to Johnny Notions that is. In her tiny hand she clutches a wooden doll her father has carved for her and all the while her younger brother tries to wrench it away.

'I want it. I want it,' he cries.

Anna slaps him in the face and he responds by kicking her in the shin. 'It's mine. Take your hands off her. Mother, tell him to leave me be,' she sobs and rubs her shin.

'Anna, don't hit your brother.'

'He kicked me.'

'Yes, but you struck him first.'

'I'm sorry. I won't do it again,' Anna pouts.

As Maggie turns away she catches Anna pinching her brother on the leg. *What a little horror,* she thinks. The sound of their quarrelling buzzes in her ears as she closes her eyes. *Perhaps if I ignore them they will stop,* she thinks, but alas the children persist.

'I'll bang your heads together if you don't stop.' She grabs Patrick and Anna's hands and guides them over to the oak tree, stooping to gather up their stockings.

Maggie rubs their pink toes with her plaid, listening to their laughter as she tickles their feet. But then something distracts her and she stops what she's doing. A young man passes by; her eyes glitter as she looks him up and down. It's the blacksmith's son, all grown and tall; her gaze lingers on his body, he's muscular and strong.

'Mother – Mother!' Anna shrieks and tugs on Maggie's skirt.

But Maggie can no longer hear them; she's deep in thought, thinking up a reason to visit the smithy and his handsome son.

CHAPTER NINE

PRESS-GANGED

There's a beggar at Canongate, under the arch of Tolbooth Wynd. He has one leg and his eyes are all misted over with white film. On a makeshift cart, he drags himself along the floor, his hair, body, and clouted-up leg crawling with vermin. There's no shoe upon his one foot and his stocking is torn. He shelters under an arched bridge and every day folk step over him as though he's not there. But Maggie can see him, she even knows his name – Hoppy Hughie they call him, who lost his leg on a man-o'-war. Maggie greets him like an old friend and places an apple into his filthy hands. 'God bless you, Hughie.'

'And you too. You're an angel,' his bottom lip quivers.

The narrow twisting wynds that lead to the flesh market are beset with ravenous dogs. The air is heavy here; fleshers, tanners and dyers, each creating a rancid stench that claw at the nostrils and cause even the strongest of stomachs to gag. Rotten carcasses litter the market square, attracting swarms of flies and other insects. Maggie walks faster as the fish market looms ahead; she greets the linkboys and listens to ballad singers singing their bawdy songs. Finally she pushes through a row of blue-gowned beggars and fights for a place beside the other fish hawkers to cry out her wares.

★★★

The cottage is in darkness, the only light comes from a fading fire. Patrick sits at the table eating cold oats; shoulders slumped as he licks his teeth with his tongue. He is lost in thought; forehead bunched together in a deep frown. The tiniest shimmer catches his eye beneath the table, the children hugging their knees. But Patrick has no time for them. He suddenly has an urge to scream and curse, and so he does, like a wild, injured animal.

'Where is she?'

The rumours are ripping him apart; he picks up his plate and throws it against the wall, it shatters into a thousand pieces upon the dirt floor. *Can they be true? These evil rumours.* He shudders, Patrick's frightened. A queer feeling comes upon him, a tightness that starts at the base of his neck, circling his throat and choking him so that his lungs feel sure to explode. After a while he becomes quiet and still, his bloodshot eyes glancing warily at two shadows beneath the table.

'It's all right,' he croaks, his voice is hoarse from spent tears. 'I was feeling a wee bit sad, but I'm better now.' He leans over a bowl of water to splash water upon his face, and all the while his body trembles.

★★★

The door is ajar; the sound of weeping resonates from within. With a sinking heart Maggie stretches out one trembling hand and pushes on splintered timber. Little by little, step by step, she enters her dwelling, feet crunching upon broken pottery. Maggie peers through the dim light, wondering why Patrick's let the fire run low. Then she notices the children beneath the table.

'What's the matter? What are you doing under there?' Maggie rushes towards Anna and Patrick with open arms. They cling to her like frightened mice, eyes and noses dripping with moisture. Maggie fumes, turning to Anna with flashing eyes. 'Where is your father?'

At that moment, Patrick emerges before her, a plaid in his hand dabbing his face. 'What have you done, Patrick? You've frightened them to death.'

'What have I done?' he hisses, rushing towards her and grabbing her in a vice-like grip.

'Let me go, Patrick. What's got into you?' She thrashes in his arms like a slippery eel.

'Where have you been?'

Maggie cannot meet his gaze, fear pierces her heart. She's wondering if he knows, if he really *knows* what she's been doing. And the very thought causes her knees to shake beneath her. She manages to break apart from him.

'I've been selling fish at market, what else?'

'Where is your creel?'

'On the steps. Have you had anything to eat?' she asks, changing the subject.

He nods. 'Aye, cold oats.'

Maggie dares to glance at him, there are bags beneath his eyes and his face is pale, a chilly feeling of disquiet settles into her bones.

'And the children?'

'Cold oats.'

From out of her creel she takes out two pies, she bartered for them earlier at the market square. She places them on the table, takes a deep breath and against her better judgement heads for the door.

'I have to go out for a short while. When are you sailing?'

Patrick groans out loud. 'You're going out? You've only just returned, woman. Sit with me.'

'Must I always be sitting with you, Patrick? You bore me with your dull fisherman talk. I've chores to do. A woman's labour is...'

'You're a cruel woman, Maggie. What have I done to deserve such coldness?'

Maggie shakes her head. 'You've done nothing, you daft beggar,' she replies, hoping to lighten his mood. 'I won't be long. I need to fetch some eggs and the widow has plenty, I am sure. Then I'll make you a good broth.'

For a while he stands there staring at her, mouth gaping open, and all of a sudden she has an awful feeling that he won't let her out... and all Maggie can think is what will she do then?

'Don't be long,' he orders through gritted teeth. 'And cover your head.'

Maggie resists the urge to jump for joy. She can't get out of the door quick enough for fear of him changing his mind. Her short raspy breaths cut through the dense air as the walls seem to disintegrate around her. 'Aye, won't be long,' she mutters.

At the corner of the harbour, Maggie tugs the kertch from her head. 'Damn the man, he has no right to order me around,' she curses out loud. *No matter,* she thinks, *soon he will be gone again, back to the sea,* and then she can do as she pleases. A feeling of exhilaration surges through her as she walks towards the blacksmiths.

★★★

As Maggie walks away, every step she takes feels like a stab through his heart. But what can he do? Hasn't he encouraged her to be independent? For a while, as he stands there with Anna clutched to his body, he contemplates shouting after her, or even begging her to come home. But all he does is say, 'wave to Mother,' before drooping his sorry head.

Once Maggie's out of sight, he places Anna gently to the ground. 'Come on. Let's see what your brother is doing.' They walk into the cottage.

'Father, may we play on the steps and wait for Mother?' the young lad enquires and without waiting for an answer he takes his sister's hand and walks to the doorway.

'All right. But stay here on the steps. I won't be a moment – I forgot to tell your mother to fetch me some bait.'

Patrick runs towards the harbour, all the while looking left and right. But Maggie's long gone; he'll have to collect his own blasted bait now. 'Damn,' he says under his breath. He walks slowly back to the cottage, the muscles in his jaw twitching. As he peers towards the cottage steps suddenly a sense of dread consumes him. The children are gone.

He bolts into the cottage, leaving the door wide open to let in some light. The room is quiet, empty – he checks behind a threadbare piece of material that serves to divide the room, but all he finds is a nasty over-flowing chamber pot. A ringing noise begins in his ears and then a sickening in the pit of his stomach. He dashes back to the open door, eyes darting in all directions, but they're nowhere to be seen. It doesn't make any sense. He has been gone but a moment. So where are they?

Then something catches his eye and he breaks into a dead run, heart pounding as he heads for the harbour.

★★★

Agnes strolls along the fisherman's way, whistling a merry tune. The boy's too slow and so she stoops to pick him up, holding him to her bosom as the lassie trails stubbornly behind her.

'Stop whining. There is nothing to fear. Your mother asked me to take you to her, nearly there now.'

'But mother has gone to the widow's house, and this isn't the way,' cries Anna.

'Shut up, girl. Do as I say, I'm your mother now.' Agnes tightens her grip around Anna's little hand. These children are hers. The voices tell her so.

'Your mother is a witch! I'm your real mother,' she declares in a sing-song voice. Anna begins to cry.

★★★

Towards the harbour Patrick sprints; the sound of Anna's cries spurring him on. He races after them, ignoring the dagger-like pain in his stomach as his arms furiously pump up and down.

'Agnes, what are you doing?' Patrick screams. He bends his face to his knees, struggling for breath. 'Have you gone soft in the head, woman? Why have you taken my bairns?'

Agnes clutches the children to her and smiles. 'These are our children, Patrick. You know that. You lay with me, did you not?'

He shakes his head, and swallows back a wave of nausea. 'That was a long time ago, Agnes, years and years ago. Have you turned lunatic? These are mine and Maggie's children.'

She cackles. 'Hah! You're not fooling me. The voices have spoken and these children are ours – yours and mine.'

With a slack jaw Patrick stares at the woman; she's insane. Why hasn't he noticed it before?

'Agnes,' he takes one step towards her. 'You've no right to take them without my permission. You must return them to me at once.' He holds out one arm, trying to ignore the way Agnes trembles, an insane stare contorting her pale face.

'But...'

'Agnes,' he pleads.

For one terrifying moment Agnes's hand encircles the tip of her fish knife, adjusting it so that she can place the boy higher up her bony hip. It takes all Patrick's composure to refrain from walking over to her to wring her damn neck, but a combination of factors prevent him; the insane glitter in her eyes, the fingernails dug into his son's leg, and the sharp silver knife dangling from her waist. While Agnes is distracted, Anna breaks into a run, travelling as fast as her little legs will carry her, straight into her father's arms.

'They should have been mine, Patrick.'

Patrick embraces Anna and gestures towards the boy. 'Give him to me, Agnes. You know this is wrong, now do the right thing – 'tis a sin, Agnes, a terrible sin.'

Agnes shakes her head. 'They're my own flesh and blood. Just like the one we lost, Patrick. Remember?'

He groans out loud. 'Remember what, Agnes? Please give me the boy, you're frightening the laddie... he's scared to death.'

'I will not,' she steps backwards and almost trips on a rock. 'Only if you leave that whore and come back to me.'

Patrick screws his eyes together, resisting the urge to curse at the top of his lungs. A long moment passes before he takes a deep breath and decides to fool her.

'Aye. You are right, Agnes, she is no good,' he says, placing Anna safely away upon a craggy rock. 'I should have stayed with you all along. What was I thinking? A woman like you is just what I need.

I must leave Maggie and come to you.' Patrick takes small steps, one at a time, closer and closer, till they are but inches apart.

'I knew you would come back to me. I knew it.' Agnes arches her neck backwards and closes her eyes, as though waiting for a kiss.

With steady hands Patrick snatches the lad from Agnes's grasp, and as he does so an unbelievable sense of relief comes over him as his laddie clutches his arms. At that moment, tears flow from his eyes, but he was not ashamed. If anything, Patrick is calm, even when he presses his face so close to Agnes's they are inches apart. His voice is quiet, but his message is clear and there is malice in his eyes.

'Listen to me, woman, and take heed because I will only tell you this once. Don't *ever* go near my wife or children again. Do you hear me? If you do, I will hunt you down, and put an end to you woman. You'll burn in the pits of hell if you try something like this again.'

And with that Patrick marches away to collect Anna, never looking back. But all the while that strange creature calls after him, so that it becomes a mantra in his ears, playing over and over.

'A curse on you, Patrick Spence – and a curse on that whore of a wife of yours. I hope she dies, do you hear me? I hope she dies.'

★★★

Patrick ignores the death curse on Maggie and decides not tell a soul. Besides, if he's learned one thing of late, it's that Agnes Lecke is a raving lunatic. Nevertheless, the curse festers in his mind and clings to his thoughts like seaweed to rocks. After all, fishermen are a superstitious lot, and Patrick's no exception.

A few days later there's a commotion at the harbour. A savage wind tears through the foreshore as pale faces look out to sea. Side by side, men and women wade into frothy waves, their backs hunched over to pull a body to shore. Upon the shingle they place it, turning it over so that they can see what's left of its face. The eyes went first no doubt, nibbled by hungry fish, but they're able to determine that it's Agnes Lecke.

127

Amidst the turmoil Patrick gazes upon Agnes's bloated corpse. And in death she looks to be finally at peace. With a sinking heart he puts his hands together in a silent prayer and hopes her curse died with her.

★★★

In times of sadness, confusion and desperation, folk will find a way to hold their head high, and after a while if all goes well, they can pretend that there's no problem at all, and that life's not just good, but glorious even. And this is how Patrick lives his life, for better and worse.

Patrick stands amongst the men, an amused expression on his face as he watches the women race to the finish line. A vision of flashing petticoats and rolled sleeves, they mean business. The competition is fierce; after all they're fighting for a much sought after prize, the entrails and offal of a sheep. Earlier that day, sixteen of Musselburgh's strongest fishwives set off from Fisher's Wynd to run a six-mile race to Canongate. And the crowd cheers as the women run their last few strides; sweat pouring from their bodies and muscles taut. Maggie and a young woman race towards the finish line. Patrick's heart leaps, Maggie looks sure to finish, but then the younger woman gets a second wind and just beats her to the line.

Maggie collapses to the ground, red-faced and covered with sweat. For a while she lies on the floor catching her breath, her face staring into a blue sky.

'Get up, lass,' he says. He knows how she doesn't likes to lose.

'I don't like offal anyway,' she shrugs.

They walk home, hand in hand until they reach Arthur's Seat where another race is underway. Twelve pregnant brewster wives are already halfway up the 822 foot summit having already raced from Figgat Burn. A Dutch midwife waits at the bottom clutching a budgell of Dunkeld aquavitae and Brunswick rum.

Maggie laughs. 'I'm glad the midwife is here. She'll not be short of customers once they descend the peak.'

Patrick nods his head in agreement. 'Those ale wives have a taste for the strong stuff; they'll race to hell and back for a wee dram.'

Maggie points ahead at the summit. 'Look at the red-haired one punching the other in the ribs.'

'And you thought your race was tough.'

Maggie places her hands on her hips. 'Our race was longer. We had much further to run.'

'Aye, Maggie, but you did not have to climb the summit with your belly full of baby.'

Maggie huffs. 'That's nothing. I've walked to the market carrying a bairn and a full creel of fish, day in day out since I met you.'

'You've been permanently with child since we married?' he asks, one eyebrow arched.

'Well it feels like it.'

'I'm teasing you. I know you fisher lassies are a tough lot. Did I ever tell you about when my mother was carrying me? Well this particular day her creel was full to the top. When her pains started midway to market she had to stop at a farm to deliver the baby. Anyway, the kind farmer, Patrick was his name; well he got his wife to look after her new-born baby while my mother continued to Edinburgh to sell her fish. And mother, well she collected me on her way home. She named me after the farmer.'

'That's impressive, Patrick. She's a fine woman, you must be proud of her.'

'Aye, I am that.'

With the sound of sea roaring in their ears and the sun sinking on the horizon, Patrick places his arm around his wife as they walk home. The sky's a hazy pink, sea birds glide in the shape of a 'v' to distant lands, and below them a frothy sea sparkles on the surface.

★★★

After he makes love to her, he falls asleep. For a moment or two she watches him, her eyes drawn to the rise and fall of his upper body. His body hair is coarse and wiry and the colour of fire, not at all like the blacksmith's. Is it wrong to compare them? Does she really care? *Better to be unfaithful than to be faithful without wanting to be,* she thinks. To hell with the kirk and the Lord, and all those who think her a whore. *Anyway,* she thinks to herself, *isn't life like being a whore? All give and take.*

★★★

Married six years, he can hardly believe it. Is it six or seven? He can't remember. Lately he dreads returning home, for fear of finding Maggie in the arms of another man, and he's terrified. The gossip persists, along with the finger pointing and sniggering. In the midst of the turmoil Maggie's conduct towards him remains flippant, dismissive even. And to make matters worse, every time he sets out to confront her, he loses his nerve. With his head in his hands, he groans out loud – what he needs is a stiff drink. And where there's drink, there's Duncan.

Duncan is in the Musselburgh Arms. He's near the bar as usual, his hands buried within a buxom tavern wench's top.

'What's down there, fair maiden?' Duncan slurs.

The wench laughs and shoves him away.

At the sight of Patrick, Duncan widens his eyes. 'What brings you here, fisherman?'

'The same as you – drink. Do you want me to buy you one?'

Duncan's eyes glitter. 'Aye, I'll have a wee dram of whisky, Patrick. Thank you for asking.'

Patrick places a drink in front of Duncan and takes a dram himself, and then another. 'That's strong stuff,' he chokes on the fiery liquid as it burns his throat.

Duncan eyes him with a curious stare. 'Take your time, son. What's the rush? Is anything the matter?'

'Everything is fine. Shall we have another?'

'Why not? Let's drink to this tavern,' Duncan raises his tankard in a toast. 'The Musselburgh Arms.'

Patrick raises his drink. 'The Musselburgh Arms.'

'That'll put some powder in your musket,' says Duncan.

Several drams later Patrick glances up at a spinning ceiling, the rafters are a blur of bottles and broken tankards, and all the while the noise of laughter and chatter drones in his ears. His tongue is swollen in his mouth, he's parched and so he plunges his hands into his pockets, the tips of his fingers brushing strange objects as he rummages around. But all he can find is a neck chief, a clay pipe and a rusty nail. He has no money and only a mouthful of drink left.

'Duncan. Where are you?'

Patrick twists around and near falls from his stool. Duncan is nowhere to be seen. A cold sweat covers his forehead as he searches the inn, shadows and distorted silhouettes dance all around him. All of a sudden he is so desperately weary, and so he allows his head to sag. Then there's a bump as the room turns on its side, as one clammy cheek presses against an ale sodden table.

★★★

The pressman stands up, buttons his coat, picks up his tankard and downs his ale in one. Next he takes out his purse and selects a shiny coin. Time is up. He moves with conviction towards his prey, a swagger in his walk. The first thing he notices is the young man's hands, palms scarred by rope, an able seaman for sure. And in the blink of an eye, before anyone notices, he drops the King's shilling into Patrick's tankard, relishing the clanging noise as it hits the bottom.

'Wake up, man. You and I have business to attend to.'

The innkeeper groans. 'Not here, take your business elsewhere.'

The pressman stands his ground, hands on hips, his long legs slightly apart. He's a formidable presence, especially once he lifts his red jacket aside to reveal his weapon.

'Mind your own business, innkeeper. Need I remind you that enlistment into the naval service is voluntary, and if numbers are low, men between the ages fifteen and fifty-five are fair game.'

'The fisherman hasn't taken the King's shilling.' The innkeeper points at Patrick slumped over the table.

'He will, mark my word. It's in his tankard; he'll sup his drink in a moment. Too much ale makes a man thirsty.'

'You should have asked for a glass-bottomed tankard, you idiot,' shouts some smart arse from the other side of the tavern.

'It *has* a glass bottom,' the pressman shrugs and smacks Patrick on the cheek. 'But he's too drunk to notice. Let's see, shall we?'

As predicted Patrick sits up and sups the last of his drink. The tavern is suddenly silent – folk waiting with baited breath for the outcome. They soon have their answer. Patrick of a sudden stands up, red-faced and swaying on his feet, a cough rattling from his throat... and then with an almighty sputter spits out the coin.

'That's it. He's all mine.' The pressman calls out to some men loitering outside: 'Grab an arm and a leg and get him on the cart.'

In a flash they are gone.

***

The man-o'-war ship is destined for battle, its purpose to fight the cause of English merchants in an age of trade wars, fighting against the French and Spanish for commercial pre-eminence. Patrick's only saving grace is that he's not aboard a slave ship. He's heard about them, and one thing is for sure, he would rather be aboard a fighting ship than on one carrying human cargo. The pressman informs him that he will be given a bounty of twenty-three shillings. He knows merchant seamen get double that, around fifty-five shillings a month. But he knows not to complain. The die is cast, and Patrick must make the best of it.

They set sail before Patrick has time to sober up. The sea is calm as he stands on mid-deck listening to able seamen's cries, already resigned to his fate. Throughout his time at sea he's amassed a great deal of knowledge, developing skills necessary for survival in a hostile environment. He's already trying to predict the wind direction and the weather, keeping a good weather eye open to the sky. If he's to survive, he must prove his worth; otherwise he will never get back to land, and back to his Maggie.

He looks out to sea. It never fails to amaze him. How many men has it claimed? Suddenly the wind direction changes and the ship lurches. A number of men cry out and clutch their stomachs, green hands, and terrified the lot of them. Most of them have never set foot on a ship or boat in their lives. They are landlubbers, for sure. How he pities them, because they're in for a rough ride. Many a man dies at sea.

★★★

Maggie sits on her steps in a daze. The rumours are rife, and for once they are not about her. They all concern Patrick. Where is he? Weeks pass and still there is no sight of him. No one seems to know where he is, not even his doting mother. Every day she walks down to the rocks to look out to sea, but he never comes. And then she bumps into her father near the market cross.

'Haven't you heard? He's been press-ganged. Where have you been?'

Maggie's hand goes up to her face, she covers her mouth. 'No. Press-ganged? I don't believe you and anyway how would you know? You never spend any time with him.'

'I was there. Well I was earlier that day at the Musselburgh Arms.'

'Was you there or not?'

'Aye.'

'So why didn't you help him? And since when does Patrick have a dram with the likes of you? For goodness sake, he doesn't even drink.' Maggie dismisses her father and makes her way to the harbour. The fishermen are bound to know something.

'He's probably gone to the fisheries or the keels at Newcastle,' an old mariner shrugs his bony shoulders. 'There's plenty of work there.'

★★★

Widow Arrock walks towards Maggie's cottage at Fisherrow with purpose in her stride. She wonders if there's any truth in the rumours she's hearing. There are a few versions. The most popular one is that Patrick has been pressed into naval service, but there is other tittle-tattle and whispers too. Some folk say Patrick caught Maggie with the smithy's son, and the widow can well believe that. But the fishermen insist that Patrick's gone off to the fisheries or keels in Newcastle, fed up with her gallivanting ways. Either way she will get to the bottom of it.

★★★

A smile masks Maggie's face as she ushers the widow inside. Her true feelings come to the surface as she closes the door behind her, cursing and shouting as she pushes Patrick's fishing gear out of the way. The cottage is a mess; dirty pots cover the table, the smell of damp clothes and overflowing chamber pots linger in the air. The children look miserable.

'What's got into you? Never heard of a washing line or a hedge to dry your clothes on? And for God's sake empty those chamber pots. The poor children, I expect they're missing their father?'

'Missing their father? The bairns are used to it. Patrick's always coming and going.'

'But not for this long, surely?'

Maggie shakes her head.

'And whose fault is that? You know there is no one to blame in this sorry affair but yourself, Maggie. If your mother was alive, well, she'd tan the arse off you.'

Maggie lets out a high pitched shriek. 'What did I do?'

'Well folk say you've lifted your petticoats for half of Edinburgh and the blacksmith's son from what I hear. Heaven above, what were you thinking? I know he's handsome and strong but he's barely off the breast for goodness sake.'

'Well what if I did! I was miserable and lonely.'

'Don't you love your husband, Maggie?'

Maggie frowns. 'What is love, Widow Arrock? My father always told me, "Maggie, love is a dung pile, and I'm the cock that crows from the top of it." He's a canny one, my father.' Maggie shrugs.

'Well that's a shame, Maggie, and typical. How fitting that a lass like you would take advice from her philanderer of a father. The apple does not fall far from the tree in your case. I can well believe you when you say that you have no idea what love is. But think about this, Maggie. That man worshipped you. He was loyal to you and laboured damn hard for you and the children, and this is how you repay him. You're a disgrace; you should be ashamed of yourself.'

Maggie shuffles in her seat, irritated that the widow should make her feel uncomfortable in her own home. And yet her most profound emotion is anger, and her cheeks burn a fiery red as she says her piece.

'Aye. He's a saint and I'm a sinner. But where was he when I was hungry? And where was he when the bairns were hungry? I'll tell you the truth, shall I? I was lonely. I wanted to feel the love of a man. And he was nowhere to be seen.' Maggie wipes a tear of self-pity from her burning cheek.

The widow massages her forehead, her eyes screwed up in her head. 'You're a selfish woman, Maggie, and you've absolutely no loyalty. Can't you see that I've come here to make you see reason? I'm trying to help you, so don't be angry with me. You've no one to be angry with but yourself. Now I'll hold my tongue. If you want to search for Patrick, I will take the bairns. But you have to vow to change your ways.'

'I will,' Maggie nods.

The widow shakes her head, not quite believing her. 'Right then. You need to visit the fisheries in Newcastle and speak to the keelmen – they might know a thing or two. Haven't you relatives near the Tyne?'

'Aye, one of my aunt's lives there. I can stay with her for a while.'

The widow claps her hands together. 'Well, that's it then. Pack up some belongings for yourself and the bairns, and then bring them to me. If he isn't at the fisheries, he's at sea, and you'll have to weather the storm.' She coughs, holding her chest. 'In the meantime I would stay clear of his parents. They want to speak to you.'

Maggie's face turns white. 'Oh no, I cannot face them.'

'You need to hurry then, lassie. Bring the children to me when you are ready and don't let me down.'

★★★

There is no better incentive than the stool of repentance to make haste. However, in order to travel from parish to parish, Maggie needs a testificate of character from the holy men she seeks to avoid. But there's one hope – Minister Robert Bonaloy. He's the only one who might be willing to help.

In a blind panic she gathers together the children's belongings.

CHAPTER TEN

FOR WHOM SHE IS WAITING COMES AT LAST

Maggie rises early in the morning; there's much to do. At the back of the pigsty she drops to her hands and knees and rakes through soiled hay for her pot of hoarded money. It's a disgusting task. As soon as the precious hoard rests within her hands, Maggie divides the money, placing half of it in a basket containing the children's clothes, and the other half in her stays. The pig and goat crowd around her, pushing their noses into her skirts. She hasn't really the time to take them but they'll starve if she leaves them alone. So along the brae she marches, with two snot-nosed children, a pig and a goat. They receive plenty of curious stares on their way to the widow's house, and if the pig didn't keep running away, they'd have got there much quicker.

At the widow's house, Maggie crouches to her knees to embrace her children. 'Now then, Anna, Patrick, come to Mother. Why the long faces? I'll not be gone long and I will bring you something when I return.'

'Why can't we come with you?' asks little Patrick, his bottom lip quivering.

She has to turn away to gather her thoughts. A moment passes before she looks at them again, and their little faces near break her heart.

'Oh, I wish that I could take you with me, but it is too far away for your little legs to walk. I won't be gone long,' she gives them both a kiss on the cheek, nods to the widow and runs from the cottage before she changes her mind.

'Maggie, wait. What about food for the bairns and the animals?' Widow Arrock stands in the doorway, little faces peep out from behind it. 'Get inside the cottage, Patrick, Anna. I won't be a moment.'

'Look inside the children's belongings, there's a bag with more than enough money. And if you need any help with the children, ask Jean Ramsay.'

The widow's beady eyes widen and one brow arches. 'Where did you get the... oh, never mind. Get gone, before I have second thoughts.'

★★★

Minister Bonaloy does her proud. Tucked beneath a rock at the bottom of Inveresk Kirk is the testificate Maggie needs to travel. With her testimony of character stuffed safely in hand, she descends the steep hill, flanked by huge stone walls overgrown with moss and ivy. Near the hay market, she climbs on-board a corn cart bound for Newcastle. And it's not until she passes Figgat Burn that she remembers that she's not said goodbye to her father or James.

★★★

During his first week, Patrick is given one of the most difficult and unpleasant tasks at sea, the devil to pay. Of course, as most able seamen know, the devil seam is the most difficult to seal with hot pitch or tar, because it's curved and intersected with straight deck planking. 'Why have they given me this damned chore?' he curses, trapped here between the devil and the deep blue sea.

Several hours pass before he returns to his starboard watch. A swabber cleans the decks ahead; Patrick walks around him and looks to the sky. He can sense a change in the weather. The wind blows most terribly, the cargo below deck tumbles and rolls.

'The top masts will be taken down if the winds get stronger,' he says to the swabber, but the man ignores him.

Soon two seamen armed with axes scramble up deck to cut away the top mast. With each dip and roll the masts slam hard against the vessel as gigantic waves rise from a savage sea. Green hands and ordinary seamen scream and bawl, but what with the crashing waves and wind shrieking in their ears, they cannot hear a thing. The sea meanwhile rages and swells, white-capped waves foam and slap the bobbing decks. And so, as the seamen battle with the waves and the winds, bellies full with sea water, their shouts get swallowed up by a howling gale. Like a monstrous creature it steers the ships towards rocks, causing exhausted men to tremble and shake. Danger looms in the overcast sky, and so they use every last amount of strength as they court death, until the fury of the waves die down.

After the storm, the landsmen stagger around in a dazed state, most of them returning to their hammocks to sleep it off, either that or to thank God for sparing them. The other men, the more experienced ones, head off to the galley. They eat in groups of eight to twelve messes. The menu is always the same, salt beef and stale biscuits washed down with grog or beer. After a good half hour of retching up saltwater, Patrick's famished. But the mess cook is far from sober, and by the time he's finished boiling up the salt beef, it's like cutting through tree bark. In the mess hall, Patrick tries a biscuit, it's crawling with weevils. He clasps a calloused hand to his empty stomach and screws up his eyes to take a bite. In haste, he grimaces and swallows it whole, weevils and all, and then another. It's a relief when they bring water from the hold. Something to wash the biscuits down with, Patrick thinks, smacking his lips. But the water is green with algae, and he watches in fascination as the older seamen sift it through their teeth.

'Drink the grog,' says one of the seamen.

Patrick shakes his head. 'Don't touch the stuff.'

The seaman sits back violently in his chair, his eyebrows raised in utter bewilderment. Patrick reaches for watery rum, not wanting to look odd. It's better than green algae for sure, but he doesn't want to become reliant on it. So, he takes a wee mouth full and hopes for the best.

Outside the galley, he passes the foremast on the gun deck. Walking calms him, taking his mind off his rumbling stomach. He walks in a crisscross line to avoid the landsmen performing menial deck duties; hauling ropes, adjusting sails and cleaning decks. He just wants to get to his damp hammock, a wee sleep before the next battle stations drill. But near a scuttlebutt of water, Patrick walks straight into a commotion. A group of men surround a drunken man, sleeping off his latest rum ration, and somebody else's by the look of it.

'Will you look at that? Someone has cut the tips of his ears off. Send for the midshipman!' one of the seamen cries.

The drunkard staggers to his feet, his tattered trews fall around his bony arse. An able seaman grabs him around the shoulders to wind a length of linen around his head, and all the while Patrick edges away. But it is too late to scarper; the midshipman arrives promptly, wearing a scowl.

'Who did this to you?' the midshipman demands of the man. 'And how could you sleep through that? They've shaved one of your eyebrows off. You!' He points to Patrick. 'Stay where you are.'

'A prank – that is all,' the man slurs. 'No harm done. They're always playing pranks.'

The midshipman seethes with anger. 'I will get to the bottom of this, rest assured.'

The raised voice carries across the ship, like ripples in a pond. The sound is akin to a siren, causing men to stop what they're doing and seek out the source. Ordinary and able seamen, even the elite group of top men, most of whom spend their days aloft in the tops gather together, all eyes on the drunk and his one eyebrow.

The midshipman rants and seethes, one bony finger pointing to the men. 'If someone doesn't tell me how this man came to have the tips of his ears off, I will stop the daily ration of grog.'

A chorus of loud groans roar out from the crew.

'I did it,' one of the grog blossoms declares.

'Did you now? Are you sure?'

Patrick keeps his head down, not wanting any part of this calamity. It never fails to amuse him how seamen will endure a flogging rather than go without their beloved grog. The midshipman gestures to the boatswain. Patrick's mouth goes dry, he doesn't want to hang around to watch the bos'uns mate deliver a punishment; just the sight of a cat o' nine tails makes his blood turn cold. But he's trapped amongst the crew, his heart racing as the drum begins to roll. He can hardly bear to look at the grog blossom as the bos'uns mate rips the shirt from his back. And all the while the crew move closer and closer to gather around them.

The bos'uns mate curses. 'Get back all of you, I say. I've no room to swing the cat.'

The grog blossom cowers as though regretting his admission of guilt. And then, by some miracle, just as the man swings the whip, the wind changes as the storm returns with a vengeance.

'All hands on deck!' the first mate's fearful cry rings out. 'Up every soul nimbly, for God's sake or we will perish.'

With the roar of the sea in his ears, Patrick watches a top man with one shoe on and one shoe off climb aloft to the foretop to take in the top sails. He's soon followed by another man and several more till they're spread across the rigging like flies caught in an intricate web. For hours the storm rages on. Patrick's knuckles turn white as he holds onto a rail to secure a rope; his face wet with wind and sea, and alive – so alive, for the sea is in his blood. Amongst the chaos he closes his eyes and prays to the Lord. His huge frame sagging over the rail as he heaves up salt water, his throat feeling like it is on fire. But when he opens his eyes there is a hope, for the sky is cloudy, and beyond the horizon is a patch of blue right in the middle. A Dutchman's breeches, a good sign, and as the storm breaks a green hand whistles.

The bos'un shudders and screams. 'For the love of God, will someone tell that waister to pipe down? Hasn't anyone told him it's unlucky to whistle when the wind is blowing a gale?'

★★★

Due to a combination of poor diet and sanitation, a number of the crew fall ill. It's to be expected really when the fish and meat are spoiled and the water is stale. Therefore, on voyages such as these many a man develops scurvy. Patrick's seen it all before, teeth falling out and the swollen tongues. Even worse, the dreaded sickness or bloody flux, that brings about a terrible lingering death. It's the tragedy of life at sea. All around them is suffering, as once hale and hearty men drop like flies. However, by some miracle Patrick remains able-bodied – but for how long?

It's not till the wee hours of the morning that Patrick slings his hammock fore and aft at his numbered peg; he's weary from manning a four-hour watch. Within his canvas is a flock mattress, and as he lies back in his damp clothes, the hammock stays quite still, while the ship rolls with it. In his hand he clutches a lock of his Maggie's hair.

'Oh Maggie, I miss you so. I forgive you,' he whispers into the night. When he finally sleeps, he dreams of his love.

★★★

The corn cart rocks side to side. Maggie peeps out of it at Never-Bow Port, and takes a deep breath as they go through the south gates that lead out of Edinburgh to England. She lies back for a while and lets the motion of the cart lull her to sleep, and her dreams are of Newcastle and all manner of lavishness, comfort and delight. But as the cart jolts and rocks, all that greets her is the smell of manure, heather and gorse. Near a great river the horse slips in some mud, and thus the rickety corn cart comes to a halt. The driver leaps from the cart, for the moment unaware of the sleeping person along for the ride. The horse is his main priority and so he makes sure that she's fine. And then he remembers the girl.

'Wake up, lassie. I'm not going any further. It's time to get out.'

'Are we in Newcastle?' Maggie rubs the sleep from her eyes.

'No. This is Kelso.'

'Kelso?'

'Aye, Kelso. If it is England you want you'd better find another cart.'

'But where?'

'Not my problem, lassie,' he says and walks away.

★★★

Snowflakes fly into Maggie's eyes like burning sparks, her ears are frozen solid. She tries to ignore the cold, but as the ice crystals crunch beneath her feet, she can hardly feel her toes. The wind presses against her face, pulling and tearing at her so that her eyes and nose smart. She pauses by the water edge, through watery eyes she can just make out a market town. An old fisherman tips his hat as she passes by. It's nearing dark, and Maggie doesn't want to spend it out of doors – so she calls out to him.

'Can you tell me how to get to the town across the river?'

'That's no town, lassie. That's Maxwellheugh, a small village. There be no bridge to it though. But there be a good ford that way.' He glances at her shoes. 'How good are your boots?'

'Well, they've seen better days. But a bit of cold water never hurt anyone.'

The old man shivers. 'Don't get your feet wet in this weather, lass, unless you can help it. You'll catch yourself the death of cold.'

Maggie turns and walks in the direction he points. The ford is not a good one. But she has no choice, she must reach the village. So, she straightens her feet and holds both arms out at her side at shoulder height. Across the rocks she balances, one foot at a time. Her progress is slow, and then she wobbles as a stone crumbles beneath her. It's a shock when she hits the water. The temperature is ice-cold, and it is as though a thousand needles are plunging into her feet. To make matters worse, a sharp stone tears through her heel, but she walks on, ignoring the pain. At the river's edge she pours out the water from her boots and winces as she places them back onto her feet. In a daze she approaches the town, her body crying out for warmth as her feet shuffle through a blanket of white snow.

A small cluster of dwellings loom ahead. Only one of them brightly lit. Maggie's breath billows out like white clouds as she stumbles towards it. Was there ever a more welcome sight? The door's heavy, she hasn't the vigour to push it open. She collapses against it and almost falls to the floor, and then to her relief someone opens the door.

'Sorry miss,' a fat man passes by, tipping his hat.

Maggie enters the tavern, unsteady on her feet, her whole person sprinkled in snow. A tall fair-haired woman approaches her with a puzzled expression, but Maggie's passed caring, all she wants is to warm herself by a blazing fire.

'For the love of God, what are you doing out on a night like this? You look chilled to the bone, child. Come – sit down and warm yourself by the fire. My name's Isobel Lidgerwood, I'm the wife of the innkeeper.'

Maggie nods and follows her to a raging fire, feeling so light-headed she might fall.

'Thank you. You're very kind.'

'No trouble at all. You're not alone are you? Surely not. A bonny lass like you.'

'Aye, I am quite alone.'

'No chaperone?' The innkeeper's wife glances at the door.

Maggie shakes her head.

The innkeeper's wife smiles, revealing surprisingly white teeth. 'Take a stool by the fire, lassie. You look chilled to the bone, did I say that already? Silly me, I forget what I say and repeat myself over and over.' She calls over to a tavern wench, 'bring us a couple of drams, Moll.'

Maggie basks by the fire, enjoying its warmth, pointing her wet boots to the hearth so that steam rises off them. 'Thank you for your kindness missus. I got wet crossing the ford. My boots are soaked and I think I cut my foot. I just need a place to stay for the night. I'll be no trouble. I'm on my way to Newcastle to visit my aunt.'

The woman turns to Maggie, her eyes like saucers. 'Hush child. You must call me Isobel. Now stay here by the fire and keep warm, you're awful pale. Let me help you take your boots off and take a wee look at that foot.'

Maggie slumps backwards, her elbow resting on another stool. Isobel takes a look at her heel, turning it this way and that, and all the while Maggie's stomach rumbles as the smell of delicious food wafts in from another room.

'It's just a scratch. But no doubt sore. How did you do it?'

'I slipped crossing the ford.'

'You foolish girl! What were you thinking walking about in weather like this? And what are you staring at, Angus McDonald? Put your tongue back in your mouth. Haven't you ever seen a bonny lassie before?'

'He's curious, no doubt. Me being a stranger.' Maggie shrugs her shoulders.

'I don't think it is that dear. Have you come far, lass? You must be hungry from your travels. Do you want something to eat?'

Maggie knocks back her dram and wonders which question to answer first, in the end her stomach decides for her. 'I'm famished, missus.'

'Please call me Isobel. And you have come from?'

'Musselburgh, near the Firth of Forth. Do you know it?'

'Not heard of it. Jedburgh and Kelso are as far as I'll go.'

A bowl of broth is pushed in front of her. Maggie devours the lot, it is absolutely delicious. Maggie's never tasted anything so good. 'Is that meat in the broth?'

'Aye, Adam slaughtered a pig earlier. He's got some fine breeding stock. Have you tasted pork before?'

Maggie laughs. 'Never, I'm from fisher folk. We hardly ever eat meat, can't afford it.' Without appearing to be impolite, Maggie allows her gaze to travel around the room. Everything is so wide and welcoming in the tavern. There are plenty of comfortable seats, two hearths, and numerous rooms with wooden furnishings. In almost every area there are large torch lights, and they flicker from crude brackets on the stone walls, casting peculiar shadows onto the floor below.

'It's a pleasant tavern isn't it, lass? You must stay here for as long as you like.' Isobel pats her hand. 'We have a large scullery for cooking and cleaning and several rooms above for staff and guests. I have a box-bed in one of the rooms; I'll show you if you like.'

Maggie is at a loss what to say. Her eyes feel heavy, as though there's grit in them; she rubs at them with clenched fists but the action only makes them feel worse. Isobel holds out a hand, she takes it gladly and rises to stand.

'How are you feeling now?'

'Middling.'

'Good, now come with me, lass.' Isobel signals to one of the tavern wenches. 'Pass us a candle and hold the fort.'

The corridor is narrow and there's an absence of torches. The silhouette of Isobel's trim figure is just visible as she climbs a steep staircase, her tallow candle flickers and sputters, giving off an evil smell. One of the wooden steps is loose and in a state of decay, Maggie stumbles on it and near twists her ankle.

'Careful, lass. You'll know every step by the end of the morrow.'

As they reach a hallway, Maggie is seized with apprehension, and as she searches in her pocket for some coins, she looks at the innkeeper's wife with sleepy eyes, while Isobel herself looks at her with bewilderment, as if not understanding how a young woman such as this could be travelling alone.

'This is the room,' Isobel opens a door.

'It's beautiful. Is that a box-bed?'

'Aye, lassie. You'll no doubt find it cosy. It has a fine mattress stuffed with wool and when you close the doors it gets very warm.'

Maggie takes a closer look. The room does not have much in terms of furnishings. But there is a chair and what appears to be a large wooden cupboard, closed on all sides by panels of oak. There are two hinged doors and a bed clear off the dirt floor by four short legs. In front of it is a large oaken chest, no doubt for storing bedding, clothes or linen.

'Thank you kindly for giving me a bed for the night. I am very grateful.' Maggie holds out a coin.

'Put your money away and get some sleep. I'll be along to see you in the morning. Sleep well, oh and there's a lock on the door – be sure to lock it, there are other lodger's here and well you can never be too careful.' Isobel bids her farewell. But before she's even out the door she turns on her heel and laughs to herself. 'I can't believe it.'

'What?' Maggie yawns, trying her hardest not to close her eyes.

'I never asked your name.'

'Maggie. Maggie Dickson.'

★★★

Isobel Lidgerwood tugs her husband's jacket again.

'Leave me be, woman. Can't you see I'm busy?' He fiddles with a wooden barrel, lifting and turning it around as if it's light as a feather, and all the while he glares at his wife with an exasperated expression.

'But Adam, I want to tell you about the girl. You know the one that arrived earlier. Can't you just stop for just a moment?' Isobel stands in his way now, interrupting his work.

'What's all the fuss?' Adam bangs down his tools, puffs out his cheeks and curses. 'I've laboured here too long, and I'm not done yet. What is it, woman? I've work to do. Didn't I tell you that I'm busy?'

'A lass just walked in, Adam, all covered in snow – with no chaperone.' She tugs on his jacket again. 'Did you hear me, Adam? She's all alone.'

'Aye, and what's so strange about that? She's probably a gipsy sorner, or a beggar.'

Isobel shakes her head and wrings her hands together. 'No, Adam. Not this one. You've got to see her. God's truth, she's a bonny one, grand for business, mind. Folk will flock from all over Kelso to see a pretty fresh face, and we need a new serving maid since Bessie left.'

Adam shivers as though someone's danced on his grave. 'Hah! Pretty faces bring nothing but trouble, woman. We don't want any of that here. Does she look strong? The last woman, Bessie was it? She was weak as a kitten.'

Isobel folds her arms over her modest bosom. 'Aye, well this lass is not weak I can tell you. She looks strong as an ox and sturdy like, and her hands are worn. She's done plenty of work for sure. You should see the size of her arms, Adam. She must have shifted some weight to get such big muscles. And that's not the only thing that's big about her. She's got a fine pair of...'

'Has she now? You're a meddlesome jade, Isobel. Always thinking of business, aren't you?' He ruffles his wife's fair hair and pulls her to him to give her a wee kiss.

'Get off me, you daft beggar. You're all bristles.'

Adam wags a finger at her. 'I'll give her a try, Isobel. But if there's any trouble, she's out on her ear. Do you hear me?'

★★★

Maggie climbs into the box-bed, closes the door hinges and then opens them, and then sneezes as a quantity of dust wafts up her nostrils. She lies back on the bed, stretching out her arms and legs on the soft mattress before turning onto her belly. The mattress smells of mildew and soft earth, and once the bedding is wrapped around her, she's snug inside.

Maggie peers into the dim light. Along the wall is a long trailing shadow, like a great slippery serpent riding crescent-shaped waves. The shapes dance and glimmer on the wall and for a while she watches them until her breathing becomes shallow, till finally she succumbs to a deep and restful sleep.

Maggie's in that most peculiar place between stirring and slumber. She can hear a knocking noise, but she can't be sure if it's reality or a dream. Before long, there's no question she's awake and so she pushes open the door hinges, climbs out the bed and steps into the dark. But who could it be at this hour? And why didn't they leave her a candle? She fumbles in the dark for her plaid, hands grasping around until she feels the familiar fabric to gather around her.

'Who is it?' she enquires.

'It is I, Adam Bell, the innkeeper,' a gruff voice replies.

Maggie unlocks the door. A middle-aged man stands outside; in each hand he carries a candle.

'I was sleeping.'

'Sorry to disturb you.' Adam sucks in his stomach and hands her a candle, with his one free hand he runs a hand through what is left of his hair. 'It's the wife. She told me to fetch you. Said something about you wanting to work the night, for food and board?'

'There must be a mistake,' Maggie shakes her head and frowns. She examines the man before her; he's rotund and as big as a bear. In the candlelight his eyes are dark like sea coal and his hair is coarse and wiry. 'I'm only staying a night. I have money to pay for the room.'

'But it's blowing a blizzard outside. Have you anywhere else to go?'

'Aye, Newcastle.'

'You're miles from there, lass. You must stay here for a while, there's no hurry is there? We're happy to have you here with us. We need an extra pair of hands, mind. We're busy since the other tavern burnt to the ground, it's those thatched roofs see. I warned them but they wouldn't listen.'

'Haven't you other serving wenches?'

'Aye, but we need an extra pair of hands.'

Maggie suspects it's a lie, but his eyes are so appealing, and she can sense his distress at disappointing his wife.

'We're short of maidservants, you see. The last one left in a hurry. Let's just say she got herself in a delicate state.' He pauses for breath and holds out a parcel. 'This is for you. The wife told me to give it to you.'

'What is it?'

'A dress.'

'I have a dress. Why does your wife wish me to have it?'

'She wants you to wear it. It's fancier than the one she said you were wearing.'

'How observant of her. Do you want me to wear it now?'

'Not right now, for heaven's sake,' he blushes. 'My son's a tailor and so if it doesn't fit, he'll alter it for you. Please put it on once I've gone and come down the stairs.'

'As you wish.'

★★★

Maggie sets the tallow candle on the oak chest and allows her plaid to fall onto the wooden chair, safe from the damp floor. The dress is of middling quality, with both legs she steps into the rustling fabric and bends over double to pull on the garment. It's a tight fit and flattens her breasts like two oatcakes, but with a little adjustment she lowers the bodice so that her breasts spill over.

In a little while Maggie descends the stairs. The pace of work is fast, but in comparison to her life as a fishwife, serving ale and victuals is like child's play. Maggie thrives in the boisterous atmosphere, and the rude and eloquent speech she employs as a fish hawker comes in more than handy.

Meanwhile, as Maggie labours over sweaty workmen, travellers and cottars, she notices Isobel and Adam observing her with appraising eyes. And by the look on their faces they appear to be more than happy with her crude charm. From across the room, Maggie gives them a little wave and returns to serving of ale. Nothing is ever too much for her and she's never fazed, and best of all she never complains.

As the night comes to an end and the last of the customers loiter behind, there's still much to do. And so, Maggie clears away pots and tankards, wipes down tables and washes a small patch of tiled floor. The fires need banking and so she fetches a poker and pushes the fuel together, and by the time she's finished her face and hands are smudged with ashes.

'Is it still snowing outside?' Maggie asks Isobel.

'Aye, it's quite a snowstorm out there, can't see your hand in front of your face. Don't you be thinking of going abroad in this weather, Maggie, you'll freeze to death.'

A young woman interrupts the conversation; she has a look of Isobel, flaxen-haired and blue eyes.

'May I be excused, Mother. My feet are hurting and I can hardly stand.'

'Have you met my daughter, Maggie?'

Maggie shakes her head.

'This is Margaret. She's been helping with the food tonight, giving Cook an extra pair of hands.'

Maggie holds out a hand to Margaret. 'Pleased to meet you, Margaret. I'll be sure to remember your name.'

Isobel's blue eyes gleam in the soft firelight. 'There's William, my son, to meet too. He's apprenticed to a tailor. But he visits from time to time to lend a hand.'

Maggie nods but she's so worn-out she's not really listening. The smoke from the fire scratches at her eyes, she yawns and stretches out her arms, causing her bosom to nearly pop from her dress.

'Better get William to alter that dress.' Adam points a thumb in her direction, his face reddening with embarrassment.

Isobel punches her husband playfully on the arm 'She looks beautiful in the dress, nothing wrong with it if you ask me.'

'The dress needs some adjustment.' Adam's word is final.

That night, despite her weariness, Maggie has trouble sleeping. And in all honesty it's not because she misses her children, or her husband for that matter. In truth, it's the salt sea air she longs for and the sound of a thunderous sea clashing against rocks.

★★★

It's nearly noon when Maggie eventually wakes in the strange attic room, horribly disorientated, and trying to figure out where she is. The tiny windows in her room are all covered in frost, and beyond the glazed panes a whiteout reflects the winter sun, brightening the darkened room. Maggie turns over onto her side and feels a foot in her back; she jumps with surprise and lets out a small squeal, taking the homespun blankets with her.

'You're pulling the blankets off me, it's freezing in here,' whines a high-pitched voice. A mass of curly golden hair sticks out from the end of the box-bed.

Maggie suddenly sits up on the mattress, her mouth gaping open.

'Don't be alarmed. It is I, Margaret, the innkeeper's daughter. We met last night.'

'I'm sorry. Is this your bed?'

'No. Father wants us to share. After what happened with the last lass and all that, well, I will explain later. You don't mind do you?' Margaret yawns and stretches. Her eyes are all puffy and creased.

'I don't mind sharing at all. Have we overslept?'

'No. Mother wanted you to sleep late so that you're rested. Wait until that miserable cow finds out.'

'What miserable cow?' Maggie's eyes are still sticky with sleep. She squints at the girl with messy yellow hair and can't help thinking that she looks like a furry farm animal.

'You'll find out,' Margaret replies and climbs out from the bed. With both hands she pushes on a small glazed window, but the window is frozen shut.

'What are you doing? It's freezing out there. Is there still snow?'

'Aye, and William's supposed to come today.'

'Who?'

'You'll find out,'

'Is that all you ever say – you'll find out?' Maggie laughs.

Margaret smiles and dresses quickly, pulling on a double layer of stockings, a plaid and a shawl to keep her warm.

Maggie wishes she had the luxury of two layers of clothes, but she's only brought a few items for her journey.

Down the stairs there are few people around. *Who do I ask about chores?* Maggie wonders and then Isobel appears from behind a door and nearly scares her to death.

'Hello, Maggie. Did you sleep well?'

'I am very well. I don't normally sleep so late, sorry.'

A number of labouring men loiter in the tavern, some of them chatting and others drinking. One of them winks at Maggie, looking her up and down until Isobel barks out some orders to them.

'Lazy beggars they are, only supposed to be fixing a leak in the roof and shifting a few barrels and what do they do? Start supping the ale, that's what! It'll be a pie or some broth that they'll want next, but they can go and boil their heads the lot of them. Anyway, how's your foot today, lass? Any better?'

'Much better.'

'Good, good,' smiles Isobel, guiding her across the room to a narrow corridor that leads to a large open door. 'This is the scullery. Cook has already made oats, so sit yourself down and fill your belly. After that I'll tell you what to do for the day, and don't even contemplate going out-of-doors, there is still a blizzard outside.'

A fat woman with a filthy apron leads Maggie to a huge table, a number of chairs surround it on the dirt floor. An enormous hearth dominates the room and several shiny pots and dangle spits flank its huge flaming mouth. For a while Maggie just stands there, watching the cook scurrying about, her fat arse wobbling as she waddles along. Eventually, the cook orders Maggie to sit, and her mouth waters as a large bowl of oats is placed in front of her.

The room has a homely atmosphere and Maggie feels warm and comfortable as she eats her meal. Meanwhile Isobel talks to cook about food and recipes. At that moment a scraping noise cuts through the air, Maggie jumps in her seat and turns around. Near the end of the table, a big strapping lass pulls out a chair, crashing down onto the seat like a sack of turnips.

'Where's *my* oats?' the sullen girl complains.

Isobel's usual cheery disposition floats from the room and her shoulders visibly sag. 'It'll be ready in a minute, patience ...'

'You've given mine to her, haven't you? All bastard morning I've been working my fingers to the bone while others are idle.'

'Hush, Helen.'

Maggie lowers her eyes to the table top before sneaking a glance at the morose, dirt-faced lassie. She has the body and arms of a prize-fighter and a face to match. The girl exudes ill-feeling and hostility, and the air soon crackles with tension. Maggie crinkles up her eyes and wonders why Isobel and the cook hover around her, in an effort to placate her, because for the most part, Maggie can't wait to get away from her. With her bowl empty she crosses the scullery to thank the cook, and to her utter dismay the cook feels obliged to introduce her to the detestable girl.

'Well, aren't you going to introduce yourself, Helen?'

'Helen Richardson, serf to all. If you want a dirty job done, ask me.' Helen does not offer her hand to the newcomer.

'Don't be horrible, Helen. Don't mind her, Maggie. She's always like that.' Isobel shrugs and takes Maggie's empty bowl.

Not wanting to spend another moment with Helen, Maggie nods to the cook and exits the room. The sound of Isobel's footsteps echo behind her as she enters a narrow corridor.

'Why do you allow her to talk to you in that way?' Maggie asks.

'Who?'

'Helen.'

'Don't worry your head about her, she's a distant relative, but more importantly she's a good worker. Here, let us chat by the fire and I'll try and sort a few chores for you to do. You've not changed your mind about staying, have you, lass?'

Maggie sits by the fire, Isobel takes a seat opposite her and does not hesitate to take her hand, and Maggie notices a small ring upon her middle finger. The innkeeper's wife has a kindly face and beautiful golden hair; she sighs and places both hands on her knees before glancing out of the distant window and wintery view. Maggie looks from the window to the woman before her.

'No. I will stay for a while.'

'Oh lass – you won't be sorry.'

★★★

In the tavern, there's a sense of expectation in the air, not that anything grand or interesting is happening. The fact of the matter is – all is fresh and new. Maggie's not displeased with her new surroundings, and the faces and activities fill her with much elation. In short, she's happy as a drunk at a lock-in. Along with Helen and Margaret, she assists in the brewing of special ale, and a good deal of chores require much elbow-grease, of that Maggie has plenty. In no time at all she's polished a number of brass objects; plates, ornaments and trinkets.

After a small meal, Maggie offers to help Adam shift small kegs to the rear of the tavern. The kegs are heavy, but after shifting many a full creel, she's brawny and tough, and so they work fast and finish in less than an hour. Before they return to the others Adam shows her the chicken coop, and clear of the coop is a pigsty packed with swine. Maggie holds a hand to her nose and hopes that they don't ask her to do any of the mucking out, it reminds her too much of home.

'Have you a husband, Maggie?'

Maggie falters, unsure of what to say. 'I don't know where he is. The fisher folk think he's in Newcastle, and so I hope to find him there.'

He whistles. 'I can't believe any man would leave you.' He glances around quickly to make sure his wife hasn't heard him.

★★★

The food is mouth-watering. Isobel and the cook seem to be in a constant competition to make the perfect dish. *No wonder Adam has a pot belly,* Maggie shakes her head. On the second night, Maggie puts on her tight fitting dress and hurries downstairs. The tavern's busier than ever, and so she circulates the room, taking orders, handing out ale and laughing as they pat her on the bottom. Of course the banter's harmless and she's never affronted, and the men laugh at her and her smart retorts, and before the night is through they come to expect it and even encourage it.

'I wouldn't mind having you over a barrel, Maggie.'

'Looks like you've drunk the barrel from the look of that stomach, Angus.' Maggie points at Angus's belly. 'Looks like you'll be dropping that soon. When's it due?'

'Maggie, will you take a walk with me to the riverside?'

'Aye, if your wife can come too.'

Occasionally, a drunken advance goes too far, but all she has to do is glance in Adam Bell's direction and he comes to the rescue. But to be truthful, by the end of the night most of the men are not fit for anything, and before long they're staggering off home to the warmth of their beds.

As the last customers disappear, Maggie walks over to her last table, and places her weight over it to scrub away sticky ale. But as she does so, all of a sudden something compels her to stop what she is doing and stare across the room. Maggie's not one for magic and sorcery, but it is as though an invisible force guides her to the figure of an exceedingly tall man, stood with his back to the door. The hairs prickle on the back of her neck; she can feel the weight of his stare as he watches her. And for the life of her she can't understand why he looks at her with amusement, and so she checks her person to see if she has food on her skirts or soot on her face.

'We are closing,' she says to him. Despite his good looks, he irks her for some reason, although she does not know why.

'Already? And I was wondering if I could stay for the night – perhaps you could find me a bed?'

'Well, you must ask the innkeeper about that,' Maggie says with a half-smile.

He walks over to her then, towering over her and using his extraordinary height to stare down at her breasts. Maggie feels the blood rise to her face and neck. When his eyes come back to meet hers, he smiles and is suddenly distracted. 'I must apologise for keeping you from your chores.'

Maggie opens her mouth to reply to him, but then the sound of Adam Bell's voice booms from across the room. 'William. Come and see your mother. She's missed you.'

Her cheeks burn, Maggie lowers her face and pushes down on the table with both hands, feeling quite foolish. So this is the innkeeper's son, William – the apprentice tailor. He could have told her who he was! The noise of laughter fills the room as Maggie crosses the floor to clear a missed table. Before long her arms are laden with empty ale flagons and broth dishes destined for the scullery. Near a blistering hearth, she bumps into him again, a drink in his hand, smiling casually at her with laughter in his eyes, and for the second time that night she has the distinct feeling that she amuses him for some reason.

Once their labour is done, they congregate near the fire, to rest aching feet and make conversation. Cook is a solitary character and prefers to stay in the scullery, sleeves rolled up, snoring like a pig next to the blistering hearth. From the corner of her eye

Maggie glances at William. He's young, no more than twenty or so with skin like a girl. His hair is thick and fair and he's the tallest man she's ever seen, and for one so young he carries himself well. Sour-faced Helen, the burly maidservant can't get close enough to him as she edges closer and closer to him as he lounges in a classic male stance, legs wide open as though airing his masculine parts. But no matter what the lass does, be it complimenting him, fetching or carrying for him, the tailor pays Helen no heed. For the most part William moves away from her as if she's a bad smell.

William's sister, Margaret is amused by Helen's conduct and for just a moment Maggie feels inclined to feel sorry for the girl. But her empathy soon disappears when the lassie storms off slamming a door behind her.

'All the lasses are like that with him.' Margaret shakes her head.

'They are? I wonder why?'

'Are you blind? He's the most handsome fellow, even I can see that and he's my kin.'

'He's all right, I suppose. I prefer them more manly myself.'

'Well, you would. You're much older than he is.'

Maggie chews on her lip and takes off her cap, shaking out her hair. 'I'm not that old. How old is he?'

'Nineteen. But he looks a little older, don't you think?'

'No, I don't. Anyway how old do I look?'

Margaret screws up her eyes. 'Six and thirty?'

'You saucy beggar. I am nearly six and twenty,' Maggie glowers.

Margaret clutches a hand to her stomach and laughs so hard, her eyes water with mirth. 'I was jesting, Maggie. Anyway, one thing is for sure – that Helen hasn't got a cat-in-hell's chance.'

★★★

It's a fine morning and Maggie's third day at the inn. From the chicken coop outside, a cockerel crows repeatedly, and the sound seems to bounce off the walls before floating away into the stale attic air. With sleepy eyes she watches Margaret tip-toe across the room, turning the key in its lock before letting her mother in, and to Maggie's consternation, Isobel's even noisier than the damned cockerel.

'On your feet now. Up the pair of you. William's downstairs. He's here to alter the dress for you, Maggie. Hurry now, he hasn't got all day. Put on the dress, girl.' Isobel wags a finger in her daughter's direction. 'And Margaret, in the name of decency and decorum, stay in the room with them.'

Maggie staggers out of bed, hair bedraggled from sleep. She holds up her arms to pull the dress over her sark, but it gets stuck over her shoulders in the process. The damned dress won't dislodge and she's trapped half-naked with her arms in the air. 'Margaret, please help me.'

A knock on the door startles them.

'It is I, William.'

'She's not dressed. Wait there.' Margaret giggles and shouts to her brother through the door.

The innkeeper's daughter shifts the dress over Maggie's shoulders, tittering all the while as she fastens it at the back. 'Your breasts are too big,' she grins, grabbing both of them with her hands before opening the door. 'You can come in now, William.'

To Maggie's mind, William looks distracted as he stoops to enter the room. There is briskness in his step, and his manner is cool and aloof. Straight away he begins to push Maggie around, turning her body this way and that to observe the cut of the dress. Maggie glances at him with indignation but he ignores her and places a pin in-between his teeth.

'I need more pins. I really don't have time for this,' he says with an impatient voice. Quantities of coins jingle in his pockets as he plunges his hands into them. He looks at Maggie coldly as he rummages about, pulling out bits and pieces until finally, after the longest time; he produces a quantity of pins and a measuring tape.

'What is that for?' Maggie gasps, her eyes are suddenly drawn to his eyes and lips.

'I need to measure you. Open your arms out wide and please be still,' he replies. With a pin still between his lips he bends at the knee and curls his arms around her stomach, arranging the tape so that it spans her tiny waist.

Maggie keeps her head high and her arms wide. His face is almost pressed into her side. Her heart pounds so hard she's breathless and her knees are trembling.

'Now the problem area,' he points to her chest.

'No one's ever called it a problem before.' Maggie gives him a sideways glance and fiddles with the front of her dress.

'I imagine not. Now put your arms down by your side,' he remarks before returning her gaze. His hands are perfectly steady, his touch delicate. The tape rests on her breasts as he mumbles a number. 'Impressive! Only one of my customers has a bosom this big and she's huge, like a great pig.'

'How incredibly rude.' Maggie's black eyebrows twist and she grits her teeth. She throws back her hair from her face and blows out her cheeks.

'Pay him no heed, Maggie. He's teasing you,' whines Margaret.

'No I'm not,' says William.

He leaves the room without saying goodbye.

★★★

Maggie and Margaret are late going down to the tavern; they prance around, throwing bodkins and ribbons at each other. In the midst of their foolery, they fuss with each other's hair. As usual, Margaret's head is a mass of unruly curls; no amount of her combing can tame it. So, Maggie takes pity on her and slowly and carefully tries to untangle it. However, the task is impossible, and therefore she ties it with a fillet.

'So what have you to tell me?' enquires Margaret with baited breath, her eyes glitter as she snatches away the comb.

Maggie ignores her. 'Your mother and father will skin us alive if we're much longer. Has William altered the dress?'

'Aye, it's over there, inside the chest. Oh Maggie, please tell me now. Have you decided to leave?'

'Aye, I have to, Margaret. I must go to Newcastle. I'll tell your folks in the morning.'

'They'll be sad to see you go, especially Mother,' Margaret lowers her head.

'Don't be sorry. It is for the best. Fetch us the dress, will you.'

Margaret helps her to dress. Maggie notices a few changes. The hem is shorter and no longer drags on the floor, and she's room to breathe in it now.

'How do I look?'

'Very respectable. The neckline is quite high. Not a bosom in sight.'

A thick band of lace conceals Maggie's décolletage, and the material almost reaches her throat, a white flower sewn to the centre. With one hand Maggie tears away the flower and throws it to the ground.

'What are you doing?'

'I don't mind your brother making me look like a prioress. But the white flower? Folk will think I'm a Jacobite!'

'No, it's white but not a rose.'

'I care not,' Maggie shouts. 'I'm not taking the chance.'

★★★

In the centre of the tavern, a group of men celebrate the birth of a baby or 'wetting the baby's head' as they call it. *It's really just an excuse to get drunk*, Maggie thinks wryly. Old Jack the chandler has his dog with him, and she chats to him for a while before changing a keg. The men are sinking down more than a few ales, and soon they'll want feeding no doubt. Thus, for most of the night Maggie is back and forth from the scullery like a blue-arsed fly.

Halfway through the night she feels his presence. She senses him before she sees him. He stands against a wall with a woman, a fine, tall woman with a firm bust. Long glossy raven-black hair cascades around her sloping shoulders and her eyes glitter like polished emeralds. William leans across her, his eyes observing her as he lightly touches her arm. With a pounding heart, Maggie observes them, her mind spiralling into an eddying darkness.

Wandering about, Maggie knows not where, she passes by the scullery, helping Cook for a while to clear her mind. But when she returns, William's still there, although this time without the dark-haired girl, and suddenly she begins to feel the walls closing in on her. With the greatest confusion imaginable, Maggie stares into William's eyes, straining to see him through the smoky room, trying to connect with him, until their eyes lock together. When they do, for the first time Maggie allows a man to enter her heart, to go beneath her skin and in her blood. And *he* whom she is waiting for comes at last.

CHAPTER ELEVEN

THE RAKE'S PROGRESS

When spring comes, Maggie's thoughts return to home. At Musselburgh, the fishermen will be barking their nets now, boiling up huge cauldrons of cutch, using a tree bark that helps to prevent damage or decay to twine. For Maggie, life is much simpler in Kelso; no trudging back and forth to market and no children to look after.

On Fastern's E'en, there's a cock-fight outside the tavern and Adam Bell takes no more than eight pennies Scots from each man. No one suffers to enter that day except folks from the village and persons whom nothing is demanded and can furnish a cockerel. After the fight, Isobel collects the killed and wounded birds, shaking her head at her husband and pointing to the crude wooden stake protruding from the ground. 'There'll be no cock-throwing, husband; I'll have you know that I think that is mighty cruel.'

Maggie shakes her head and wonders why Isobel finds cock-throwing abhorrent – but cock-fighting acceptable, to her mind the two things are both unkind. As Maggie helps Isobel to pick up the cockerels a holy man approaches from the rear. A heavy Bible protrudes from his puny arms as he walks towards them with a slight limp.

'You're too late, Minister. The cock-fight's over.'

The minister cuts him off. 'I'm not here for such folly. I'm here about the woman, the stranger working in your tavern.' He looks around with beady eyes, his eyes settling on Maggie. 'Ah – there she is, I believe she is unchaperoned and I must ask to see her testificate.'

'Let me deal with this,' whispers Adam to Maggie.

'There's no need,' replies Maggie.

'I insist,' Adam folds his arms over his body.

'Has she a certificate of good character?' the minister persists. His eyes stare towards a tankard of frothy beer.

Maggie gestures towards a jug. 'Would you like a drink?'

'No. I've other matters to attend to, and so I wish for you to make haste. Have you the papers, woman?'

'Yes. I will fetch them at once.'

The minister takes the paper with shaky hands, unfolding the wrinkled piece of paper and holding it up to the light. Carefully he folds the document back to its original form and ambles away. He's just nearing the edge of the village green when he stops abruptly to shout out to the innkeeper: 'I expect to see her in kirk, Adam Bell – and that ungodly son of yours.'

And with that, he's on his way.

★★★

At Pasch, folk celebrate the return of spring, and the festivities spill out onto the village green and nearby meadows scattered with gorse and ling. Delicious buns and breads are baked and pipers and maypoles are everywhere, and all around people are joyful and happy. A small crowd congregate outside the tavern, singing and dancing and being merry. Maggie never gets a moment's peace; she's rushed off her feet and her arms are aching from carrying tray after tray of ale or food.

'Is that for me, pretty wench?' A military man in full uniform reaches out for Maggie's last tankard of ale. An overpowering whiff of masculine scent comes off him as he searches for a coin.

'Aye, if you have the right money.' She places her drinks tray on the ground.

He tosses a coin inside her dress; finger's lingering over the lace panel. 'What a fine dress, but I wager you'd look even better out of it.' His eyes glitter with roguish mirth.

Maggie smiles and salutes him. 'You should not take liberties with poor tavern girls...'

Suddenly from out of nowhere, William squares up to the man. 'Is this man bothering you?'

'Nae, of course not. The man is thirsty and wants a drink, that's all. Now if you'll excuse me, I have customers to serve.' Maggie picks up her tray and walks away.

But as Maggie dashes away, it soon becomes apparent that William's not finished with her. He's close at her heels, ignoring a young woman with fiery red hair tugging at his arm. But Maggie's no time for this; Adam's already calling out to her to fetch more ale, and if she does not respond soon, he'll kick up a right fuss. Nevertheless, William for some reason keeps on at her – until finally she stops what she's doing to confront him. And as she turns to face him, he stares down upon her with contempt in his eyes; and Maggie can't help but notice how the muscles in his jaw twitch and pulsate.

'What is it, for heaven's sake?'

'I was jesting with you that day – about the dress. You're not really fat like a pig.'

So that was it. He wants to apologise, Maggie thinks, but she's wrong.

'You're just a little fat. Here and here.' William places his hands on both of her hips.

Maggie shrieks and pushes him away, but he seizes her with firm hands by the shoulders. 'William – I despair of you. Why are you always so pig-headed? Every time we meet you're either scowling or quarrelling with me.'

'Nonsense. You should learn to govern your tongue, woman. You're imagining things and you're a little fool. Now dance with me.'

Maggie shakes her head and points in the red-head's direction. 'You're jesting. Dance with her instead, she's more your height.'

'I'm not leaving till you agree to dance with me.' His eyes crinkle at the corners and there's amusement in them.

'You'll have to wait forever, then.'

And with that William grabs Maggie, curling his hands around her small waist. They swirl around in time to the music, Maggie's dress billowing around her. She feels her face begin to burn, imagining the gawping faces all around at the sight of them together.

'I told you I don't want to dance with you.' Maggie struggles from his embrace but he's much too strong, his arms hold her fast as he presses his body against her. 'Why would you want to dance with a fat pig like me anyway?'

'I was just teasing, Maggie.'

'That's a falsehood.'

'William. William!' the young redhead shouts. 'You said that...'

William pays no heed to the woman. But the redhead is not one for being ignored, and so she calls out to him again and again, until he can bear it no more.

'Alright, woman, I am coming.'

But before William breaks apart from Maggie he stoops and whispers in her ear, sending delicious tingles and shivers up her spine. 'I enjoyed that.'

It's a strong desire Maggie feels as she walks away from them. A great ache forms in her throat and she swallows hard and tries to regain her composure, but to no avail. When she glances back at them, William holds the woman close to his body, and her neck is thrown back in rapture. A sharp pain throbs in Maggie's chest like a cold steel dirk twisting within.

A man taps Maggie on her shoulder. 'Here, wench – fetch me some ale.'

Maggie collects a new tray. Upon the table she places a tankard and jug. She moves slowly, her face wrenched into a scowl. As she proceeds with her chores, she is very distracted.

'Stop, stop, you're spilling ale all over me,' cries the man. His clothes are saturated with beer.

'I'm sorry,' Maggie reddens with embarrassment and wipes his garments with her apron.

'You should watch what you're doing, lassie. Your attention's elsewhere.'

★★★

With each passing season the air becomes warmer. It's Maggie's nature to gravitate towards water and the next best thing to the sea, the river, has its charms. There are all kinds of wildlife here; strange fish, insects and plants. Just the other day an angler pointed out an otter with one of the jumping fish trapped in its strong jaws. But even here, and despite such tranquillity, William continues to invade her thoughts.

Before evening comes, Maggie helps Cook with some chores. Beads of sweat form on Maggie's brow as she works with the vigour of a scullery maid. She washes the pots, turns the dangle spit and sweeps the floor. A quantity of leftover mutton fat sits in a basin near the door. Maggie picks it up and brings it to her nose. It smells foul.

Cook takes the basin from her and grins, her teeth are all yellow. 'You can make some rush lights for me. We've collected rushes from the river all summer, so you might as well make yourself useful and do some now.'

'But I can't remember how to do it. I wasn't listening when my mother taught me.'

'Lord Almighty, every lassie knows how to make a rush light. Didn't you used to put up a new length and mend the rush when it burnt out as a child?'

'No, not really.'

'No matter. Here – take a rush. You peel a rind from the pith and take care to leave only a strip of rind. And when the rush is dry – dip it through the grease, and keep it well under mind and then lay it on the side to dry. That's it.'

Maggie nods.

'You can catch a breath of air when you're finished. I loathe to see you moping about.' Cook sniffs and seems content at the prospect of solitude. The scullery is her domain and for the most part she prefers it to herself.

★★★

With her fingers still greasy with fat, Maggie ventures out of doors. The sunshine feels heavenly upon her skin, how she loves the sting of sunrays upon her face. Chickens cluck nearby and beyond the coop is a bird-house and clear of it a fruit tree in bloom, masking the scent of fowl and swine with its sweetness. She leans back on a wall and closes her eyes, releasing her grip on her cap so that it falls to the dusty ground. *A few minutes more*, she thinks, *and then back to the grind*. When the time is up, she bends to pick up her cap, and as she does so, suddenly there is a sharp sting to her backside.

'Ouch! What on earth...?.'

'I couldn't resist that.' A bare-chested man grins from ear to ear.

Maggie looks at the young man. He's a stocky fellow, with a face full of freckles and watery blue eyes. Maggie's seen him around delivering kegs of ale. Her brows knit together as she thinks for a moment, but the name will not come.

'You can't remember my name, can you?'

'No – I'm not good with names. What is it?'

'Michael. The brewer's son. I'm the man who delivers your ale.' He slaps her shoulder in a playful manner.

'Be off with you, laddie. I've matters to attend to and so have you, no doubt.'

The young man leans in close, and he smells of whisky or brandy, or perhaps both.

'Where did you get the scars on your body?' Maggie enquires.

'From Castle Floors, up river. They put me in the dungeons in an iron maiden and tortured me. It's like a coffin see, with spikes inside that pierce your skin and makes you bleed all over from your fingers to your toes. I was in there for weeks I was, in agony covered in sores.'

Maggie's eyebrows arch. 'You're spinning a yarn.'

'I am not.'

'So they're scars from an iron – what did you call it?' She shakes her head and laughs. 'You're jesting with me, aren't you?'

He frowns and takes her hand, guiding her fingers to press against his upper body. 'No, I wouldn't joke about something like that. Feel the marks with your fingers – see they're all over me. '

★★★

The cellar is clear. It's taken up most of their morning, and by the end of it Adam Bell's covered in sweat. He turns to his son and tries to a smile, but William can tell that it's forced. His father mounts the cellar stairs with slow heavy steps, and it's so unlike him, just a few months ago he watched his father run up those steps. Mid-way up the stairs, his father pauses for breath, his body hunched over. 'I think I'll stay here a wee bit longer, son, you go up without me.'

'Damn it,' William mutters under his breath. It never occurred to him before, but he suddenly realises his father is getting old. There's a slight curvature to his spine he's not noticed before, and his father's eyes are dull and haggard.

'Come on, old man – you're worn-out from drinking too much ale, and eating too many of Cook's pies.'

'Mind your business. I'm just grand. It's you that looks ready for some shut eye. Be off with you and back to the tailors. I can finish off here on my own.'

'Are you sure?'

'Aye, get yourself outside, William. Have a breather before you return to work. See you tomorrow.'

Without a word, William climbs the rest of the staircase, but before he reaches the top he hears voices, two of them, a man and a woman. Laughter follows, a feminine titter mingling with a deeper, heartier laugh. His curiosity stirred, William presses himself against the door, eavesdropping on the conversation, one eyebrow arching at the scandalous exchange. When he's heard enough he presses two hands against the door, and it makes a great creaking noise as he opens it and steps out into the summer air.

'William,' gasps Maggie. 'I didn't realise you was there.'

'I didn't think so, sweet,' William remarks with a sardonic air. His eyes glower down upon her as she removes her hands from the brewery boy.

William turns to the lad. They are of a similar age but William towers above him. 'What was it you were just saying about an iron maiden? Brewster is the name – is it not?'

'Aye, Michael Brewster's the name. It was nothing, just a bit of tomfoolery. I was just larking about here with Maggie.' Brewster tugs his linen shirt on quick sharp.

William turns to Maggie. 'Maggie, are you really that gullible? They're smallpox scars, not torture marks. Haven't you ever seen smallpox scars?'

'Aye,' she replies.

'Where's your cap?' The muscles jump in his jaw.

'What business is it of yours?' she declares.

'This is my father's tavern. So it *is* my business when one of our maidservants acts like a slatternly slut.'

'From what I am told, that's the way you like them.'

William's taken aback, a wench with a smart mouth. He likes a lass with spirit, but not one who coverts with a brewery lad. A look of lazy amusement crosses his face as she crouches to retrieve the cap. And he can't help but stare at the curve of her bottom as she bends down.

'What's keeping you? Haven't you a tavern to be off to?' William barks to Brewster.

Brewster makes no answer and backs away with sagged shoulders to grab a barrel. So, with Maggie now gone and the brewery lad at work, William storms off to the smoky twilight of the tavern, to pour himself a wee dram before he returns to his work.

'Bit early for that?' his mother remarks, eying him with a strange look.

He knocks it back in one and shakes his head. 'I'll be off now, see you later.'

On his way out he passes Brewster, fists clenching as he bangs into his shoulder. Suddenly, a strange compulsion comes over him to knock him off his feet. And then, all of a sudden, he arrives at his senses, and wonders why he's just acted as he did.

★★★

Never before has Maggie felt such pain. It started in her jaws at first with a dull ache, and then travelled to her neck, throat and gums. The hurt is unbearable and because of the swelling to her face, everywhere she turns people look at her and shake their heads, as though feeling her pain.

'Shouldn't she see a tooth puller or blacksmith? There'll be one at the travelling fairs,' Adam asks his wife. 'She's putting the customer's off their ale.'

'No need, Adam. I know how to cure it. It's simple. When I was a wee bairn in Jedburgh, my mother used to suffer with toothache. And what she used to do is find a nail, a new one if possible and scratch her gum with it. Then all you have to do is hammer it into an oak tree. It works every time.'

Adam Bell grimaces. 'That's an old wives tale like when you take a poker, heat it on the fire and burn your earlobe.'

Maggie shudders, her eyes are watering with the throbbing pain. But she doesn't fancy burning her earlobe or scratching her gum with a nail. In her desperation, she even tries a strange concoction, a potion made up of squashed fisheyes that tastes so foul she has to gag into a pail. And then it comes to her, a cure her mother used long ago. Orris plant – she remembers how her mother used to search for it high and low.

The following day Maggie feels much better. At the crack of dawn she starts her chores; cleaning, sweeping, and fetching water from the river. Just before noon she scrubs a small tiled section of the scullery floor, kneeling down on all fours before Cook returns. The stone floor is cold and hard on the knees, so Maggie puts her back into it, pressing down on the wooden scrubbing brush with all her might. After a while she gets a rhythm going as she pushes back and forth. A section of her long hair escapes from her cap and tickles her neck; she brushes it away with impatience and works up a sweat. Nearly done, she scrubs harder, just a few more tiles, and then she hears a cough. Maggie stops what she's doing and continues to look down at the floor. She knows without looking that it is William. He coughs again, this time louder. Maggie takes a deep breath and tilts her neck back; her eyes are dark, hot and naked in their longing for him. She pushes down on her hands to stand.

'Don't get up on my account; you're doing a fine job. Pretty as a picture,' William remarks with a smile.

'How long have you been there?' Maggie stares into his face. How she yearns to know the secret of him.

'Long enough,' he holds out a hand for her.

Maggie takes his hand, allowing him to help her to her feet. 'I'm sopping wet. I must change my apron.'

He holds her hand for the longest time.

'Maggie…' he says with a serious face, and then without uttering another word he hurries away.

★★★

In the morning, Maggie strolls to the Baxters to fetch the bread to be baked in the communal oven. The bakery lies to the west, and so she continues on her way until she passes an oyster hawker crying his wares. Just the sight of him causes Maggie to grimace as he struggles with the burden of his creel. Rooks caw and leaves rustle in the trees as she follows a cobbled path and passes a barefoot child; he's small and puny, hugging his knees to his body on a cold stone step. He makes a right din, and thus Maggie stops to stare at him. He reminds her of her own son, little Patrick, so she ventures towards him with a kindly face.

'What's the matter?' She observes him with curious eyes. He's seen at least seven summers. 'Why are you crying, little one?'

'Father sent me for some more ale, but my feet are sore and cold and I hurt them on a big sharp rock.' His speech is interrupted with bouts of sobbing and hiccups. He wipes his tears onto a filthy sleeve.

'Where do you live?' she asks him, helping him to wipe his runny nose with her plaid.

The boy shrugs and sniffles, reaching for his horn beaker of frothy ale and holding it to his thin body. 'Over there. It is a long, long walk, and if I spill a drop I'll get a smack 'round the lughole.'

Maggie holds out a hand to him, sucking in her breath as she observes open sores all over his scrawny legs. 'Come on, I'll help you. What's your name?'

The boy stops weeping and rubs his eyes red-raw.

'David.'

Maggie lifts the child. He's as light as a feather, not even as heavy as an empty creel. 'Point the way, little one,' she says. 'No fear, little one. I'll go slowly. We won't spill a drop.' She walks a good way before her back starts to ache, his tiny hands clutch around her neck and his breath is sour.

After a while she stops between a tannery and dyers. The smell is appalling. 'You're choking me,' she coughs.

'Here we are!' he shouts right down her ear.

Poor little rascal, she thinks, *he's stuck out here at the edge of the village, near this stinking smell, and he's a bag of bones.* She waves to him as he walks carefully to his doorway, not spilling a drop of the precious ale.

It is a good quarter hour before Maggie's back in the village. There's a queue at the Baxters and so Maggie taps on the floor with one shoe, how she loathes to wait. As usual, when there's not much to do, the women gossip. It doesn't matter what the subject is, they talk about anyone and anything, to spread denigration, vilification, and mindless tittle-tattle. What an utter waste of time, Maggie thinks and then for once her ears prick up as she recognises a name.

'Aye, Bell, he got the last tavern wench. Well, you know – he took her maidenhood, can't keep it in his trews that one.'

Maggie's face flushes. A rush of heat sears to the base of her scalp as her pulse quickens. The women continue, clucking and squawking like hens in their scandalous corner of chitchat.

'Aye, you know the one, Ethel – the handsome tailor.'

'Handsome sailor?'

'No, you cloth-eared idiot. I said tailor. You know the tall one with fair hair, apprentice to that fellow across the way at the tailor shop. Oh come, Ethel, you can't miss him; he's the kind that makes a lassie weak at the knees. He's been with loads of lasses, can't get enough of them. Apparently he has a box of fairings of all the lassies he's been with – ribbons, hair, and even garters and stockings, so they say.'

Maggie's had enough. She takes hold of her bread and storms outside for some air. And once again she wonders why he arouses such intense feelings in her. But deep down she knows why: she's insane with jealousy.

★★★

Every day, from the moment she wakes up, Maggie's thoughts are of William. Invariably he's busy at work, meeting women or simply amusing himself. With a swollen heart she tallies up the days since she saw him last. Oh how she suffers for him – how she longs for a sign or indication that he cares for her, but it never comes. For the most part, since that day outside the cellar door, and the antics of the brewer's son, he's distant and aloof. And when he does talk to her, she has the distinct feeling that he's never quite taking her serious.

★★★

Angus McDonald claims he can't find a wise-woman, and because of Maggie's success with the orris plant, he's on a mission to find a cure. It's common knowledge that if one ventures over the heather brae, past a pair of rowan trees, and beyond a tiny burn, there's a low wooden structure that could almost pass for a home. It's inhabited by an old hag, who has knowledge of plants and herbs. And when Maggie reminds Angus of this he laughs and says: 'She's no wise woman, that old crone is away with the fairies and soft in the heid.'

'Well I can't help you. I can do without your bothering me now, Angus. I only know a couple of remedies for headaches or ague and

I am certainly no wise-woman. You'll have me hanging from a tree come candlemas. Folk will think me a witch,' she shivers.

'Will you look at me,' he throws up his hands and strokes his balding head. 'I'm not getting any younger and it's time I got me a wife. There must be a cure for thinning hair. Are you listening to me, Maggie?'

'Aye, I am and don't look at me. I am already wed.'

'Oh yes, and where is this husband of yours?' he scoffs and swings a hand around the room.

'At the keels in Newcastle, so I'm told. How the hell should I know? I'm just his wife!' Her eyes narrow and then she has an idea.

'Angus. It's suddenly dawned on me. I *do* know of a cure. It is a little odd I might add, but I'm sure that it works.'

Angus practically slavers and his eyes near pop from his head. 'What is it?'

'You just take a little dove dung and slap it on your head twice a day.'

From the corner of her eye Maggie catches a glimpse of Adam Bell collapsing into heap of laughter at the corner of the room.

★★★

A lively fire crackles in the hearth as Helen, the sullen maidservant scurries about the scullery. The witch never shuts up, and Maggie loathes the sound of her grumbling and cursing as she performs her detested chores. In the midst of her complaining, shovel-faced Helen bawls. 'Where's Cook? Why I am making the broth? I've a hundred things to do and it's left to me to sort out the food to serve this noon.' She chops some meat, screws up her nose and leans forward to inhale its smell. 'For goodness sake, it's rancid.'

Maggie approaches Helen with caution, wary of her bared teeth. 'Rotten?'

'Aye, do you have to repeat everything I say, silly girl? Can't you smell it?' Helen wipes her hands on her apron, leaving a quantity of blood smeared marks.

'Put some spices on it to disguise the smell,' offers Maggie.

'I can't do that. It'll make folk ill. That bastard flesher! I'll tear his eyes out, I will. He's sold me rotten meat again. Isobel will be vexed with me. How could I have been so foolish? I should've noticed the smell at the flesher's stall.' Helen shakes her head and then bites her nails, then almost chokes as she spits out the rancid taste.

'Can't you buy some more?'

'No money left,' she moans.

'I have.'

Helen's eyes narrow into slits. 'And where on earth would a tavern wench get money from. Did you steal it?'

'Of course not.' All of a sudden Maggie wishes she hadn't offered to help. 'I was simply trying to help you, Helen, but I can see that you require no charity from the likes of me.'

Helen scoffs and turns her nose up. She opens the door and tosses the meat to the pigs. Sneering, she heaves herself away from the door, bringing with her a stench that causes Maggie's nostrils to burn with repulsion.

'Well, do you want some money or not?' Maggie enquires.

'No.' Helen shakes her head.

★★★

The inn is rowdy. The fire-place in the tap-room is large enough to accommodate a small crowd, and to be sure they are crammed in tonight. There is not a high-back settle empty and folk stand shoulder to shoulder scraping roughly-plastered walls. Yarns are spun, scandal slyly discussed, and countrymen take their tankards with a sense of a good day's work behind them.

A stranger enters the tavern, all eyes stop to stare. He's a tramping man and stays for one drink, but before he leaves folk have discussed him from the hair on his chin to the cut of his coat. Time is called. One by one, the inn empties of customers. Maggie stays busy. Adam's already gone up to bed and Isobel's yawning. The hour passes slowly; Maggie's worn-out and could do with a rest. But the pigs need feeding, and Helen's busy clearing up.

Maggie walks over to Isobel and asks, 'Who's feeding the pigs?'

'William. I'm worn-out, lassie. I'm going to bed. William will lock up.'

'Shall I go up too?'

'Aye, but be sure to wipe down the tables first.'

Maggie scratches her head and frowns. 'But I've just done that already.'

'Well do it again, please. We've a wake on the morrow.'

Maggie gives Isobel a side-ways glance as she walks from the tap-room, and though she wants to ask her why she has to do the tables again, she holds her tongue. The fragrance of cooking, tobacco and sawdust penetrates every nook and cranny of the room, a feral cat lingers near the open door. As the last of the stragglers leave, she takes a minute and sits down near the hearth, and suddenly she realises that she's not alone. She spins around. William's behind her with both elbows resting on his wide-spread legs, holding a whisky glass in two hands.

'Want some?' He leans over her and brushes her shoulder with his face. With gentle hands he presses a glass to her lips. 'Drink some more.' His eyes dip to the swell of her breasts.

Maggie turns red and swallows. Her fisher lassie banter evades her. She just can't find the words. Suddenly she has a miserable sense of inadequacy, and to cover her embarrassment she looks down at her shoes. A dozen times or more she thinks of something interesting to say, but her confidence wanes and she mourns the minx of bygone days.

'Cat got your tongue, Maggie. You had no difficulty frolicking with the brewer's son and his poxy scars.'

Maggie shudders as his lips graze her neck. 'You're drunk.'

'I am not,' he slurs. He leans in even closer to spin her a yarn, a joke about his manhood, implying he has length as well as girth, and all the while his hands linger over his groin. 'What tiny hands you have,' he takes her hand and presses it against his own. Hers look like a child's next to his.

★★★

To get to the tap-room, Adam must pass the main door, and to his amazement it's still open and hasn't been locked. He kicks out a mangy cat and storms across the room, not surprised by the blatant flirting. Adam has no option but to intervene. What was his idiot wife thinking leaving these two alone? His son is not to be trusted where the lasses are concerned; he cavorts with lots of lassies, especially the pretty ones. But none of them have been as bonny as Maggie. Adam sighs and runs a calloused hand through his hair. He's fond of Maggie, but when all is said and done, it would be a shame if she went down the same road as the last maidservant.

'Fetch a keg from the cellar, son.' He gives Maggie a long hard look.

William chews his bottom lip and runs a hand through his golden hair. 'Must I? Can't it wait?'

'Aye, the sooner the better.'

'How many?'

'Just the one,' orders Adam. 'And William? Take your time.'

For a short while, Maggie, William and the innkeeper stand in silence near the bar, the quiet suddenly interrupted by the sound of William's boots stomping away. Adam rummages beneath the wooden counter, picking up one object after another, till finally his son is far from sight. He continues to search until he locates a couple of candles; they are long and tapered and give off a queer smell.

'Light these will you by the fire, Maggie, and then sit down.'

Maggie obeys him at once and takes a chair near the hearth, once seated she begins to bite her nails.

'Are you vexed with me?' Maggie asks.

'If you're expecting moral indignation, you will not find any here. Hush child. I know that you have done no wrong. I would just ask that you listen to me and pay heed to my counsel. So hear me out and hear me well. While you are living in my tavern you are under my protection, and that means abiding by my rules, is that understood?'

'Aye.'

'I don't mind the banter with the customers; it's good for business mind. But don't cavort with my son, lass. You may think that he's taken a fancy to you, but he has not, mark my word. William is like that with all the lasses.' He pauses, his attention suddenly drawn to her bewitching eyes. 'I've no doubt that you are a chaste woman and protect your good name and reputation, Maggie. But you have a husband, lass. Perhaps it's time that you continued your journey to Newcastle or back to where you came from.'

Her reaction is not what he expects.

'There is no need, Adam – honestly. I am settled here and this will not happen again, I assure you. Please allow me to stay a while longer.'

'I'll speak to Isobel,' he replies in a stern voice, although he already knows her wishes concerning Maggie.

★★★

Maggie runs up the stairs to the attic room, locking the door behind her. She feels like she's been slapped in the face and her stomach is in knots. How dare Adam speak to her like that – and the irony of it, because for once she has done nothing wrong. It was his precious son making advances at her, not the other way around. In Musselburgh, she would have shouted a man down for talking to her like that, including her own husband.

From behind the doors there is a creaking noise as the hinges to the box-bed open. 'What's wrong?' Margaret Bell peers at her from beneath her covers.

'He scolded me.'

'Who?'

'Your father.'

'No. Why?' Margaret's hand flutters in front of her mouth.

'He caught your brother cavorting with me.'

'Is that all? He frolics with all the lasses, Maggie. You must have seen him. He's with a different one near every week.'

Maggie sighs. 'I think I've heard this a hundred times.'

'But it's true. You'd be wise to avoid him, Maggie. Let him take his pleasure with the new girl, Moll, or her pal with the scar.'

'I won't have any man telling me what to do. Do you hear? I shall be mastered by no man, least of all your father.'

Margaret tuts. 'This is his tavern. He is your master here.'

Maggie shakes her head. 'I'll do as I damn well please.'

★★★

On market day, Maggie's sent to buy victuals for the inn. She barters a price for vegetables and meat, and the grocer cannot do enough for her and throws in a basket of shiny green apples. At the rear of a market she bumps into little David again, and to her utter consternation, he's barefoot, half-naked and begging for scraps. As Maggie gets closer to him she notices his ears are thick with dried blood. So before he runs away, she scoops him up in her arms and hands him an apple.

'What you doing here, little rascal? And don't eat so fast, you'll choke and get the hiccups. Is that a jug of ale for your father? I'll help you to carry it home again if you like.'

The lad nods. 'Aye, missus, he drinks it all the time, 'til he falls to the ground or his bed.'

Maggie looks at him sadly. 'Where's your mother?'

'She died when I was a bairn. I don't remember her.'

'Do you want to come with me and have something to eat?' Maggie ruffles the boy's hair and as she does so a lump swells in her throat.

'Aye, I would like that, missus. I'm starving, haven't eaten in days. Have you got any bread?'

'Don't call me missus. Call me Maggie. And no, I haven't any bread, but there's plenty in the tavern.'

★★★

All is quiet in the scullery and so Maggie tip-toes inside before Cook returns. The boy's like a ravenous fox and Maggie constantly has to remind him to chew slower as he devours his food. Maggie winces as she looks at him, he's so thin, like the linkboys in Edinburgh, and so

179

she fusses around him, fetching tasty morsels for him to eat. A mutton pie, a bannock smothered in cheese, and a cup of milk fresh from the dairy. With his dirty sleeve he wipes away a milky moustache, his eyes widening as a strange woman enters the scullery.

'What's he doing here? The lad's probably crawling with lice, get him out,' whines Helen.

Maggie pulls a face. 'Have a heart, Helen. He's all skin and bone. Anyway I'm taking him home now and I won't bring him here again,' she lies.

Maggie fumes and swings to the right, almost colliding with William. That's all she needs, another person to order the laddie out. But William takes one look at the boy and drops to his knees beside him.

'Who's this fine young laddie, then?' William winks at the boy and playfully punches his tiny stomach.

'William – the boy should not be here,' Helen hisses.

Maggie cuts in and points a finger at Helen. 'Honestly, you are one miserable cow. Come on, David and don't forget your jug of ale.'

They stroll hand in hand towards the tannery, enjoying the wind in their hair. Maggie stops for a breather and kneels before the child. 'Next time I see you I'll get you some shoes and we'll sort out those sore legs.'

'Don't need shoes, Maggie. And I don't want to wear any and you can't make me.' David scratches his head and holds out his arms for Maggie to carry him. 'Who was the giant in the scullery, Maggie?'

'That's William, the Master's son. He's going to be a fine tailor one day.'

'You like the giant too, don't you, Maggie?' David laughs and blows a kiss.

'Aye, I do. He's a fine man. Now stop wriggling about like a worm.'

CHAPTER TWELVE

SINS OF THE FLESH

By the main hearth, Maggie sits in contemplation. For the first time in a while she thinks of her husband, and whether she loves him at all. But she cannot find love for him, not now, not since he abandoned her. Thus, in just a small space of time, her deliberation fills her heart with anger, causing her hand to shake and form a fist, and how she curses Patrick for deserting her and leaving her alone. And yet she misses him – sometimes, and the children, more often than not in the wee hours of dawn, when all is quiet except for the chirps of song-birds.

All morning, she reflects on her matrimony. Even in the beginning, her eyes would stray and linger on other men. It's her nature to be seductive; didn't her father warn her so? In truth Maggie's inclination towards wanton behaviour has caused her to tread a reckless path. Hasn't her life thus far been one continuous quest to allure any man who takes her fancy? She revels in such hedonistic and selfish games. Maggie's used men and discarded men, without a sentiment of guilt. In truth, other than her husband, she's not formed one single affecting attachment – until William that is.

What passion he stirs up in her, and how he blights her soul. She presses a hand to her heart and curses the day she met him. Is it possible to feel so wretched in love? As she peers across the room to steal one fleeting glance at him, her heart leaps, but she can no longer look at him, for fear of betraying her heart. And so, with her hands still clutched to her breast, Maggie takes a deep breath and resigns herself to the fact that she, and she alone has allowed herself to become trapped in an intricate web of obsession and love.

★★★

The Beltane day celebrations cause much animation. At the tavern, Adam and Isobel busy themselves planning a May celebration to run the same time as the fair. When the day arrives fires are lit across the entire village, and later on, a procession is led by a piper. As expected the tavern bustles with energy, and folk buzz here and there like busy little bees.

Halfway through the day, Maggie notices that Adam is short. He's suffering from one of his headaches that make him see stars. But no matter how many times Isobel tries to cajole him to take to his bed, she's always met with a shaking head.

Maggie overhears their conversation as she fetches more ale.

'Go to bed? How can I do that? These barrels won't shift themselves, wife. Are you going to move them?'

'No,' replies Isobel with a tight face. 'I'm off to the scullery, then.'

Maggie smirks as Adam follows her, staying close to his wife's heels. He's really got it in for her.

'I've not finished talking to you yet, wife. Don't walk away from me – now listen here. Cook's working far too slow. Tell her to hurry or she'll be feeling my foot up her backside, do you hear me, Isobel? I'm tired of telling folk what to do and them just nodding at me like an idiot.'

'What's got into you, Adam Bell? You've been sore all morning. It's me who should be in a temper because I haven't had a decent night's sleep now for over a week because of your snoring.'

'Snoring? Hah! I don't snore.'

'Oh yes you do, and I wish you would stop.'

'Aye, I'll stop snoring…when you stop breathing!' He turns his temper on his daughter then. 'What are you gaping at, Margaret? Haven't you chores to do? Have you fetched the water yet?'

Margaret's shoulders droop and she looks at the floor. 'No. I was just about to do it, Father. But it's me back, I can't…'

Adam cuts her off then, wagging a finger in his daughter's face. 'Stop slouching and look at me girl. I've had quite enough of your pathetic excuses. Now get your backside down to that river to fetch some water. Maggie will help you. And you can use that.' He points to a wooden stoup on the floor.

Margaret Bell sticks out her bottom lip, pouting like a wee lassie. 'Oh, Father, I loathe going to the river. Why can't you send Helen? My back is sore, really it is.'

Adam's voice booms. 'I'm not going to tell you again. Get gone before you feel the back of my hand.'

Maggie rushes to Margaret's side and places a soothing hand on her shoulder. But the lassie's having none of it and snatches up the pail and stoup, banging it against a wall on her way out.

'Wait for me,' Maggie cries, shuffling behind with more pails. But Margaret is already out the door.

'For goodness sake,' Maggie complains. 'Can't you wait for me, Margaret?'

Just before she reaches the way out, Maggie stands aside to allow William to enter. Though, to her surprise he deliberately blocks her way and stares down at her with his come hither eyes. And so, she finds herself trapped in a narrow corridor, just William and her, between a wall and his lanky frame. Maggie's heart races in anticipation. She waits – and all the while a delicious tingle builds up deep in her core. *If he touches me once it will all be over*, she thinks... she closes her eyes. When she opens them he is gone.

At the riverside, while she is collecting water, Maggie scratches her leg on a rock. Then later, when she's feeding the animals, one of the dumb beasts bites her. So as the afternoon draws to an end, Maggie wonders what else can go wrong.

'What's up with your miserable face?' Cook asks, breaking her usual silence. 'It's not the end of the world. You can help me make oatcakes in a moment, there's never enough to go round. Oh, and stay clear of the Master, he's in a foul mood.'

'Don't I know it,' mumbles Maggie, hoping there might be time for a bite to eat before the night time customers arrive.

★★★

The tavern is hectic. Maggie can't keep up with the demands. She scurries from one end of the room to the other, her arms heavy from carrying tankards. Her eyes look left and right, searching the room for Adam, Isobel or Margaret – but there's no one to help.

'Where is everybody?' Maggie utters under her breath. Her feet are smarting and her back aches. She leans her weight over the counter for a while to catch her breath. A customer screams down her ear for her to take his order, and so she places her fingers in her ears and walks away. But the man persists and follows her through the scullery, the beer cellar, even the chicken coop. But the only person she can find is sour-faced Helen.

'Where are the others? Isn't Moll and the other girl here tonight?'

'I have not seen any of them…' answers Helen. 'Oh, there they are.'

'Where?' Maggie peers through the tobacco smoke.

'Over there – with William,' she points ahead.

Maggie turns to the irate man. 'Helen's not busy; she will serve you at once.'

The look Helen gives Maggie as she walks away, but Maggie does not care. She's discontent and weary from holding the fort. And so she proceeds to the back of the tavern, to one of the high-backed settles, a group of three occupy one, William, flanked by two idle maidservants.

'Haven't you ale to serve, Moll? And you, Prissy or Missy or whatsoever your name is. I'm running around ragged while you lot have a get together…'

Moll pulls a face at her. 'What business of it is yours? Keep your nose out, wench.'

'It's my business when I'm the only one doing any work,' Maggie complains, folding her arms over her breasts and turning to William.

'She's right,' adds William, holding her gaze. 'You two should make yourselves busy. It's not fair that Maggie has to cope alone.'

'Hah!' Moll sniggers. 'Didn't I tell you, Missy? While we satisfy his body, his mind's filled with her.'

William seizes Moll by the wrist, tightening his grip. 'Hold your tongue, Moll. Or you'll be out on your ear. Have I made myself clear?' William releases his grip.

'Aye, you made yourself clear all right. Come on, Missy. Let's go. I've had enough of the earache.' She knocks into Maggie as she passes by.

But Maggie doesn't feel a thing. Moll's words are buzzing in her ears, over and over. *His mind's filled with her.* She closes her eyes, summoning up every smile, touch and furtive glance. Had she imagined it? Surely not.

'To hell with it – I can't go on like this anymore,' Maggie curses. Suddenly, it becomes her resolution to find him and tell him how she feels. High and low, Maggie searches for William. But he is nowhere to be found. With a groan, she picks up a tankard of ale and knocks it back in one, banging it down on a nearby table before reaching for another and then another. Before long, the room begins to spin; ale dribbles the length of her chin as she walks a zigzag line. Outside she slumps against a moss-stained wall. The disgust goes to the very bottom of her, clawing at her black heart. And a weakness runs through her body, causing her to fall to her knees and stare up at a star-filled sky. *I want to sleep*, she thinks sadly, *and dream not of him.* A small bright moon shines brilliantly ahead, and she fancies it is laughing at her, hoping to break her soul.

A customer pushes into her as she re-enters the inn, knocking her sideways, straight into the arms of William. Maggie winces as his fingernails dig into her arms.

'Where have you been? What on earth has got into you, Maggie? Have you been drinking the ale? We brew strong stuff here you know, not like the weak stuff you have with your meals.'

Maggie's words come out in a drunken slur. 'I know, I know. It's just I can't bear to see you cavort with the other lassies anymore, William. It's breaking my heart. I don't want to feel the way I do about you, but I can't stop myself, William. I love you. I always have – since the very first time I saw you.'

His face turns pale, but there is a glint in his eyes. He glances around the room with wary eyes before pulling her to him, sniffing the liquor on her breath. 'You love me? You're talking nonsense, you silly fool. You have a husband, woman,' he hisses through gritted teeth.

Maggie laughs. 'What husband? I can't see him, can you?'

He tightens his grip around her arm. 'You need to sober up.'

William takes a deep breath and presses one hand into the small of her back, ushering her from the room before folk can guess what state she's in. They're alone at last, surrounded by dirty pots and empty pitchers in a small room off the scullery, out of sight from Cook. With steady hands he pours a quantity of water in a bowl and motions for her to come to him. 'Splash some of that on your face, and drink a little.' He sits behind her watching her bend over the basin.

Maggie feels his eyes upon her, imagining his hands taking hold of both of her hips from behind. But he does nothing and so she turns around and makes her move. Upon his lap she climbs, legs straddling him, pressing warm thighs against his skin. Beneath his clothes she can feel his arousal, and she kisses his lips over and over, and to her amazement he kisses her back and entwines his fingers through her hair, pulling her face closer to his. And then, as quickly as it starts – it ends.

'Maggie, I can't do this.'

'Don't you want me, William? What's the matter? Am I not bonny enough?' She swallows away tears. In her heart she expected rejection, but when it comes it's a bitter blow.

He shakes his head and puts his face in his hands. 'Oh, Maggie, give me strength. I have never desired a woman more and you are beautiful. But I can't do this – you can hardly stand up, woman. You're drunk. You will not even remember in the morning.'

She shivers and bites her lip. He's loosened her stays when she'd jumped on him, causing her breasts to spill out of her dress.

'Give me strength, will you cover yourself, Maggie.' He takes off his woollen jacket and places it around her shoulders.

'I'm not drunk,' she slurs. 'And since when have you been chaste? Can't you take me somewhere, just you and me?'

'No. I bid you a goodnight, Maggie. Let's forget this ever happened.'

And just like that he's gone.

★★★

Weeks turn into months and all the while he avoids her. Not knowing how to return the woollen jacket without raising suspicion, she keeps it like a prized possession, her very own piece of William. And then a strange thing happens. All her life, since she was wee girl, she's looked at men – young men, mature men, they've all turned her head. Yet now she ceases to look at the opposite sex. From that day forward, Maggie sees only one man – William Bell. And she cannot see past him.

***

At the end of May, a function's planned and with it the inevitable hard work that is necessary to prepare for such an event. The occasion is a much needed distraction for Maggie, and so she throws herself into her chores with much vigour. When the day comes, early in the morning, Isobel takes Maggie aside and explains the initiation rites for apprentice to journeyman; and from the look of her she doesn't seem to look forward to the event.

'I abhor initiations, Maggie, but they are good for business mind, so I can't turn them down. You mark my word; they'll make a right racket and be a right rowdy lot.'

'Surely not as noisy as a wake?' Maggie asks.

'Aye, Maggie, I'm afraid so. Plenty of sweaty men wanting to eat and drink, smoke baccy or take snuff. Let's be ready for them, shall we?'

Helen scowls, eyes darting left and right about the whole room. 'Is Margaret shirking again?'

Isobel snaps at Helen. 'Nae, what makes you think that? She's outside. Go and fetch her, will you?'

Helen shakes her head. 'I'm wanted in the scullery. Send Maggie.'

It's warm outside and so Maggie removes her plaid. The summer breeze caresses her skin and whips her hair up. For a while she just stands there, taking in the swaying trees and rustling leaves before looking for Margaret. Near the coop, Maggie bumps into William. 'Morning.' Maggie feels her cheeks grow hot.

William tips his hat.

'Have you seen your sister?'

'I haven't seen her. If she's not in bed she'll be with the chickens. Look inside the coop.'

Sure enough Margaret's in the chicken coop, talking to the birds as if they were her own children.

'Come on, Margaret. You're wanted. Your mother needs your help.'

★★★

Timing is everything when it concerns a festivity. Since the crack of dawn, Cook has been busy preparing food, and the result of her laborious exertions produces a mouth-watering smell that wafts throughout the inn and beyond. Maggie sweeps and cleans, and whilst she does she sings an old Scottish ballad about three sisters in a forest – a song her mother used to sing to her as a child.

'What are the oil and wood shavings for?' she asks Margaret.

Margaret shrugs. 'No idea.'

The apprentice men flock in around noon, and it does not take long for the banter, joking and ridicule to begin. In the course of the revelry, Maggie watches the master cooper place a coarse hand on his young apprentice, raise his tankard and make a toast.

'Here's to wealth, health and happiness. You now have the full protection of the Cooper's Guild. Oh, and give me back that hammer I loaned you,' he laughs, punching his young protégé in the arm.

The men raise their tankards and cheer and shout. Next they grab the young apprentice and strip him naked. Maggie averts her eyes, thinking there's more meat on Margaret's scrawny chickens.

'Come here, beautiful,' shouts the nude apprentice from the other side of the room. 'It's not every day you see such a fine body as this.'

Maggie ignores him and continues with her work, clearing the tables and fetching more ale. And all the while the young men become rowdier, shouting and grabbing the nude man, smearing him with oil and wood shavings, before placing him in a barrel. And as if that's not enough, to further humiliate him they douse him with beer and roll him all around the room.

'Did you get a good eyeful then?'

'Good eyeful at what?' Maggie feels the weight of William Bell's stare.

'The naked lad. You were making eyes at him.'

'I was not making eyes at him. And I don't know about lad. He looked all man to me,' she utters, deliberately provoking him.

Quick as lightening, William seizes her, wrapping his hand tight around her wrist, pulling her to him. She has to tiptoe to look into his eyes. 'Don't push me, Maggie.'

Maggie rubs her tender skin as he storms away. The coopers' shouting and laughing rings in her ears as she runs from the room. How dare he hurt her like that. She has a mind to speak to him and chastise him for his conduct. It takes an age to find him, but when she does, she's surprised to find him in the cellar, pounding on the door. She places a tentative hand on him and meets his hot gaze. And for the longest while they stand facing each other, as though reading each other's wicked thoughts.

An explosion of stars burst beneath her eyelids as William pushes his body violently against her. Maggie bangs her head against the cellar door, and her knees buckle beneath her. Just before she hits the floor, a long limb pushes between her legs to prop her up against the door. Maggie throws her head backwards, almost biting her tongue… she's scared and yet excited at his savage onslaught. With firm hands, he stretches her arms apart so that she's pinioned against the door.

'I warned you, but you would not listen to me.'

As William's lips graze her ear, his groans drive her insane. His need is great and there's urgency to his passion as he tears at her clothes. The sound of spent desire echoes in her ears as he claws off her stays and bites her shoulders, breasts and neck. Beneath her many petticoats, his hands caress and slide, exploring her, inside and out. His tongue finds her own as his fingers dig into her round buttocks to lift her feet from the ground. Maggie wraps her warm thighs around his waist; he adjusts his underclothes and allows his large manhood to spring hot against her thighs. Maggie groans with delight. She's never wanted a man like this in her whole life. She almost screams and begs for him to take her there and then, but there is no need; his desperation surpasses even her own. Without warning, William pushes between Maggie's thighs. He's not gentle, and his want is so fierce he enters her quickly and with a force that startles her. His manhood's huge, and with every thrust she feels a stabbing pain, crying out so loud, he places a hand across her face to muffle her cries. The ache that sears through her stomach is unbearable, but as his thrusts became slower and not as deep, she finds herself pushing against him with her own desire.

'Do you want more?' he teases and stops moving inside her. 'Beg me. You love it don't you, you little witch. I'm going to give it to you hard.'

'I beg you,' she sobs over and over.

Still inside her, he carries her into the cellar and lowers her to the floor. He plunges deeper and deeper. A shiver runs through her as he presses his mouth to her ear and groans out loud.

'You can't get enough of me, can you? You want me to push harder, don't you, witch? Don't you?' His hand covers her mouth again as he forces himself deep inside her, and just when she thinks it will never end, his hot seed spills inside her.

'Holy Mother of God,' she cries, and sinks her fingernails into William's back.

When at last their ecstasies are over, Maggie places a hand over her stomach and winces. Her insides feel like they've been torn apart, but her lips curl upwards with blissful joy. William turns on his side to face her; he traces a thumb over her swollen lips, provoking in Maggie a passionate longing for him to take her again.

'Look at me,' he demands, cradling her face in his hands. His fair hair is ruffled and dishevelled; his scent is of sex. She cannot shake the feeling that she's been here with him before, like she's known him all her life. He moves closer to kiss her and then rests his golden head between the peaks of her breasts.

'We have to go,' his hot breath tickles her skin. 'Before I want you again, and you're such a noisy one, Maggie. We'll be heard for sure.'

'Why?'

'Why? Because if I stay here with you, you little witch, this will never go down.' William points to his swollen manhood. 'Damn, it's so hard, it's smarting. Get dressed. We've been fortunate so far. No one's heard us. Now let's part, lass – while all is well.'

Maggie closes her eyes. She can't bear to watch him dress and then just walk away as though nothing has passed between them. So in a state of anxiety she says: 'If I'm quiet, can we do it again?'

He laughs and throws her clothes at her. 'Most lassies are too sore for another bout. You're a randy one, Maggie. Get dressed.' He ascends the steps.

'William,' she calls to him, trying to mask the desperation in her voice.

'What?' he stops midway up the cellar steps.

'Don't go. When will I see you again?'

'I've had my fill of you, Maggie – and from the look of you, you've got more than you bargained for.'

Maggie's mouth twists, her voice is harsh and angry. 'Damn you, William. Damn you to hell.'

★★★

The month of May passes quickly. When June arrives there is fine weather and summer flowers. Along with the village girls, Maggie holds a banquet to lay up the Johnmas flowers. As is the tradition, the village lassies search the countryside for the ribwort plant, collecting two flowers, one bigger than the other (these are supposed to represent the girl and her sweetheart) before removing the florets and rolling them into a dock leaf to be buried in the ground. The following morning, if the florets reappear on any one of them, it's a sign of happiness.

The following day, Maggie rises early to dig up her Johnmas flowers. Fingers clawing at the soft earth to retrieve her pale flowers, but to her dismay they have no florets, and so she throws them to the ground and stomps all over them, cursing out loud.

★★★

Nearly a year has passed since Maggie dropped her children at the widows, along with the pig and the goat. To her mind it feels like much longer. Maggie wrings her hands and shudders inside, it no longer matters how much time's passed. Since that day in the cellar, Maggie's in a state of distress, miserable and wretched in love. *We should be bed fellows by now,* she thinks, *so why doesn't he come to me?*

'You are slow in seeking me out – come to me,' she whispers into the night.

★★★

Adam needs new tallow candles and torches but he can't find them anywhere. The rush lights are useless. They burn for a mere ten to fifteen minutes, and to make matters worse if they're not placed at the right angle they burn for even less.

'Maggie,' Adam calls to her. 'I want you to go to the chandlers and the tailor's shop on a few errands.'

Maggie shakes her head. 'Can't Helen do it? I'm busy.'

'And what the hell are you doing? It's quiet.'

'I told Margaret I'd clean out the chicken coop.'

'She can do it herself, the lazy mare.'

Adam's eyes are swollen and bloodshot. He's not slept a wink of sleep and his head's aching all over. He frowns and peers into Maggie's face, taking her chin in his hands and turning it left and then right. Next, he takes his neck chief and spits onto one corner of the fabric before furiously wiping her face. 'Is that rouge?'

'Rouge?'

'You know the stuff whores wear. Red paint.'

'No, my cheeks are hot. I'm not feeling well.'

192

'Have you a fever?'

'Nae.'

'Well, a bit of fresh air will do you good.' Adam rummages beneath the bar, tossing objects into the air and creating a right mess. 'Where is my money? I know I put it here somewhere. Hah!' He hands her a few coins.

'What's this for?'

'Buy some candles and torches from the chandlers, we are all out.'

She nods curtly. 'I thought you wanted me to go to the tailor's?'

'Did I?'

'Aye.'

'Well in that case I am glad you reminded me. It completely slipped my mind. I need you to tell William that I need his help. It's me back, see. I hurt it the other day.'

'I'll tell him.'

★★★

Maggie peers into the reflection of the milky glass window, adjusting her hair. A face stares out at her, the face of an older woman. She hardly recognises herself. Maggie wonders if she's still bonny as she stares at her thick lashes. There are fine creases at the corners of her eyes, laughter lines her father calls them. She turns from the window and takes a deep breath.

The shop consists of one long narrow room, and there's a smaller room at the rear. A large wooden table dominates the floor; an assortment of fabric is scattered upon it, surrounded by scissors, ribbons and pins. Except for herself and William, the shop is vacant; he sits cross-legged upon the floor mending a shirt. For a while she observes him with needle and thread, intent in his work, the outline of his spine visible through his leine as he bends over.

'William, it is I, Maggie.'

'What brings you here?' His manner is distracted.

'Your father sent me. He needs help shifting barrels. It's his back; I think he's hurt it. He's getting older, you know…'

William throws down the shirt, tugging furiously at his apron. 'Don't you think I know that, Maggie? He knows that I'm busy, aren't we all? I'm working flat out here and there is just the two of us. But still he persists in badgering me to do one job after the other. Can't he ask Patrick Murray of Cherry Trees?'

Maggie pulls her plaid around her; she looks nervously at her shoes. 'I'm sorry. I'm sure he can manage without you.'

'Aw – tell him I'll be round later.' He picks up his scissors and sets to work.

'I'll be off then.'

Suddenly William's on his feet, his scissors and material dropping to the floor behind him. Maggie's heart leaps, but there's awkwardness between them, and for the longest time they just stand there at a loss for what to say.

'About that day, Maggie. What can I say?'

'Nothing.' Maggie's head sags. She can no longer conceal her irritation, disappointment and frustration. 'I expect nothing from you.'

'Likewise. Perhaps you should run back to your husband. I'm sure he's more a man than I.'

'You are cruel. I've told you how I feel – but you continue to insult me.'

William leans towards her, his hand cupping her face. 'You have no idea how I feel. I curse you, woman. I've not slept a wink from the time when… you know, or been with any other lasses since. I don't want to feel this way about you, Maggie, but I just can't stop thinking of you. I want you out of my mind; you're a damn affliction.'

William's hands are hurting her now; his fingers scraping against her cheeks. But Maggie's oblivious to the pain. 'I'll never stop wanting you, William.'

'No,' he shakes his head.

'Why must you treat me this way?' Maggie beats him with her hands. 'Why not give us a chance? I love you.'

'Because I am you – can't you see that? I am you. You and I are one and the same. We're utterly selfish, the pair of us, unwilling to sacrifice our desires for the sake of another – it would never work.'

'It would, it would,' Maggie sobs. 'I'd sacrifice everything for you. Haven't I already? I've left my children, my husband...'

'The reason you left has nothing to do with me, Maggie. Now I've said my piece. You must forget about this now and...'

'Please, William, you're breaking my heart,' she pleads, her hands sagging to her side.

'No.'

Maggie turns and faces the window. She closes her eyes and thinks back to the first time she saw him in the tavern, staring into his beguiling blue eyes. But it's no use her trying to persuade him; she knows he's made up his mind.

'Very well,' she mumbles, a thousand miseries in her damp eyes.

He nods and folds his arms across his body. 'Tis wise to be prudent, Maggie – you don't want to end up on the cutty stool, do you?'

'Course not. But that's not the reason you won't see me again, is it? It's because I mean nothing to you.'

Her heart thumps as Williams's hands caress her face and neck; his fingers linger at the base of her throat before he pulls away. 'I haven't any time for this nonsense, Maggie. Accept it's over. It never really began.'

'You're an animal,' she steps backwards, edging towards the door. 'You've used me just like you have other lasses. You treat all women the same.'

William strides past her, blocking the exit. 'I gave you what you wanted. You practically begged me, woman.'

Her eyes are sad, like the dark pools of a peat bog. She's no fight left in her and there's a sickening feeling in her muscles and bones. 'I must go. I don't want to quarrel.'

William's eyes soften; he fumbles for a moment with his jacket, unclipping a small pin from the cloth. 'Take this – go on, take it as a token of my affection.'

Maggie stares at the silver brooch; it feels cold in her palm. 'What is it?'

'A luckenbooth. This was pinned to my shawl when I was a wee bairn. I want you to have it.'

She lifts her eyes from the brooch, lifting her head in hope. 'So you'll see me again?'

'No,' he groans.

A look of disgust crosses Maggie's face. 'Well I curse the day I met you, William Bell. I will plague your thoughts now and forever and never forget it.' She runs from the shop, tears rolling down her face.

She leans against the tailor's door. A mother bird feeds her chicks on a rooftop, their high pitched cries soaring over faded grey tiles. Nearby, a wood pigeon competes with the racket, puffing its breast in and out, adding to the din. Maggie sighs and takes a deep breath – she has to go back in, but her throat's so tight she feels sure to choke. She pushes open the door.

'Now Maggie…'

'Shush,' she stands on her tip-toes and places a finger to his lips. And then she walks to his work bench, reaches for his cutting scissors and snips off a lock of her hair. 'Here,' she says, 'a fairing to add to your other conquests.'

William shrugs and ties the lock of hair with a scrap of scarlet material, and then places it inside a leather pouch. 'Tell Father I'll come by at dusk. Goodbye, Maggie.'

She swallows a lump from her throat. 'I love you, William. I knew it the moment I first saw you.'

Every step she takes towards the door, she yearns for him to reciprocate her love, but he remains rooted to the spot and says nothing.

CHAPTER THIRTEEN

MAGGIE CONCEALS HER SHAME

The sour girl Helen is a nightmare to work with. No matter what Maggie does, Helen will not smile or be civil. It's as though a strange entity had climbed within Helen's body and sucked all the goodness out of her. *Evil, that's what she is*, decides Maggie. *The lass thrives on misery and maliciousness.*

'Get out of my way,' Helen pushes past her.

'I'm not in your way, you feckless idiot.' Maggie ignores her, having had quite enough.

'I'll go to the Master and tell him you've been cavorting with his son,' she hisses.

'What's there to tell,' says Maggie. 'He's not set foot in this inn for days.'

★★★

Isobel glances at the two lasses from across the room, shaking her head as she runs a smooth cloth over the bar. There's trouble brewing, of that she's sure. She only has to look on the faces of the lassies to see that. Helen in particular looks ready to roll up her fists and do battle, and so she tugs on her husband's sleeve.

'Adam. Will you look at those two? There's going to be trouble, I'm warning you now.'

'I'll not get involved in women's quarrels, so leave me be, Isobel. They're just having an argument; you know what lasses are like. They're not happy unless they're quarrelling like cats.'

'I disagree. Maggie's a placid girl. It's our Betty's girl, Helen, that's the trouble...'

197

'I know, I know, but she's kin, so my hands are tied.' He scratches his beard and places a hand on his wife's shoulder. 'Helen's an awkward girl no doubt, but she's got the stamina of a carthorse, and besides – if we interfere we'll probably just make it worse.'

Then, to Isobel's surprise, her husband stops talking and squints ahead, his whole concentration suddenly focused on the two girls.

'Did you hear that?'

'Nae,' says Isobel. 'What did they say?'

'Be quiet, woman. I just heard them mention William's name. Let me listen to what they say.'

★★★

The two women stand toe to toe, finger pointing and prodding one another. For every step Maggie takes backwards, Helen inches forward, spewing her venomous bile. With her fists clenched by her side, Maggie stands her ground.

'Leave me be, Helen. You're just jealous.'

'Hah! Jealous of you? You're nothing but a whore. You should go back to where you came from and find that illusive husband of yours. If you've still got one, that is!' Helen sniggers.

'I'll go when I'm good and ready. And I stand by my word, you are jealous. You're sweet on the Master's son, but he's no interest in you whatsoever.'

'And I suppose you think he likes you? He's diddled every lassie in this tavern, except his mother, and it wouldn't surprise me if he's been there as well.'

★★★

Adam and Isobel overhear the whole conversation.

'Helen. Come here, at once,' Adam bellows.

'She made me to say it – she's caused nothing but trouble since the…' cries Helen.

'Pack your things and get out.'

'But…'

'Out!' Adam shouts, his eyes flashing with anger.

Maggie has no pity for the lass. After all is said and done, Helen has no one to blame but herself. To be honest, she can't wait to see the back of her. For the sake of Adam and Isobel, though, Maggie tries to muster up some understanding and compassion.

'I am so sorry. I didn't mean to badger her. No matter what I did she wouldn't take to me. That must have been hard for you, her being kin and all.'

'It's all right, lass,' Adam says handing her a glass. 'Just get that down you. Let's drink to happier times now that she's gone. Good riddance.'

'Happier times,' Isobel raises her glass.

Maggie joins in with the toast. 'Who will do her work?'

'You and Margaret can take on her chores between you, just until we can hire another girl.'

Maggie forces a smile. Her stomach churns at the prospect of extra work, not because she's afraid of hard work, mind. No, life as a fisher lassie has put her in good stead in terms of hard labour. But extra labour means more time in the tavern, mixing with all kinds of folk, be it baker, flesher or worse still – the prying eyes of old and wise women who might guess her predicament. It's no use to pretend; in her heart she knows. Maggie's carrying the child of William Bell.

★★★

The months pass slowly and to conceal her shame, Maggie develops a routine. In the morning, if she feels nauseous, she disguises her retching as a coughing fit. Once Margaret has left the room, she crawls out of bed and dresses in haste. The child grows quickly, stretching out her stomach like a man with a large ale belly, and when it kicks her beneath her ribs, Maggie grimaces in pain.

At first it's easy to pretend it's not happening, but as Maggie's belly grows, so does her fear. And that fear lives with her every single day. She shudders and wraps her arms around herself – the horror of being discovered and the inevitable consequences is something she dare not contemplate. With her own eyes she's witnessed an adulteress's shame, and to be sure she does not wish to endure that.

★★★

Adam Bell senses trouble, and he can't comprehend what irks him so. Of late an atmosphere exudes within the tavern, especially last thing at night, once they congregate near the fire. Awkward silence, stilted conversation, forced smiles – Adam feels sure it has something to do with Maggie, and so he contrives to send her on her way.

As fortune has it, Adam's elder brother needs help in his inn in Berwick. A month or so ago, Adam's brother's wife became ill, and so he's desperate for an extra pair of hands. Adam rubs his hands together with glee, he can think of just the person to send to him.

'I'll go,' Isobel declares with bright eyes.

'You will not,' Adam elbows her in her arm. 'Your place is here with me. Maggie will go. I am sure she will go if I ask her. It will do her good; a step closer to Newcastle and her husband, as far as I'm concerned. Haven't you noticed the way she looks at William, or the way he looks at her for that matter? I'm sure there's something between them, I can feel it in me bones.'

'Nonsense.'

'Anyway, I've made up my mind. I'm sending Maggie; hopefully it will be the last we see of her. The new girl can take up her workload.'

★★★

Therefore, the following day, Maggie finds herself bound southward for Berwick, in a rickety old cart. The blue-grey sky is scattered with birds, their wings spread out to a dying sun. The driver's a quiet fellow with a rough and sullen face, and for the duration of the journey, he offers little in the way of conversation. For the most part of the trip, Maggie stares ahead to take in the rough moorland. Trees are sparse and the ground is bleak and deserted, devoid of houses and people. The further they go, the fiercer the weather becomes. An incessant wind blows, and with the wind comes the rain. Maggie takes in the bleakness and she wonders how anything can survive this wild terrain.

'Are you sure this is the right tavern?' Maggie taps the driver on his shoulder.

'It's a wild and rough terrain, lassie. Not suitable for the likes of you if you ask me, but here we are.' He stops the cart and jumps out.

Out of the mucky cart Maggie steps, near twisting her ankle as she hits the stony ground. The driver catches her arm and she thanks him, and to her surprise he smiles and tips his hat.

'There's a door ahead. I'll be off now, wishing you good fortune.' He glances nervously at the door before climbing into his seat. In a flash he's away, whipping his horse into a frenzy so that it gallops off. For a while she watches him, disappearing into the horizon, like an apparition, and when she turns around she has the most beautiful coastal view.

But the sea will have to wait. Maggie stops near a huge oak door, her bag at her feet. She hears a great deal of noises from behind it, like rusty bolts and metal scraping. The door creaks open, and out of it comes a man, the spitting image of Adam Bell, although older and fatter.

'Who is it?' he enquires in a gruff voice.

'Maggie Dickson, sir. Your brother, Adam, sent me.'

'Ah – so it is you, the lassie from Adam's inn. How is my brother?'

'Good,' she replies.

'I bid you welcome to Cross Key Inn. My name is Joseph, Joseph Bell. Come in, rest your feet.' Joseph takes her hand and squeezes hard. His hand is warm.

'Can I take a moment? It's a while since I've been near the coast and I've missed it so.' Maggie turns towards the glorious view of the sapphire sea.

'Aye, I'll be just inside.'

Maggie inhales the salt sea air, closing her eyes so that the smells and sounds become heightened. Her senses sharpen; she can hear gulls and a roaring sea crashing against rocks. There is a freedom here that's part of the air and sea; and so she's compelled to stumble away down the rocks, with the call of a thundering sea in her ears. Near the foaming surf, Maggie rips the cap from her head, so that her dark hair falls wild upon her face… and for the first time in a long while, Maggie feels at peace.

★★★

'You took your time,' Joseph smiles and takes her arm. He guides her to a small room littered with old tubs, crates and hogsheads. A hideous looking man works in the corner, shifting sand-covered crates, and his figure casts a monstrous shadow on the lime-washed wall. For just a moment, a candle illuminates his face, and Maggie peers at him with a surprised expression, her countenance turning grave. He has the perfect shape of 'S' burned into his forehead.

'The S is for slave. He's a runaway collier serf. The first time he ran, they set to work with the branding irons, once they caught him that is. But those bastards won't catch him again, he's with us now. Does he scare you, lass?'

Maggie shakes her head. 'Nae, not at all.'

'Good, good,' he smiles. 'Can you brew ale and cook? The wife's ill and, well, we're behind with stock. I might be able to find another pair of hands to assist you if it's too much to ask'

Maggie's brows knit together. The prospect of working with another woman who might guess her condition she likes not. 'No need. I am sure that I can cope alone. I mightn't be the best cook, I warn you, but I can brew some fine ale. Where is your cauldron?'

The look of relief on his face is plain to see. *Good*, she thinks. *Now that he's satisfied that I can manage the workload alone, I am safe.* From the corner of her eye, Maggie glances at the collier serf again. He drinks from a horn beaker and the sight of him swigging back his drink makes her mouth water.

'Listen to me clacking on like an old hen. I'll show you the brewing vessel later – once you've had a bite to eat and something to drink.'

Joseph leads her to a large room thick with peat smoke. A table stands in the middle, and there is a loaf and a jug of water sat upon it. He gestures for Maggie to sit herself down and takes a chair from across the room, dragging the chair legs all the way with a piercing shrill. Joseph's large belly disturbs the table as he sits beside her. With a blunt knife, he scrapes mould from a hunk of bread, and then cuts it into thin slices, before cramming a few into his own mouth. With a flick of his wrist he throws a few slices at her.

'Drink up,' he says, passing her a cup. 'We'll soon have much to do.'

★★★

They stand inside a storage room; Maggie and Joseph, near a window, watching the customers arrive. In they come, like a flock of drenched rats, mangy and flea-bitten and covered in sores. Whole hoards of them arrive; dirty thieves, beggars, and gipsy sorners, puffing on their clay pipes and staring warily around them. Even from in here, she can smell the reek of sweat and tobacco. The rowdiest of them congregate near a half open door. At first Maggie assumes they're all drunk; what with the incessant singing, shouting and swearing. But on closer observation, she realises that they are quite sober. After a while, on further observation, Maggie assumes that they are on guard of something, standing rigid like sentries at the door, hair ruffled from wind.

'Who's serving the ale?' she asks.

'The collier you met earlier. Just till we go in, then no doubt he will join them. Are you ready to go in and face that ungodly rabble?'

'Aye – but before we do, why do they keep going outside?' she asks Joseph.

'Checking the weather, no doubt.'

'Why?'

'You ask too many questions, wench. Your curiosity will not be met well here.'

Joseph claps his hands together. 'Right, let's go in then. Once you get behind this bar, stay behind it. Take heed, because I say this for your own good. Don't mix amongst the men; I will take them their ale – all you need do is pour it.'

The bar is made up of beams salvaged from shipwrecks, so Joseph says. In a rare moment of quiet, Maggie presses her face against a weather-beaten window,and can just make out the shape of a tiny ship on the blue horizon, its sails a washed-out white.

'Maggie!' shouts Joseph, no doubt for more beer.

She turns her attention from the window and pours more ale. He takes it through to a group of men passing and trading contraband; brandy, tea, tobacco and wine, most of it covered in seaweed and sand. And all of a sudden she notices the pistols. Near every one of the men carries one in their belts and the air is suddenly charged with menace, causing a shiver to run up her spine.

Just after midnight, Maggie's directed to a second floor. The quarters are mildewed and damp, and upon the dirt floor are empty barrels covered in grime. At the farthest corner is a huge bay window, and beneath it a bed of dirty straw. And so, as Maggie yawns and lays her plaid upon it, she hopes she's not to stay here long. It takes an age to fall to sleep, for the inn is still alive with the sound of activity and noise. But soon, as her breathing becomes shallow, she is able to dream of distant lands – and of William. In the wee hours a scraping sound echoes from outside, like chains and strange metal objects being dragged about. *What now?* she wonders, pushing upwards to peek through the lattice window. A single lantern illuminates below, and a group of men follow behind, carrying ropes, lanterns and axes, their shiny pistols glinting in the dim light.

In hindsight, it's a rather romantic image of them Maggie has that first night, because with time she will discover what a vile breed of men they are, these brutes – holding men, women and children down in the water, or killing them with rocks. In time she will discover how they smash up wrecked ships with pickaxes and shovels, to relieve them of goods, while dead bodies float all around them, belly-up, teeth broken, seaweed in their hair.

Like most peasant folk, she turns a blind eye. Maggie sees nothing and watches the wall. There is a code of principles here that's easily learned, so Maggie does not see the tubmen carrying off their spirits in half ankers, or the batsmen defending contraband when smugglers make a landing. And of course she's not aware of the barrels with false bottoms and the customs men and riding officers constantly snooping around. Maggie's not a fool and she's not about to betray a confidence, especially since they've been so kind.

'I need extra transport for a shipment tonight,' moans Joseph one day. 'The tubmen have toiled too long and are weary, so I must labour alone.'

'Use old Ned's horses up yonder,' Maggie says crossing her arms.

'Nae, he won't – not even if I set all his hay-ricks on fire.'

The air crackles with tension as Joseph stomps about. To Maggie's relief he soon finds a man for the job. All it takes is a meaningful wink to a nearby farmer, who leaves his stable doors unlocked that night. In the morning, Joseph returns the horses to the farmer's stalls, muddy and exhausted – and a keg of best brandy in the corn bin.

★★★

One morning, as a hint of dawn seeps through the wooden lattice of her window, Joseph storms into Maggie's room. And for the longest time, all Maggie can feel is her own racing heart and the trembling of her body. With terror in her eyes, she realises that from where he stands, he might see her bulging stomach. She clenches the mattress with both hands and sits up, hoping with a sinking heart that he has not guessed her secret.

'No need to get up, lassie. I just came in here to tell you you're not needed anymore. My wife, you see, she's much better. I owe you my gratitude,' Joseph says.

Maggie stares up at him with sleep-filled eyes. 'What for?'

'For coming so promptly to Cross Key Inn. We're a rough lot but you rolled your sleeves up and worked hard, never complained once. Hah! You've even helped us hide our smuggled goods in the caves. Have you enjoyed your stay?'

'Aye, I learnt a great deal.'

'Did you now?' he laughs, and throws his head back. 'I've a soft spot for you, Maggie. I think we understand one another. You've got a wild spirit, but more importantly I think you're a lassie I can trust.' He waits for her reply.

'You've my trust and my loyalty, Joseph. Now leave me in peace to get dressed.'

Joseph heads for the door, but before he gets there he turns and says: 'I'll sell this tavern in a few years, Maggie. It's yours if you want it, for a fair price. You've got guts in you – I can see that. What do you think?'

Maggie looks at him, wondering how on earth she could afford to buy an inn. 'You own the inn and don't lease it?'

Joseph nods. 'Aye, lassie. You've seen the business I do here, it brings in more than enough to live comfortably. Almost all the inns round here finance smuggling, because we're able to sell contraband straight across the bar. Think it over.'

Maggie smiles and wraps her plaid around her. 'I'm afraid I'm in no position to accept your offer, Joseph. There's the money and my husband and…'

'That might change in a few years, wait and see.'

She wonders at that. Later on, as the carter cracks his whip and she's on the way, Maggie suddenly realises that she's at liberty to go where she wants. She calls out to the carter. 'How long would it take to get to Newcastle from here?'

'At least two hours,' he says in a gruff voice.

'No matter.' She nods, and her thoughts suddenly return to the father of her unborn child.

★★★

When summer arrives, a peace settles over Kelso. Birds sing, drowsy bumblebees hum in the hot air, and butterflies flutter and dance through the trees. Near the water's edge, vibrant flowers spread their petals to a hot sun. By the river, Maggie feels safe enough to remove her plaid, her hair blows in the soft summer breeze, and little David sits by her side, dangling his bare-feet into the cool water.

The boy points to a large ripple in the water. 'Did you see, Maggie? That must have been a big fishy swimming there beneath the surface. It was as big as a cow.'

'Don't be daft, laddie.' She shakes her head. 'It was probably a salmon or trout and none of them are big as cows,' she smiles and chuckles to herself. For a while they just sit there, side by side, comfortable in each other's presence. Deep within the green foliage of riverside, Maggie's attention is drawn to the marsh. Her eyes follow its course until the figure of a man protrudes from the rushes like a strange freakish plant. With shaky hands she gathers her plaid around her. 'Come on, laddie. It's time to go.'

'Why must we go, Maggie?' David whines.

'We just do,' she says staring at the strange man.

★★★

On the Sabbath, at kirk, Maggie stands in her usual position, behind the Bell family, alongside maidservants and rosy-faced dairymaids. As the sermon drags on she sneaks a glance at William, but his gaze is fixed firmly ahead. Since her return from Berwick he's visited the inn twice, and on both occasions he's helped his father and promptly returned to the tailor's.

With each passing day, it's becoming harder to conceal her shame. Before long, the four walls of the inn became an insufferable prison, hemming her in and pressing down upon her oppressive thoughts. That night, as Maggie lies on her box-bed, her bulging stomach clear of Margaret's feet, she dares to dream of the living creature that lives in her belly and of his father, who will never hear the cry of his first born child.

★★★

On Monday morning, Maggie and Margaret carry peat from Pelstone Crag. On Tuesday they take dirty linen to the river to be laundered and on Wednesday they sell eggs and chickens in the market square. The market buzzes with activity, hawkers and buyers bartering for fresh goods, it is familiar territory, and not something Maggie's keen to return to. A quantity of pigs and goats roam free causing havoc and a scold's ducked in a local pond.

All her life, Margaret Bell has lived in Maxwellheugh. She knows and loves this area well. From the corner of her eye, she observes Maggie with wary eyes, she's definitely stouter – and as Maggie bends backwards to relieve her sore back, her plaid gapes open to reveal a slight swelling in her stomach. Hence, Margaret Bell's suspicions are roused but not confirmed. With a sense of doom, Margaret walks beside Maggie, her thoughts of condemnation and shame; she shudders and gazes into a leaden sky. Heaven above, if her fears are realised, Maggie's in for a miserable time.

Flurries of clouds stretch out in the sky as they walk home. Margaret's silent and morose, her lips pursed together in a perpetual scowl. She wants to voice her concerns to the girl walking beside her, but she's at a loss for words, and when her mouth finally does open, the speech is clumsy and stilted and she's unable to articulate.

'I need to… what I'm trying to… Maggie, I hope…'

'For God's sake, Margaret – spit it out.'

'Have you something to tell me, Maggie? A secret perhaps?'

'No, why do you ask?'

'Are you with child?'

'No, no, I am not,' Maggie walks faster, shaking her head.

Margaret grunts. 'Oh my dear God, I knew this would happen. It is William's child, isn't it? My poor mother, she'll be mortified if she finds out. It's happened before, not long before you arrived here. The girl who ran away, we never heard from her again.'

'I'm not. Please believe me, Margaret,' Maggie pleads.

Margaret Bell bites her lip. 'You know what to do, Maggie. Do you understand my meaning? You *know* what to do. You're a married woman estranged from her husband.'

An almighty shudder passes through Maggie's body, a tortured expression contorts her pale face and tears roll down her cheeks. 'But...'

'Hush. I won't tell a soul; this is between you and I, Maggie. And it will stay that way as long as you do as I say. Now wait here, I won't be a moment.'

★★★

But Maggie does not wait, because suddenly she's overcome with a strange desire, and before she knows it she's sprinting through the air, arms pumping up and down. The wind whips up her hair, and with it goes her cap, and on and on she runs as though her life depends on it, until there's no breath left in her lungs. At the end of the wynd she stops and bends double, gulping like a fish out of water. But still she pushes on until she stands beside a heather brae. A sense of dread fills Maggie's heart as the wise woman opens her door.

'I've no herbs left,' she mumbles. 'But I've got this.' She hands Maggie a clout of dead worms and a rusty nail.

And thus, in her desperation, Maggie follows her inside.

CHAPTER FOURTEEN

ON THE BANKS OF THE TWEED

When it began the morning light was just peeking through slate grey clouds, a crow was cawing from the top of the chicken coop, and the sounds of Isobel and William quarrelling echoed from below. With both hands Maggie pushes herself from the mattress and takes care not to disturb Margaret as she rolls out of the box-bed.

In haste, Maggie pulls on her clothes, her face contorting as a tightening ache surrounds her stomach. She recognises the cramps in her stomach immediately. They come in waves, starting in the lower back and tightening like a belt around the belly. With a sickening heart, she knows these contractions will come closer and closer together – until, well she daren't think about it. Nevertheless, for the moment she's able to cope with the pain.

The sound of Margaret's soft snoring suddenly vexes her. In a short while, Maggie might need the room to herself, of that she's sure. *Why is Margaret always so indolent*, she wonders. Thus, Maggie reaches into the box-bed and places a hand on the sleeping girl.

'Wake up, Margaret.'

Margaret opens one eye. 'All right, all right, just a moment more.'

'No, you must get up now, Margaret. Your mother just called you downstairs. I'll go down and tell her you're coming, so hurry,' Maggie lies.

Once downstairs, Maggie enters the scullery. Cook is busy and doesn't give her a second glance. Therefore, Maggie is free to do her work, without fear of folk seeing her pain or guessing her predicament. But in less than an hour, Maggie's in a state of panic, staggering around with wild, terrified eyes. In no time at all, she has no alternative but to get to the attic room, away from prying eyes.

In a daze Maggie flees the room, her face flushed and covered in sweat, at the end of the corridor she bumps into Isobel.

'Oh, lass, what ails you? You're burning up.' Isobel feels Maggie's forehead with the reverse of her hand.

'Must be something I ate. I feel terrible, Isobel. May I be excused?'

'Aye, you must have caught a winter chill. Take yourself off to bed, lassie. It's best that you rest. I'll be along later with some water and a cloth for your forehead.'

'There's no need,' Maggie mutters.

'Nonsense. Now off you go.'

★★★

A cold sweat coats her forehead as she enters her room. Knees shaking and weak, she places a hand on the wall to steady herself, determined not to fall.

'This isn't happening; this isn't happening to me,' she says to herself. And then, before she has time to reach a basin, Maggie retches into her hands. Before long, the tightening pains are minutes apart, and are so unbearable, she falls to her knees. With her elbows resting on the box-bed she presses her face into the mattress and screws up her eyes. In desperation, Maggie wills the agony away, but the contractions keep coming, like the sea tide's inexorable waves. She sobs, she takes shallow breaths, and her fingernails dig into the mattress as another cramp passes. *Isobel*, she could walk in here any moment. In haste Maggie undresses and staggers to her bed in her sark.

A moment later the door creaks open.

'Here I am, Maggie. How are you feeling? Oh dear, you look awful. I'll leave you some water and check on you later.' Isobel fusses with her covers and feels Maggie's forehead again. 'You're hot as an oven, lass.'

'No. I'm fine. I just need to rest. There's no need for you or Margaret to check on me, really. I will be all right.'

Isobel pats her on the arm. 'Well, if you are sure, lass.'

Just go, please go, thinks Maggie, grimacing as Isobel strolls out of the room.

Maggie rises from the box-bed. Hands over head, she strips off her sark and places one hand over her swollen stomach. Suddenly there's an unbelievable pressure in her stomach, forcing its way down. Maggie drops to the floor again, crawling on hands and knees beneath the box-bed to drag out linen and clouts. She takes small linen squares and twists it into a spiral shape to stuff into her mouth, after that she shuffles backwards till her naked body blocks the door. Then, with her last ounce of strength she reaches up to turn the key in the lock.

Very slowly and with great effort she pushes herself off the door onto all fours. Her ears are ringing and a mist covers her eyes, as though she's immersed in murky water. Through the haze, Maggie bites down on her length of twisted linen and pushes her feet against the door for leverage and at that very moment a great quantity of water bursts from her body. And then everything goes black.

★★★

Something wriggles beneath her; Maggie won't look at it, because she doesn't want to acknowledge it. As she struggles to lift her cheek from the floor, strange gurgling noises come from beneath her. After a while, she can ignore it no more, so she pushes on her hands and sits straight. It is tiny and struggling for breath. Without hesitation she places a finger in its throat and nostrils, and then taps it on the back. It lets out a hearty wail – and to silence its cries, she places its mouth to her breast, but it won't suckle – it is too weak.

Maggie's numb. She feels nothing. Her eyes are cold as she pushes the child farther beneath the box-bed, and the very act allows her to detach herself from it. Not merely as a cover or a lie, but to deny the child its existence from the outset – in an act of self-preservation – and to remain near William.

★★★

'Ah – there you are, Maggie. Are you feeling better this morning? I was terribly worried about you lassie,' Isobel holds a tray of dirty tankards, no doubt from the night before.

'Aye, much better. What do you want me to do?'

'Do you feel well enough to fetch some water from the river, lass? I can't find Margaret anywhere.'

By the time Maggie returns from the river her napkin's soaked with blood and her thighs are chaffed. As she waddles and staggers to the tavern door, a high pitched voice calls out to her. It is young David. Her heart sinks – she hasn't the time or vigour to help him today. Maggie just about manages to carry the water pail to the door; she really needs to rush upstairs to change her soiled padding, and so she ignores David.

'Maggie! Maggie! Where have you been?' David runs into her arms, sulking as she pushes him away.

'You cannot stay, David. I'm too busy, lad. Run along now, that's a good boy.' Maggie doubles over, her teeth clench as she rests the pails to the ground.

'I'm hungry, Maggie. Have you got a pie for me?'

'Nae, come back tomorrow. I'll give you some bread.'

'Oh please, Maggie.'

'You're a little beggar, you are. Go round to the back door.'

His eyes are bright as she hobbles out of the door, practically slavering at the sight of the oatcake she holds out for him.

'God bless you, Maggie,' he says, with a mouth full of oatcake.

★★★

It's funny how when someone longs for something and craves for something so much, it never comes. And then, when they least expect it, or perhaps when they no longer want it, it lands at their feet, like an unwanted guest or a toy that has lost its appeal.

'Maggie? Maggie, can't you hear me?'

The voice is warm like honey and instantly recognisable, and yet at this moment in time, she hasn't the energy to acknowledge it. But alas, as the voice persists she turns wearily around to face him.

'William,' is all she can think to say.

William leans in close. 'You look awful.'

'And fat like a pig?'

'Now come on, Maggie, that was a long time ago and I was just tormenting you. Is everything all right? You don't look too...' his forehead creases with concern.

'I am very well, thank you.'

'Why were you ignoring me?'

Maggie opens her hands out wide. 'I wasn't ignoring you. I just couldn't hear you, and is that any wonder with this almighty din going on?'

'Look at me,' William demands.

'Why?'

He touches her hand, ever so gentle. 'You looked troubled. Has someone affronted you? Have I upset you?'

'No – everything is just grand.' She grits her teeth to block out the hurt.

His eyes flicker and dart in all directions. He looks confounded. 'I never thought I'd say this, but I feel wretched and I'm sorry. Can you forgive me?'

Maggie's eyes widen and her heart thumps. 'There's nothing to forgive.' She tries to move away but he grips her hand.

'I must see you later.'

'After all this time you want to see me? Now?'

'Aye.'

'Month after month I have waited to hear you say those words, William. But really, your timing couldn't be any worse.'

His eyes widen with surprise. 'So be it.'

★★★

That night, her usual nightmare is replaced with a wondrous dream. In the dream there's a beautiful baby boy with flaxen hair and blue eyes, and the tiniest nose. And they're a family, all three of them, and so happy. She holds out her child to his father, and

214

William lifts him from her arms, his mouth widening with a proud smile.

'What shall we call him?'

'What do you want to call him?'

'James,' Maggie claps her hands together. 'James – after my little brother.'

'James he shall be,' William declares in a proud voice.

And then she wakes and the real nightmare begins.

★★★

Hoarfrost covers the banks of the river. She walks briskly past Castle Floors and glances at the fabulous castellated parapets and pepper pot turrets, her pail swings side to side, banging against her legs. She slips in the ice, but Maggie doesn't feel a thing, she's completely numb.

A queer feeling descends upon Maggie as she reaches the Tweed. At the water's edge, the sight of the tumbling waters prove too much for her, and thus she's overcome with sorrow. Tears roll down her face as she retrieves the bundle from the pail. With a sob, Maggie places it within some tall reeds on the river bank, thinking it will be washed away.

★★★

On 9 December a fisherman baits his fishing line on the banks of the Tweed. He curses under his breath, his line's become snagged on a weed and so he pulls and tugs until finally a small bundle appears. And to his horror, it's a dead child, perfectly preserved, and on further inspection he's able to determine that it's male. The fisherman duly informs the magistrates and the local Justice of the Peace is quickly acquainted with the dead child. In a short amount of time, a midwife and several women who have borne children are quickly assembled and ordered to inspect it. All of them give their opinion that the child has been lately thrown in the river.

The body's then moved to the Gospel Kirk in Kelso under the supervision of Minister James Ramsay. Meanwhile, the Justice of the Peace calls upon his constables to go along with the midwives to make a diligent search through the town of Maxwellheugh for any women with the usual mark of one who has brought forth a child.

On a cold winter day, William Pringle, the present Baillie of Kelso is summoned to investigate the matter of the dead child found on the banks of the River Tweed. Pringle's an utterly diligent man and after a small amount of enquiry he's directed to the home of Easter Mosereys and his sister, Elizabeth, who quickly inform him that a stranger resides in Maxwellheugh. And that stranger is a young lassie, who goes by the name of Maggie Dickson. Interestingly, according to Easter, she works in the inn of Adam Bell and Isobel Lidgerwood and as coincidence has it, the River Tweed flows directly past their inn.

***

In winter, the scullery is by far the warmest room in the inn. Maggie sits with young David by the large hearth, the pair of them warming their hands and faces in the soft flow of flames. Cook pays no heed to them as she peels her turnips, and all the while she sings one of her Irish ballad songs.

'A coin for your thoughts, laddie? You're staring into the flames like you've seen a ghost.'

His eyes light up. 'I'm wishing you could be my mother, Maggie. You're kind – and you always help me carry my father his ale, and give me bread and apples and...'

Maggie laughs. And it feels as though she hasn't felt joyful or untroubled for so long. She hugs David to her and ruffles his hair. 'I already have a son, David and a daughter as well. Besides your father would miss you I am sure.' It's cruel to give the lad false hope, so Maggie shakes her head and takes him by the arms. 'I've got to leave here soon, David. It's time I returned to my own kin.'

'You can't, Maggie. I want you to stay here.'
She bites her lip and looks at him. 'I'm sorry, David.'

★★★

The mind's a mighty and powerful thing, and if a person wants to forget about something and remove it from their memory, if they try hard enough, they can. In the wake of her trip to the banks of the Tweed, a new harder Maggie emerges: cold, indifferent and keen to go back to where she came. Time has left no mark on her face, she's bonnier than ever, but there's hardness in that fine-looking face that was not there before. With purpose in her stride, Maggie sets off in search of her employees, to tell them her news.

The sound of Maggie's footsteps echo into the cold air as she marches along the grey slate floor. She continues down a long winding hall before entering the main room. A group of people stand in its centre, turning to her with slack mouths and expressions of horror — the innkeeper, his wife, Margaret and William.

'Is it true?' William rushes towards her, seizing her by the wrist. 'Oh, a plague on you, tell me it isn't true, Maggie.'

Adam shakes his head violently. 'Step away from her, William. The magistrate will be here any moment.'

William ignores his father and cries out: 'The child — was it mine?'

Maggie trembles and dares not look him in the eye; he will forever be associated with a child that she cannot acknowledge or claim as her own. A solitary tear escapes from the corner of her eye, and other than that Maggie displays no emotion. But somewhere deep within her soul, Maggie's heart breaks for William. How she wishes she could hold him till they are both lifeless and covered in earth — her William, the object of her obsessions and desires.

'You have killed me,' he whimpers.

'The devil I killed you — you denied me and doing so betrayed your own heart,' Maggie hisses.

'I beg of you,' he sobs. 'But why? Why did you murder our child?'

'But I didn't,' she says, wiping angrily at her tears. 'You are cruel, William. You are always cruel where I am concerned. Why did you deceive your own heart? You never cared for me. You despise me.'

William pulls Maggie into his arms. 'You drive me insane with your notions, woman – you always have. Won't you quit tormenting my soul?'

'I've wanted nothing but the earth for you, William. And my life thus will be richer because of you.'

'You're a little fool.' He kisses her. 'But how can I forgive you after what you have done?' William groans a curse and pulls Maggie closer. But then the door crashes open and before Maggie can reply to him, he's swept away.

★★★

The Baillie enters the tavern, aware of the guffaws behind his back. He is conspicuous because of a ridiculous and exceedingly large wig. To hell with their sniggering, he cares not what they think of him; he never ever leaves his house without his precious wig on. Once inside the tavern, he chooses a chair, sits down and crosses his legs. For a while he neither speaks nor looks around. Instead, he takes out a leather-bound book, and then a quill and stretches out his arms. His eyes sweep about the room; it takes him all of five seconds to determine who the Dickson girl is. With a little wave of his hand, he greets the women assembled.

'Good afternoon, ladies. So where is the woman?'

'Here she is, Baillie. Margaret Dickson,' a woman says.

Of course, he was right. He is *always* right. He writes down the name in his leather book. 'Ah – so this is the wench. So what are we waiting for? Oh yes, I remember, the doctor of medicine. We need to determine if she's recently brought forth a child.' The Baillie's eyes become drawn to the wee lassie suspected of infanticide; in the soft candlelight her face is childlike. He crosses the room in order to take a better look at her, and then motions for the women to move away.

'A private word, if I may. Do you know who I am?'

Maggie nods. 'The Baillie.'

'I understand that you are married but un-chaperoned, and a stranger to this village.'

'Aye, sir,' she says.

'So you've been working as a tavern wench? In close contact with many different men each night, I expect.'

'Aye, I suppose so.'

'Have you been chaste?' the Baillie whispers into her ear. As he does so his lips graze her hair. 'I wager that you've been flat on your back since you got here.'

Maggie flinches. 'I have not, sir.'

He sniggers and rises to stand. 'Are you sure that you had no carnal relations with a man here?'

Maggie closes her eyes. 'Nae.'

'What a pity you could not confide in me. I could have been an influential friend, and believe me, you could benefit from one right now – because to be sure you will hang.'

★★★

Meanwhile, outside the tailor's shop, William Bell is like a haunted man. Everywhere he turns she is there forever etched in his mind. He takes a respite, filling his lungs with air before stepping inside. Without meaning to he slams the door, and so he eyes his Master with apologetic eyes and marches inside. He assumes his preferred position, cross-legged on the floor, but it soon becomes apparent that his mind is not on his work. After a while he throws down his scissors and puts his head in his hands.

'What's got in to you, Master Bell?'

In a choked voice he answers: 'I've just a few things on my mind.' And off he goes into the rear of the shop to search amongst his things. With trembling hands he opens drawer after drawer, throwing things up into the air and onto the floor, until he finds what he's looking for.

He cries out and slumps to the floor. The soft leather pouch has a worn cord drawstring; he unties it and releases the treasure inside. It falls into his hand, tickling his palm, a lock of shiny chestnut hair bound with scarlet material. He brings it to his lips and kisses the soft locks. 'Maggie, Maggie – why did I forsake you?'

CHAPTER FIFTEEN

PUT TO THE GAD

On 9 December, in the year of our Lord 1723, the Baillie orders two kirk elders and one Anna Pringle – a midwife, to make a diligent search of Margaret Dickson. The midwife immediately takes charge. In a quiet corner, safe from the eyes of inquisitive men, she commands Maggie in a gruff voice to remove her clothes.

'Make haste, woman. I need to see your breasts.'

Maggie's stomach heaves. It's useless to object; swiftly the woman removes Maggie's plaid, stays and shift. And in short, she is neither gentle nor kind.

'And the petticoats – take them off now.' Once Maggie is quite naked, the midwife hands her the plaid to drape around her, and then crosses the room to hand the garments to the kirk elders to inspect. 'Gentlemen, please examine the clothes for signs of blood.'

After that, to Maggie's dismay, the midwife makes her lie back on a crude bed to perform an examination of sorts. She pokes and prods with sharp fingernails, all the while muttering pious citations. Maggie's face is aflame, and as she grips the sides of her trembling skin, the deed is not done. Like a hideous nightmare, the woman persists, until finally, and to her utmost humiliation, the midwife draws a small amount of milk from sucking.

In a loud and powerful voice Anna Pringle declares: 'Can I state for the record, the said woman, Margaret Dickson, has been found to have green milk, green meaning freshly delivered of child. And furthermore she has an empty feeling in her stomach and her body is tied around with a napkin, as is customary with women after childbirth. Get dressed,' she says and hands Maggie back her clothes.

221

Maggie dresses in a hurry, aware of strange men straining their necks in the shadows. Before her stockings are both on, the Baillie is seated before her. In his hands is his leather-bound book and quill.

'Where was the child born?'

'In the attic bedroom.'

The Baillie writes the information down in his book. 'I understand that you share a room with – a Margaret Bell, is that correct? The innkeeper's daughter is called Margaret Bell. Is that right?'

'Aye.'

'How confusing – two Margarets. Margaret Dickson and Margaret Bell, tut tut. What a nuisance – how unfortunate! We must be sure we refer to you as Maggie to avoid confusion. Ah, if my memory serves me right she is the sister of William Bell; yes, we must speak to him later. Now then, let's get to the heart of the matter. How on earth did you give birth alone without alerting Margaret?'

'She was not there.'

'Well where was she?'

'I don't know. Working or in the chicken coop.'

'So you gave birth alone?'

'Aye, but I think I must have fainted.'

'Fainted before, after or during the birth?'

'I can't remember,' Maggie draws a hand to her face.

'Well, what did you do once the child was born?'

'I tried to suckle it but it was too weak.'

'Did you tie the cord?'

'I – I cannot recall…'

'Well, did you or didn't you?'

'I – I, no.'

The Baillie stops her here and throws up his hands. 'What did you do with the soiled linen and the afterbirth?'

Maggie explains. 'I burned the soiled linen and the afterbirth.'

'And then?'

'I pushed it beneath the box-bed and returned to the tavern. When I went back later it was blue and cold. I think it must have died not long after it was born, but you… see I had to get back to work or they would have discovered something was wrong.'

The Baillie pinches the bridge of his nose. 'Now listen to me, Maggie. This is very, very important. Did you tell anybody that you were with child?'

'No one knew I was with child,' she nods with conviction.

'No one?'

Maggie shakes her head no.

'Did you murder your child?'

'I did not. To do so would be a mortal sin.'

'But you left the child to die near a freezing river – did you not?'

Maggie's eyes glitter as they meet her inquisitor, challenging him to doubt her. 'Sir, I'm guilty of many, many things, and I have sinned. But I did not kill the child. It was sickly and weak and died of a natural cause. You must believe me. There is not a mark on the child.'

He closes his eyes and exhales noisily. 'Who is the father?'

The Baillie is met with silence.

★★★

Late in the evening, Adam Bell guides the Baillie to the attic room. The Baillie considers it his duty to make a search of the box-bed and the attic room. The Baillie wheezes as he climbs the steep stairs to the top floor and every few steps or so he pauses to take a breath.

'She slept in there,' Adam points into a room sparse of furnishing, its only furniture a huge box-bed, a chair and an oaken chest. 'Maggie shared with my daughter.'

The Baillie nods and proceeds to search the room. He immediately opens the box-bed's hinged doors and turns the feather mattress. But he finds nothing. Not that it matters – the marks on her body are proof enough. But nevertheless, it is a puzzle how she's given birth alone without leaving a single trace or clue.

'I have spoken with a Helen Richardson – she was a maidservant here. Is that correct?'

Adam's brow furrows and the muscles in his jaw twitch. 'Aye, I had to let her go. She was a difficult woman.'

'Well the young woman claims that Maggie offered her money? Do you know where this money might be and how she acquired it? The lassie thought it might be beneath the mattress in this room.'

Adam breaks into laughter. 'Pah! Maggie has no money, the lass is talking nonsense. A tavern wench lives a hand-to-mouth existence. What utter drivel.'

The Baillie nods but examines beneath the mattress one more time – just to be sure. 'All right. I am satisfied.'

★★★

A smile of satisfaction crosses Margaret Bell's face as her father follows the fat Baillie downstairs. Pringle is a crafty old sod, but Margaret's one step ahead of him. It doesn't matter how much money the quality have, they always wanted more. So, earlier that morning, and tipped off by Maggie, Margaret crept into her attic room and searched beneath the box-bed to locate the heap of money. Later on, when no one's around, she returns the money to Maggie – who quickly stuffs it into her stockings.

'Margaret. I must sew this into my petticoats. Can you fetch me a sewing needle?'

Margaret can't bring herself to look into her eyes. 'It's done,' she answers in a sad tone.

★★★

That evening a cart arrives to take Maggie away, and she is not permitted to say goodbye. With a crack of a whip the cart moves away from the bleak landscape, leaving behind the peasant houses, inns, taverns and kirk that Maggie came to know so well. And as night falls, Maggie's eyes are drawn to the tumbling waters of the

Tweed, and beyond to the twisted trees that follow the river path, their thirsty roots clawing into the river bed.

At the gaol in Jedburgh, it soon becomes apparent that the foremost priority is to secure the prisoner. Thus, the turnkey puts her to the gad, securing her ankles with shackles connected to a chain of four feet, joined to a large iron bar, six inches off the ground.

'What is this place?'

The turnkey sniggers. 'Welcome to Jedburgh Tolbooth.'

Upon the damp floor she prays for her mortal soul, pressing her hands together and dodging the rats that scurry near her feet. To the right of her, an old woman rocks back and forth and pulls out her hair. To the left, an emaciated man smashes his head against a dank wall. A clanking noise slices through the air each time he lunges forward and causes blood to seep from the shackles.

'What am I praying for?' she mumbles through gritted teeth. 'God will never hear me in this awful place.' In the dim light Maggie's eyes strain to make out shapes in the dark, a mass of bodies cover the far wall, some of them moving, some of them not.

The old man all of a sudden comes to life and says in a raspy voice: 'Sometimes folk pass foodstuff and drink through the bars. Good Christian folk – hoping to secure a place in heaven. Aye, the same folk peep through the bars to gawp at us, as though we're animals or worse.'

Maggie lowers her head and wonders at the shame of it.

'Have you any money, wench? You'll need it or you'll be begging like us through the bars. Money can make your time in prison more comfortable like – especially bonny lasses like you. Those prison guards get mighty lonely on a cold night, do you get my meaning?'

Maggie shivers and shakes her head, thinking the old man a fool. Besides she can look after herself, at least she thinks she can.

The old man laughs. 'Not a talker then? Well, I'll tell you a few things – if you have money, hide it well because you'll need it. First you must pay a fee to the prison guard, and then you can buy food, drink, bedding, warmth by a fire. Or you might simply want to be left alone…' The old man's brows lift, surprised at her cool reaction.

'Ah, it'll be a letter to friends or family that you'll be wanting. Well that can be bought too, because everything has a price in gaol.'

Armed with this piece of information, on her third day Maggie seeks out a Mr Kerr in order to arrange for a letter to be sent to Musselburgh to get word to her folk. A strange expression crosses the guard's face as Maggie dictates her letter to him. And as she leans over his shoulder to admire his beautiful handwriting, she wonders how on earth such ugly fat fingers can produce fine and beautiful script.

'Who taught you to write, Mr Kerr?'

Maggie watches him shrink like a hermit crab retracting into his shell; he is such a nervous little man, the kind unable to meet your eyes or make conversation. And then there's his stature. He reminds her of a dog that's just been beaten, cowering in the corner with its tail between its legs.

'I was taught in a dame school and then a parish school. We had to learn the catechisms by rote and were tested all the time. Later we had to learn to write them down.'

'What happened if you failed the test?'

He fetches a sigh. 'We were thrashed with a birch or a wooden rod. Weren't you taught the same way?'

'Nae, my brother and I never learned the catechisms. And I certainly did not take a thrashing from the rod. Maybe if I had if I would not be here.'

'I take no pleasure in punishment. Reform and education – that is the answer.'

Maggie changes the subject. 'But how did you learn the words not in the catechisms?'

'Self-taught – I spell out the words as I hear them.'

★★★

She's not had a drink for more than a day. Some folk lap at foul puddles on the filthy floor or even lick the damp walls but Maggie can't stomach that. So she pays a gaoler for a cup of small ale and hopes that someone will come soon, perhaps with a jug and a hunk of fresh bread. A faint noise resonates in the distance; Maggie tilts her head to the left. She has become accustomed to the sounds of a tolbooth, the clanking of the chains, the groans of the ill and the soul-destroying finality of a door being locked. The slightest noise incites Maggie, most of all the sound of a great door being opened and the prospect of a visitor.

A mass of expectant eyes focus on the door as the lock turns, while those with no hope turn away, their anguished faces, demoralised and forlorn. Maggie trembles with elation as a man walks the length of the room, all those days and nights lying alone, frightened and desperate on her filthy straw bed suddenly taking its toll.

'It's me,' the voice whispers.

Maggie peers through the murky light, gradually the silhouette in front of her becomes brighter and she can make out the form of her brother, James, glancing all around him with horrified eyes.

'James.' But all she can do is cry, for the sight of his face reminds her of all that she has lost, and the family she's left behind.

'Maggie, don't cry. You must be brave.' He wipes away a tear that has rolled a clean streak down her dirty face.

'How on earth did you get yourself in this mess?' James hands her a clean rag to wipe her face.

'Where do I begin? Has Patrick returned?'

'No one's seen or heard of him. Nothing.' He clasps her hand to him. 'Anna and Patrick have grown, they long to see you.'

'How will I see them?'

'You'll see them as soon as you are released, of course. This whole thing is just one huge misunderstanding; we must fight this, Maggie. Come on, don't give up – be strong.'

'It's hardly encouraging in a hole like this, James,' she says.

The sound of a quarrel interrupts them as a decrepit old man fights a woman for a piece of bread covered in mould. A large man stands between them breaking them up.

'Who's that man staring at us?'

'That's Black Bill, he's an Egyptian.'

'Well I don't like gipsy men. Stay away from him.'

Maggie nods to Black Bill. He's a large man with a jagged scar stretching the length of his forehead. He has luminous skin, the colour of rich coffee.

'Wouldn't want to get on the wrong side of him,' James fidgets.

'Don't vex. We are just friends watching out for one another. Gaol is not a safe environment. He watches my back and I watch his.'

'As long as that's all he watches.' James shrugs and allows his gaze to return to the gipsy. 'Aye, I can see that he spends a great deal of time watching you.'

For a while they sit side by side, holding hands. James turns to Maggie and opens his mouth to speak – but is hushed before he opens his mouth.

'Shush, for goodness sake, James. I will be careful. Please leave me be.'

'All right. I was just going to ask you, Maggie, what are you going to do? Have you an advocate?'

'Aye, but I cannot understand him and his fancy words. He says he is to plead for my defence. Does that mean he's on my side?'

James tilts his hat and scratches his head, then presses his hat down carefully over his ears. 'Aye – I imagine so. It means he works for you and that he'll try to make the jury believe that you're innocent. You are innocent, aren't you, Maggie?'

Maggie swallows hard, not meeting her brother's eyes. 'Aye, but they won't accept the truth. They say I'm accused of child murder and that if I'm found guilty, I'll hang.'

'Hang?' James turns away from Maggie clutching his stomach as though it hurts. 'Please tell me you have pleaded your innocence.'

'Of course I have, James. A hundred times, but they won't listen.'

A rag rests in Maggie's lap, she holds both ends and twists with her fingers, tightening the tension until the material warps and distorts into a coiled snake.

'Stop it. Give it here.' James snatches the rag from her lap and flings it to the floor. 'If you have told them you are innocent, why don't they let you go?'

'Because I have been accused of infanticide and concealment of being with child...'

'Infanticide?'

'It means the murder of a new-born child.'

James sucks in his breath. 'Oh, Maggie. Why did you go there in the first instance? You should have come home to Musselburgh, you know, after you left the child at the river's edge.'

'It does not matter, James. They would've found it and traced it back to me.'

'Well, why didn't you reveal that you were with child and face the consequences? You didn't get into that state on your own, what about the father? He could have shared his half of the blame.'

'Oh, James, it's no use looking back now. What's done is done.'

James shivers and wraps his arms around his body. For a while they just sit there opposite one another, at a loss for what to say.

'Father sends his love, and Widow Arrock. Do you have a message for your children?'

Maggie struggles to stand; the shackles are heavy and meddlesome and make a clinking noise all the while. 'Aye, tell them I love them.'

★★★

A sinister presence seems to lurk within the walls of the prison late at night. With some of the money from her petticoats she purchases a small cell off the main prison with a fire and a clean bed of straw. Soon, Maggie's joined by a thief, a prostitute, and the burly gipsy – Black Bill. And for the majority of time, Maggie's days are a miserable affair, most of them spent politely declining the gipsy's advances, and hoping he's gracious in her numerous rebuffs of him.

To Maggie's relief, after a couple of weeks, Black Bill finally relinquishes and turns to the prostitute for consolation. And for this she is thankful, because the last thing she needs is another child growing in her belly. Nevertheless, she's far from a saint and in moments of weakness Maggie finds herself drawn to Black Bill and his chivalrous ways.

Mr Kerr, the nervous gaoler, visits from time to time to teach Maggie to sign her own name instead of writing an X. When this happens Black Bill sulks in the corner, doing anything and everything to distract them. But Maggie never lets him get away with such nonsense and takes Bill aside, explaining that Mr Kerr's a good man to be acquainted with – because he knows his letters and numbers. And if Maggie needs a message sending to Musselburgh, he's the man to get it done.

★★★

In the middle of March, Maggie receives important news. She's to be moved to Edinburgh Tolbooth to await the beginning of her trial. Thus, with the stench of Jedburgh clinging to her skin, Maggie staggers out of doors, squinting into a searing bright light. The journey doesn't take long and they are there in a few hours. With the wind and rain in her hair, she closes her eyes and pretends she's at Joppa shore with the sound of a thundering sea in her ears.

The tolbooth stands in the centre of Edinburgh's old town, across from St Giles. Maggie knows it well. She's passed it many a time as she's cried out her wares. A formidable building with slit windows and large heavy doors, on the ground floor there is a shop and a thieves' hole. The felons are held upstairs, and just like Jedburgh, it has thick iron bars on the floor where prisoners are chained and put to the gad.

They ascend curved steps; gaolers escort Maggie on both sides. At the top of the staircase is a tunnel. Suddenly they're plunged into an inky darkness. She gasps and reaches out ahead into a sinister passageway but there is nothing but blackness. A gaoler locates a torch and the tunnel soon flickers with weak amber light. She stumbles along with trembling knees, a feeling of suffocation descending upon her. Before long, Maggie struggles to breathe and places a hand to her breast.

'I've bad feelings. Like feelings of darkness and sickness, as if I've reached a place where there are no boundaries between the living and dead. I can't go any further...' she wails.

The gaolers laugh uneasily and move her along. 'We feel it every time we go down here. Now walk on.'

They proceed to a huge barred entrance. At the other side of the door a large cage dominates the main floor. A man sits cross-legged inside the enclosure, rocking back and forth. A quantity of spittle oozes from his mouth, and his eyes look like a crazed animal's.

'What's that?' she asks a gaoler.

'That's where we keep the dangerous and violent prisoners. Perhaps you would like to join him for the night? Keep him company.'

Maggie shudders.

'The gaol does a good trade here; you'd be wise to pay a fee – a lassie like you.' His eyes look her up and down as though she's a greased-up mulatto at a slave market. He licks his lips and stretches out one hand to fondle her, but before it reaches her a loud slap rings in the air as a hunchbacked man cuffs him across the head.

'Leave the lass alone, she hasn't even got to her cell yet. Be off with you, lecherous fool. I will deal with her.' The hunchback takes hold of Maggie's arm.

With his shoulders forward, and his lower back curved, he shuffles forward passed the cage. As they proceed further into the tolbooth, he takes Maggie aside and pulls out a small book and a bag of coins.

'Now, have you some money?'

Maggie nods and hands him a few coins. 'Will this do?'

The hunchback nods his head and takes the money; despite the dim light he manages to record something into his small book. 'I heard you ask about the cage. Well, if I was you, I'd stay well clear of it. The fellow in it now – well he's evil, the devil's own, he is. Do you get my meaning by that? Insane is what he is.'

Maggie glances back at the barred enclosure with cautious eyes, wondering how a person can become so low as to be treated like an animal.

The hunchback continues. 'Aye, he's insane all right. Bit someone's nose off, he did, last week, a guard. Aye, bit it clear off, he did, and let me tell you there was blood absolutely everywhere. We picked up what was left of it and ran to the barber surgeon's to stitch it back on. But it was no use; he'd eaten most of it.'

'I'll stay well away,' nods Maggie.

'That is wise.'

★★★

He directs her to a solitary cell, inhabited by a few miserable creatures. In the pitch black, Maggie's confinement enhances an acuteness of hearing and her senses become sharper. The days pass slowly, and for the most part she spends them sleeping, because in a land of slumber she can escape this godforsaken den of misery. One morning or night – she has no comprehension of time – Maggie's ears prick up at a sharp high-pitched noise. Her back pushes off the moss-stained wall to peer beyond the shadows to the huge iron door.

Maggie hears the steps first, and then a key turning in the lock. Finally the door flies open and Widow Arrock waddles in, wearing her best plaid pulled high around her head. A guard lights her way, keeping his eyes firmly ahead till she's directed to Maggie. In haste, he turns on his heel, taking his torch with him, and thus plunging them into darkness.

'Miserable blighter could have left us the light,' the widow complains. 'And what sort of greeting is this! Embrace your dearest friend.'

The widow's whiskers prickle Maggie's face as she holds her in her arms. Nevertheless it feels good to be embraced by a friend. Maggie points to her bed of straw and motions for her to sit. 'There are shops below. There is bound to be a chandler.'

Then, before the widow contemplates whether or not to go to the chandler, the gaoler returns with his torch. For a while he hovers over them, and then he gets a good look at the widow's face and promptly turns his back to them. The widow stares at Maggie from beneath scraggy brows, ugly as ever.

'Well, I suppose this stinking flea-pit of a bed is better than sitting on the dirt floor. I bring you news, not that you deserve it. Your children are well and your father and brother send their greetings.'

'What of Patrick?'

'Still missing, but I suppose after everything that has happened, can you blame him?'

Maggie hangs her head in disgrace. 'Oh, for the love of God, I wish you could bring me words of comfort and not moral indignation…'

'You've not a soul to blame, Maggie, but yourself. I took the children so that you could go to Newcastle to find that husband of yours, but you never got there, did you? Never got past Kelso, is that right? You're fortunate to not feel the back of my hand, young lassie.' She pauses for breath.

Maggie holds out an arm to the widow and with her lips trembling says, 'I wish I could… oh, I never intended for things to turn out this way. There's nothing I can do about it now, is there? Don't you think I feel wretched enough?'

The widow takes her hand and squeezes. A tear pools in the corner of Maggie's eye.

Maggie forces a smile and asks, 'How are the children? Have they been good?'

'Aye, they are very well. Don't be troubled concerning them, they are well cared for – Jean Ramsay has them now. And James looks after them occasionally.' The widow suddenly shudders. 'Lord above, this is a rat-infested hole if I ever saw one.'

'Aye, it is not a pleasant place,' Maggie says.

The widow grimaces, somehow bringing more symmetry to her face. 'The sooner you are out of this awful gaol the better, Maggie. Has your court date been set?'

'No,' Maggie shakes her head.

'Well, I expect you'll hear something soon.' The widow pats her hand.

'Aye, I expect I will.'

★★★

In May, one of the bigwig's clerks arrives, a fleeting visit, to impart vital news. It soon becomes evident that he has little interest in anything Maggie has to say. He hasn't even the decency to acknowledge her with his eyes, preferring to talk to a spot directly above her head. With a handkerchief pressed against his mouth, his words are indistinguishable and mumbled.

'I cannot hear you. Can you say that again?' Maggie asks.

The clerk takes the handkerchief away for just a moment. He immediately gags. 'It's the smell – gets me every time. I don't know how you can stand it.'

'It's a case of having to.'

'Never mind. The reason I am here is to inform you that the date of your first court appearance has been set.'

'When?'

'June.'

'Can I ask for somebody to inform my friends and family?'

'That can be arranged,' he answers, returning his handkerchief to his face.

★★★

When the weather turns sultry, the stench in the gaol is unbelievable. Sickness is rife in Edinburgh Tolbooth and gaol fever takes many a poor soul. Isaac the flesher died two days ago. And because the prison guards are too busy to collect his body, his remains are pushed into a corner. Somebody's already claimed the blanket that covered his corpse. He lies uncovered, in plain view for all to see, and it isn't a pretty sight. A mass of flies descend on him to lay eggs in every orifice. Soon maggots emerge and spew from his mouth, ears, nose – and worse. Rodents fight for his dead flesh, gnawing and chewing him, and somehow creating the illusion that he's alive and twitching in his sleep.

Maggie tears her eyes away from him; the smell that comes off him is unbearable. She sniffs her ragged clothes and her nostrils burn. The scent of death lingers everywhere; flesh, fabric and hair. Maggie has strange fancies of doom. Death is everywhere, and she knows the dead are known to terrorise the living. With the passing of time dark thoughts begin to taunt her – Maggie no longer cares. She peers into the dim shadows. A fat rat scurries along the floor, its long slimy tail trailing and swishing in the shape of a letter 'S' behind it. The rodent scratches about in foul straw, his pointy nose seeking prey and then he finds it. An old infirm man lies next to Maggie. He's delirious and unaware of the mangy rodent. Maggie stares in horror as it climbs up his body, proceeding to chew his ear. The poor wretch doesn't even have the strength to brush it off. And then all of a sudden, a calloused hand seizes the rodent and sends it flying in the air – like a flying trapeze act.

'Bastard rats,' rages Black Bill.

★★★

Minister Bonaloy thinks he's a worldly man, but as he descends into the miserable hole of Edinburgh Tolbooth, he realises that he is most definitely not. Horrible sights are everywhere and the stench; well it's enough to knock a man down. Surely Maggie's not survived this awful experience, but then he sees her.

Upon a bed of filthy straw Maggie lies in a stupor. She's much changed, hardly recognisable because of the weight she's lost; he winces at the sight of her fettered feet, bloodied and full of sores. With a tentative arm he reaches out with his hand and strokes her matted hair, rousing her from sleep.

'Maggie.'

'Minister Bonaloy?' her voice cracks with emotion.

'Yes, it is I, Maggie. I've come to pray for you and comfort you.' He holds out his hand.

In a weak voice she mutters, 'You've come to ask me to confess and repent.'

'Let God be the judge, Maggie. I'm here to offer you my support and say a few prayers.' He lowers his head and begins to recite a prayer.

'I have sinned,' she sobs. 'Many, many times – and I've had impure thoughts…'

'Hush…'

'Please let me continue, Minister Bonaloy. I've been a slatternly witch – and I have strayed from my wifely duties many times. But I did not kill it. I could never murder my own child.'

The minister shakes his head and his eyes fill with sorrow. 'Your crime is one of ignorance, Maggie. And ignorance is the source of all evil. The knowledge of God is easily obtained. Your ignorance made you a faithful factor to the devil and evil. As a consequence you will be punished. But take comfort in the Lord, Maggie, because if you repent, He will forgive you. Have you anything to say?'

'Nae, my fate is in God's hands.'

★★★

The hunchback gaoler does not attach himself to prisoners. But one prisoner is suddenly a concern. She is a bonny one; well, she was once he thinks, still is – in a way. As he peers down at her scrawny frame, he realises she's been in exactly the same position for days. He shakes his head with frustration and wonders how she's got beneath his skin, this fisher lassie at death's door. With his boot he nudges her, but there is nothing, no noise or movement. He nudges her again and is relieved to hear her moan. In haste, he shuffles off into the darkness, his ghastly hunchback shadow falling behind him.

'Ague,' says the hunchback to the gipsy, Black Bill. 'Weren't you with the girl at Jedburgh gaol? She has a fever. I'm afraid she won't last much longer.'

'Let me tend her.' The gipsy stands his ground and hands him a coin.

'It's up to you, gipsy. It is gaol fever, I tell you. You could go the same road as she's going if you go to her, and you'll be no use to anybody then.'

★★★

The hunchback takes him to Maggie, and as he does so, Black Bill wonders what compels him to her – this strange lass he barely knows. Once he fixes his gaze upon her, he speculates no more. His eyes linger on her slender ankles; he steadies his rough hands and gently lifts them before turning her feet to examine the wounds.

'Oh, lassie,' he winces. Her feet are festering. 'I wish I could take you away from this wretched gaol.'

Somehow he manages to obtain a damp sponge to press against Maggie's face. Afterwards, he strokes her hair and holds a cup of water to her parched lips. And slowly and carefully he cleans the wounds around her ankles, all the while keeping one eye on her.

Suddenly Maggie cries out in delirium. 'I can't bear it any longer. William, please help me. I need you.'

'It is I, Black Bill. Who's William?' He can't help feeling irritated, jealous even.

'The child, William. I want to tell you…'

'Shush, Maggie.' Bill holds her hand.

'It's you I love, only you. I can't see past you.'

In a couple of days, thanks to Bill's intervention, Maggie's fever breaks and she's able to sit up and take a little refreshment. But nevertheless, Black Bill stays by her side, and with his care and devotion, Maggie is soon feeling much better.

'Drink the broth.' He places a protective arm around her shoulders, and guides the bowl to her mouth.

★★★

A clerk arrives with news of her trial again.

'How long will the trial last and who will be there?' Maggie enquires; she wrings her hands and gazes ahead. She's never set foot in a court in her life and she wonders if folk will be allowed in there to witness her humiliation and shame.

'These things take time. Lord Advocate Robert Dundas will be there. I don't expect you've heard of him, well never mind he's a very important man, having said that he is the most important man in court. Have you met your advocate yet?'

'Advocate?' Maggie frowns.

'Yes – counsel for your defence?'

'Nae.'

'Well, you will, no doubt. Warrants have been issued for those people attending the trial, witnesses. Do you understand?'

Maggie nods her head, but she really has no confidence in the matter. In short, she is perplexed; foreboding has left her crumpled and weak. She hasn't the faintest idea what he is talking about. All she can fathom is that her first court appearance is sometime in June, and she knew that already.

As night falls Maggie succumbs to fatigue, ignoring the groans of prisoners and scratching rodents. In her miserable cell she allows her eyes to fill with the vision of a starlit sky, focusing on one bright burning star, letting its light grow bigger and brighter until it materialises into a halo of golden light.

'William,' she sobs.

CHAPTER SIXTEEN

PUNISHING THE POOR

A large coat of arms dominates the back wall of the courtroom. Its sombre walls lined with long sheets of polished mahogany, a contrast to the dull slate floor. As Maggie enters the dock a strange sense of foreboding washes over her. A number of law men observe her, peering down their noses at her with haughty, self-important postures, most of them old men with pot bellies and sagging jowls. For some reason they remind her of Alexander and the bathhouse, though he was neither fat nor old. *Perhaps it is the wigs,* she surmises. A memory surfaces from the back of her mind: Alexander strutting around like a peacock in Dawney Douglas's, showing off his gold fob watch.

'It's a beauty, a real work of art. Look at the movement.'

'What movement?' she'd asked, trying to muster up some interest.

'Never mind, silly girl,' Alexander had said. 'This watch was designed by a master watchmaker in London. Oh what was his name again? I always forget it. Clarence or Marcus? Thomas. That's it. Thomas Tompian.'

That night, Alexander sipped too much claret and the small pocket watch slipped from his waist coat onto the cold floor. Once in her hand, the shimmering gold suddenly became interesting, so much so that Maggie had been unable to part with it.

The memory of Alexander and the watch fades...

In the dock, she stands directly facing the witness box, away from the partitioned spaces for jurors and privileged spectators. Maggie's chains cut into her ankles. She's barefoot and the ground is cold. Her face peers into the crowded galleries. A huge swell of sadness rolls through her as she glances around the room. She doesn't recognise anyone. *Why hasn't anyone come?* Her head hangs low until a flash of pale yellow hair juts out from a crowd, and all at once Maggie's face becomes ashen at the sight of it. A guard stretches out his hand to steady her.

'Stand straight before you fall down,' barks the guard through gritted teeth.

On the other side of the room the Lord Advocate enters the courtroom and bangs down his gavel, the sound compelling the full power of the court. A hush fills the room as his monotone voice drones on: 'Therefore, necessary it is for the complainer to have our warrant and diligence for citing that said Margaret Dickson come appear before the Lord Justice, General Justice Clerk and Commissioner of Justiciary, the said twentieth day of July next to come within the tolbooth or Criminal House of Edinburgh realm and ask that ye summoned are assessed here to not exceed the number of forty-five persons together with such witnesses as best know...'

Maggie's advocate takes her by the arm and leads her from the court. She follows as fast as she can in the chains, grimacing as he steps on her toes. They come to a private room, a dusty room at that – and he enquires if anyone could bear witness to her bringing forth the child.

Maggie's weary, hungry and parched. 'No, sir, I cannot.'

The advocate groans.

'I'm confused, sir. Might I enquire what is happening? I do not understand...'

The advocate throws down his papers. 'The date for your trial has been set, woman – did you not take heed? Now, I will ask you again. Can anyone bear witness to you...?'

'Nae.'

The advocate stares at her insolently. 'Hear me well, I am a man of little patience and so I will speak plainly to you in the hope that you will see sense. The fact that you did not seek assistance in bringing forth a child is detrimental to your defence. Do you understand?'

Maggie glances at him, bemused by his frustration. The advocate is an average man, in as much that he is of average height, weight and appearance. But when it comes to questioning folk he is far from middling.

The advocate persists. 'There must be somebody who knew of the birth – a friend you confided in perhaps?'

Maggie fetches a sigh. 'Aye – Margaret Bell suspected I was with child, but she did not assist me with the birth. I had the baby alone and fainted. The child fell into a pool of blood, but I lifted him from it, quick, mind.'

The advocate screws up his eyes and pinches the bridge of his nose. 'So you gave birth alone, with no one to help you? You must know that is an offence in itself. What of the necessary preparations for the child? Did you buy linen or clothes for the future baby?'

Maggie wonders what on earth these questions have to do with anything; a nauseous feeling begins to swell in her throat.

'I did not, sir. I did not prepare linen or clothes because I wanted to push away the fact that I was with child and pretend that it was not happening, like it was all a bad dream. Do you understand? Can you understand? I was scared to death. My mind was not right.'

The advocate slaps his forehead. 'So you just thought you could cross your legs and it would all go away?'

Maggie flashes her eyes at him, an uncontrollable rage building inside of her. 'How foolish of me to think you might understand. You're a man, and a rich one at that. You've never had to give birth alone, have you? Or been so frightened that your hair falls out in great clumps? And am I correct in assuming that you've never gone hungry, or struggled in life, fearing for your job or your children, or the prospect of public humiliation and condemnation?'

'Ah, so that was it. You killed the child rather than suffer public humiliation or denounce the father. I hope he was worth it, Margaret Dickson.'

A quiet descends on the room. The advocate glances at his fob watch and breaks the silence. 'How long have you been separated from your husband?'

Maggie's eyes look upwards to the cobwebbed roof beams. 'A year or more, perhaps, I cannot remember. And you need not ask me where he is, he never bothered to tell me. Just ran off, he did, to the fisheries or off to sea again, leaving me all alone with the children.'

The advocate pauses and seems to consider her words. 'Well now, Mrs Dickson. I've listened to you and it's obvious that you are an able woman, so listen to me. A man *has* to provide for his family. You cannot blame a man for wanting to put food on the table.' The advocate rubs his long fingers over his chin. He scribbles a few notes onto a paper and curses as he smudges a quantity of ink on his fingers. 'The reason I asked is that married women are not normally charged under the concealment of pregnancy act...'

'Why not?'

'Consider the facts my dear – does a married woman have to hide the fact that she's with child?'

Maggie shakes her head. 'No.'

'And why does she not need to hide the fact?'

'Because a married woman has a husband, and everything is as it should be.'

The advocate stares into her eyes. 'Correct. In any case – I am your counsel for defence and I will do my very best for you, rest assured. But bear in mind that although you are indeed a married woman, your husband was away when you concealed the child. So not only are you guilty of adultery, you are guilty of murdering your infant child. This places a great deal of pressure on me in terms of persuading the jury that you are innocent of this crime.' The advocate pauses for breath. 'Do you understand?'

'Aye.' Maggie nods.

'Now then, please think of anyone who can help us in your defence.'

★★★

The voices in the courtroom grow increasingly hushed as Lord Advocate Robert Dundas arrives, and it is as though his formidable presence commands authority and respect from all present in the room. Upon his head he wears a white wig. His eyes are clear blue and sparkle with cleverness and his robes are fashioned in the traditional Scottish way.

Once court is in session, there is complete silence, and so the softest noises are audible. Thus, as the trial begins so do the whispers and muffled coughs as folk push and shove one another to catch a glimpse of the unfortunate fishwife accused of murdering her child, a married woman they say, pregnant while her husband was at sea.

'Look at the state of her, so thin and scrawny,' whispers a peasant woman straining her neck.

'I was told she was bonny. Is that her?' Another peasant woman points a bony finger in Maggie's direction.

'Aye – pestilence has come upon her for her sins.'

A strange sound vibrates inside Maggie's ears, like the droning of honey bees. Her hair is stuck to her face with sweat and tears, she brushes the hair away and stares ahead, and all the while her fear grows.

The Lord Advocate reads out the circumstances of the case. Next the counsel for Maggie's defence calls witness after witness, not one of them helpful in terms of Maggie's defence. His Majesty's Advocate responds by producing several witnesses who reveal that Maggie has been frequently pregnant. And others state there were signs of her having delivered a child and that a new-born infant had been found near her place of residence.

The next witness for his Majesty's Advocate, a respected surgeon, deposes that, putting the lungs of the infant in water, they were found to swim, which was proof that the child was born alive. For it is the received opinion that if no air be drawn into the lungs, they will not swim. But alas, this circumstance is a matter of doubt and ambiguity, even among the gentlemen of the faculty.

Anna Pringle, the midwife, testifies that Maggie had the appearance of a woman who had brought forth a child. And William Pringle, the Baillie, testifies that Maggie revealed she had been involved in adulterous affairs with several men throughout her marriage to her husband, Patrick Spence. And thus, as the evidence mounts against her, Maggie squirms in her seat.

A loud voice calls: 'I call William Bell.'

The crowd roars and all eyes turn to the witness box, curious eyes straining to catch a glimpse of the innkeeper's son whom the fishwife begotten a child by.

The King's Advocate stands proud and tall, but William dwarfs him as he stands opposite to take an oath to tell the truth. He looks uncomfortable and anxious, and several times he is warned to pay heed and stop looking at the accused.

The King's Advocate says in a loud and clear voice: 'Several people, who were questioned during the course of the investigation, including your own mother, father and sister, admit that *you* had a close relationship with the accused, Margaret Dickson. Is this true?'

William nods. 'Yes. It is true that I had a close relationship with Maggie Dickson.' He glances at the prisoner again, visibly distressed by her appearance.

The courtroom becomes quiet, the air pregnant with anticipation.

'William Bell. Are you the father of the dead child found on the banks of the river Tweed?'

The courtroom bursts into a deafening noise, forcing the Lord Advocate to bang down on his gavel with all his might.

'Aye,' William states. His gaze falls on Maggie so that their eyes lock. 'It is quite possible that I am the father of Margaret Dickson's child.'

Incredulous gasps fill the courtroom. Maggie makes no noise because she has no breath. She struggles to draw air into her lungs and there is a throbbing in her heart.

'You admit this and yet you have no doubt heard that Margaret Dickson is a married woman and has admitted to fornication with several men. So, in fact, the child might not be yours.'

William's face contorts, as though disgusted by the insinuation. 'To the best of my knowledge she had carnal knowledge of one man at the Kelso inn, and that man was me!'

The King's Advocate waves a dismissive hand at William Bell. 'Very well, Mr Bell. I have no further questions. Remove the witness.'

A pain fills Maggie's heart as he passes by. Unable to control her emotions, she lets out a grief stricken wail. And as they lead William from the courtroom they exchange one fleeting glance.

With each passing moment, Maggie's counsel for defence grows paler. In a vain attempt, ashen-faced and at times with a slight tremor in his voice, he tries to build a good case. But in truth – it's an impossible task. He leans in close to Maggie and whispers to her. 'Counsel is not permitted to contradict the facts provided by the King's Advocate and word-of-mouth statements are perfectly acceptable. I'll defend you to the best of my ability, Mrs Dickson, but this is it now, this is our last chance.' He walks from the dock to approach the jury.

'Ladies and gentleman of the jury, as you are aware counsel for the accused is allowed to sum up as much evidence as he can muster on his client's behalf, and be the last speaker before the jury withdraw to consider the verdict.' Maggie's advocate pauses for effect and then points to the accused. 'Look at her. A poor fishwife abandoned by her husband, trying to find him all alone without a chaperone. And what is her defence you might ask? Well, let me tell you, Margaret Dickson has been separated from her husband for at least a year. And it is a well-known fact that the concealment of pregnancy murder act only applies to unmarried women, as those who have husbands are under no temptation to murder their children. Furthermore, as you may remember, the hydrostatsy test, which involves the child's lungs in the sink or swim theory, should be treated with much doubt as the results are indefinite.' The advocate clears his voice and removes his spectacles, turning away from the accused to face the jury. 'Ladies and gentlemen of the jury, you have listened to the evidence and must come to the most logical conclusion. Margaret Dickson is innocent of concealment of pregnancy and the murder of her child.'

★★★

The wait is torturous, like she's coming to the end of a long hard journey, but in truth Maggie is terrified. Once the verdict is in, Maggie shakes uncontrollably, her stomach churning as the guards drag her from her filthy cell. Outside, her eyes adjust to a searing light and her leg chains clank and rub as she hobbles along the dusty street. A scorching sun burns in the summer sky, its hot rays beating down on her pale face.

The courtroom is full. People crammed in like herrings in a creel. In the centre of the galleries, familiar faces peer out from the crowd – James, Johnny Notions and Minister Bonaloy. At the very rear, a large group of fishwives stand united, shouting out their support for the Musselburgh fisher lassie. Maggie rubs her eyes; the courtroom has become a blur. She tries to move her arms and legs but they feel like lead weights. She shakes out her feet to bring back some feeling but the chains bite into her ankles and trip her forwards and her fingers wrap around the back of a dock to steady herself. Maggie's face droops forward. All of a sudden she longs for her mother's arms around her, and as she stares into space, her eyes like glass, her head suddenly jerks forward as the Lord Advocate clears his throat, keen to deliver the verdict. Maggie is ill-prepared for his words.

Oh my God, she thinks in horror. *This is it.* Suddenly she finds it hard to breath and all she can hear is the sound of blood rushing through her head as her mouth dries.

'The court has found that the libel as founded upon the act of parliament, sixteen-ninety, relevant to infer the pains of death, and confiscation of all movables, but sustains the defence of her revealing her being with child relevant to restrict the same to an arbitrary punishment.' Cries echo throughout the courtroom as the Lord Advocate continues. 'Margaret Dickson, you are to be taken from this place to a place of execution and there you will be hanged by the neck until you are dead. May the Lord have mercy on your soul.'

'This can't be happening to me,' Maggie sobs, searching through the crowd for the face of her father. She strains to hear the cries of her friends and family, but her hearing has become distorted and muffled, as though someone has placed their hands over her ears.

'Order, order! Let there be silence in this court! Execution date is set for Wednesday, 2 September 1724.'

In spite of her distorted hearing, Maggie's guessed the outcome. After nearly eight months in gaol, it has come to this; they are going to hang her. Maggie tugs at her shackles and struggles to remain standing, her legs buckle and give way beneath her. A guard catches her and allows her to slump to the floor.

'I did not kill my baby, I swear it. It was born dead,' Maggie cries.

A familiar voice cries out in the crowd. 'Never fear, Maggie. We'll fight for you. We'll walk to London to King George if we have to.'

Maggie's father stands to the side of Johnny. He makes a fist in what she assumes is an indication for her to be strong, but how can she be strong when her legs have turned to water?

Two guards pull her to her feet and drag her away, back to the gaol.

★★★

William Bell needs air. He stops and stands motionless outside, fighting to control his emotions. He's pale and overwrought and his lips are bloodless. His brows furrow, thinking it all out. *How could this happen?* He clenches his teeth as his father approaches, suddenly realising the gravity of the outcome and the horror takes his breath away.

'I'm sorry, son.' Adam places a hand on his son's shoulder.

'I must go to the tolbooth to see her.'

'No, William. It's over and what's done is done. You can't go there; they won't let you in, anyway. Come on, lad, don't be a fool. With time you'll forget all about this nonsense.'

William glares at his father; he's surprised at his callousness. 'What's done is done? What do you mean? I'm as guilty as she is – and yet I get off scot-free,' William says, sounding choked.

Adam grumbles, 'Come on now, William – she would have ruined your life and reputation. See sense, lad. Maggie should not have let you bed her in the first place.'

'Aye, but she did. And despite that she did not denounce me. And it pains me to say this, father – but I do not regret it, do you hear? I do not regret that night. Not even if she haunts me for the rest of my days...'

★★★

A week after her trial, Maggie's sat next to Black Bill. He's to be executed in the morning, and if one listens carefully, there is the sound of clanking and hammering as they erect the gallows at the north-east corner, near the foot of the West Bow. In less than a month it will be her own hanging, and the very thought brings a shiver to her bones.

Black Bill moves closer to Maggie. His eyes shining like black pools. 'Will you lay next to me tonight, lass? I have not felt the arms of a woman for such a long time and I won't take any liberties – I vow...'

'Hush, Bill. I know you won't. It is the least I can do.'

It pains Maggie to look at his miserable face, a sad contrast to the proud gipsy man she knows him to be. Gaol does that to folk; it breaks spirits and reduces all but the insane to shadows of their former selves. When night falls, Maggie grants Black Bill his wish and turns her thin body to his, allowing his head to rest against her breasts. He shrieks and jerks backwards.

'Ouch – what is that?

'A luckenbooth. I always wear it close to my heart.'

'Well it just scratched my face, can't you take it off?'

'Never,' Maggie shakes her head. 'Now go to sleep, Bill.'

'I don't want to die,' he whispers.

'Hush now, I am here for you.'

★★★

In the morning, when they come for him, Black Bill keeps his nerves in check. There is no bravado about him, rather a calm, sorrowful look. As the guards lead him away, the wild creature flips in his cage, and his arms crash against the heavy iron bars as froth protrudes from his mouth. He chants: 'Dead man, dead man, dead man!'

Meanwhile, Black Bill's mouth twists with mirth. As he approaches the cage he stops and pauses to bang on his bars. And the guards suck in their breath at this brave feat, as they never get close and tend to poke things in with a stick.

'Who rattled your cage?' Bill bellows at him.

The caged man stands perfectly still, his face like stone. No one has ever seen him keep quiet or still for so long. All of a sudden he erupts into laughter and mimics the gipsy. 'Who rattled your cage?'

★★★

Gaol is an empty and lonely place without Black Bill. Four days after his execution, a prisoner, one Maggie is not acquainted with, manages to acquire a broadsheet of his crime. Therefore, in haste, Maggie contrives to possess the broadsheet, and exerts herself to this stranger, in an effort to acquire the paper. However, once the precious document is in her hands, her face falls in disappointment – damn, she cannot read. In the end the old hunchback guard takes pity on her and snatches it from her hands, saying through gritted teeth: 'For goodness sake, give us it here, you bunch of half-wits. I'll read it for you if you want – although I have a much shorter version for you: he was a highwayman and that is that.'

'Please,' Maggie pleads. 'I want to know the details of his crime.'

A group soon circles the disfigured man, all struggling for a spot of their own. Maggie, impatient as ever, prompts him to start. The hunchback clears his throat before reading. 'That upon the twelfth day of December, William Leslie, alias 'Black Bill,' did commit the heinous crime of highway robbery. A Mr McFadden had set home in his carriage after a successful day at the races and was carrying £150. All had seemed well and quiet until he was stopped by a well-dressed man of dark complexion wearing a green velvet coat with gold buttons. Furthermore, the dark man who was riding on a black horse and carrying a pistol demanded that Mr McFadden hand over all of his money and jewels. Initially, Mr McFadden refused until he was hit with a pistol over the head. Eventually his manservant became injured in the struggle. The man escaped quickly on horseback with the £150 and a precious Thomas Tompian pocket watch.'

Maggie gasps and repeats the words, 'precious Thomas Tompian watch.' She tries to remember where she placed *her* precious watch – the one she took from Alexander. Maggie bites her lip and near chokes with hysterics. She's hid an incredibly valuable watch in a stinking pigsty.

The prison guard hushes her and continues to read from the broadsheet: 'A sergeant was quickly ordered to search for the highwayman and a cash reward was offered for the capture of the perpetrator of the crime. A man fitting the description was quickly found and lodged in Jedburgh Tolbooth, and subsequently taken to Edinburgh Tolbooth to await trial. Black Bill was found guilty of highway robbery and sentenced to death by hanging.'

The gaoler returns the broadsheet to Maggie, a cheerless look on his face. 'Your turn next.'

★★★

It was the dream, the one she's suffered with for years. That damned tapping noise followed by clanging and hammering. Disorientated, Maggie turns on the filthy straw and realises it's not the dream – it's real. They are building the gallows for her.

Minister Bonaloy arrives, a Bible in his hand. Maggie rocks back and forth, her lips so dry they are stuck together. She tries to speak to him but nothing comes out and as he reaches for her hand she begins to cry.

'The sheriffs are coming,' says the minister. The minister winces as they drag her outside and in vain he tries to shield her from the coffin that sits on the cart outside – but she's already seen it.

'Who paid for the coffin?' she enquires.

'Jean Ramsay,' he replies. 'Folk are wondering how on earth she paid for it.'

Maggie knows how.

Before the cart sets off, she reaches a tentative hand out to Minister Bonaloy and looks him deep in the eyes. 'Will you tell my children that I love them, and that I am sorry for all that has happened – and kiss them for me?'

The minister nods. 'It shall be done.'

'And there is something else. If Patrick should return, will you tell him that I begged for his forgiveness? And will you tell him that I am sorry for being an unfaithful wife and that I love him?'

'Oh, Maggie – is it foolish of me to think that might be hard for him to believe? After all that has happened?'

Maggie stares into his fine face. 'He will believe, Minister Bonaloy, because I have no reason to lie – not now when I'm about to die.'

'Never mind, dear, let us pray together.' He offers her his hand.

'Aye, let us pray. I'm ready. I am ready to die.'

CHAPTER SEVENTEEN

THE HANGING – 2 SEPTEMBER 1724

'Honest John' Dalgleish holds the unenviable position of Edinburgh executioner. It's not the greatest job in the world, but someone has to do it and that someone might as well be him. When John's not hanging or scourging folk, he's expected to keep busy and that involves keeping the streets clean of stones and swine. Stranger things are found lying in the wynds – a dead baby inside a sheep's bladder for instance, being kicked about by the beggar boys. But then there's not much that surprises him in his line of work. John's hardened to it all, and he more than anyone realises life is cheap. People live and people die and life goes on.

Nevertheless, it's a living and in short, John Dalgliesh is a livery of the city – a public servant. For obvious reasons he's not a popular man. But having said that he obtains no pleasure from watching folk suffer and there are times when he feels he can no longer stomach the job. It's not all doom and gloom though, there are a few perks to being a lockman; such as all the free fish and peat he's entitled to – and better still, all the ale he can drink during a punishment. Scourging in particular is thirsty work.

Many a public executioner abuses their power, but not Johnny Dalgliesh – he's indeed an up-right character and just man. Only the other week someone asked John how hard he beats his criminals, and he said: 'I lay my lash according to my conscience.'

The hangman's house lies at the foot of the fish market. It's a modest lodging but serves his needs. As always, at the crack of dawn he awakens, he stretches and yawns. A prickling sensation begins at the base of his neck, spreading all across his scalp with a searing heat. *Another hanging*, he thinks, wiping the sleep from his eyes – nothing remarkable except for the fact that he knows the woman, a Musselburgh fishwife by the name of Dickson, a popular lassie. He's taken fish from her creel many a time.

'Damnation,' he curses under his breath. As he dresses in haste he hopes the crowd won't give him any trouble. He must take his staff – just in case.

Delicate hands cut at a chunk of bread, knife protruding from elegantly tapered fingers that might have played a fine instrument or painted art. He eats his bread with haste, swallowing before he chews properly, not savouring the taste but mechanically so; to him it's just fuel. A hand to his mouth, he wipes away crumbs then gathers a length of hempen span in his arms before closing the door behind him.

Outside Hingie House, he pauses to lean on his door; the sun beats down on his face, scorching his eyelids. When he opens his eyes all he can see is a fireball, a blinding light that makes the streets appear ghost-like and eerie. A knocking noise echoes in the distance. The banging noise of a hammer as the gallows is erected.

★★★

Horse and cart rattle downhill towards the Grassmarket, a spacious and stately rectangle 230 yards in length. They proceed along the north-east angle along an acclivitous and ancient winding alley towards the gallows situated at the foot of the West Bow. The minister shudders at the sight of the scaffold flanked by tall tenements, the windows of which afford a grandstand view. A young drummer boy bangs on his drum ahead of a sweating horse and guards surround the cart to protect the prisoner from the rabble. Outside a tavern, the wagon comes to a halt and one of the sheriffs jumps out to speak to the innkeeper.

'One for the road, Maggie?' a sheriff asks, and mimics the act of taking a drink.

'Nae, I'll stay on the wagon.' She turns to Minister Bonaloy. 'The tavern's where all this trouble started.'

The cart moves off again, rattling down the steep hill. Maggie sits in the cart, perched on top of her coffin, her hands tied together in front of her so that she faces the back – they tied her thus to spare her the sight of the scaffold looming ahead. Not because they care mind – no they tie all condemned folk this way to avoid escape attempts from terror-struck prisoners. Minister Bonaloy prays at Maggie's side, uttering words of comfort. The road is narrow and winding and all around them folk crowd around the cart, packed shoulder to shoulder to get a view of the condemned. At the head of the procession, the chief sheriff and hangman lead the way, and at the rear more guards keep the rabble from the cart. Maggie's crying, tugging at the rope with her hands. The minister reaches out and continues his prayers but Maggie can't hear him – a tall man with golden hair has burst his way through the guards.

'Maggie!' he screams.

William Bell chases the cart, arms pumping up and down; he is near – just within reach. Maggie tugs on the rope again and before long her hands are loose, she stretches out a hand – and as their hands entwine, Maggie passes him the silver luckenbooth.

★★★

Mr Cunningham, the baker, is excited as he hangs his floury apron on a rusty nail protruding from his flaking lime-washed wall. The streets of Edinburgh are heaving with activity, pie-sellers, beggars and whores weave their way through a massive crowd. As he opens and locks the door behind him, he hears the macabre beat of the drum-roll that marks a hanging day. Into the dense crowd he is drawn, hands guarding his pockets, vigilant and cautious of the pickpockets and thieves. The crowd is raucous and stirs along like a great ebbing tide, sucking Mr Cunningham into its current. He finds a spot at the West Bow well beneath the inscription 'Nisi Dominus Frustra.' He's familiar with Edinburgh's motto – 'Without God Everything Fails.' As he climbs onto a small platform to gain a most splendid view, a sea of bodies cover the Grassmarket. Thousands have turned out to see the wanton fishwife hang. The rat-a-tat of drums pulse through his body as the woman's crime is read out to the crowd.

'I'm innocent,' she cries.

The crowd roars.

Mr Cunningham observes the damned woman with abhorrent fascination. With curious eyes he observes her family and friends standing near the gibbet foot, bidding her a tearful farewell. As the drum beats to a crescendo she remains calm and admits being unfaithful to her husband but denies murdering her child. Finally, a great hush descends over the crowd. Hecklers at long last silenced as anticipation and expectation crackles all around.

'She's all skin and bone,' a fat water-carrier cries out.

'The tolbooth's left its mark on her. That's what happens when you drown your baby,' someone replies.

'Some say she's innocent.'

'Aye, that's what they all say.'

★★★

John Dalgliesh circles the scaffold. He's forgotten something, he's sure of it, but what? He checks the rope again – it's a new one and he can find no fault. The fishwife stands next to her minister, he can hardly bear to look at her – it's her face and the slender sweep of her shoulders. His hands are steady as he places the noose around her neck. The hangman glances at her again, she shows no fear, except for a slight tremble in her knees. He can't help noticing her skin, so pale and white that he can make out spidery blue veins in the sides of her face and neck.

'Turn around. I need to tie your wrists.'

'I won't be able to climb the ladder.'

His face reddens. 'Aye, up you go then – I'll tie them later.'

At the base of her spine he presses his hand, guiding her up the ladder, one rung at a time. His eyes become focused on her clothes, all ragged and torn, her soft skin visible beneath.

'Stop,' he commands in a gruff voice. He peers up at his assistant perched atop the crossbeam of the gallows and nods his head. With a sweep of his arm he throws up the loose end of the rope and watches him secure it properly. 'Done?' he calls out.

'Aye, it's secure.'

'I'm tying your wrists now. If you struggle, I'll hang you myself with me bare hands, do you hear me?' He jumps off the ladder.

The drum-roll grows louder, tension building as he places two rough hands either side of the ladder. He curses and pauses to wipe sweat from his forehead. An awful feeling festers in his stomach as he handles the ladder once again and at the same time he looks up to the shadowy silhouette perched upon the top rungs. All is quiet – he takes a deep breath and twists the ladder.

'May the Lord have mercy on your soul.' The hangman turns the ladder away.

'Her hands have come free,' a woman screams. 'She's trying to pull the rope from her neck.'

But the hangman has turned to stone. His feet stick to the ground and his legs turn to mush and all the while he screams inside. He can't believe his eyes – the lassie's hands have worked their way under the noose, somehow trapped after the drop took place. Her feet thrash in empty air, writhing in the painful agony of death.

'Cut her down,' a man screams.

'Shame – shame on you!' another man in the crowd yells.

Suddenly the feeling in his legs returns and he springs to action. 'Where is my staff?' the hangman curses. He knew he'd forgotten something – how could he be so foolish? 'I need a stick. Has anyone got a stick with a cleek?' He ducks as stones and rocks are hurled at him.

'No, you incompetent fool!'

The hangman lunges at a poor cripple. 'Give me the stick now or you will be sorry.' He snatches it away and recoils as the crowd surges towards him – holding out the stick to keep them away.

'For God's sake, get back. This poor woman is suffering and needs to be dispatched.'

He picks up the stick and gives the fishwife a few whacks, but before he knows it he's on his knees being pelted with stones. They stamp on him, curse and spit – then everything goes black.

★★★

Mr Cunningham, the most respectable baker, crosses himself and shudders, he can't bear to watch. He closes his eyes to the hideous spectacle playing out in front of him and waits for the screams and shrieks to die down. Folk elbow and shove him in the ribs and shout down his ear, before long he's tempted to peek out once again. He takes a deep breath, opens his eyes and stares at the gibbet.

'Where's the hangman?' he questions a pie seller.

'He fell. He's with his assistant now. They were separated in the confusion – haven't you been watching?'

The hangman emerges covered in muck and blood, his assistant helping him to stand. A light drizzle begins to fall, clinging to the shape of the hanged woman's curves. The baker holds his breath and quivers at the macabre spectre, his eyes lingering over her for the longest time.

'Watch,' the pie seller points to the corpse dangling from the gibbet. 'The hangie's about to pull down on her legs.'

'Whatever for?'

But before the pie seller can answer, the hangman wraps his strong arms around her and tugs down on her legs; it would seem to snuff out any life left in the poor woman.

★★★

John Dalgliesh slumps to the floor beneath the gallows, his body bruised and sore.

'Fire and hell, man. Where were you? Did you see what happened?' he mutters to his assistant.

'Aye, I'm sorry, Jock. I saw them throwing stones but there was nothing I could do – I was pulled into the crowd and I thought the sheriff…'

'No matter. Fetch us a dram, will you. I could do with a stiff drink.'

The assistant nods and pauses before running off to a nearby tavern. 'I'd give it an hour at least before you cut her down.'

'Fear not – that graceless wife will hang till I'm satisfied.'

Beneath the gibbet, the fishwife's friends and family flock together to wait for him to cut her body down – he can feel the weight of their stares. Before he takes his knife from his belt, he downs his drink in one and wipes his mouth with the back of his hand.

'Stand back, the lot of you,' he hisses.

His hand trembles as he severs the rope, her body falls with a thud to the soft ground. He drops from the crossbeam, landing awkwardly on his feet and wincing in pain. The friends and family move fast – fighting their way through the rabble to bring the cart and coffin, eager to protect the body.

'How much longer?' an ugly old woman complains.

John Dalgliesh pays no heed to the old crone and drops to his knees to press and ear to the corpse's breast. The ugly woman gives him a vicious stare as though he's violating her corpse and so he continues to ignore her and cuts the noose from her neck.

'You incompetent fool,' hiss the fishwives. 'Just give us the body.'

He's used to the insults, the cursing and jeers. And in his own way he understands their animosity and fear. The hangman backs away from the body, his hands gripped tight around his knife, not taking his eyes off them. He's curious to see how long it will be before they have to fight. As it happens they don't have to wait long – Munro's surgeon apprentice men are on the prowl.

★★★

There isn't time to mourn, and no amount of sobbing is going to bring her back. Widow Arrock tears her eyes from Maggie's body and decides to take charge. She pushes her way through the Musselburgh fishwives, rolls up her sleeves and makes herself known.

'The men are bringing the coffin over and the cooms must be nailed fast. Help me place the body in the coffin.'

The carter cries to them from the cart, cursing and swearing for them to make haste. As soon as the coffin hits the ground they lift the unroped body and place it in the wooden box.

'That's it, in she goes, now get her on the cart quick,' nods the widow, nearly stumbling to the floor in the hurry.

Together they gather around the coffin, nervous fingers curling and clawing beneath the wooden base. The journey to the cart is further than they think and as the sun beats down the coffin bobs along like a boat on rough sea. The manoeuvre prompts an almighty commotion playing out in front of them like a horrendous dream. The body snatchers come from nowhere, taking them by surprise – armed with hammers, and every splitting blow pierces their hearts as they are swept away in a hurricane of shouting and brawling.

'He's smashing the lid through! Get him!' shouts one of the fisherwomen with murderous fury, baring her teeth and nails. The other women follow suit, barking like bitches and driving the men away.

'There's no time to bang the lid down,' the carter gestures to the fishwives. 'Get it on the cart and let's go now, before they return. We can nail the lid down later.'

★★★

With the coffin safely on the cart, the carter cracks his whip. At top speed, he proceeds away from the Grassmarket toward the safety of Inveresk Kirk. As the makeshift hearse rattles and bumps across the cobbled wynds, the carter feels mighty relieved to leave the body snatchers and apprentice surgeons far behind.

The cart-horse whinnies as the splendid spire of Duddingston Kirk comes into view, encircled by a fine blue sky. The mourners follow on foot behind him, complaining of sore feet and parched tongues. The weather is sultry and Duncan's eyes light at the sight of a tavern in the distance. 'I need a drink.'

'Trust you. Anyway – where are we?' the widow sighs.

The carter shouts out to all: 'Peffermill, and that's the Sheep's Heid.'

The carter halts the cart and pats his horse. 'The horse needs water. I'll leave the cart and coffin out here while we all go inside.

So if it's drinks you're wanting or a wee dram, go and have one now before we set off again.'

★★★

'To Maggie,' Johnny Notions raises a dram, his arm wrapped around Duncan.

'To Maggie,' Duncan tastes his drink before lifting his tankard in a toast.

'She was quite a character,' grins Johnny.

'Aye, she was that,' Duncan wipes away a tear. 'A remarkable woman was my Maggie. I can't believe she is gone.' He gestures to the other women inside the inn. 'Look at them all – the widow, Jean Ramsay and the fisher lassies, aye, they're a rowdy lot. But she...' His voice cracks with emotion. 'She was a free spirit and she did as she damn well pleased.'

'She paid for it too, Duncan.'

'Aye, she did.'

★★★

The joiners trudge along with heavy limbs to the tavern up yonder, covered head to toe in saw-dust, their throats dry and parched from the fine powder lodged in their throats. A jug of frothy ale is just what they need to wash it away. They walk side by side, an old man and a young apprentice, neither of them a care in the world as they approach the inn.

A cart and coffin stands opposite the Sheep Heid, unattended in a sheltered corner, one half in the shade, the other half drenched by a scorching sun. Shadows fall on the wooden box in the shapes of twisted branches and shimmering leaves. A horse whinnies at the front, drinking from a pail of water.

'Wonder why that's there? Has someone drunk themselves to death?' the old joiner laughs at his own joke.

'How should I know? Shall we take a look?'

'Aye,' they nod to each other and walk towards the cart, their faces bright and curious.

The older man leaps onto the cart, screwing up his eyebrows and tracing one hand along the wooden chest. 'Looks a bit battered, as if someone's been throwing it around.' He inserts a finger into a centre of the of the coffin lid.

'Jack. Don't do that!'

'Why? Whoever's in it is dead, laddie.'

'Aye, I know, but you're giving me the creeps.' The lad shudders and presses his palms together as though in silent prayer.

Meanwhile old Jack examines the cart, looking for free tools. And then, he turns, sharp-like on his heel and points to his friend. 'What are you doing?'

'What do you mean?' says the lad.

'The scraping noise, it's not funny. Give over.'

'I'm not making a scraping noise, Jack.' The laddie's face turns pale as he hears it, like rats scratching their way out of a wooden trap.

'Are you sure, laddie? You'll feel the back of my hand if I find out you're jesting.'

'It's not me, Jack – honest. It's coming from the coffin.'

'Oh my Lord.' Jack shakes his head and leaps from the cart, his heart racing as he runs into the tavern.

★★★

Everyone is merry in the Sheep Heid, just as a good wake should be. A singsong is in process, snuff's being passed round and there's even a round of free drinks. Then the joiners storm in looking like a couple of demons banished to purgatory. A tension crackles in the air as the funeral entourage crowd around the two trembling men. As usual, the widow takes charge, pushing the officious carter and Johnny Notions aside.

'Get them a drink and a stool,' she shouts gruffly, before passing them a wee dram of firewater to calm their nerves. She turns her attention to the older man as she can get no sense from the laddie. 'What did you say your name is?'

'Jack Bytheway. I'm a joiner from the sawmill. You know the one behind the tavern.'

The widow nods. 'Now then, tell me what you think you heard – and slow down.'

Jack Bytheway stares at the widow with wide-open eyes. The pulse in his neck twitches beneath his leine. When his words finally come they are awkward and clumsy and so he has to slow his speech down. 'A noise came from the coffin, a scraping and knocking noise, and honest to God, I'm not jesting, it scared me to death.'

Duncan turns pale and puts his drink down.

Johnny turns to Duncan and laughs. 'This is a prank.'

'Hush. The man is trying to speak.' The widow prompts the joiner to continue.

'It is not a prank. I speak the truth – there was a scratching sound coming from inside the coffin. I heard it, and he heard it too. Honest to God!'

Duncan bolts for the door, Johnny Notions close at his heels as the others follow slowly behind. The widow at the rear shakes her head and says, 'It's probably a rat in the cart or a mouse – nothing to fear.'

But despite the widow's words, the funeral entourage keep a wary distance from the battered coffin, their faces turned towards the cart and coffin, waiting for a noise. A moment passes in silence, the widow folds her arms over her bony chest and approaches the two joiners – her bony finger pointed to their faces. 'You feckless idiots. You should never make jokes concerning the dead, I've a mind to…' and then, all of a sudden, the scraping noise returns.

'I told you,' Jack Bytheway nods and holds out his arms.

Johnny holds his breath; a cold sweat covers his pale face as he turns to Duncan. 'Aye, must be a rat,' he adds with nervous eyes. 'Let's take a look.'

★★★

They stand either side of the cart. Johnny holds one hand over his eyes in a gesture of pain, making a little crack between two fingers and peeking through. Through the gap in his fingers he can see a dark wood coffin, partly smashed in at the centre of the lid. A scratching noise reverberates from inside it, causing the two men to shiver and shake.

'Open the lid,' Duncan suddenly comes to life and panics. 'Come on, Johnny.' With one leap he is on the cart, his hands on the coffin.

Johnny's feet stay firmly on the ground. 'Calm down, Duncan. Now let's not get excited. There must be a reasonable explanation.'

'Open the damned lid, that's my daughter in there. Get in this cart now.'

Johnny jumps on to the cart and gestures to the carter. 'Where are your tools, man?'

The carter shakes his head and takes a few awkward steps backwards. 'I've a hammer and a spade under that hessian sack.'

'Pass us the spade,' says Duncan, stretching out a hand. 'Are you ready for this, Johnny?'

Johnny's terrified; his stomach is in knots. 'Aye – as ready as I'll ever be. You get the spade beneath the lid and I'll help to lift it.'

As the tip of the spade slips beneath a gap in the lid, Johnny is suddenly frozen with fear – and it takes all his resolve to gather his wits and strength as the sound of metal scraping wood cuts through the air.

'Curl your fingers under the wood and lift,' Duncan commands.

Johnny's lips are trembling. He swallows back bile and yanks up the lid with Duncan, lifting it away with one last heave.

Out the corner of his eye, Johnny watches Duncan fall to his knees, his mind filling with thoughts of fallen angels and ethereal creatures, the likes he's never seen before. And then his eyes are drawn to a searing light, streaming downwards onto the coffin and casting a heaven-like glow upon her white face.

A few brave souls strain their necks to see within the coffin. And then, something truly remarkable happens. *A miracle of the Lord*, thinks Johnny, as an unearthly groan echoes into the air. The corpse draws up her limbs and arises from within the coffin causing terrified onlookers to take flight along the dusty road as fast as their legs will carry them – with one exception.

★★★

Peter Purdie opens his bag and stares into the man's eyes. 'Did you bathe? Bathing increases the movement of blood.'

The man nods.

'Have you a calm mind?'

'Aye.' The man holds out his arm.

Purdie places a tourniquet on the man's arm and a gives him a stick to grasp. He urges the man to squeeze, and soon the man's veins swell.

He makes an incision and lets the blood flow into a bowl. After that, he bandages the man's arm and is on his way, thinking he might have a wee dram before returning home.

A few drams later, Purdie puts on his hat and makes his way to the road. But as he proceeds to the door of the Sheep Heid, a great deal of people block the exit outside. He pushes his way through them, and comes to a cart and horse. A minister greets him with an ashen face and stammers: 'She sat up and they all took to their heels.'

Purdie frowns. 'Who sat up?'

'Maggie – oh, dear Lord, the dead woman in the cart.' The holy man is making no sense so Purdie jumps onto the cart. He cannot believe his eyes – a young woman sits upright in a coffin. A man kneels before her, hands held up in prayer.

'Maggie. You're alive,' the man in prayer cries. 'But how can this be? I saw him pull down on your legs with my own eyes.'

But as the man continues to pray, the woman's eyes roll back into her head and she falls backwards into the coffin. 'Who is she?' he asks the man on his knees.

'My daughter. Please help her. Please.'

'She's out cold. May I examine her?'

The father nods, his lips stretch out horizontally into a grimace.

Purdie puts down his bag to examine the girl; his fingers immediately trace the deep red ligature marks around her neck. *Surely not?* he thinks, shaking his head. 'What happened to her neck?'

'She's just been hanged in the Grassmarket.'

'You're jesting. And she's come round. How incredible!' Purdie grabs his bag and gestures to the other man in the cart. 'Who are you?'

'Johhny Notions, a family friend, and this is the woman's father, Duncan. Can you help her?'

'Aye.' He turns to the father again. 'I'm a blood letter – will you let me open a vein?'

'Yes – yes – anything. You must do anything you can to revive her.'

Purdie opens his bag and gets to work. 'Now I'm going to breathe a vein in her arm.' He takes the woman's pale arm in his hands and makes a small cut. Almost immediately, her blood flows into the bowl. Suddenly Maggie stirs again and murmurs, 'Oh dear.'

Purdie lifts her then to a brae at the roadside, and in a short while the blood returns to her lips and cheeks. He glances around, the escapees having conquered their fears have returned. At once he cries out to them: 'Is there anybody here who will help me get blankets and hold her in the cart? She's had a terrible shock.'

An ugly old woman answers, 'Aye – I will hold her.'

They lower the poor woman onto a pile of blankets in a corn cart and Purdie makes sure the old woman holds her by the arms and shoulders.

'Thank you,' the father says. 'My Maggie is alive because of you.'

'No – no – it's divine intervention. The works of God are works of wonder.'

★★★

The weaver's cottage is in darkness. A young man weeps on his knees, praying to God Almighty for sparing his sister. It is a miracle of that he is sure. James is dumbstruck. The news has hit him like a thunderbolt and causes him to weep like a small child. His head aches and his throat is swollen and dry.

'Can it be true?' James asks the master weaver again, a bewildered expression on his young face.

'It must be, James. Your sister is alive. They've sent for a magistrate to guard her and they're on their way.'

James hears them before he sees them; they seem to come slowly down the hill with a soft buzzing sound, occasionally interrupted by shrieks and screams. James closes his eyes and swallows, when he opens them his eyebrows raise and pull together and his stomach churns. In one swift motion he opens the door and takes a deep breath.

A cart lies abandoned near a patch of thistles; and within it is a wooden coffin, upturned and on its side. But where is Maggie? His eyes gaze upon the many men and women, but he cannot see her. Eventually James moves from the door and takes small tentative steps towards the cart. A thin woman probably overcome from all the commotion is supported in Johnny Notions arms, as they come closer a feeling of dread sends shivers up his bones.

'No – no – no. Maggie? That cannot be Maggie. What has happened to you?'

'She's not come round yet.' Johnny strides past James and kicks open the door. Minister Bonaloy follows close behind with his good book in his hands.

They place her on a clean straw bed and all James can do is gape and stare. Around her neck are angry red marks and her face is deathly pale.

'Don't vex yourself, son. She will come through – God knows she is strong.' His father places an arm around him.

'But look at her, Father. She is all skin and bone.'

'Aye – she is. But she is alive and that's all that matters.'

They feed her broth and whisky and Minister Bonaloy prays over her until the magistrate arrives. Before long folk arrive from every corner of Scotland, as the news of her failed hanging spreads like wildfire. The cottage buzzes with activity – friends and neighbours, some with tears in their eyes come to visit her, others to take a wee look at her neck. But for the most part, they stand gathered around her bed, gazing upon her face in a meditative silence – and better still they leave gifts or money.

★★★

Throughout the next day, Maggie raises no hopes that she is recovering her strength. She remains in a deep sleep, occasionally broken by bouts of delirium. James does his very best to console her as she thrashes about on her bed. Before long he is exhausted, and therefore Minister Bonaloy takes a seat beside her to watch her and pray. And he's mighty happy to be beside this extraordinary woman fresh off the scaffold, reading out from his much-loved Bible in a soothing tone – that is until she screams out: 'Let me be gone, for I am to be executed on Wednesday.'

★★★

The following morning sees a marked improvement in Maggie; she is able to sit up and complains only of tenderness to her neck. And amidst the turmoil of well-wishers and visitors, Maggie suddenly remembers that she is a mother and cries out for her children. Minister Bonaloy promptly puts down his Bible and ventures outside to fetch the widow and Maggie's bairns to be reunited with their mother.

It seems to take an age for the children to arrive. For some reason they do not come to their mother's bed at once. Maggie is puzzled, as she lies propped up in her bed she fidgets and curses and wonders what is taking them so long.

'Where are they?'

A door opens. Two reluctant children are pushed inside. Meanwhile Maggie is lost for words. To the casual observer this sad little threesome would appear but strangers to one another, an emaciated woman and two terrified children.

'Have you forgotten me, Patrick?' Maggie holds out a trembling hand.

'Greet your mother, go on, laddie – don't be scared,' barks out the minister.

'She's not my mother.' Young Patrick backs away from the straw bed.

Maggie shakes her head at Minister Bonaloy and sinks back onto her pillow. 'It's all right, none of this is their fault. It's all mine for leaving them for so long. I've been a terrible mother.'

At that moment little Anna walks over and takes a seat on the straw bed beside her. All eyes widen as her little hands linger on the red marks around Maggie's neck. 'What happened to your neck? Did you fall over?'

Maggie chokes, her words come out broken. 'Aye, I fell. Did you miss me, Anna?'

'I didn't miss you, Mother. I had Buttercup.'

'Who's Buttercup?' Maggie frowns.

The widow titters and places a hand to her mouth. 'Your old goat. Anna would sleep with the thing if I let her.'

'I've been replaced by a goat,' Maggie nods. 'Serves me right.'

★★★

On the proceeding Sunday, Maggie decides to attend a public worship, at which the minister has agreed to preach a sermon applicable to her case. Maggie fasts and prays and gives gratitude for her deliverance. As the sermon comes to an end the crowded congregation surge forward and nearly crush Maggie against the kirk wall. Duncan, Johnny and James gather around her to push away the crowd, trapped between a rabble of people and a trembling minister.

'For goodness sake, I just want to thank God for sparing me,' she cries into the dense crowd.

The kirk minister turns pale. 'You're all in danger of being trampled. Follow me now.'

And so the minister is obliged to conduct them out of the kirk through a backdoor, denying many a glimpse of 'Half-Hangit Maggie.'

★★★

The following Wednesday, one week after the hanging, Maggie returns to the Fisherrow cottage along with the bairns. She glances around the cottage at the fishing gear; the creels and skulls. Everything is not as she left it, someone has tidied up and everything is spick and span. With her hands she removes the scarf from her neck to reveal her scars of her shame.

268

The widow stays for a wee while to settle the children and help make up a fire.

'Will you be all right, Maggie?' The widow holds out a hand.

Maggie nods and wipes away a tear.

'What have I done?' she whispers as the widow departs. 'I must devote myself to solemn fasting and prayer.' Maggie drops to her knees.

'Where has the widow gone?' sobs little Patrick.

'Hush,' Anna pouts. Her eyes widen as the door flies open and a gust of wind fills the room. 'Father!' she gasps.

Maggie gulps. Her husband is very much changed. And her mind reels and turns like cogs on a wheel to discover the reason for this transformation. She looks him over. He carries a lantern and it swings from side to side. His figure is the same, although he appears stronger – but then he always was as strong as a horse. Then, as her eyes sweep over him, she notices his mouth, one side of his lips is raised and his head is tilted back slightly, as though he is looking down at her, the focus of his disgust and contempt.

'That's enough praying, Maggie. You'll wear out your knees.'

'Patrick, Patrick,' she crawls on her knees to wrap her arms around his legs.

'It's been nearly two years since I saw you last, Maggie. I have continued to exist only for you. You have no idea how many times I yearned to see your face,' his voice quivers as he pulls her to her feet.

'Patrick. There is something I must tell you.'

'No matter – I know everything. The widow told me about the hanging and mouths are no doubt clacking everywhere. I could hang you by the scruff of the neck myself.'

Maggie's hands flutter nervously to her rope-scarred neck. 'Are you going to leave? Please don't leave me, Patrick – can you forgive me?'

Maggie stands very still, her hands at her sides so that he does not see them tremble. She dare not move for fear that he might have a swift change of mood and grab her by the scruff of her neck.

'After the hanging, they pronounced me dead and I thought to myself that means we are no longer wed. You are free to marry another if you wish…'

Patrick pulls her into a fierce embrace. 'To hell with them all. As far as I'm concerned you are still my Maggie and we are still wed.'

★★★

The next morning, Maggie wakes to find Patrick snoring by her side. She kisses his rough face and creeps from the bed, taking care not to wake him. Due to two mischievous children, the cottage is already a mess and needs a good sweeping and dusting. But for now it can wait.

The usual sounds come from the harbour; iron ringing on iron, hammers striking nails, sending a shiver up Maggie's spine. She doesn't want to think of the hanging but images come to her all the while, triggered by the smell of old rope, or the feel of the deep welt that encircles her neck. *What if they decide to hang me again?* she wonders, as sadness fills her heart. When Patrick stirs he places one arm around her and sets her mind at ease.

'They can't hang you again, Maggie. It was God's will that you lived. The law can't meddle with that, no matter how high and mighty. And besides, I won't let them. They'll have to hang me first.'

★★★

If there's ever a place to forget your worries, it's the sea. The harbour's a magical place at dawn and as Patrick and Maggie walk bare-foot towards the crashing waves, the two children lag behind admiring the sailboats and fishing boats beside the shore. For a while they rummage through the sand and rock pools, collecting shells, starfish and crabs.

'I'm going to swallow the anchor, Maggie — I've thought it through and it's what I want,' Patrick declares, nodding his head.

'Patrick? But you love the sea.'

'The time has come for a change, Maggie. Besides I need to be closer to home – to keep an eye on you.'

Noisy gulls screech above. Patrick grasps his wife's hand and pulls her into his arms. All the while she feels her mouth going dry, trapped like a songbird in a cage, suffocating within his arms.

'Maggie, Maggie!' a voice interrupts them.

James runs towards them, his face red. A strange looking man follows behind him carrying a leather bag and papers.

'A doctor from the Surgeon's Hall in Edinburgh wants to see you, Maggie. I expect he's one of Munro's men. He'll pay you for your time. And don't be surprised if you're presented with a magistrate, too.'

'What?' Maggie gasps.

Patrick releases Maggie from his arms. 'Don't fret. Everything will be fine.'

'I hope so.' Maggie clutches his hand, digging her nails into his fingers. 'What do they want? Haven't I already paid for my sins?'

★★★

Near the cottage he waits, at the bottom of the steps peering at his fob watch as though he is short of time. If first appearances are anything to go by, the doctor seems a pleasant enough man. But as time passes he becomes brutally succinct to the point of downright rude. In a brusque manner the doctor explains that in the interest of medical science, he feels it necessary to examine Maggie in order to determine how she managed to survive the noose.

Inside the cottage, he removes his thick coat and puts on his blood-stained apron. The learned gentleman carries the all-pervading odour of decay, a nasty remnant of the dissecting room, not to mention fingernails clogged with putrid flesh. Maggie shivers and holds her breath as he approaches her, her eyes gaping at his macabre bag of medical tools. Her first instinct is to run and be away from the man. But on reflection she realises that by doing this she will gain nothing, and besides if she refuses him, other medical men might follow to satisfy their curiosity, so better to be done with this now.

'What do you want me to do?' she asks, not meeting his eyes.

'I won't be a moment.' A smudge of ink streaks his fingers as he scribbles some notes. 'Now then, basically, I need to perform an examination that involves a physical bodily inspection. And then I will ask you several questions regarding the hanging. Is that clear?'

She nods and looks at him with haggard, desperate eyes. 'Will it hurt?'

'After what you've been through – I imagine not,' the doctor continues. 'Do you realise how fortunate you are? You could have regained consciousness on the dissection table, and then – well, I shudder to think.'

Maggie rocks backwards and forwards in her chair as the doctor talks, biting her nails.

'Your survival is nothing short of a miracle! I refused to believe your incredible tale when I heard it, dismissing it as pure nonsense. Though I must say I am glad to be proven wrong. You're the talk of Edinburgh. 'Half-Hangit Maggie,' they're calling you. Do you know that?'

'Aye, I could do without the fuss,' she shrugs.

The fire crackles as he motions for her to sit forward in her chair. 'Now be still so I can take a wee look at that neck,' he says.

★★★

It's all over and all the fretting was for nothing because the doctor was a kind and gentle man. He didn't bleed her or hurt her in anyway. Once the examination and inquisition are over the doctor packs up his medical bag and makes his way to the door.

'Count your blessings, lass. I'm quite sure that the man who bled you had nothing to do with your recovery, but no matter. I'm glad he was there anyhow. Peter Purdie, you say?' He turns to Patrick and smiles. 'Your wife is very well, sir. Except for the ligature marks – I expect it will leave a scar but that's a small price to pay for her life. Good day to you both.' He tips his hat.

★★★

After the doctor leaves they sit for a while by the fire. Maggie's restless still, imagining all sorts of horrors that await her. After a while there is the sound of a horse galloping outside, and then a series of blows onto the cottage door. Patrick opens the door and realises that the magistrate has arrived.

'What is it?' he says to the man.

'Does one Margaret Dickson live here?'

'Aye.'

'Please inform her that I have come to deliver her an important message.'

Maggie peeks out from behind Patrick with wide eyes, and wasting no time, the magistrate takes out a document and nods to her: 'Are you Margaret Dickson?'

'Aye,' she says in a hoarse voice.

'After much deliberation, it has been decided that the said Margaret Dickson shall not be hanged a second time. The legal authorities have pointed out that as the certificate of execution was indeed signed, they therefore have no further claim on you. I must also inform you that as a consequence, the said Margaret Dickson's marriage to a Patrick Spence has been legally dissolved.' Satisfied that his message has been delivered, he passes Patrick the document and walks off in the direction of the nearest tavern.

Maggie chokes. Her voice, when it comes, is thick with emotion. 'I'm safe, Patrick. They can't touch me now. I've been given my liberty.'

Patrick lifts her from the ground, sweeping her up off her feet and twirling her around.

★★★

Inside the Musselburgh Arms, a large party toasts Maggie Dickson's health.

'To Half-Hangit Maggie.' They raise their tankards.

Musselburgh being a small town, word soon gets round and the tavern buzzes with well-wishers and folk hoping to catch a glimpse of the woman who survived a public hanging. Maggie mingles and dances with the fishwives while the fishermen puff on their trusty pipes. In the midst of the crowd, Minister Bonaloy walks towards his most infamous and miraculous parishioner, taking hold of her arm.

'I am delighted for you, Maggie. There is nothing to fear anymore.'

She shouts over the revelry. 'I am thankful to the Lord above, Minister Bonaloy. And from this day forward I intend to live out the rest of my life to the full.'

The minister glances at the blacksmith's son, he's a handsome young lad and folk would have to be blind not to notice how he follows Maggie around with his eyes.

'Are you all right, Minister Bonaloy?' Maggie enquires.

'Grand,' he lies and heaves a great sigh. He sits heavy in a seat and massages his temples. 'Maggie, my dear, have you considered a nunnery?'

Spellbound on the young blacksmith, Maggie never hears him.

CHAPTER EIGHTEEN

THE LUCKENBOOTH

Maggie steps over Duncan. He arrived at the cottage late at night, stinking drunk and passing out on the floor. No one's bothered to move him.

'Wake up, you daft fool!' she shouts, prodding him with her foot.

'Have you got a few groats for your dear father?'

Maggie shakes her head. 'So you can return to the alehouse? No!'

He struggles to sit straight on the floor, scratching his scraggy head. 'Can I have a wee bite to eat then?'

'Aye, now move yourself, you daft ass. You're making this place untidy.'

'This pigsty?' he mutters.

'What was that?' asked Maggie.

'Nothing, help your dear father to stand, will you?'

Maggie struggles to lift him; her stomach's so huge it's awkward to perform the simplest of jobs.

'Jesus. You're a dead weight.'

'Don't say the Lord's name in vain.'

'Pish,' she laughs.

★★★

The widow's door's twisted, probably due to the ivy creeping around its oak frame. Making a fist Maggie knocks and waits. But there's no response. She knocks again and hears a clinking noise. A great shiver runs along her spine as she remembers the chains she once wore.

'Who is it?' a faint voice reverberates through the door.

'It's me – Maggie. Maggie Dickson.' Maggie stares through a crack in the door, squinting past dark shadows.

'Wait a moment.'

After a long while the door creaks open.

'Oh dear God, what have they done to you?' Maggie gasps, gawping at the widow. She looks like a grotesque mythical creature. Her clothes are a stinking mess. Placed upon her head is an ugly metal mask, fashioned to resemble a monstrous creature, its exaggerated tongue curling upwards.

The widow tries to talk but it comes out muffled. 'They put the branks on me.'

'What?' Maggie says.

'The branks – they put them on me.'

'I can see that, but why?'

'I don't know, some disagreement with the miller's wife,' the widow declares, spreading out her arms in front of her. She hobbles into the house, her chains clanging with every step.

'You're chained to the fire?'

'Aye, the gaoler did it. He comes once a day to take this awful thing off. Once he's given me some bread and water he puts the bridle back on and beggars off.'

'I see. How long do you have to keep it on? '

'God knows, lass. I don't know how much longer I can stand it. It's the metal part, it makes my mouth dribble and it's so heavy it's hurting my neck. I can't get a wink of sleep. How could anyone get a moment's rest with this on their head?'

Maggie grimaces and turns away from the old woman. *Another man-made invention designed to create human misery*, she thinks, before adding, 'Let me wash your clothes and tidy this place for you.'

'Would you? You're a kind, lass. I've a mind to rest my weary head.'

First Maggie sorts the chanty – it's near overflowing. Then she tidies the cottage, sweeping and taking away half-eaten food covered in mould. The hearth needs cleaning and new peat placed inside. Maggie looks for kindling and a bucket to fetch fuel.

'Can you take off your clothes? Have you a clean sark?'

The widow points to a wooden box.

'Here, let me help you.' Maggie passes her clean linen.

'I'll have to step into it, lassie, and I'm a wee bit unsteady on my feet. Will you pull it on for me? Excuse my filthy body; I haven't been able to wash properly.'

'No matter. So you got into a disagreement with the miller's wife again, did you?'

The widow tries to nod. 'Aye.'

'You need to learn to bite your tongue, old woman,' Maggie says pulling on the clean sark.

'I could do with a wee nap, Maggie.'

'Lean your head against the wall.'

Before Maggie departs she spreads a blanket over the widow's knees and stokes up the fire. She's careful not to slam the door as she closes it behind her. Once outside, she turns on her heel to return home. Suddenly a man collides with her causing her to jump backwards, shrieking with terror. 'Minister Bonaloy! You scared me.'

'I'm sorry. How is she?'

'Not good. The poor thing has had no sleep. Anyway, now that she's finally resting, it would be a shame to wake her.'

'The baby's getting bigger,' he says glancing at her stomach.

'Aye, and it kicks all the time.' She places a hand over her bump.

Maggie twitches her head in the direction of the widow's cottage. 'I'll check on her later. I've got to go now so – good to see you, Minister Bonaloy.'

He nods and then suddenly calls after her. 'Maggie!'

'What is it?' Maggie shuffles on a spot, keen to be on her way.

'I was wondering – well, I don't mean to pry or pressure you, but I assumed you and Patrick would marry again, before the new baby comes.'

'You're not prying at all. We've been so busy since – well, we've had people bringing gifts, money, and some folk just wanting to touch me thinking I'll bring them good fortune or something. Lord knows why!'

'Would you like me to arrange something? It's not every day a holy man gets to marry a woman to her widower.'

'All right, I'll speak to Patrick. We'll need to make some arrangements. He's swallowed the anchor, you know. He's a labouring man now.'

'Aye, I heard.' He tips his hat and walks away.

★★★

At the end of the night they congregate near the fire, all huddled together for warmth. For a while Maggie stares into the crackling flames, wondering if the widow has finally managed to get enough sleep. An amber glow fills the room, beyond the fishing gear her eyes are drawn to her fish creel, Maggie's heart thumps in her bosom and her face grows hot.

'Do you want some? And stop biting your nails,' Patrick gestures towards the cooking pot.

'No, thank you. Just been to Widow Arrock's cottage. She's in a right state. Come here, Anna. Your hair is a mess.' Maggie takes a bone comb and proceeds to run it through her daughter's hair.

'Arrgh, get off me, Maggie. I don't want you to comb my hair with that louse trap.' Her little head shakes from side to side in an effort to avoid the comb.

Maggie smacks her around the head. 'Stop calling me Maggie. I'm your mother. Who taught you to call it a louse trap?'

'Widow Arrock.'

Maggie laughs, amused by the child.

'Who's making that awful noise?' Patrick kisses his soon-to-be wife.

'Your scraggy-headed daughter, who else? She doesn't like having her hair brushed and tied with a fillet.'

Patrick lifts both hands into the air. 'I wonder where she gets that from.' He turns to young Patrick. 'Do you want some oats, son?'

The laddie nods his head. 'Are we going to the harbour to work on the boat again on the morrow?'

Patrick's eyes crinkle when he smiles. 'Yes lad, first thing – once we've had something to eat. An empty sack won't stand up on its own, you know.'

'I thought you swallowed the anchor?' Maggie places her hands on her hips and her lips curl into a scowl.

'I have. Just helping one of the fishermen with his boat, that's all. I'm teaching the lad a few things.' He winks at his son.

★★★

They marry the following Sabbath in Minister Bonaloy's home. Andrew Hay, the master weaver is a witness, and Maggie's brother, James. There are no celebrations or revelry of any kind. They marry and then they head home to the bairns.

That night they go to bed once more as man and wife.

'Was it strange to marry me a second time?' She traces her fingers around the scars on her neck.

'No, you'll always be my wife. I thought of you every day on that man-o'-war ship.'

She closes her eyes and thinks of what she was doing while he was away, willing away that familiar ache from her heart.

★★★

Almost a year to the day since her trial began Maggie gives birth to a healthy son. They name him James after her brother, and he's baptised privately in the home of Minister Robert Bonaloy on 20 July 1725. Witnesses present are Andrew Hay and William Cass.

Ever since Patrick was press-ganged into the navy, he expresses an ardent fear of being taken again. On the rare occasions that he helps out at the harbour, Patrick keeps a low profile. But every now and then, Maggie catches him looking out to sea with misty eyes. She knows the longing, she feels it too, that constant craving for something out of reach but irresistible. Nevertheless she continues to fast and pray every Wednesday and tries to be a good wife.

★★★

The following market day Maggie returns home early without her kertch and her plaid torn. She slams the door so hard they near come off their hinges.

'What's the matter?'

'I can't do this anymore, Patrick. It's impossible.'

'Do what? You're not making sense.'

'Sell fish, here or in Edinburgh. They follow me everywhere, tugging on my clothes, pointing or shouting "Half-Hangit Maggie!" They stole my kertch today for a souvenir.'

'Is it that bad?'

'Worse. Look at the state of me – they near tore off my clothes today. If it wasn't for the chandler from the Cowgate, I'd be still there trying to fight them off. Thank God he let me take refuge in his shop.' She lifts her tattered sleeves. 'Just one person it takes to recognise me and then all hell lets loose.'

Patrick shakes his head and does his best to console her. 'Well, what shall we do? What can we do?'

'I want to move away from here, Patrick. I want to make a fresh start away from here.'

Patrick pushes her away. 'But I've lived in Musselburgh my whole life, and all our friends and family are here. What about James and your father?'

'We won't move far. Folk can always visit.'

Patrick's forehead furrows. 'Can't we think about it? I just don't know lass, it's a big decision and we haven't much money, remember?'

'Nonsense. We've plenty, what with all the well-wishers and gifts.'

'I suppose it would be good for the children. But this is our home and all I've ever known.'

'You've travelled across many seas, you daft fool. A house is just wattle and daub. Think of the bairns, Patrick, they've been through enough. The other children keep teasing them and singing a song to them, one about me.'

'I've heard it. Merry wives, welcome to Meg Dickson – is that the one?'

'Aye, that's it. Well that's settled, then. I have somewhere in mind.'

'Not Kelso?'

'Of course not,' she replies. 'Berwick. How would you like to run an inn in Berwick?'

★★★

It's always hard to say goodbye, but it has to be done. Patrick's parents, James, Minister Bonaloy and his kind wife, Betty, all have to be thanked. Hand in hand, Patrick and Maggie walk from house to house to say farewell to the fisher folk, Jean Ramsay and Widow Arrock.

On the day of the move Maggie looks around the empty cottage with fresh eyes. Looks like someone has ripped the soul out of this place, she thinks and proceeds to the hearth. Her knees creak as she bends to pick out a large chunk of peat. This will be the first thing she places in her new home in the Borders. *One more thing to do*, she thinks. Lifting a shovel she walks out to the pigsty as her family wait outside. At the far right-hand corner she begins to dig till her back's drenched with sweat. She removes the object from its pouch – it's larger than she remembers and heavier. When she turns it up towards the sunlight it glitters like molten gold. Engraved onto it is a picture of a sun and moon, she polishes it with her sleeve and drops it into her stocking.

★★★

It took a good few hours to reach The Cross Keys, what with the three children wanting to stop and pee every hour or so. Anna and little Patrick stare all around them at silver-birched trees, and along the broadest of paths, a golden light lingers on their white sunlit limbs – and beyond lies a purple pathway sprinkled with moss. As they approach the coast the terrain became sparse of houses and trees, and soon a sparkling blue sea can be seen on the distant horizon.

At a huge oak door they wait. Patrick holding onto Anna and little Patrick's hands, Maggie with her new baby on her hip, listening to the sounds of rusty bolts and metal scraping as the door is pulled open.

'Welcome to Berwick. Joseph Bell holds out a hand to Patrick, clapping him on the shoulder and greeting him like a long-lost relative.'

'Pleased to meet you,' Patrick smiles. 'These are our children – Patrick, Anna and baby James.'

Joseph crouches to his knees, ruffling Anna and Patrick's hair and making a fuss of them. 'I expect you two are hungry. Go with your father to the scullery, there's lots of food. Follow your noses.'

Joseph and Maggie are alone. 'Good to see you, Maggie. How are you, lassie?'

'A lot has happened since I saw you last,' she blurts out.

'I heard, and in my opinion 'tis not a fitting punishment for a lass in trouble,' he grumbles and points above. 'And he agrees and all. It was God's will that you survived. Come here, lass.' He gives her a bear hug.

'Joseph – you asked me once if I wanted the inn. Well, here's your answer.' Maggie drops the solid gold fob watch into his hand.

'Where on earth did you get this?' His eyes bulge. 'On second thoughts, don't tell me.'

Maggie whispers in his ear. 'Be careful how you get payment for it. It's worth a fortune. It belonged to a fine gentleman friend.'

Joseph nods and touches the tip of his nose. 'I know a man who can fetch me a pretty sum for this. Still got a bit of business going on here – I think you know what I mean, don't you, Maggie? I have my contacts.'

'Oh, I almost forgot.' She climbs on the cart and lifts up a blanket. 'This is my father.' She points at a man snoring on his back, a flask of whisky nestled within his arms. 'He'll be our best customer.'

★★★

It was the right decision. The children flourish and Patrick's happy, despite the ruffians he has to mix with (he's met rougher men at sea). Maggie, because of her previous experience in Kelso, is a dab hand regarding tavern work. Trade picks up and much to Maggie's irritation, folk still come from afar to see the miraculous Half-Hangit Maggie. But in short, their custom is most welcome.

With the passing of time, Maggie becomes acquainted with Joseph's wife, Bessie. One day, as they brew ale together, curiosity gets the better of Bessie and she asks Maggie a question. 'What was it like, Maggie?' she whispers.

'What?'

'The hanging, of course – what else would I be asking you? What did it feel like?'

'Funny, no one's asked me about that for a while.' Her hands move to her scarred neck. Maggie no longer wears a scarf.

Bessie places a hand on Maggie's shoulder. 'Do you mind me asking? Sorry, lass.'

'It's fine. Well, what can I say? It hurt and I couldn't get my breath – it was like being strangled or choked. Once he pushed me off the ladder the rope jolted and my hands became untied. I managed to get them under the rope, but then the hangman hit me with a stick until I let go. After that everything is a blank, Bessie – I really can't remember. The next thing I recall is waking in the coffin.'

'But they say the hangman pulled down on your legs and that you were suspended from the rope for over an hour. Can't you remember any of that?'

'No – none of it, Bessie. But would you want to remember?'

'No, lass. What a nightmare. I know I shouldn't say this, and don't let Joseph know I've told you, mind – William Bell sent word.'

'William. My William? What did he say?' Maggie chokes.

'He wants you to come to him. He says he wants to take you somewhere else to live – far from here.'

Maggie's face turns pallid. Her legs tremble beneath her. She stretches out a hand to lean on a chair to lighten her weight. With her pulse racing, she inhales deeply and places one hand over her pounding heart.

'Will you send him a message?' Maggie asks.

'Of course,' Bessie stares at her with huge eyes.

'Tell him that I have a husband and children, and that I am loyal to them. I've put them through enough hell already. I just can't, Bessie. I love him still, but I just can't.'

Bessie pats her hand. 'I'll let him know. And you've made the right decision, lass. And I hope you are content now. After all, what does a passionate heart bring but trouble and turmoil.'

'Aye,' Maggie answers. 'I suppose I am content now, Bessie. Since Patrick and I have reconciled, well, he's been different like – how can I say? He's become more masterful, and as a young woman I resisted such control. A woman will try to dominate a man, but really inside herself she wants to be dominated. And if that man softens and bends to her will, well, need I say more?'

'Wise words, lass. I'm glad you've found peace.'

'Well, I don't know about that,' Maggie replies, a twinkle in her eye.

★★★

Maggie walks over to the sleeping child. As her eyes gaze upon him, her heart sinks as she remembers the one she left at the river's edge – and the man she will forever hold in her heart.

'Sleep well, little one,' she whispers.

★★★

Maggie Dickson lived in Berwick for many years, and presented her husband with several more children, all credibly born. And Maggie, in spite of her narrow escape, was not reformed, but lived and died again, in profligacy. To her dying day, she constantly denied that she was guilty of her alleged crime. And she was living as late as the year 1753.

William Bell's life was short and painful. His profession as a tailor rendered him bandy-legged and arthritic as a result of sitting cross-legged hour by hour, for many years. The cloth particles he continually inhaled gave him respiratory problems and, in addition, he suffered chronic back pain. William never married, nor had children, and it was said that he died tragically before he reached the age of forty, and that he died alone. When they found his corpse, clutched in his hand was a lock of dark silky hair tied with scarlet material, and in the other a silver luckenbooth.

Lightning Source UK Ltd.
Milton Keynes UK
UKOW04f0239171213

223155UK00001B/16/P